"I'd like to hire you for the position of my assistant."

"But I have no

"Experience and ___ more than book learni ___ proven yourself ___

Maeve thought of ___ sne'd treated and seen worsen and eventually die. Less than two weeks ago, she hadn't been able to save her own da. But right now, her sisters needed her to agree to this. Their welfare depended on someone earning a wage.

"We accept your kind offer," Maeve said. She prayed her abilities were enough that she would be a help.

"Very well then. The three of you should go get settled. Afterward, you can return and help me store the supplies."

"We're indebted to you, Dr. Gallagher," she replied.

Gathering their things, the sisters made their way back out to the corridor. Once the door closed behind them, Bridget grasped Maeve's arm through her sleeve. "I think he likes you."

Cheryl St.John
and
Renee Ryan

The Wedding Journey
&
Mistaken Bride

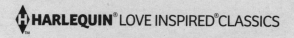
HARLEQUIN® LOVE INSPIRED®CLASSICS

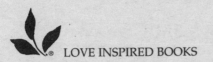

LOVE INSPIRED BOOKS

Recycling programs for this product may not exist in your area.

ISBN-13: 978-1-335-45461-4

The Wedding Journey & Mistaken Bride

Copyright © 2019 by Harlequin Books S.A.

The publisher acknowledges the copyright holder of the individual works as follows:

The Wedding Journey
Copyright © 2012 by Harlequin Books S.A.

Mistaken Bride
Copyright © 2012 by Harlequin Books S.A.

Special thanks and acknowledgment are given to Cheryl St.John and Renee Ryan for their contribution to the Irish Brides miniseries.

CONTENTS

Cheryl St.John's love for reading started as a child. She wrote her own stories, designed covers and stapled them into books. She credits many hours of creating scenarios for her paper dolls and Barbies as the start of her fascination with fictional characters. Cheryl loves hearing from readers. Visit her website at cherylstjohn.net.

Visit the Author Profile page
at Harlequin.com for more titles.

THE WEDDING JOURNEY

Cheryl St.John

God resisteth the proud, and giveth grace
to the humble. Humble yourselves therefore
under the mighty hand of God, that he may exalt you
in due time: Casting all your care upon him;
for he careth for you.

—*1 Peter 5:5–7*

"My dream is of a place and a time where America will once again be seen as the last best hope of earth."
—Abraham Lincoln

Chapter One

June 1850, Castleville, Ireland

Lilting over the roar of the ocean, the haunting notes of a flute raised goose bumps on Maeve's arms. There were no men in the Murphy family to carry the plain wooden box holding the remains of their father on their shoulders, so she and her two older sisters followed behind as the men of the village proceeded from the small stone church up a grassy incline to the cemetery.

The gathering reached the crest. Here the sound of thundering waves far below the cliffs grew to a crescendo, nature's hymn as familiar as the expansive sky and the salty tang of the ocean.

Beside Maeve, her sister Bridget wept into her handkerchief. She'd worn a somber secondhand brown bonnet, fashionable some ten years ago, yet still serviceable. "What's going to become of us without Da?"

Maeve comforted Bridget with an arm around her shoulders. "Shush now, *ma milis,*" she said, calling her sister *my sweet* in their native Gaelic tongue.

"We'll come up with a plan." The eldest of the three, Nora, always had a plan. The sisters were stair steps in height and age, Nora being tall, Bridget in between and Maeve petite.

Most of the simple graves were marked with stones, others with weathered wooden crosses. Goat's-beard grew in thick patches throughout the grass, the yellow blooms a cheerful contrast to the mood. A hole had been dug in the rich black soil, and Maeve had only to glance about the crowd to note which of the young men's hair was damp from exertion. She spotted two familiar heads of curly red hair. She would thank the Donnelly brothers later.

Reverend Larkin had prayed over members from every household represented at the graveside today. The famine that had taken its toll on their countrymen had spared no family. Hunger, sickness and poverty were all these people knew, but the believers of Castleville clung to their faith. Now the reverend stretched his hand toward the pine box as six farmers dressed in their Sunday clothing lowered it by ropes down into the earth.

"Jack Murphy, your daughters long for one more day spent at your side. When we lose someone we love, it seems that time stands still. What moves through us is a silence, a quiet sadness, a longing for one more day, one more word, one more touch."

The ache in Maeve's chest threatened to cut off her breath. Security had been whipped out from beneath her with the death of her father. The pain of never seeing him again, of never hearing his thick brogue, was almost more than she could bear. She worked to hold back the grief and fear bearing down on her—and to steady Bridget, who swayed on her feet.

Their female friends and neighbors wept softly into their handkerchiefs and shawls. The men stared at the ground and worried the brims of their hats as a red-billed chough flew in a lazy circle overhead.

"We may not understand why you left this earth so soon," the reverend continued. "Or why you left before we were ready to say goodbye, but little by little we shall begin to remember not just that you died, but all the days that you lived. We will see you again some day, in a heavenly place where there is no hunger or sickness. No rocks in the fields. Now, Lord, bless the daughters of Jack Murphy. Keep them safe from harm and provide for them by Your bounteous grace and mercy."

Reverend Larkin turned and nodded at Nora. "You first, dear."

Maeve's oldest sister seemed taller than her already admirable height while she kept her back straight and stepped forward. She wore her chestnut-brown hair fashioned as she always did, in a practical bun, so not even a single strand of hair caught in the breeze. Kneeling, she picked up a handful of earth and dropped it into the grave. The clods hit the coffin with a dull thump. Bridget followed, her dark wavy hair hidden by her bonnet, with Maeve going last.

She performed the task quickly, without thinking, without gazing upon the pine box, but still she imagined her father laid out in his frayed suit. He wasn't in that lifeless body, she reminded herself again. He'd gone onto glory and was right this moment looking down from beside her dear mother. They were together now in a place where there were no potatoes to dig or mouths to feed.

Scully and Vaughan Donnelly rolled back their sleeves over beefy forearms and shoveled dirt upon the casket.

Maeve watched for a few minutes until Mrs. Donovan, who'd been a dear friend of her mother's, pressed a coin into Maeve's hand and hugged her soundly. "I'll be prayin' for ye, I will."

Maeve swallowed the sob rising in her chest and pressed her fisted hands to her midriff. She accepted condolences and pennies from her neighbors. Her fellow countrymen were poor, so these modest offerings were sacrifices they couldn't afford. Their gifts humbled her. The fact that so many had come to the funeral at all was enough to touch her heart.

It was a workday, as was every day in County Beary, except the Sabbath, and the landlord didn't take kindly to a day off.

"I still be missin' your beautiful mother," a longtime friend told her and enveloped her in a warm hug. "Colleen and I were dreamers, we were, as girls, but these times steal a woman's dreams. Don't let anythin' or anyone take your dreams, lassie."

The woman joined her daughter and together they walked through the knee-high grass.

After extending their sympathies one at a time, the rest of the mourners headed back down the green hillside toward their homes and fields.

With the ocean pounding below, the Murphy sisters stood on the lush green crest above the village until they were the only ones remaining.

"Mr. Bantry already has someone waiting to move into the cottage, he does." Nora spoke of their landlord. "We'd better go pack and clean."

Maeve set her jaw. "I'll not be cleanin' the house that ill-mannered tyrant's forcing us out of."

"Our mother kept that cottage clean all the years she lived within its walls, and we'll not be shaming her by leaving so much as a speck of dust."

Nora was right, of course. She was always right.

"What's to become of us, then?" Bridget asked.

"Mrs. Ennis said we could board with them temporarily." Nora showed them the wrapped bundle she held. "She gave us a loaf of bread."

"They have seven mouths to feed as it is." Maeve took off down the hill and her sisters followed. A startled grouse flew out of the tall grass.

"Our neighbors gave me coins." Bridget extended her hand.

The three of them compared what they'd received. The total was pathetically insufficient and would barely purchase a week's food. Their cupboards were empty. That morning they'd shared two partridge eggs Maeve had found.

Maeve led the way around a field bordered by a low rock wall. They crossed a stone bridge over a creek and continued toward the only home they'd ever known. The stone cottage greeted them with a lifetime of memories. Their mother had died here ten years previous, during the worst of the influenza epidemic. Their father had repaired the thatched roof numerous times, and the newest foliage showed up distinctly against the old.

Inside, Nora set the bread on the scarred cutting table. Bridget removed her bonnet. The three of them gathered around and studied the golden brown loaf reverently. "The Ennises couldn't afford to part with this," Maeve said.

"Our neighbors are a generous lot, they are," Nora agreed. "The Macrees brought bramble jam earlier. We could each have a slice with it now."

Bridget shook her head. "We should save it. I'm not very hungry."

"My stomach is tied in knots, as well," Maeve agreed. "We'll want it later. It will last us through tomorrow."

Nora wrapped the bread in a clean square of toweling. She brushed her hands together. "Very well. We'll pack."

"Pack. Where shall we go?" Bridget asked.

Nora placed her hands on her hips. "We must each find a husband immediately."

"And not marry for love?" Bridget asked with a horrified expression. She placed her hat on a hook by the bed they shared. "We should stay with the Ennises. We'd still be near the village and the young men we know."

"No proposals have been forthcoming yet," Nora reminded her. "All the men here are as poor as we are. None can afford to take a wife and work a piece of land on his own. Honora Monaghan married one of the Kenny brothers, and now she has to live with his whole family."

"Perhaps Mr. Bantry will allow us to work this land ourselves," Bridget suggested. "We've worked it alongside Da all these years. We're as capable as any man."

"Mr. Bantry has his own kinsmen waiting to occupy the land," Nora replied.

Maeve picked up her mother's Bible and touched the worn cover. "May God turn Bantry's heart, and if He doesn't turn his heart, may He turn Bantry's ankle, so we'll know him by his limping!"

"Mind your tongue, Maeve Eileen Murphy," her eldest sister admonished. "And spoken while you're holding our dear departed mother's Holy Bible."

"I learned the saying from her, I did." Maeve laughed, the first sound of merriment in this house for many weeks. "We'll simply have to find work," she told them logically. "And you know as well as I there's not a job to be had in all of County Beary. We must travel to County Galway."

"We can use Mother's trunk." Nora removed an oil

lamp from the top and pulled the trunk into the center of the room that served as their kitchen and living space. "We'll have to sort out all the things we can't take."

They found a few neatly pressed and folded aprons, a piece each of their baby clothing, a bundle of letters and a few daguerreotypes, one in an aged frame.

Nora picked up the likeness of their beautiful mother and caressed the frame with farm-roughened fingers. "What would Mother have done? She was practical above all else."

"Where did practicality get her?" Bridget asked. "She never had a day's happiness."

"Romantic notions won't put food on the table." Holding the frame too tightly, Nora's fingers poked through the fabric backing. She turned over the frame and examined the hole. Peering more closely, she worked three folded pieces of paper from inside. "Whatever are these?"

The younger sisters crowded in close for a better look. The first paper Nora unfolded was a letter, the second some type of legal document and the last a pencil drawing of a house. "How odd."

"Read the letter," Bridget coaxed and reached to take the drawing.

"'May 1824,'" Nora began. "'My dearest Colleen, I know you have made your choice. My heart is broken, but I understand your decision. I've gone to America, to Faith Glen, the village in Massachusetts we spoke of so often. The town was founded by an Irishman. It is just ten miles from Boston, yet I have heard it is so much like Castleville, though, of course it is another world. I have purchased a small home for you—'"

"Who's the letter from?" Maeve stepped in closer to have a better look at the handwriting.

Nora waved her away. "Let me finish. 'I have purchased a small home for you on the water's edge. Should you or your kin ever be in need of a place to go, know this house is yours. With undying love, Laird.'"

The three sisters stood in stunned silence for a full minute.

"I told you she whispered the name *Laird* with her last dyin' breath." Bridget looked up from the letter to Nora's tense expression. "But the two of you insisted she was just trying to say *love*."

"We didn't know any Laird," Maeve said.

"Until now." Bridget gave a satisfied nod.

"What's this mention of undying love?" Maeve asked.

"Dated a year before I was born, 'tis." Nora turned her attention to the pencil drawing Bridget held, and the three of them studied the depiction of a home near the ocean. The artist had even drawn flowers blooming in gardens on two sides.

"Mother was in love with this man!" Bridget's expression showed her shock. "He bought her a house in America, but she stayed and married Da? I can't conceive of it."

"There must be a logical explanation," Nora said.

Bridget's hazel eyes were bright with excitement. "The cottage sounds ideal. We should go there."

"They say there's so much land in America that anyone can own a share." Maeve took the deed from Nora's fingers and examined it. "The soil is rich and there's plenty of rain. There are schools and jobs. Western men are hungry for wives."

"That may be so, but it takes more than we have to purchase ship's fare and travel there. Fanny Clellan sold both her cow and her mother's brooch to buy a ticket. We don't even *have* a cow." Nora snatched the paper back. She pointed to the date. "This deed is over twenty-five years old, 'tis. The house is most likely occupied—or it could have been destroyed."

Maeve went to the coffee tin and dumped out the contents on the kitchen table. Bridget added the coins they'd received that morning, and the two of them tallied the amount.

"This could get us to Galway," Nora pointed out.

"But we'd have no food or lodging," Maeve argued. "We have something we can sell to buy tickets to America."

"Don't even speak of it." Nora gave Maeve a cautionary glare.

Maeve went back to the trunk. "Once we land we could find an inn and secure jobs. We can look for this house in Faith Glen and learn if it's still there. Think of it! We might have a comfortable place to live just waitin' for us." She knelt and took out several objects that had been packed in fabric at the bottom.

Bridget unwrapped one and held up a silver sugar bowl, followed by the teapot. "I never saw Mama use these."

"I never did, either." Maeve unwrapped a creamer. "They've always been in the trunk."

"They've been there as long as I can remember," Nora said. "Da once told me Mama got them from a woman she worked for. He said she had saved them for a rainy day. Even when times were the worst, she held on to them."

"This is the rainiest day I can think of," Bridget commented.

Maeve gave her eldest sister a pleading look. "It would be a fresh start, Nora. We have nothing left here."

Nora looked about the barren room, her concern clear, but her resolve crumbling. "Even selling that, the tickets would take every last penny."

"Perhaps there are positions aboard one of the sailing vessels. None of us minds a good day's work." Excitement laced Bridget's tone.

Nora refolded the papers and carefully tucked them inside the Bible. "I suppose it can't hurt to go see how much the tickets actually cost and learn if it's even possible for us to hire on."

Bridget shot a delighted bright-eyed gaze to Maeve. A broad smile lit her sweet face. Reaching for Maeve's hands, she squeezed them until Maeve winced. "We're going to America! Can you conceive of it?"

"Only if we can afford to buy fare," Nora reminded.

Maeve tried to hide the jitters weakening her knees. If they didn't have enough, they'd have to find a way by the end of the week. They couldn't remain here. Butterflies fluttered in her stomach. What did three simple village girls know about traveling aboard a sailing ship? What if the deed truly was worthless and there was no place for them once they arrived?

The sense of hopelessness she'd lived with for months had lifted, however. They were taking action to change their situation. Even if the house was gone, anything was better than this. God had already seen them through difficult times. All they had to do now was trust Him.

"Into Your care we place ourselves, Lord," she prayed aloud. "Show us the path You would have us take and bless us as we seek a new home and a new start. Thank You for hope."

Chapter Two

Two weeks later, Minot's Ledge, Port of Galway, Ireland

"Move aside!" A barrel-chested man carrying an enormous crate on his shoulder jostled passengers awaiting their turns to board the *Annie McGee*. Overhead, gulls with black-tipped wings cawed and swooped.

Maeve and her sisters backed out of the way. All of their earthly possessions had been whittled down to the trunk, which had been stored aboard earlier, a few crates, a donated bandbox and a battered satchel. The pungent smells of fish and brine burned Maeve's nose.

The rude man set down his burden at the foot of the gangplank and headed back to a wooden cart, which interrupted the line of waiting passengers. The harnessed mule jumped nervously at the man's approach, and the fellow picked up a switch and waved it in a threat.

The mule sidestepped, rocking the cart precariously.

"Stand still, you good for nothin' bag o' bones!" His accent plainly emphasized a lack of Irish heritage.

With a loud bray, the frightened animal kicked out with his hind feet, solidly connecting with the cart and tipping the entire thing backward.

Crates toppled onto the ground as a piercing cry rose.

"There's a lad beneath the cart!" someone called.

High-pitched screams raised the hair on Maeve's neck.

The burly man grumbled and, together with several bystanders, righted the cart back onto its wheels.

"Aren't you the doctor's assistant?" a gentleman in a black suit asked the grumbling bear of a man. His face showed noticeable concern. "The lad here's bleeding."

"Filthy urchin shouldn't have been beggin' on the wharf," the big man snarled. He picked up one of the spilled crates and headed for the gangplank without a backward glance.

Maeve didn't hesitate to set the satchel she held at Nora's feet and rush to the fallen boy's side. She'd seen more than her share of sickness and injuries over the past few years, and the lack of a proper village doctor had given her plenty of opportunities to pick up numerous nursing skills. She didn't know if she could help, but she'd do whatever she could.

The scene was alarming. Blood flowed from the boy's thigh at a steady rate. Thinking quickly, she untied the scarf from around her shoulders, twisted it into a rope and tied it about his leg.

"I have need of a stick," she called.

"Will this do?" A nearby woman shoved an ivory comb into her hand.

Maeve tied the tails of the scarf around the comb and twisted until the makeshift tourniquet cinched tight and the flow of blood ceased. Certain the bleeding was stopped, she lifted her gaze to the frightened boy's dirty face. Tears streaked the grime on his pale cheeks, and wide frightened brown eyes appealed to her.

"You're going to be all right," she assured him. She

glanced into the crowd. "Has someone sent for the doctor?"

"Yes, miss," a female bystander replied. "My husband alerted the sailors on the gangplank. One of 'em rushed aboard."

"It won't be long now," Maeve assured the boy. "What's your name, laddie?"

"Sean," he replied, his lower lip trembling. "Sean McCorkle."

"Is your family nearby?" she asked.

"Aye. Me two brothers. Emmett be right over there."

Maeve glanced about and spotted the younger boy he'd indicated standing several feet away, wearing a terrified expression. Both of them appeared dirty and uncared for.

"'Tis the doctor comin' now," the woman called to Maeve.

Stepping around passengers, a tall man hurried forward. His chocolate-brown gaze analyzed the scene, taking in the patient, the improvised tourniquet and lastly Maeve. He leaned over the lad, looking into each eye, and then pressing long fingers to the boy's sockless ankle above his battered shoe. The doctor's black hair glistened in the morning sun as he bent to examine the wound.

The scent of sandalwood clung to his clothing and drifted to Maeve's nostrils. His efficiency impressed her.

He raised his head, piercing Maeve with an unsmiling, yet admiring look. "That was mighty quick thinking, miss."

"I did what I could."

He knelt and effortlessly picked up the boy. Maeve stood as he did, keeping her grip on the twisted scarf and comb secure. "I'll take him to the dispensary, where I can treat him."

"His name is Sean McCorkle. Says he has brothers, but he didn't mention parents."

"It will be helpful if you hold the tourniquet in place while I carry him aboard." He called to one of the sailors. "Find this lad's family! McCorkle's the name."

As dirty as he was, Maeve couldn't imagine his family or home. "Where's your mother, Sean?"

"She be with Jesus, miss. Don't have a da, neither."

She exchanged a significant look with the doctor.

His contemptible assistant chose that moment to return for another armload. The doctor stabbed him with an angry dark gaze. "What happened here, Hegarty?"

"Filthy beggar got in the way. Shouldn't be underfoot, that one."

A man with coal-black hair sticking out from beneath his cap stepped forward. "Takin' a switch to the mule, Hegarty was," the man supplied. "Frightened the poor beast into tippin' goods all about the wharf and spilt the cart right atop the laddie here."

"Cruelty to animals and children isn't acceptable behavior under my employ," the doctor proclaimed, already walking away with the boy. "Pack your belongings and leave the ship immediately. You no longer have a job."

Hegarty dropped the crate with a resounding crash and brushed his beefy hands together. "You can keep your measly wages. Too many smelly Irishmen aboard this vessel for my taste, anyhow."

The doctor directed an undiscernable look at Maeve. It was apparent from his speech, he was every bit as Irish as she, though obviously from a higher social class and far more educated. In those brief seconds it didn't matter. The obnoxious man had insulted the majority of people on the wharf.

"Are you boarding the *Annie McGee?*" At her nod, the doctor asked, "Can someone see to carrying your belongings?"

"Aye, my sisters."

"Call to them, if you will, please. All of you can come aboard with me."

Quickly, she turned and called out before the crowd had time to close in behind them. "Nora! Bridget! Bring everything and follow us!" She addressed the doctor again. "You're taking him aboard the sailing vessel?"

"Can't very well leave him here unattended, can I? We've no other choice."

"He said he was with two brothers, but I saw only one, I did. A lad younger than this boy."

"The crewman will search them out," he replied. "I suspect if there are brothers, they've either sneaked on the ship already or will board as soon as they have the opportunity."

Maeve left her last footprint on the soil of her native land and stepped onto the wooden gangplank.

Reaching the deck, she kept pace with the long-legged doctor, and they made their way to the companion ladder. He descended ahead of her, and she leaned as far forward as she dared without toppling over to keep hold of the tourniquet.

Once below deck, he led the way along a corridor until they reached a closed door. She had a free hand, so she opened it and stood back. The doctor was so tall, he had to bend to enter the room, but Maeve walked through upright. Her sisters followed, with Nora bending to fit under the doorway.

"Set your belongings inside the door," he instructed.

"I apologize for my lack of manners, ladies. I'm Dr. Flynn Gallagher."

"Oh, goodness, no," Nora objected. "You were involved with an emergency situation and could hardly have been expected to tip your hat."

"He isn't wearing a hat," Bridget said with a grin.

Nora ignored her. "I'm Nora Murphy. This is Bridget, and your capable helper there is Maeve."

He had already laid down the boy and was now washing his own hands in a basin. Beside it was a stack of folded towels and linens. The dispensary was impeccably clean.

"Will you assist me?" he asked Maeve.

Clearly he had no one else to help now. She couldn't have imagined that Hegarty fellow would have been of much use anyway. The doctor took hold of the comb while she washed her hands as thoroughly as he had.

Dr. Gallagher's brows rose in obvious appreciation for the care she took. On her return, he handed her a small brown bottle and a cloth folded into a square.

"What will happen if his brothers aren't found?" she asked. She didn't want to see this lad separated from his family.

"Where do you suppose your brothers are right now?" Dr. Gallagher asked Sean.

Sean didn't meet his eyes. He was sweating from the pain.

"They're stowing aboard, aren't they? Was that what the three of you cooked up?"

"What would happen to them if they did?" he asked.

The doctor nodded at Maeve. "We'll see them eventually. Go ahead."

She uncapped the bottle, held it well away from her nose and caught a whiff to test its contents. Knowing full well what it was and what he intended it for, she poured a small amount on the cloth, capped the bottle and held the fabric over the child's nose. "Close your eyes now, laddie. The doctor's going to fix you up as good as new, he is."

Dr. Gallagher cut away Sean's trousers, covered him with toweling and doused the area with alcohol. The boy's eyes were peacefully closed as he proceeded.

"I'll need a good helper for this voyage. I'd like to hire you for the position of my assistant."

"But…" Caught off guard, she looked up. His diligent attention was fastened on his task. "I have no formal training."

"Experience and quick thinking are often worth more than book learning, Miss Murphy. You've already proven yourself more than competent."

Maeve thought of all their neighbors and her own parents whom she'd treated and seen worsen and eventually die. Two weeks ago she hadn't been able to save her own da. She didn't know if she had the courage to take care of any more sick people. "I don't know."

The handsome doctor glanced toward Nora and Bridget as he took instruments from a small metal box and threaded a needle. "How shall I convince your sister to become my assistant?"

"May I step closer to speak with her?" Nora asked.

"Have you a weak stomach?"

"I'll be averting my eyes, if that's what you ask."

He gestured for her to come forward. "Yes, come speak to her."

Nora shot Bridget a glance and hurried to Maeve's side, deliberately keeping her eyes averted from the surgery.

"This is a divine opportunity," she whispered in Maeve's ear. "Think on it. We spent nearly every last penny on tickets and have nothing left for emergencies or even lodging when we get to Boston, should our plans fall through. We tried in vain to seek positions before the ship sailed. And now this perfect opportunity is presented to you and you want to refuse it?"

"If it aids your decision," the doctor interrupted. "I'll secure positions for the three of you. The cook always needs help preparing meals for the crew, and only an hour ago one of the passenger families was inquiring about a governess."

Maeve looked up into Nora's pleading blue eyes. Her sisters needed her to agree to this. Previously they'd been turned away each time they'd sought work on the ship. They'd risked the voyage anyway, but their welfare depended on someone earning a wage.

"We accept your kind offer," Maeve said with a surprising sense of anticipation. She prayed her abilities were enough that she would be a help. The thought of learning from a skilled physician buoyed her enthusiasm.

"Very well, then." Within minutes, he had neatly sutured a punctured vein as well as the flesh on Sean's leg. "Your quick thinking spared the lad's life. He might have bled to death if you hadn't fashioned that tourniquet."

"I knew what to do and I did it."

"I can finish up from here. The three of you should go get settled. Afterward, you can return and help me store the supplies. We'll have plenty of time to discuss working arrangements once the ship is underway."

He glanced at Nora. "Is one of you better with children than the other?"

"That would be Bridget," Nora replied. "I've had more experience in a kitchen."

"The family I spoke of are the Atwaters," he said to Bridget. "They have three daughters with whom they need help on the voyage. Mr. Atwater believed he had a governess, but at the last moment, she disappeared with their silver spoons and the cobbler's son. I'll send a note of recommendation with you. You can inquire above about his present whereabouts."

The doctor cut away the remainder of Sean's trousers and rolled them into a ball for the rubbish bin. "And I'll let Mr. Mathers know he can expect you in the galley tomorrow bright and early," he said to Nora.

"We're indebted to you, Dr. Gallagher," she replied.

"Not at all. I'm sure you'll each make a valuable contribution to the voyage." He inquired about their cabin number and gave them simple directions.

Gathering their things, the sisters made their way back out to the corridor. Once the door closed behind them, Bridget grasped Maeve's arm through her sleeve. "The angels surely blessed that man with staggering good looks." She gave Maeve a grin. "I think he likes you."

"What a nonsensical dreamer you are," Maeve replied. "He was as staid and solemn as a grave digger."

Perhaps that comparison had been thoughtless, so soon after burying their father, because Bridget got tears in her eyes. Maeve too often spoke without thinking.

Other passengers had begun boarding the ship, carrying their belongings and herding children. Nora led the way, turning a grateful smile on Maeve. "Thank you. This income sets my mind at ease."

"Now we'll all feel more prepared to dock in America," Maeve assured her.

They'd been assigned a small cabin that housed twelve bunks anchored to the walls by chains. On either side of the door were lockers with padlocks. Several other women had already chosen lower bunks and stowed their things, so the sisters chose beds near each other, with Bridget above Nora and Maeve on the next top bunk. This would be the first time they'd slept in separate beds, so the closeness would be a comfort.

Quickly, they stored their clothing and the food they'd brought, so they could hurry above.

Back on deck, Bridget was first to the railing. Maeve and Nora stood on either side. A small crowd stood at the wharf, waving scarves and hats. Maeve didn't recognize any of her countrymen, but she waved back. What a monumental moment this was. A life-changing day. To embed the scene in her memory, she took in every rich detail.

"Weigh the anchor!" came a shout, and she turned to spy a bearded man she assumed was the captain. A tingle of expectancy shimmied up her spine. She held her breath.

The anchor chain had become entangled with the cables of several fishing boats, so the moment lost momentum and her nerves jumped impatiently. At last, with much squeaking and creaking and dripping seaweed, the anchor chain was reeled in. The sound of men's voices rose in a chant as the sailors unreefed the enormous topsails and the bleached canvas billowed against the vivid blue sky. The sails caught the wind and the ship glided into the bay.

Goose bumps rose along Maeve's arms and the thrill of expectancy increased her heart rate.

In a matter of minutes, an expanse of water separated them from land, and the lush green coast with its majestic steplike cliffs came into view. She strained to see far enough to recognize the familiar outcroppings near her village, but of course the Murphy sisters had traveled a far piece to get to the ship, and it couldn't be seen from here. Perhaps when they were farther out in the ocean.

Maeve glanced to find Nora's face somber, her expression tense, as though concerned for their future. Between them, Bridget's soft weeping caught her notice. Always sentimental, a friend to all, Bridget would miss their friends and the people of their village. Her love for their community had been tainted by that despicable Daniel McGrath leaving her brokenhearted at the altar, however. It gave Maeve a sense of satisfaction to know that Bridget was leaving him behind once and for all.

Maeve put her arm around Bridget's shoulders and gave her a comforting hug. "'Tis a brand new start, *ma milis*."

Bridget dabbed her eyes and nose with her plain white cotton handkerchief and gave her a tremulous smile. "I'm glad to start over. But I shall miss what used to be. Before Mother and Da died. Before the famine. But I know we have much to look forward to. In America we'll solve the mystery of that letter and learn who Laird is. We'll live in the lovely house by the ocean and plant flowers."

Nora moved to stand on the other side of Bridget and wrapped her arm around her waist. "Don't raise your hopes too high, just in case."

"At the very least we can learn who that Laird fellow was to Mother," Maeve said.

She turned from the diminishing view of their homeland as they cleared the breakers and left the lighthouse behind to face her sisters. "We're headed for the land of opportunity."

She didn't know what the trip held in store, but she liked the way it had begun. The doctor had treated her—and her sisters—with dignity and respect. Bridget's teasing comments flashed through her mind, but she quickly set them aside. Yes, Dr. Gallagher did possess startling good looks, no doubt about that. Looking at him nearly took her breath away. She would have to work on composure.

The last person he would ever find of interest was a simple farm girl away from home for the first time. Ignoring her own attraction meant her new job was going to be challenging in more ways than one.

Chapter Three

"Come in," Flynn called at a rap on the closed door.

"Couldn't find any of the boy's kin around Minot's Ledge," a bearded sailor told him, setting down the last of the supply crates. "Inquired along the wharf, and learned he was beggin' handouts from the passengers waitin' in line. Villagers from nearby say he's an orphan."

"That goes along with his story. In which case I doubt anyone's looking for him," Flynn replied. "Soon as he's on his feet, he can be my errand boy."

"Looks mighty scrawny," the man noted with skepticism. "Don't know how much work you'll be gettin' out of 'im."

"You'd be scrawny, too, if you'd never had a mother to put meals on the table."

"I'm supposin' you're right about that, doc. My dear ma, God rest her soul, set out a feast every noon and evenin'. Miss her cooking somethin' fierce, I do."

Flynn thanked him for searching, and the man went back to his tasks.

Before Sean awoke, Flynn washed the boy's grimy face, hands and bony arms. For sure, the lad needed a good scrubbing, so he did the best he could. After removing his ill-fitting shoes and seeing Sean's dirty blistered feet, he got more clean water and soap, scrubbed, then treated and bandaged both.

It was obvious this boy had gone without proper clothing and food for some time. Bones protruded at his wrists and ankles, and his ribs stood out in sharp relief. What was wrong with the world that children starved in the streets? The signs of such clear poverty made him feel shame at the thought of his own life of wealth and privilege.

He thought of the petite little miss he'd hired as his assistant. He was used to ladies who never mussed their elegant dresses and who always had every hair in place. They were at home in drawing rooms and shone seated at elegantly appointed dining tables.

Maeve Murphy, on the other hand, he could picture running barefoot across a meadow or gathering flowers and wearing them in her hair. She was natural. Unaffected.

And he had no business thinking about her. He had no room in his life for complications, not even a beautiful, obviously compassionate and capable distraction.

Sean opened his eyes and blinked. "Am I dead?"

"You're not dead, laddie. You're stitched up and in my dispensary aboard the *Annie McGee*. You'll be good as new in a few days."

The boy's face blanched even paler, and he raised his head off the pillow. "What of me brothers? Am I at sea all alone?"

"I sent someone to search, but he didn't turn up any brothers."

"Gavin and Emmett are surely worried by now." Tears glistened in his eyes.

"I suspect you were planning to board the ship without paying passage." He raised a brow. "Am I correct?"

Sean gave him a sheepish nod.

"It's also my guess that your brothers found their way aboard. That both of them were nowhere to be found on the wharf is a good indication. Did you arrange a meeting place, the three of you?"

"Aye. On the foredeck at sundown."

"I shall be there on your behalf."

The boy's expression turned to one of terror. "Will they be thrown overboard? I heard sharks follow the ships."

"No one will be throwing children overboard," Flynn assured him. "And this isn't one of the coffin ships of years past."

Flynn himself had lobbied for legislation to put an end to the overcrowded and filthy, disease-infested vessels. Now there were passenger limits and a doctor aboard each ship. He was putting in his own time to see that the plan was fulfilled.

"Lie down and rest now. I'm going to get you something to eat so you can build up your strength."

"I have no way to be payin' you for tendin' my leg," Sean said in a thick voice. "Or for food."

Flynn got a knot in his chest. It took him a moment to speak, so he busied himself rolling a clean length of bandage. "If not for my fool assistant, you wouldn't have been injured, so the responsibility lies with me. You owe me nothing."

"Thank you, sir. I'll keep you in me prayers, I will."

Flynn covered him with a blanket and at last met his brown eyes. Young as he was, those eyes had seen the worst side of life and known more misery than any child should. His mention of prayer caught Flynn off guard. Perhaps the lad had more sway with the Lord of heaven than he. He hoped so, for the boy's sake. "You're welcome. Now sleep."

* * *

Bridget had gone off to meet with Mr. Atwater and acquaint herself with the family, so while Nora made up their bunks, Maeve headed up to locate the line for their daily allotment of food.

The topsails snapped in the wind that had swiftly carried the *Annie McGee* out to the ocean. The sharp cliffs of her homeland were still visible, and the sky was vivid blue. She paused at the rail to gaze out over the water and have another look at the receding cliffs. From here they all looked the same, so spotting Castleville was hopeless.

Was anyone she knew back home watching the ocean and seeing this ship on the horizon? She had spotted vessels many times, never dreaming she'd ever be aboard one.

The sun's reflection on the water nearly blinded her. She blinked and refocused on the person beside her.

The tall woman wore a flounced dress and matching capelike jacket, with six inches of lace at her wrists. Requirements for boarding had specified no crinolines or hoops, so her layered skirts hung shapelessly and a little too long on the deck.

Maeve's plain brown dress was far more practical, though poverty had driven her choice, not fashion or even practicality. The woman's dark auburn hair was parted in the middle and severely drawn back. She stood gazing at the horizon, and appeared to be a few years older than Maeve's mother had been when she'd died.

"I'm Maeve Murphy," she said by way of introduction. A good many people were going to dwell in close quarters for the duration of the voyage; she might as well get to know a few of them.

The woman turned and glanced down at her, taking in her long red curls and plain dress.

Maeve felt at a distinct disadvantage, being petite and obviously from a different social station. She resisted the urge to smooth her worn skirts with a calloused hand. They were fellow countrymen, after all, embarking on a journey together. There was no reason they couldn't be friends.

"This is all so exciting. I've never before been away from Castleville. Have you traveled aboard a ship before?"

The woman's chin inched up until she was literally looking down her nose at Maeve. She took a handkerchief from her sleeve and held it over her nose as though she smelled something odiferous. "Someone of your station should not be speaking to a lady, unless first addressed. You've obviously had extremely poor training. Where is your mistress?" She glanced around. "Shouldn't you be seeing to her needs instead of bothering passengers?"

Maeve drew a blank. No words formed, and humiliation burned its way up her neck to her cheeks. She'd never been dressed down in such a rude manner, but then she'd never mingled with anyone other than the people of her village—simple people just like the Murphys. The doctor had been kind and mannerly, so this woman's rude behavior caught her off guard. "I have no mistress. My sisters and I are taking this voyage to Massachusetts together."

"Then it will serve you well to learn your place. Never address a lady unless spoken to. And I certainly have no intention of speaking to you again." The fabric of the woman's skirts swooshed as she gathered them and marched off as though she couldn't get away fast enough.

Maeve stared at the two elaborately braided buns on

the back of her head. The deliberate shun pierced her previously buoyant mood.

Maeve was from a poor family. The landowners and their families lived very different lives from hers, but she'd imagined that in a situation like this, the boundaries would be less severe. Apparently there was no escaping the attitudes of those with more money than humanity.

She gave the ocean one last look and made her way across the deck until she found the line for food supplies and stood at the end. The man ahead of her was dressed in a black suit and stylish hat. He glanced at her, but since her previous lesson still stung, she kept her silence.

Minutes later she was joined by a woman in a pretty white-on-tan silk dress with a flounced skirt and long puffed sleeves. Surreptitiously, she admired the woman's pretty dark hair, and the way it gleamed in the sunlight and remained gathered within its confines, but quickly turned away.

The woman spoke from behind her. "Aren't you the young lady who helped that boy on the wharf this morning?"

Surprised, Maeve turned to face her. "Yes, ma'am. The lad's name is Sean McCorkle."

"That was very quick thinking, indeed. I dare say the lad might not have survived had you not gone to his aid when you did."

Pleased by the woman's friendly manner, she warmed to her immediately. "Dr. Gallagher is a fine surgeon," she replied. "Sean should be on his feet in no time."

"Have you chosen a spot on deck for your evening fire yet?" the woman asked.

"Not yet." A brisk gust of wind caught Maeve's hair, and self-consciously, she quickly fashioned it into an unruly fat braid and tucked the end under her collar. She would find a bit of twine when she got back to the cabin.

"I'm Aideen Nolan. I'm traveling with my aunt, Mrs. Kennedy."

"A pleasure to meet you, 'tis. I'm Maeve Murphy. My sisters and I are headed for Boston—well, a small village nearby called Faith Glen, actually."

The woman glanced at the nearby passengers. "I suggest we reserve our spaces next to one another. That way we'll be assured that at least one of our nearby supper companions will be familiar. Unless, of course, you have other plans. I'm probably being presumptuous."

Maeve gave her a bright smile. "No, we hadn't made plans yet. I'd very much like to find a place near yours. I'm confident my sisters will be glad for friendly company, as well. I've already had an encounter with a rather unpleasant woman who put me in my place for speaking to her." Maeve glanced down at her clothing. "Thought I was someone's maid, she did."

"I'd wager that was Mrs. Fitzwilliam," Aideen said. She leaned near and spoke quietly. "The gentleman just ahead is her manservant. I know her from the ladies' league in Galway." She took a brochure from the deep pocket of her skirt and flipped it open. "This list of preparations and rules for the journey instructs us to select the areas where we will be cooking our meals for the next several weeks." She glanced at Maeve. "Are you familiar with cooking procedures?"

"Indeed I am," Maeve replied with a sigh. "My sisters and I have been preparing meals since we were quite young."

"I shall be forever indebted if you will show me how."

Maeve had suspected from her dress and speech that Aideen was well-to-do, and her admission confirmed that thinking. "I'd be happy to tutor you, but you won't be indebted. Communities help one another, and we're going to be a community while we're aboard. Like a village on the sea, wouldn't you say?"

"Yes, I definitely would. My aunt and I had rooms in my grandparents' home until recently, and they always had a cook. Neither of us have ever attempted our own meals."

"My dear da passed on, only twelve days ago, God rest his soul. My mother's been gone ten years now. We've had a lot of experience at creating meals from nearly nothing."

"Next!"

Maeve turned to accept a burlap sack and a piece of chalk from a sailor whose face was coated with smoke and soot. "Daily allotment for three," he said. "Find yer cook spot and mark it with yer name or yer mark. Respect yer neighbor's planks and douse yer fire promptly at eight. Next!"

Maeve accepted a surprisingly heavy bag and a square of chalk, while the man recited the same instructions to Aideen. Together the two women headed away from the line in search of the fireplaces.

Along both sides of the foredeck, sections had been marked off with jagged stripes of black paint. For the most part, the areas were all the same size. The hands had obviously counted rows of deck planks in making the partitions. Each rectangular section held a curved brick cooking pit, partially open to one side, with three iron bars on the other to confine the coals.

They stood planning their strategy, hoping to predict which spot would be most protected from wind and weather. Praying they had it right, Maeve and Aideen wrote their surnames with chalk in side-by-side plots.

Setting down the bag, Maeve looked inside and

found half a pound of rice, a small slab of bacon, flour and a tin of peaches. "My sister is a better cook than I am, but these are basic foods and there's not a lot we can do with them. We should take them to our cabins now, and we'll prepare them side by side this evening."

"I look forward to meeting your sisters." Aideen gave her a grateful smile. "I hope we'll become fast friends."

Maeve returned below deck, where she stored the food in their locker and gave Nora the key to wear around her neck. "I met a lovely young woman, and we saved our cooking areas beside each other. You will meet her and her aunt this evening. She was delightful, she was. From a rich family, I'm certain, but she struck up a conversation and wasn't the least pretentious.

"Wait until you see her hair, Nora. It's dark and sleek. I didn't see it without her bonnet, of course, but I could imagine it's nothing like these wild ringlets."

"She sounds very nice, indeed." Nora had finished making their beds in her efficient and tidy manner, with corners tucked and pillows fluffed. "On the doctor's recommendation, I met with Mr. Mathers, and he assured me of a job with his staff. The galley is surprisingly roomy and clean. I'll learn my duties tomorrow," she said. "The others are men, but he said there would be another woman besides myself. The chores don't look like anything I haven't done a thousand times."

"I hope he gives you a chance to show what you can do and doesn't have you washing all the dishes. The crew would miss out if you couldn't cook for them."

"You're a sweet lass. Biased, of course."

"Dr. Gallagher is expecting me back in the dispensary to help organize supplies." Maeve located a faded apron in her bag and slipped it on over her dress. "This will have to suffice for a uniform."

"It's clean and adequate," Nora assured her. She

rested her hand atop Maeve's as her sister reached into her bag for her comb. "Thank you for accepting the doctor's offer, Maeve. I know you worry you're unqualified for a job with so many responsibilities, but you always did your best to help Mother and Da and our neighbors in Castleville. The local women declared you the most knowledgeable and dependable midwife in all of County Beary. I've no doubt you will be a benefit to the doctor."

"I'm hoping to learn from him." Maeve braided her hair as neatly as she could manage and secured it with a length of twine. For the first time she wondered what other passengers like that Fitzwilliam woman would think of her helping the doctor. Maybe they would simply see her as his servant, and find that acceptable. Was that how the doctor saw her? She surely didn't look forward to any more encounters like the one with Mrs. Fitzwilliam.

"The three of us will have an income…all because you so bravely went to that boy's aid."

"Helping him was simply instinctive," she replied. "Not heroic."

"Tell that to the lad who is alive, thanks to you."

"God provided the way for us," Maeve told her eldest sister. "He used what could have been a tragedy to find us jobs and bring the boy onboard. It will be interesting to see what develops next with Sean."

"Only you would find the silver lining in an otherwise cloudy situation."

Maeve stretched to her fullest height to give Nora a peck on the cheek. Nora leaned forward to accept the kiss. She took Maeve's face between her hands and looked into her eyes. "Mother always said you were like a bright star on a dark night. Even as a wee bairn, you saw everything differently than the rest of us. 'Tis a quality I admire."

"Nothing would get done without your practical thinking and logical planning," Maeve reminded her. "Sometimes I wish I was more like you."

"You're perfect just the way you are." She released Maeve. "Now go about your duties at the dispensary."

Maeve turned and headed for the door. For the first time in as long as she could remember, she was looking forward to something.

Chapter Four

A knock sounded on the door. Flynn looked up as Maeve Murphy opened it and peered in. She had bound her wild red hair and donned a plain coarse apron in preparation for her duties. He liked that she was efficient and punctual, adding those qualities to her quick thinking and kind manner with the boy. So far he liked everything about her.

"Come in, Miss Murphy. I've only just opened the first of the supply boxes." He gestured to the wooden crates lining the wall in the rectangular room.

She walked toward him, her bright blue gaze taking in her surroundings. In the morning's confusion he hadn't looked her over, and he did so now. She was a tiny thing, her flaming red hair creating ringlets that framed her cheeks, while the rest had been contained in a braid. Her skin appeared as fragile as porcelain, with healthy pink cheeks and a mouth like a China doll.

If a person judged on appearance, he'd think she was nothing more than a sweetly pretty girl, and overlook her wit and courage. Not many people had the knowledge or the compassion to jump to the McCorkle boy's aid the way she had.

She glanced with keen interest at the sturdy cabinets

with chicken wire instead of glass in the doors, where only a few bottles and tins stood. "If you'll be so good as to acquaint me with your system, I'll store the supplies."

"We'll both work on it." He led her to the other room, where Sean lay sleeping on a low cot, a blanket pulled to his chin.

"How is the laddie doing?" she asked softly.

"Very well, indeed," he replied. She smelled good, too, like clean linen and spring heather, and his reaction startled him. He hadn't noticed a woman in that way for a long time. He took an unconscious step away.

Her inquisitive gaze took in her surroundings, fastening on the storage cabinets and workspaces. There were no rimless surfaces in his dispensary. Everything had been designed to accommodate the normal rock and sway of the ship or even a storm. He explained his mortar and pestle for grinding roots and seeds, the scale and weights for measuring ingredients, the piece of marble on which he prepared salves, sets of measures, dosage spoons and a plaster iron. The young woman listened with interest and apparent understanding. She asked surprisingly insightful questions. He was glad now that he'd learned of Hegarty's true nature before the ship sailed. Maeve Murphy looked to be the better choice.

He described the contents of each crate as he carried and opened it. Between each ocean voyage, he spent weeks preparing bottles of saline draughts and barley water, jars of calves' foot jelly and plasters. He saw to it that those who fell sick on a ship he worked received the best care possible. His meager pay didn't begin to cover the cost of medicines, but he drew from his inheritances and vast investments.

He'd left his father's practice over the objection of his family to make a difference and to forget. He truly believed it was his calling to help people so desperate to start new lives that they risked a journey like this. Everyone he encountered had a dream of a new beginning he didn't share. He didn't think about his future, only about the work he had to do today.

"I wish I'd had half as many cures when my friends and neighbors were ailing," she said wistfully. "I may have been able to save more of them." Tears shone in her wide blue eyes as she gazed at a bottle of vitriolic acid.

Uncomfortable with the intimate glimpse at her suffering, he placed the bottles he held inside the chest and withdrew from his pocket the key he carried at all times. "We'll lock the mercury, laudanum and calomel in this chest under the case here." He stood slowly.

"Truth be told I wouldn't have known what to do with half of them." She raised her gaze to his in an earnest plea. "I'd like to learn."

He couldn't ignore her sincerity. "It won't be a bother to share their uses and common dosages," he said. "You have a natural instinct, Miss Murphy. I might even learn a few things from you."

He handed her his checklist and a pencil. As they worked he explained the contents of each bottle and their uses. She knew most of the more common medicines and was fascinated by others. He also took the opportunity to educate her a bit about ship life.

"They're electing the council today," he mentioned.

"What does that mean?"

"Each voyage the male passengers meet and select a group among them to form a council. When problems arise—and they will—these men govern by representing the passengers."

She couldn't imagine what would come up that would require their government, but she trusted the process.

"Are you ever on the council?"

"No, I'm technically not a passenger. I'm part of the crew."

When Sean woke up, Flynn's new assistant efficiently saw to his needs, inquiring about food supplies and then making the boy a gruel of millet and rye flour. Though Flynn grimaced at the concoction, the boy lapped it up and lay back with a contented smile.

"You're a blessing, you are, Miss Murphy," Sean said to her, his dark eyes adoring. "I be grateful for your care."

"You might well change your mind when I wash that head of hair of yours. It's going to need a good scrubbin'. I'm going to fill a pail now, and you can lie right there with your head over the edge of the table."

"I'll catch me death of cold, I will," the lad howled.

Flynn turned aside to hide a grin. "I have free access to the barrels of rainwater, Miss Murphy. Just ask a sailor for help toting buckets."

Sean's smeared face showed his concern. "I'd just worked up a good skin coverin' afore the doctor began to scrub it away."

"It's June, not December," she argued. "You'll not catch cold. And it's a good thing the doctor got a start on scrubbin' off the filth, otherwise we may have mistaken you for a bit of firewood lying on the wharf. You'll be washin' your face and hands every mornin' while you're here."

As she argued with the boy, her brogue got amusingly thicker. Flynn chuckled.

The room grew silent, and he turned to see the both of them staring at him. Perhaps his laugh had sounded as rusty to them as it had to him. "I don't think you're going to win this one, laddie. We'll find you some clean clothing, as well."

"Aye, sir," Sean said, putting aside his bowl. "Thank you, Miss Murphy. 'Twas a delicious gruel."

"I don't know that it was delicious," she said with a raised brow. "But it will build up your strength. Tomorrow I'll make you a flavorful potato soup that will stick to your ribs."

The boy beamed at her promise. "I'll not fight you on a quick washin' today. The doc's already done me feet."

She'd known just what to do with the meal to make it palatable, and Sean had eaten it as though it was fare fit for a king.

Flynn didn't know Maeve's background, but her clothing, while clean and pressed, indicated a lack of means. Her older sister had whispered how desperate they were to earn a wage. And Sean, an orphan, surviving in the village streets... Flynn had no concept of such poverty.

His privileged life had been glaringly different from the ones these two had lived. His family owned property in three countries, had a home in each and employed servants to do the work and the cooking. There was no such thing as a simple meal where he came from. Four courses served with silver utensils and gold-monogrammed china was the norm.

Even he himself owned land and a house in England and had purchased a home in Boston. His lifestyle was extravagant compared to those of his poor countrymen. But money didn't mean happiness or contentment, he knew for a fact. It was heartwarming that Maeve seemed satisfied with next to nothing. It said a lot about her temperament...and her faith.

Flynn got called away several times that afternoon to tend passengers unaccustomed to the sea. Many lay on their bunks with heads swimming and stomachs roiling. There was nothing to be done for them, save bathe their heads in cool water. Since they weren't ill or contagious, he assured each one they would feel better in a day or two and advised them to stay on deck, rather than below.

As the day waned, the doctor sent Maeve on her way. She felt good about her day's work and confident she'd earned her wage. She passed a man with an easel set up at a good vantage point and paused to watch him sketch the horizon, with its craggy cliffs and white-crested waves. Minutes later, she joined her sisters on the foredeck. A piece of paper fluttered from beneath the edge of one of the bricks that made up their cooking pit. Nora reached for it and unfolded the note.

Immediately, she handed it to Maeve. "It's for you."

My dearest Miss Murphy, she read silently. *My aunt and I have been invited to dine in the captain's cabin this evening. Please accept our regrets, and we will look forward to meeting with you as soon as possible. Sincerely, Aideen Nolan.*

Bridget, who'd been reading over her shoulder, found a small keg and perched on it. "The Atwaters were invited, as well. After this evening, I'll be eating with them and their daughters most of the time. This dilemma never entered my mind. I don't know the first thing about proper etiquette. I can't let on and make mistakes or they'll think I'm not an appropriate governess."

"Nonsense." Nora paused in piling wood in their brick hearth. "You're a fine young woman, with the common sense God gave you and the convictions of your beliefs. You will make a wonderful role model for the children."

"I'm sorry you didn't get to meet Aideen and Mrs. Kennedy this evening," Maeve added. "They might be a help in teaching you proper etiquette, so you may in turn teach the children. Aideen is the friendliest person I've met so far, she is. Not haughty like some of the others."

"The kitchen help are all quite nice," Nora added. Together, she and Maeve started a fire and put on a pot of water for rice and tea. Nora cut their small ration of bacon into six slices. From the other nearby cooking pits came the mouthwatering smells of frying bacon. Maeve's stomach growled.

She marveled as the heavens changed color. The smells were unfamiliar here. Of course the salty tang of the ocean was predominant, but there were no green scents. Grass, flowering bushes, heather had all been left behind, and she found she missed them. The smell of tar reached them from time to time, and always the smell of cooking food permeated the air.

As the sun set lower in the sky, the wind grew more chill. They bundled themselves in their shawls and unobtrusively glanced at the neighboring passengers.

"Tell us more about the Atwaters," Nora said.

"There are three young daughters," Bridget began. "Laurel is eleven. Hilary and Pamela are younger. When I arrived, Laurel actually looked at my dress and asked if I'd come to clean their stateroom." She smoothed her hand over her skirt, as though the memory still stung.

After her encounter with Mrs. Fitzwilliam, Maeve could certainly understand.

Bridget glanced up. "Not that I wouldn't have, mind you, had that been the duty assigned me."

"They have a stateroom?" Nora asked. She had mixed ingredients and set the dough on a smooth clean brick beside the fire to rise. Once it was baked they would have bread for tomorrow morning.

"Aye. It's well-appointed, with room for the girls to do lessons. Hilary has brought a canary aboard, and little Pamela has an array of China dolls like I've seen only in catalogues."

"A canary?" Nora set out a small jar. "Our rations contain enough molasses to sweeten our tea. I should think it was unnecessary to bring a bird aboard a ship."

Bridget shrugged. "Perhaps she simply enjoys the songs, and her parents indulge her. I glimpsed a life unfamiliar to anything we know. The girls bicker among themselves and argue over who gets the largest or best portions or whose shoes are prettier."

"Mother would never have allowed us to behave in such a way," Nora said.

"She was strict, but she disciplined us with love," Bridget agreed.

They bowed their heads and held hands in a familiar circle.

"Father God, we come before You, grateful for this opportunity You've given us," Maeve began. "We are thankful that we could buy tickets and amazed at Your provision in giving us jobs so quickly."

"Thank You that we are not going hungry," Nora added. "This is more than adequate food for Your humble servants."

"And thank You," Bridget added softly, "That none of us has the seasickness."

"We ask that You heal Sean McCorkle's leg now," Maeve added. "And watch over his brothers, wherever they are. In Jesus' name we pray..."

"Amen," the sisters chorused and gave each other tired, but joyful smiles.

The wind had come up, so Nora tied a scarf over her hair before dishing the rice onto three tin plates. Bridget divided the bacon equally. This allotment of food was more than they were accustomed to, and Maeve truly did feel blessed. She vividly remembered many times when Nora had told them she'd already eaten and split pitiable amounts of potatoes between the two younger girls.

"There's a can of peaches," Maeve told Bridget, and her sister's eyes lit up.

The boat rocked upon the waves. The wind tossed Bridget's hair. Maeve looked upon each of her sisters with a fond smile, and hope buoyed her spirits. *Thank You, Lord.*

Flynn had been standing in the same spot for nearly half an hour. He'd glimpsed a shaggy-haired boy earlier, but the lad had slipped away before he could speak to him. So he waited.

Finally, a boy sitting on a coil of rope caught his attention. Flynn hurried over. "You Sean McCorkle's brother?"

Smaller and even skinnier than Sean, the boy's frightened brown gaze darted about as though seeking an escape. "Who are you?"

"I'm Dr. Gallagher. I have Sean in my dispensary. If you want to see him, come with me."

The boy shot Flynn a cautious look. "What're ye gonna do to us?"

"Put you to work to earn your passage. How does that suit you?"

"You're not gonna make us walk the plank?"

Flynn chuckled. "I promised Sean I wouldn't feed you to the sharks, and I'm a man of my word. Now get your brother and bring him back here."

The boy scrambled to his feet and ran off, arms pinwheeling as he nearly toppled forward in his haste. A few minutes later, he returned with a young man of about eighteen in tow. "This here's Gavin."

"What've you done with Sean?" The tall lanky boy squinted with skepticism.

"Cleaned and sewed up his leg. The Murphy girl saved his life, you know. Has big plans for washing Sean's hair. Can't wait until she sees the two of you. Fresh water is rationed, but I get a larger portion for medical purposes. Come on."

"Where you be takin' us?"

"To the dispensary so you can see your brother. Have you had a meal today?"

"We ain't hungry."

"I doubt that's true."

"How do we know you won't get us down there and put us in stocks?"

"No stocks aboard the ship," he replied. "Are you coming?"

The boy glanced at his little brother. "Aye."

They followed Flynn down the ladder and along the passageway. Flynn opened the door and stood aside for them to enter. "He's in the side room over there."

The tall young man inspected his surroundings before moving to the door and peering into the other small room.

"Gavin!" came Sean's gleeful shout. "Is Emmett with ye?"

"Aye, he's right here, he is."

The two boys crowded at Sean's side and gave him awkward hugs. Emmett, the littlest one, pulled back with tears streaking his dirty cheeks. "We was afeared you be dead."

"No, the redheaded Miss Murphy saved me life for sure. Her and the doctor here. They been real good to me, they 'ave. The doc said he'd give us jobs, so we can earn our fare."

Flynn moved to stand closer. "You two will have to

take baths. And we'll find you clean clothes. Can't have the captain catch you looking like that."

"Can they sleep 'ere with me?" Sean asked. His desperate expression threatened to open a crack in the barrier around Flynn's heart.

"I have a stateroom," Flynn replied. "There's plenty of room for pallets, so the three of you can be together." He pinned Gavin with a probing look. "I'd appreciate your telling me why you were planning to stow aboard."

It was plain Gavin didn't fancy sharing his business. "We been stayin' in the back room at Ferguson's Livery. Old Mr. Ferguson left the door unlocked 'til we was in at night. But he died, and his missus sold the livery. The new owner shooed us out, so we was sleepin' under wagons and in back o' the millhouse. Sean here overheard stories of America. We came up with a plan to make our way there. I'm gonna find work and Sean and Emmett can go to school."

"Well, that sounds like a fine plan. I admire men with foresight. What happened to your parents?" Flynn asked.

"We ain't seen our da since Emmett was a wee babe. He just up and left, he did. Ma took care of us best she could, but then she took sick an' died."

Flynn wasn't surprised to hear their story. Death and hunger had been part of everyone's story over the past several years. The plight of the Irish had been grim for anyone not born into a wealthy family. "First things first," Flynn said. "Let's get you bathed."

"Why are ye and Miss Murphy so firmly set on bath takin'?" Sean asked.

"Because cleanliness is important. You should bathe and wash your hands often to prevent disease."

"What kind o' disease gets on yer hands?" Gavin asked.

"I've studied epidemiology for most of my career."

"Epi— What?" Gavin asked.

"Germs. Bacteria. Skeptics will say something you can't see can't hurt you, but that's not true. And in truth you *can* see germs, just not with the naked eye. In fact, I'm sure I can show you something that will convince you to wash your hands."

"What's that?"

"Before we get you in the tub, I want both of you to scrape under one or two fingernails, and place the dirt on a glass slide. Then I'll show you through my microscope what is living there."

"Living?" Sean asked, with a squeak.

Flynn grinned. "But not for long. Let's heat water." Instinctively, he knew his new assistant was going to be pleased when she saw the McCorkle boys clean. He looked forward to her reaction.

Chapter Five

The following morning, the Murphy sisters shared bread in their cabin before going their separate ways. Maeve arrived just as Dr. Gallagher peered out from the dispensary.

"Thank you for being punctual. I'm going to go above deck to boil water and then carry it back."

"I could do that for you," she offered.

"I spent the night here with Sean. I'd like a few minutes of sun and fresh air, if you don't mind. I'll probably eat before I return."

"Yes, of course! Take all the time you need. How is young Sean this morning?"

"Already talking about that potato soup you promised him. The galley help will provide you with anything you need for our patients. Simply introduce yourself as my assistant. You can make a trip to the galley after I return. I won't be long."

He headed away from the dispensary.

Maeve found Sean awake and obviously listening for her. "Mornin', Miss Murphy!"

"Good morning, Sean. Did you sleep well?"

"Yes'm. Didn't much notice the ship's sway. This 'ere cot is comfortable and the doc found me brothers."

"He did? My sisters and I prayed for them. And for you, too."

"Yes, he did. He made 'em take baths and then he put 'em up in his stateroom. He stayed here with me all night, he did. He told me after I eat, he will carry me to lie on his very own bunk."

She was glad to hear that the doctor was looking out for them. It was bad enough that Maeve and her sisters had been left with no family, but at least they were adults. The McCorkle lads were little more than babies. "Are you boys alone in the world?"

"Yes'm. We're headed to America so Gavin can work and me an' Emmett can go to school."

"You look well today. How are your brothers faring?"

"They're clean for sure. An' the doc showed us germs what was *livin'* under their fingernails!"

She wrinkled her nose. "That's disgusting."

"Yes'm, 'tis. You can be sure I'll be washin' me hands afore I eat from now on."

"Well, it was an effective lesson, to be sure."

A rap sounded at the door.

"I have to see to the caller," she told Sean.

Two women stood in the corridor. The younger woman's ebony hair had been brushed to a sheen and fashioned stylishly upon her head. She was strikingly lovely, with aristocratic cheekbones and dark winged brows over deep blue eyes. Her dress had been designed to fit her tall slender frame in the most flattering way, and she carried herself with confidence. Maeve had never laid eyes upon a more beautiful woman.

Maeve stepped back and gestured for the two to enter. Immediately, she hid her work-roughened hands behind her back and wished she'd had something nicer to wear, even though she was only coming to work.

After the upbraiding she'd received the previous day, she said nothing.

The shorter woman was older, and obviously the younger one's mother. She had the same black hair, though silver strands laced her temples and a shock of silver had been artfully drawn back from her face. Maeve had never seen a woman of her age without creases or lines in her face. Her hair and a few nearly imperceptible crow's-feet at the corners of her eyes were the only subtle clues to her age.

The older woman considered Maeve with disdain and dismissed her as though she wasn't there. She guided the one Maeve assumed was her daughter into the dispensary.

Now Maeve was faced with a dilemma. She hadn't intended to speak until spoken to, but she couldn't very well let these two stand there without telling them Dr. Gallagher wasn't in. She took a breath.

"Flynn?" the younger one called and glanced expectantly toward the back room.

Maeve released the air in her lungs. *Flynn?* "The doctor's not here at the moment." She glanced at the younger woman and then away. "He should arrive soon."

The woman's glance traveled from Maeve's face and hair to her shoes and back up. She towered over Maeve by a good eight inches. She narrowed her eyes. "Don't devise any designs for the doctor's attentions."

Maeve couldn't have been more startled. No words came to her.

"Flynn's family and mine are close. He and I are cut from the same cloth." She let her gaze fall again, as though pointing out the world of difference in weaves of cloth.

Maeve resisted touching her skirt with a self-conscious hand.

"Our fathers have made arrangements, and Flynn and I have an *understanding.* So don't imagine your undeveloped charms will hold any appeal to him when he has someone like me."

Maeve remained speechless. What might she have said to that?

The dark-haired young woman turned her back and faced the other direction.

Perturbed at their rudeness, she tamped down growing irritation and went about her chores.

Several minutes later and not a second too soon, the doctor returned.

"It's a pleasure to see you this morning, Kathleen. Mrs. Boyd, how are you faring?"

"I am well, thank you," Mrs. Boyd replied.

"What brings you to the dispensary so early?"

"It's Kathleen," the older woman said. "She barely slept a wink last night. Her ears hurt severely."

"Did you meet Miss Murphy?" he asked.

The two Boyd women didn't look at Maeve.

"They only just got here," Maeve answered. "We didn't have an opportunity to chat." She offered Mrs. Boyd a sweetly antagonizing smile, and immediately regretted it.

The woman's nostrils fared.

"Miss Murphy has filled a position as my assistant. She's as efficient and capable as they come. I can already tell she's going to be my right hand during this voyage."

Kathleen shot Maeve daggers. "How unfortunate for you, Flynn. I heard you had no choice but to hire someone off the dock."

"And she's already proven herself. Look how Hegarty

turned out, and he had references. I wouldn't have selected her if I hadn't thought she possessed the skill required for the job. Miss Murphy, this is Miss Kathleen Boyd and her mother, Mrs. Estelle Boyd."

Maeve gave a polite nod. "'Tis a pleasure to meet you both."

"Let's have a look at those ears," he said and reached for Kathleen's hand to help her up the wooden step to the examining table.

She stretched her long pretty neck to accommodate him and batted her thick lashes.

"You've traveled by sea before." His words reiterated what Kathleen had revealed about their relationship. "Have you had problems in the past?"

"Yes, I felt this same way last time."

"Are you experiencing any vertigo?"

"Why yes. Yes, I am."

"That should go away in a day or so as your body grows accustomed to the ocean. Any queasiness or vomiting?"

"A little."

"Excessive tiredness?"

"Yes, now that you mention it. But I can't sleep."

"How about a tingling in your feet?"

"Yes, the tingling definitely kept me awake most of the night."

"I suggest you spend as much time above deck as possible. It helps. There's nothing I can do for you. You might want to place a cold cloth on your forehead. Don't drink any alcohol or eat apples."

"Shall I bring her back for another consultation?" Mrs. Boyd asked.

"It's always a pleasure to see you both," he answered politely.

At a knock, Maeve crossed to usher in another young woman.

"I'm not feeling well," she told Maeve. "I'd like to see the doctor."

"He'll be right with you."

With his smile in place, Flynn ushered Kathleen and her mother out of the dispensary. In passing, Kathleen inspected the incoming patient with a frown of concern.

Once the door was closed, Dr. Flynn whispered to Maeve, "I made up the tingling feet part."

Maeve raised her eyebrows in surprise. Kathleen had gone right along with his list of symptoms, making it obvious she'd only come to see the handsome young doctor—and perhaps to warn away his new assistant.

"What can I do for you this morning?" he asked the young woman who'd just arrived. Maeve already had a nagging suspicion that no matter what the complaint, this case would have a similar outcome.

"I fell against a doorpost when the ship tossed. I believe I've injured my shoulder."

"Miss Murphy will help you slip one arm free, so I can examine your shoulder." He turned away and washed his hands.

The young woman gave Maeve a disapproving glance.

Maeve gestured for her to sit upon the examining table. "What's your name?"

She unfastened the back of the other woman's rust-colored satin dress. The fabric was like nothing she'd ever felt, and the buttons were tiny carved ivory disks. Beneath it she wore a fine silk chemise.

Flynn dried his hands and joined them.

"I am Miss Ellnora Coulter. Having just finished school in London, I'm traveling to the States with my parents. My father has investments in Boston."

Her English was proper with no hint of a brogue. Maeve glanced at Dr. Gallagher to gauge his reaction to the pretty young miss. He didn't seem interested in anything but her shoulder as he moved close. "I don't see any bruising. Help her back into her sleeve, Miss Murphy."

Once her dress was in place, he probed the area with his fingertips. "Does this hurt?"

"Yes."

"This?"

"Yes, indeed. It's quite painful."

Without a warning knock, the cabin door opened and Nora entered, stooping to accommodate her height. Her face was flushed, and she wore an expression of worry and concern Maeve had seen far too often. The surprising thing was that she cradled a bundled apron against her breast.

"Nora?" Maeve said, turning to meet her. "Whatever is…?"

"I was in the storage apartment, searching for a bag of salt, when I moved aside a sack and heard the oddest sound, like a mewling. I thought perhaps a kitten had been closed into the depot of provisions. Just look now what I discovered lying between the sacks of oatmeal, Maeve."

Her sister lowered the apron to reveal what lay within its folds. Maeve stepped close, and her heart caught in her throat.

An infant, obviously no older than a few hours or possibly a day at most, lay with eyes pinched shut, fists at its face, turning its head this way and that with mouth wide open.

Maeve stared in astonishment.

Chapter Six

"A baby? Nora, you found a *baby* in a storage bin?"

"Not in a bin. Between bags of oatmeal, almost right out in the open and near the entrance to the apartment. Is the little *grah mo chee* all right?" After referring to the infant as *sweetheart,* she handed off the bundle to Maeve.

Maeve took the baby just as Dr. Gallagher joined them. Nora explained again where she'd found the child. "Someone had wrapped a flour sack around her and left her like that."

He peeled the apron all the way back, revealing the pink infant's froglike legs and several inches of umbilical cord still attached. Her skin still bore streaks of mucus and blood.

"She's a newborn," he said unnecessarily. He glanced at Maeve. She hadn't seen him wear this look of discomfort before. "I haven't had much experience with infants." And he stepped away. "I'll get a basin of warm water so you can bathe her, and then I'll listen to her heart and lungs."

"What about my shoulder?" Miss Coulter called from the examining table.

"Your shoulder will be fine," Flynn told her. "I think it's just a little bruising."

"Perhaps you could call on me tomorrow to make sure I've improved."

"Certainly," he replied and saw her to the door.

Maeve exchanged a glance with her sister. "An unending stream of young ladies have sought medical attention since yesterday," Maeve whispered. "The good doctor is obviously prime husband material."

Nora only had eyes for the baby in Maeve's arms. "Will she live, Maeve? She's puny, is she not? You've seen a lot of babies born. What do you make of this one?"

"Let's clean her up and look her over." Maeve asked Nora to spread out towels on the examining table and proceeded to sponge the infant with clear warm water.

"All babies this young look puny," she told her sister. "She's average from what I can tell. She seems perfectly healthy and quite obviously hungry, the poor dear."

Once the baby's skin was clean and dry, Maeve made a diaper from the cotton bandages Flynn kept stacked nearby. Flynn opened a drawer on the other side of the room and offered a folded shirt.

Nora accepted the garment. She studied the intricate embroidery and monogram and asked a question with her expressive blue eyes.

"It's just a shirt," he said. "Cut it up to make her gowns. I have plenty more."

Nora used his bandage scissors to cut off the collar, sleeves and buttons and crudely fashion a garment.

"She appears fine," Maeve told her. "But we need to feed her."

"Rice water?" Nora asked.

"No, milk is best."

"It will have to be goat's milk." Flynn took a small

tin container from inside a cabinet and headed for the door. "The sailors have a nanny aboard. I'll be back with milk."

Nora glanced about. "How will we feed it to her?"

Maeve handed her the now-squalling baby and searched in earnest for a feeding method. "We could soak towels...or gauze."

She opened a cabinet and picked up a length of rubber tubing. "Better yet. We'll use this."

"That?" Nora asked, cuddling the infant.

"Aye. It's pliable, see. We'll puncture a couple of needle holes in it for the milk to come through and bend it like so. The baby will suck on it."

"Are you sure?"

"Stick your finger in her mouth and see if she doesn't latch onto anything."

"I've just washed all the sailor's breakfast dishes, so I expect my finger's clean enough." Nora offered the baby the tip of her index finger, and the crying stopped immediately. Nora got tears in her eyes. "The poor *grah mo chee* is so hungry."

"We'll have her fed in no time." Maeve placed the tubing in a kettle of water. "I'm going on deck to boil this."

Nora's eyes widened. "And leave me here alone with her?"

"You'll be fine," Maeve assured her. "Just cuddle her, as you're doing. She likes your warmth and the beat of your heart. If you'd like conversation, Sean McCorkle is lying in the next room."

"Who would leave their newborn baby on sacks of meal, Maeve?" Nora looked into her sister's eyes with a look of concern and disbelief. "She's only just been born, wouldn't you think? Aboard the ship...maybe right there in that storage apartment?"

"Seems likely, it does. But why her mother abandoned her is a mystery. If she'd died, someone would have found her body—or at the very least we'd have heard of a death."

"Maybe her mother couldn't care for her," Nora suggested.

"Her mother was the one with milk to nourish her," Maeve reminded her. "She could have cared for her better than we."

"Perhaps something happened to her and she was unable to return. If she was a stowaway, like those boys, she may have been hiding in that storage depot."

"We'll do everything we can. Have a seat. I'll be right back."

The situation did puzzle Maeve. Perhaps the woman would show up. Perhaps the infant had been left there by accident. Maybe she'd been taken from the mother. There were too many questions to think about, without any facts, so she set about doing what she could to help.

Flynn explained the situation to a couple of the sailors seated near their pens of chickens and only several feet from the goat's enclosure. The men generously gave him a cup of milk and told him to come back any time he needed more.

The newborn's presence knocked him a little off-kilter. Returning to the dispensary, he regarded the situation. He'd cared for children aboard ship, of course, but he hadn't been in close proximity to a baby only hours old since his own son had been born. The thought caused him more pain than he could deal with now.

Two years ago he'd lost his young wife and tiny son to the deadly cholera that had spread through Galway and so much of Ireland. His countrymen referred to potato blight and epidemics as *an Drochshaol,* the bad times, which were still prevalent and still a threat to lives and livelihoods. He'd read that after thousands had died, nearly a quarter of the remaining people had fled to other countries.

An Drochshaol was personal to Flynn. Unbearable. He'd studied to learn how to treat people and heal them. He'd devoted his life to medicine and research...but when the shadow of death had come to his own door, he'd been unable to do anything to save his wife and child.

He'd cared for them feverishly, night and day for weeks. Jonathon had gone first. Sturdy and strapping though the boy had been, his eventual dehydration caused by vomiting and diarrhea had been more than Flynn could stave off.

Grief-stricken, he'd buried his son and turned his attention to his wife, only to lose the same battle. Once they were gone, he had avoided people—even his family. He hadn't wanted to practice medicine, turning instead to research in an all-consuming drive to understand and eliminate the contamination that caused so many deaths.

He rarely let himself think about Jonathon or his failure to save him, but the memories of all he'd lost stalked him in the night, haunting his dreams and stealing any peace he hoped to find.

The risks to a newborn on this ship terrified him. And the dilemma of caring for a baby posed a problem, as well. Perhaps, if no mother was found, they could find a family to take in the infant for the duration of the journey.

He approached Maeve and Nora. "Boil everything that touches this baby," he told them. "Boil the cups in which we carry the milk." He glanced at the tubing. "You're using that to feed her? Did you boil it? Good.

Wash your hands thoroughly." He handed Maeve the half-full cup. "Throw out any she doesn't take and get fresh each feeding. I'll notify the captain that she's been found. A search to turn up her mother will come next, I have no doubt. Shall we find someone to care for her?"

Nora appeared stricken at the idea. "I can take care of her!"

"Nora, what about your kitchen duties?" Maeve asked.

"You and Bridget can help. We'll share her care and feeding." She gave her younger sister a pleading glance. "Please. She's so tiny and alone. We know she'll be safe with us—and under the doctor's supervision. With someone else we can't be sure they'll care for her properly or give her the attention she needs."

Maeve looked at the fragile little human being in Nora's arms, now frantically sucking at the pinpricks they'd made in the tubing and swallowing in noisy gulps. "I have helped care for a good many newborns. 'Tis not such a hardship."

She glanced at Flynn, and her compassionate blue gaze shot him through, touching a tiny crevice in his hardened heart. Thoroughly impractical though it may be to have an infant strapped to his assistant or a kitchen worker, the warm burst of admiration he felt at their earnest concern and willingness to take on this task couldn't be denied.

He didn't let himself look at the baby, but the sound of her sucking speared his heart. He gave Nora a stern look. "Clear your intent with Mr. Mathers. Assure me you have his approval and promise you'll take no safety risks in the galley. If you're to be near fire or water, you will give your turn over to one of your sisters."

"Yes, of course," Nora acknowledged quickly. "Thank you, Dr. Gallagher. God bless you."

"I'm going to assign one of the McCorkle boys to run errands for you part of the day. Emmett is the youngest and most agile, so he will run for milk and carry messages between the three of you." He looked at Maeve. "Thoroughly instruct him on sanitation."

She nodded her understanding. "Certainly, doctor. I'm relatively sure he already comprehends hand washing. Sean filled me in on their lesson. It made quite an impression."

Flynn asked Nora to place the baby on the examining table once she'd burped. "Let's have a listen now." He glanced up and then away. "The two of you may call me Flynn when there are no patients or other passengers present."

Maeve gave him one of her stunning smiles. "Thank you, Flynn."

A soot-faced cabin boy appeared then, extending a piece of paper. Flynn took it and read the hastily scrawled note. Seemed the captain had invited him to dinner in his cabin that evening. "Tell Captain Conley I'd be happy to join him and his wife."

The lad nodded and hurried off.

Once Flynn had listened to the baby's heart and lungs, he left Nora to diaper and dress her as best she could.

"Are we going to try to find the baby's mother?" Maeve asked in a near whisper.

He gestured for her to follow him into the smaller room. "One of us can go to the captain while the other stays here."

"I'll go," she offered.

He nodded his approval.

Maeve told Nora what she was doing and left to find the captain in the chart house. "May I have a moment to speak with you?" she asked.

Once she'd explained the situation, he removed his cap and scratched his head. "Never had this happen b'fore. Plenty o' babies been born aboard, but none have been deserted."

"I was thinking you could go over the ship's manifest," Maeve suggested. "See how many women of childbearing age are aboard and then question them."

"Sounds like a logical plan. Come with me."

She joined him in his cabin, where Mrs. Conley was cheerfully humming and scrubbing potatoes. Their cabin had a tiny kitchen area with hanging pots and pans that swayed with the ship's movement.

The captain set the heavy manifest on the scarred table with a thump and opened to the last pages.

After hearing Maeve's story, Martha Conley joined their efforts. She got a paper, pen and ink to make a list, then pushed them toward Maeve. "Your writin's probably better'n mine, dearie."

They came up with thirty-nine possibilities for someone who might have given birth.

Martha took a knife from a crock and slit the paper in half, handing half to Maeve. "We'll each take half. Do you think you can talk to nineteen women today?"

Maeve nodded. "I'll do as many as I can this morning and the rest after I'm finished in the dispensary."

"We'll compare this evening, then," Martha said.

After visiting with fifteen women, Maeve determined all of them unlikely to have given birth to a baby and abandoned it. Five were pregnant and three had new babies. The rest were widows. With four remaining on her list. Maeve went about her duties. She didn't hold much remaining hope for finding the baby's mother.

At noon she carried a meal to Sean, who had been moved to the doctor's quarters and made comfortable. She looked about the physician's neat room, noting rolled pallets where the three McCorkle brothers had slept. Books lined specially made shelves with brass bars to hold the volumes in place, and more were stacked here and there, where Flynn had left them. The doctor had a private cabin, with more space than she and twelve others shared each night.

She pictured him here, poring over his books. It was curious that a man of his age, especially one so handsome and intelligent, didn't seem to be married. But he must be single. If he wasn't, he wouldn't have taken a position like this.

Sean was glad for company, so she stayed while he ate his potato soup. "Dr. Gallagher said in America boys like me learn numbers and words. He said he'll help find us a family to stay with, where we can do chores an' go to school."

He talked her ear off before she could get away. Half of his sentences started with *Dr. Gallagher.*

Upon returning to the dispensary, she gathered containers and went to the foredeck to boil more water. While it cooled, she absorbed the warmth of the glorious sun and gazed across the vast Atlantic. The water's surface was crowded with slimy-looking objects of varying size, form and color, some of them resembling a lemon cut in half. In the distance two ships on the horizon kept the *Annie McGee* company. Were those ships as laden with immigrants escaping lives of poverty as this one?

Nearby, male passengers in three-piece suits and ladies in finely made dresses strolled the deck or sat upon wooden folding chairs. The women held parasols over their heads to protect their skin from the sun, reminding Maeve that she'd been standing there too long. She covered the pots of water and carried them back to the dispensary.

"It's a beautiful, sunny day."

Dr. Gallagher had been seated at his small writing desk making notes since she'd left. He didn't look up.

"Did you stop for a meal?" she asked.

"Lost track of time," he replied distractedly.

A commotion sounded in the corridor, and the door burst open. A woman's screams raised the hair on Maeve's neck. A sailor leaned in and spotted her. "The doctor in?"

"He's right here. Is someone sick?"

"We got her right here." He backed into the room, carrying one end of a blanket, upon which a woman lay, writhing in pain.

Flynn shot up and ran to meet them as the second man, a passenger dressed in plain clothing, entered with the other end of the blanket.

The reason for the woman's distress was immediately obvious. Her skirts were blackened, with much of the fabric burned away, right down to her pantaloons. The sickening smell of scorched wool reached Maeve.

Chapter Seven

Maeve swallowed and took a deep breath to stay calm.

"Caught her skirts on a cook fire, she did," the passenger said.

"Are you family?" Flynn asked.

"Aye, she's m'wife," he replied.

Maeve had treated burns before, and she knew how much pain the woman suffered. "Laudanum?" she asked automatically.

"Chloroform first," Flynn answered. "Bring her over here to the table," he instructed.

Maeve doused a square of gauze. "What's her name?" she asked the husband.

"Goldie," he replied in a thick voice. "Goldie McHugh." He cleared his throat, but didn't tear his stricken gaze from his wife.

"The doctor's going to take good care of you, Goldie." Maeve smoothed the woman's hair at the same time she placed the gauze over her nose and mouth. "Just take a few deeps breaths now. You'll sleep."

The woman's eyes, filled with pain and fear, met Maeve's in those torturous few moments before her lids drifted closed and she lay blessedly still.

"Now prepare a dose of laudanum," Flynn instructed.

He turned to the husband. "Miss Murphy and I are going to have to cut the remainder of her skirts away to see how severe her injuries are. I understand your concern for your wife, sir, but the fewer people in here while we treat her, the better her chances."

"I'm not leavin' my Goldie like this," the man argued.

"Understand now, she is at risk for serious infection, and until we can see how badly she's burned, your presence places her in jeopardy."

His words were severe, but Maeve comprehended his concern to keep the room and the wounds as clean as possible.

Goldie's husband seemed taken aback by that information and stood with his mouth clamped shut.

"Every second I spend with you is a second I'm not attending to your wife," Flynn added.

Maeve watched their interaction with deep compassion for the man and appreciation for the physician's wisdom.

At last a look of resignation crossed the big man's face. "I'll be in the corridor."

As soon as the door had closed, Flynn was all business, cutting away the remaining skirts as close to the burned area as possible. Maeve removed the woman's shoes and cut the remaining portions of Goldie's wool stockings away. Maeve assisted him as he used a large pair of tweezers and removed bits of fabric seared to the lower portions of Goldie's legs.

Each time flesh was revealed, Maeve marveled that there was skin intact beneath the scorched fabric.

"I don't want to peel away skin, but I can't leave this fabric stuck to the burns," he said as though thinking aloud.

Maeve studied the patches. "We could soak rags in

vinegar and lie them over the wounds to keep it all wet while you work."

"That's a sound idea." He gathered rags and a basin of vinegar and plunged the fabric down in the liquid.

"I honestly expected to see much worse," Maeve confessed.

"As did I. She's extremely fortunate. Seems whoever doused the flames did so quickly enough to spare her." He draped the wet rags over her shins. "How would you have treated this patient back home?"

"With whatever was available. Potato peels work well. I once made a liniment of turpentine and yellow basilion. But I most appreciate the properties of cotton ash paste."

"That's my first choice, as well. How did you make yours?"

"Burned cotton wool and mixed it with any oil available. Usually linseed or olive."

"Cotton wool ashes are in the big jar in the base of that cabinet." He gestured with a nod as he lifted the corner of the rag and loosened a bit of fabric from their patient's leg. "This is coming right off. Go ahead and mix the ashes with peppermint oil to make a paste."

She did as directed, stirring the blackened concoction that smelled better than it looked. She placed the container and a wooden spatula at the ready.

To their amazement, once Flynn was finished removing fabric, there were only half a dozen small patches of seriously burned skin and a few blisters. Goldie would definitely be in pain, but she would heal.

Flynn took the container and carefully smeared black paste on the woman's shins. "We want to keep this dressing fresh and the skin completely covered for a few days."

Maeve nodded.

"How did you learn all you know about methods of healing?" he asked. Her instincts were impressive.

"My mother had a good many home remedies," she answered. "I was always interested in her methods, and she was eager to teach." The stick he used became too glommed with paste, so she handed him a clean one.

"I have always found it fascinating how our ancestors used home remedies—roots, flowers, herbs—with excellent healing properties," Flynn commented. "I have often wondered about the first people who tried such a remedy. Where did they get their ideas?"

Maeve shook her head in reply. "There was an elderly woman in our village who tended the sick for many years, until she grew too old and feeble. It was then her nephew and his family took her in. She sat in a chair just outside their front door the last years of her life. Sharp as a tack, she was. Anything I needed to know, I went to her. Plus, much of my education came by accident and necessity."

"You have a natural instinct," he told her. "I saw physicians graduating with less skill than you. What is it you plan to do when you get to America?"

"Have you heard of a place called Faith Glen?"

"Indeed. It's not far from Boston."

"Is it pretty there?"

He glanced at her and then back down at his work. "It's on the coast, so the countryside is green and lush. A welcoming little village, much like those in Ireland. Without the lava beneath or the eroded cliffs, of course."

"I can see it now," she breathed.

"How did you learn of Faith Glen?"

"After my father's death, my sisters and I found a letter written to my mother many years ago. In it, the writer explained he had bought her a cottage in Faith Glen. We had nowhere to go, because the land

we farmed had been given to the landlord's family…
so we decided to set about learning if this deed is legal
and if the house is still there. Have you ever heard of a
man named Laird O'Malley?"

He finished the task and draped clean cloth over
Goldie's legs. "Can't say I have, no. Is he family?"

"We're not sure who he is—or was. But he thought
enough of our mother to buy a house and deed it to
her." After checking that Goldie still slept soundly, she
cleaned up supplies and put away containers. "We've
left behind everything we ever knew on the chance
that there's a new beginning for us in that village. We
spent all we had on fare and food to last this journey.
Working on the ship will give us a little money to live
off, but once we reach our destination, we'll need jobs."

Flynn covered Goldie with a crisp clean sheet. "No
doubt the wondering is a burden to the three of you. Will
you find this house? Does this O'Malley fellow exist?"

His perception warmed her even more to the man.
"We've had to turn the worry over to the good Lord,"
she told him. "He tells us not to be afraid, because He
is with us and takes care of us no matter what. I believe that."

The doctor rolled the scraps of burned fabric and
Goldie's ruined skirts into a compact ball. "I'll burn
these on deck later."

"I can do it."

He listened to Goldie's heart and tested her pulse before looking up at Maeve. "She's doing well. I want to
keep her dosed and unconscious for the rest of the day."

"It will be the kindest thing to do."

"And it will prevent movement and dislodging of
the dressings."

"I will stay with her."

"Maeve," he said, "if the house in Faith Glen isn't

there or is occupied—if you can't find this O'Malley fellow or anyone to recognize the deed, I'll make certain you find quarters in a good boardinghouse. You and your sisters won't be left with nowhere to go. I give you my word."

Maeve's eyes filled with tears she rapidly blinked away. "Thank you. My sisters will be as relieved as I am to hear that." She chanced a direct look at his face. "You're a kind and generous man, Flynn."

He dropped his gaze to the patient. "I'd like to think someone would do the same for my sisters."

"You have sisters?"

"Two of them. Spoiled and pampered. One is getting married next month."

"Where is your family?"

"Galway," he replied. "That's where I lived before…"

"Before?"

"Before I researched and traveled. I'll be talking to Goldie's husband now. I'm grateful I have good news for him."

He strode to the door and ushered the man inside.

The entire time he spoke with the man about his wife's injury and fortunate circumstance, Maeve counted her blessings. Their future was still uncertain as far as the house in Faith Glen went, but at least Flynn's assurance they wouldn't be on the streets set her mind at ease. She couldn't wait to tell Nora and Bridget, but first she had another four women to locate.

His capable—and undeniably beautiful—assistant had generously offered to check on Goldie that evening while Flynn enjoyed a leisurely supper in Captain Conley's cabin.

Flynn had sailed the *Annie McGee* on several occasions and had previously sampled a delicious and hearty lobscouse, unsurpassed by any other stew he'd ever tasted, prepared by the captain's missus. This one was tender lamb with chunks of potato and turnip. Her biscuits were gold and flaky, and he was grateful to Maeve for the opportunity to enjoy this meal without having any fear for his patients' well-being.

He had to wonder, however, what she and her sisters dined on this evening. The daily allotment consisted of meal and usually another staple, sometimes ham or bacon because it could be stored in salt. Perhaps he could beg a dish of lobscouse from Martha Conley to carry back for her.

From across the opposite side of the table, Kathleen gave him a generous smile, while her mother chatted with Martha. Martha Conley had apparently invited the Boyds because she'd known Flynn for years and knew his family and hers were close. His father had suggested Flynn marry her, but Flynn didn't have those kind of feelings for her.

He could never look at Kathleen with love or passion. She was indeed lovely, educated and brought up to run a household. Any man would be fortunate to gain her attentions. Her social status made her appealing to a man, and her family was wealthy, qualities that would make her a good match one day soon.

Flynn couldn't think of marrying again. He did not feel at ease with the idea—and especially not with someone he considered a friend.

Currently, he divided his time between Boston and Galway, with lengthy trips to Edinburgh, where medicine was beginning to advance and he had opportunities to work with colleagues and study the groundbreaking practices of Joseph Lister.

There would come a day when he wanted a family and a home, but he couldn't work on it now, even if he did become a bookish recluse. Perhaps one day he'd find a woman content with his overzealous commitment to medicine, but it wouldn't be Kathleen.

He couldn't marry for love: love hurt too much. Nor could he marry someone he didn't love, even though that sort of marriage might neatly and efficiently preclude any chance of additional hurt or grief. It was plain he couldn't marry for any reason.

"How is the McHugh woman?" the captain asked.

"She's doing very well. I confide I didn't have a good feeling when I first saw her, but her husband and several sailors put out the flames before her skin was badly damaged."

"The good Lord was watching over her, He was." Martha placed a bowl of golden brown custard on the table.

"I agree, Mrs. Conley. There's no other way she could have been spared from a worse fate, but by divine intervention."

"Is that dwarfish person still assisting you?" Estelle Boyd asked.

Flynn blinked in consternation. "Who?"

"The girl with the blinding red hair."

"You must mean Miss Murphy," Martha said. "I think she's a lovely little thing, and her hair is as bright and pretty as can be. 'Tis a true Irishwoman who has skin and hair like that."

Estelle's caustic comments about Maeve didn't sit well with Flynn.

Kathleen gave him an apologetic smile.

"Did you notice the ships to the south this day?" Captain Conley asked, changing the subject.

"I didn't see them myself, but I heard they were in sight."

The captain nodded. "By tomorrow we should be able to make them out and recognize the vessels."

"Will you be staying in Boston for any length of time after this voyage?" Estelle asked. "Kathleen and I are planning to host a celebration once we find a suitable home."

"What will you be celebrating?" Martha asked.

"Our move to America," Estelle replied. "So many of our friends and acquaintances have moved to London or New York or Boston that we've been sorely alone. The merchants haven't been stocking items we require, and even the sempstresses have taken other employ."

"*Sempstress* sounds so primitive, Mother," Kathleen chided. "In America they use the word *seamstress.*"

Estelle rolled her eyes. "*Seam*stress, rather."

"Aye, these tryin' times have been hard on Irish in all walks of life," Martha agreed. "Shipping or sailing seems to hold the most promise."

"They say the cities along the coast of America are brimming with jobs, and merchants are doing well," Captain Conley said. "Immigrants are heading west, and they need supplies for travel."

"I should warn you we're not considered the cream of society in America," Flynn told Estelle. "The English have been there for quite some time, and they've already set the standards."

Estelle didn't appear pleased by his pronouncement, but he thought it better she be forewarned to the snobbery that prevailed.

"We are people of means," she informed him. "We shall buy a home and prove ourselves in the community."

He hoped she was right, but he felt no assurance of that.

Flynn was enjoying a bowl of custard when there was a hard knock at the door. "Cap'n, sir!"

"What is it? Come in."

The sailor entered and stepped to the captain's chair, where he leaned to say something in his ear.

Conley shot his gaze to Flynn. "Excuse us, ladies. The doctor and I are needed."

"Thank you for the exceptional meal, Mrs. Conley," Flynn said, standing. "Excuse me, Kathleen, Mrs. Boyd."

Outside in the corridor the captain turned to Flynn. "Seems someone's found a young woman's body. Do you know who it is?" he asked the sailor ahead of them.

"No, sir."

On deck, the crew had considerately rigged canvas to hide the girl's body from the eyes of the passengers. She lay in what would have been plain view where she'd fallen. This wasn't the area where the passengers had their fires, so only a few passengers who'd been strolling the deck stood nearby.

Flynn glanced up. "Looks like she fell from the fore-castle onto the deck."

"Passengers aren't allowed up near the crew's quarters," Captain Conley said.

"Nobody saw her or knows what she was doin' there," the nearest crew member told him.

Flynn stepped closer. It had been obvious even from a distance that the girl was dead, but gathering all the details was part of his job. Her curly mane of dark wavy hair was matted with blood. He brushed a skein from her neck and pressed his fingers against her vein. No pulse, as he'd expected.

"She's dead."

"Does anyone know this girl?" Captain Conley asked.

A young woman of maybe sixteen or seventeen who clung to her mother's hand, raised stricken eyes. "I—I have talked to her before."

"Do you know her name?"

"She told me her name is Bridget."

Flynn's heart stopped for half a minute. Maeve's sister? The one working for the Atwaters? His chest felt as though someone had rested a weight upon it. Maeve would be devastated.

How was he going to tell her?

Chapter Eight

A knot formed in Flynn's throat. "Bridget is the name of one of the Murphy sisters."

"We'll lay her out before you get the others," the captain said. "This isn't a pretty sight for her kin."

Flynn waited with the captain while several men brought a coffin with holes drilled in the side and sand in the bottom. He'd seen burials before, but the box was still a shock. He helped place the body in the coffin, and waited while the deck was scrubbed clean.

When all was presentable, he went in search of Maeve.

"I'll be fine sittin' here, Miss Murphy. You go eat your supper."

"She's had another dose of laudanum, so she will sleep a couple of hours," Maeve told him. She left Goldie's husband seated at his wife's side and called on the last women on her list before joining Nora for a meal of stirabout and dried apples beside their firebox. Maeve held the squirming baby while Nora cleaned their dishes. Bridget had gone to have dinner with the Atwaters.

"I called on half the possible women aboard this

vessel today," she told her sister. "To no avail. Mrs. Conley took the other half of the list, so I still need to meet with her."

"She took her milk and slept in her sling most of the day. I even had a few minutes here and there to cut some of this fabric in preparation for sewing her clothing."

"That's what newborns do." Maeve changed the square of flannel the child wore for a diaper. A few of their fellow passengers had generously given them scraps of material and a few pieces of cast-off clothing. "Right now she's easy to care for. Meet her needs and she's happy. Will you have time to wash these tomorrow?"

"I thought I'd wash them out tonight, while we have a fire going. I can hang them in the morning. Laundry days are designated on Mondays and Thursdays, unless someone has a baby. If there are diapers that need to be laundered, we can hang them any time we please."

"I'm sure that rule is in place as a favor to everyone," Maeve replied with a smile. "Isn't she the prettiest little thing? Look at her silky fine hair. I hope it's not curly."

She bundled the infant in a lightweight square of cotton to keep her secure and protect her head from the breeze. It was still light enough to make out her features and her delicate fingernails. Maeve touched her incredibly small, soft hands with wonder.

Nora finished her chore and came to sit beside them. "She is indeed a pretty baby. I've been thinking, Maeve. Our *grah mo chee* needs a name."

"She probably has a name already," Maeve said.

"No one has claimed her, and it looks unlikely that you're going to find her mother or anyone who knows of her existence. For now we're all she has, and we can't go on calling her baby."

"You call her *grah mo chee*," Maeve added.

"Her name isn't *sweetheart*. She needs a real name."

"I suppose you're right." Maeve waited, because she knew Nora had already thought it through.

"I was thinking Grace or Faith."

"I like them both."

"Grace it is, then?"

"Grace is a fine name."

Nora took the baby and nestled her close. "Baby Grace, we are going to take care of you. You have our promise."

Maeve smiled at her sister. She couldn't have anticipated Nora's fascination with the little one. She was quite obviously besotted with the child, as were Maeve and Bridget. No baby ever received so much attention and affection in their first day as this one.

They hadn't been paying attention to their surroundings, so the swift approach of booted feet upon the planks caught Maeve unawares. She glanced up, even more startled to find Flynn, his stark expression serious.

"Dr. Gallagher!" she said. "What brings you here this evening?"

"Please. Stay seated." His forehead was wrinkled with concern at the sight of her and Nora sitting together, and he looked around, as if he'd hoped to see someone else with them. "May I join the two of you?"

"Yes, of course. Have you eaten? I can offer you tea."

"Nothing, thank you. I'm afraid I have some bad news for you."

"What is it?" Maeve asked. "Is it Goldie? She was sedated when I left, and her husband was right at her side."

"No," he answered. "That's not it."

Maeve waited for whatever it was he had come to say.

"This is going to be difficult." He glanced from side to side, as though reconsidering or perhaps not wanting their neighbors to overhear. His expression was decidedly pained. "Perhaps this isn't the best—"

"We have a guest? How delightful!"

The feminine voice caught Flynn's attention, and he turned as Bridget approached. She wore a bright smile, and as usual her hair had escaped its confines and trailed down her back.

"The Atwaters chose to share the evening with their daughters, so I was dismissed after supper. Their cook is traveling with them. We had the most delicious fish and potatoes."

Color drained from Flynn's face. He jumped to his feet and stared at Bridget. "You—you had supper with the Atwaters?"

"Yes. I've just left there."

"Why, I—I don't know what to say." He grasped Bridget's shoulders and tugged her to him, hugging her soundly before releasing her. "I'm so glad to see you."

Even in the semidarkness, Bridget's blush was apparent. She was quiet for a full minute, which plainly showed her astonishment.

Maeve was dumbfounded, as well. His demonstrative behavior was completely out of character.

"Forgive me," Flynn said, his voice low. "That was forward of me, but I believed... Well, I..."

Maeve and Nora were on their feet now. "What did you think?" Nora asked the doctor.

"I was so glad to see your sister alive and well," he explained. "You see, there was an accident earlier. A young woman who looks just like Bridget here fell from the forecastle and was killed."

Bridget gasped, and Nora hugged the baby to her breast.

"How dreadful!" Nora exclaimed.

"And you saw this young woman?" Maeve asked.

"Aye. She had the same hair as your sister. Similar clothing."

"And that's what you'd come here for? Thinking you were going to tell us our sister had fallen to her death?"

He nodded, clearly disturbed.

"Oh, my goodness," Maeve breathed.

"That was kind of you, Dr. Gallagher," Nora said. "And very brave. Thank you. Now I'm believing some other poor girl's family will be grieving her this night. Let's pray."

And just like that, the Murphy sisters joined hands, Maeve and Bridget taking his on either side. Maeve's hand was small, the bones delicate in his palm, though her grasp was strong, and she had small calluses at the padded bases of each finger. He tried to picture her with a pitchfork or behind a plow, but couldn't get the image to gel.

Nora led them in a simple, but heartfelt prayer for the family of the deceased girl.

"And thank You for our friend, Lord," Maeve added, squeezing Flynn's hand. "Bless the good doctor's hands as he treats patients and assists You in healing Your people. Amen."

The sisters chorused their *amens*. Visibly shaken, Flynn sat at their fireplace with them, as much for the tea as to steady his turbulent emotions and jumping nerves. Nora refilled his cup. "I must return and let the captain know we haven't correctly identified the girl."

"As soon as you've finished your tea," Nora insisted. "You had a bad scare."

Flynn experienced broad relief that all three sisters were alive and well. The captain would need to search for someone who knew the identity of the dead girl. The fright he'd had while thinking it was Bridget Murphy was more stress than he needed this night. He sipped his tea and focused on remaining calm.

The weather was appropriately dismal the following morning. Dark clouds hung over the ocean and a fine mist dampened hair and clothing, chilling those who stood on deck. Both Bridget and Maeve had secured their curly hair with nearly an entire tin of pins and wore hats, as well, since their tresses turned into unruly corkscrews in this wet, bleak weather.

There was much ceremony, and faces were somber as Captain Conley and the crew prepared to deliver the coffin into the sea. Those who'd brought instruments along played hymns. Bundled passengers lined the deck in wait. As mostly Irishmen were aboard, the eerie sound of bagpipes floated across the dreary gray ocean.

News had come that an accounting of passengers and crew had turned up the identity of a young woman traveling alone. As coincidence would have it, the dead girl's name had been Bridget Collins. Her belongings had been stored in hopes of finding relatives once the ship docked. No one the captain had spoken to remembered much about her. She stayed to herself and cooked her meals alone, not speaking to the other women in her cabin. Everything about her was a mystery.

Maeve had come above deck with Flynn and the McCorkle brothers. They stood together, watching as the plain coffin was raised with rope and swung out over the water.

"What's them holes for?" Sean asked.

"So the box takes in water and sinks faster," Gavin replied quietly.

Sean's Adam's apple chugged up and down several times. He reached for Maeve's hand and squeezed it.

The sailors maneuvered the ropes so the coffin slid out of the loops and into the water.

A woman passenger with a fair, lilting voice began a hymn, "'Fairest Lord Jesus, ruler of all nature. O thou of God and man the Son.'"

People joined in the singing, Maeve and her sisters included. "'Thee will I cherish. Thee will I honor, Thou, my soul's glory, joy, and crown.'"

Beside her, Flynn's deep baritone joined in. "'Fair are the meadows, fairer still the woodlands, robed in the blooming garb of spring. Jesus is fairer, Jesus is purer, Who makes the woeful heart to sing.'"

Everyone who'd spoken of the dead girl had lamented over the fact that no one had known about her or her circumstances. Some said she'd deliberately jumped to her death; others speculated she'd been dallying with a crew member. In any case, it was a sad and lonely way to die and be buried.

The sound of the bagpipes caused Maeve a healthy pang of homesickness, but she soon recalled the hunger and suffering and reminded herself why they'd cut ties and set sail aboard the *Annie McGee*. It was a harsh fact that not all who had boarded would set foot in Massachusetts. But she'd do her best to assist the doctor in making sure as many arrived safely as it was in their power to help survive.

She made her way through the dispersing crowd to where Martha Conley stood. "I apologize for not coming to see you last night. The day was longer and more exhausting than I could have expected."

"Don't give it another thought, dear. You had your hands full." She tucked a strand of gray hair under her cap. "I didn't have any luck. How about you?"

Maeve shook her head. "Nothing."

"Could be someone's lying," Martha suggested. "Or the baby's mother might not be listed on the manifest."

Maeve met her eyes. "A stowaway?"

Martha shrugged. "We get plenty of 'em. You did your best, child. I'm just thankful you and your sisters are willing to care for the babe."

They parted on that note. Not long after their conversation, she returned to assist Flynn as he changed Goldie's dressings. The woman was staying awake for longer periods with less medicine. "Heard tell a poor girl died," Goldie said.

"Yes, ma'am," Flynn replied.

"Do you think I can go back to my cabin soon?" she asked. "Truth be told, I get more time with my husband here, since we're separated in men's and women's cabins otherwise, but I don't want to be takin' up space someone else could use."

"It's up to you, wherever you're most comfortable," Flynn told her. "As long as you keep the wound clean and covered with the dressing, you'll do fine. If I send along a bottle of medicine for pain, I think we could let you go tomorrow."

"I have little to pay you," Goldie told him with an embarrassed shrug.

"The shipowner pays me by the trip," he told her. "You don't owe me anything."

"I do think I owe you, but I thank you nonetheless."

"Miss Murphy will show you how to get around using crutches, but I want you to stay off your feet as much as possible."

"Anything you say, doctor."

That afternoon, Maeve tended to a gaggle of female patients with questionable complaints. Most were disappointed they didn't get to see the doctor, and two were downright rude, but by now she was accustomed to their behavior and prepared to deal with them. With all this attention, it was a wonder the doctor didn't have an inflated sense of his own importance, but he seemed to take it all in stride, often exchanging a private look with her that said he was on to these women's tactics.

When she got to the deck later, dark clouds hung low in the sky, making it seem later than it was.

A crewman cried out from the rigging above. "Fire to the east! All hands on deck! All hands on deck!"

Startled, she oriented herself to figure out which way was east. Passengers had already run to the side of the ship.

An odd light burned a quarter of a mile away. One of the ships that had been keeping pace with them was on fire. Alarm spread through the crowd watching the scene on the other ship.

Maeve's heart kicked blood more quickly through her veins. No doubt there were hundreds aboard that vessel, people just like these around her—people just like her.

Sailors climbed the rigging above for better vantage points and called updates to their fellow mates.

Smoke billowed into the night sky, eerily lit by the flames fueling it.

"'Tis a sail ablaze now!" a man called down.

"They're handing buckets up to the riggers," another said.

The water probably added to the amount of smoke. Maeve prayed for the safety of the passengers and crew.

Captain Conley called orders that had something to do with the sails, and the *Annie McGee* bobbed closer to the other ship. His next command was to furl the sails and drop anchor.

Too many passengers had moved in front of Maeve, so she worked her way through them to reach the rail. The others could see over her head.

Objects in the water became visible, but from this distance she wasn't sure what they were.

"Lifeboats and swimmers!" came the call from above.

Swimmers? In these shark-infested waters? Her heart dropped to her stomach.

"Excuse me, please. Excuse me." Flynn worked his way to the rail beside her.

"Man the lifeboats!"

Crew members urged the bystanders away from the side, so the rowboats could be manipulated with ropes and pullies.

"Two men in each boat!" Captain Conley ordered. "Away!"

Flynn hurried forward.

"You're needed here," the captain said to him. They looked at each other for several seconds, and then Flynn backed away.

Two sailors climbed into the boat and were lowered down over the side.

"Go for my bag," he said to Maeve.

Obediently, she turned and ran to do his bidding.

"We'll need an area where anyone injured can lie down and I can treat them. Preferably not too far from a fire."

Maeve designated a place on the deck, added fuel to the fire and spread out blankets in preparation for patients.

It seemed as if an eternity passed before the boats from the *Annie McGee* reached people floundering in the water.

Turning to those standing nearby, she called, "More blankets! We'll have to get them warm when they get onboard. Bring as many blankets as you have."

The passengers jumped into action, some moving no

farther than their fireplaces for a blanket, others disappearing down the ladder to their cabins below. The pile of blankets grew.

The first boat came near, and those paying attention above tossed down ropes, which the sailors hooked. The boat was hoisted upward, dripping water.

Ingenious brackets fit the boat snugly against the side of the ship, so it was held steady.

Maeve had counted eight heads besides those of the sailors as the boat had neared, so she grabbed blankets and passed them out.

"I'll check each person for injuries first," Flynn called to everyone within earshot. "If I deem him well, take the person to your cook fire and get him warm."

Flynn's assessment consisted mostly of asking each dripping-wet and shivering refugee if he or she had been hurt.

One had a long gash on his arm. Flynn wrapped it tightly and sent him with Maeve.

The next boat was full of dry passengers, who had obviously climbed into a boat and not jumped into the water.

A barrel-chested fellow she'd seen a time or two led a dripping-wet, sobbing woman to Maeve. "Doc said she has a bump on her head."

Sure enough swelling over her left eye prompted Maeve to look into the woman's eyes. "We'll get you warm and keep a cold compress on that."

Bridget and Aideen showed up just then. "What can we do to help?" Bridget asked.

"I see the two of you have met."

"We were just getting ready to start supper when all the excitement started," Bridget replied.

"Bridget, I could use a plaster for this woman's head,

if you please. I'll tell you exactly where to find it in the dispensary and how to prepare it."

"All right."

Aideen and Bridget ran errands for both Dr. Gallagher and Maeve as the survivors were brought onto the ship. There were very few injuries. Mostly things like contusions and scrapes from the passengers panicking and jumping overboard.

They learned the other ship was the *Wellington,* and it had left a port just west of them within hours of the *Annie McGee*'s departure. Once the initial emergency was over, Bridget and Aideen went back to their cook fires.

"I don't know what will happen," Flynn said to her. "We can't go forward with this many additional people."

Concern and disappointment rolled over Maeve like a wave. They couldn't go back now! Perhaps they could find a port where the additional passengers could await a new ship. She worked hard to place herself in the others' shoes and not think selfishly. What if the situation had been reversed? She would want someone to take her and her sisters in and see to their welfare.

"We can't share what we have and go forward?"

"There are laws," he told her. "Set in place to prevent overcrowding and disease. There isn't enough food or water to accommodate this many more people for the duration of the trip. The risk of disease increases with each person who is added. The most likely solution would be to put them off somewhere, but it would take us out of our way."

She didn't even know how to pray, but she silently asked God to assist these people and help her overcome her selfishness.

As darkness fell, there were no longer flames licking at the other ship. It rested on the waves like a painting she'd once seen. Bobbing at sea lent the ship a different feel. How far would dropping anchor set them back? Where would they go from here?

From where she sat, watching over two resting patients, Maeve observed as yet another boat was stabilized and two men stepped out onto the deck. Captain Conley was there to meet them, and the men walked away together.

"That must be the *Wellington*'s captain. I think I'll go join them to see what's happening on the other ship."

The additional passengers they'd taken on were distributed at the other cook fires around the decks.

A short, round woman with a headscarf over her hair joined Maeve and offered food she'd prepared for the two patients. "All the others are eating meals with our people."

Maeve thanked her. The woman and man, who hadn't met each other before ending up here, sat forward and accepted bowls of rice.

"Everythin' got so confusing," the woman told them. "Fire was licking up the mast and people were screaming and running. I kept thinkin' we'd only just left everything behind to start over, and now we'd be killed at sea."

"The sailors were telling us to remain calm," the man said. "But it's hard t' stay calm when a ship is burning out from under ye in the middle of the ocean."

"I can only imagine how frightening that was," Maeve told them.

Flynn returned less than half an hour later. "Seems there's not much damage. People panicked, as is their nature, and yet the fire was being brought under control. The sail will be mended overnight, and the captain plans to continue forward come morning."

Relief warmed her heart. "Thank You, Lord."

"There's nothing more we can do," he told her. "Everyone should get a good night's rest. You did an excellent job this evening. I was wise in my decision to hire you. I'm going to go check on Goldie now. Her husband is with her, and I'm sure they're hungry for news of what's been happening."

His praise warmed her cheeks. She was exhausted, but she felt good about how she'd handled herself. She'd had many doubts about her abilities, but if things continued this way, her job would be tiring, but nothing she couldn't handle.

It was late for supper, but that evening the Murphy sisters finally had a chance to help Aideen Nolan and her aunt with their cooking. After the near-panic earlier, it was good to develop a routine and grow familiar with each other. The women shared their histories and how they'd come to be here.

Mrs. Kennedy had been married to a clergyman for only six years before his untimely death. She'd been a widow since the early thirties, and had become a milliner to support herself, but her parents had insisted she come and live with them, so all her earnings went into savings. When Aideen's father, Mrs. Kennedy's brother, had died, Aideen had come to live with them, as well. Aideen had never married and was an accomplished sempstress.

"That explains your beautiful clothing." Bridget fed Baby Grace warm milk with the rubber tubing. "I can't help but notice the soft fabric and the lovely embellishments."

Maeve had admired their beautiful clothing, too. She had a difficult time imagining the luxury of a cook and a housekeeper, though they must have missed the companionship of others their own ages, living with

Aideen's aging grandparents. Unlike the other well-dressed passengers, these women didn't turn up their noses at the sisters in their plain browns and grays.

"What is our fare this evening?" Aideen asked.

Maeve showed her the bag of meal. "Stirabout again."

Bridget groaned and shifted Grace to her shoulder.

"We brought additional rice and sugar in our provisions," Nora said. "Why don't we make rice pudding as a treat?"

"Don't you need eggs?" Mrs. Kennedy asked.

"We have eggs," Nora told her.

"However did you preserve them for the trip?"

"Dipped them in paraffin and then packed them in our flour bin," Nora replied.

Bridget glanced at her older sister in surprise. "Nora, your impracticality on the matter of using our eggs just for a treat is astonishing."

"We deserve a celebration," she said simply. "We thought we were witnessing a disaster, but it all turned out just fine."

"Dr. Gallagher predicted we'd have had to make for port somewhere out of our way if the *Wellington* had been badly damaged." Maeve placed her palms together. "Thank You, Lord, that didn't happen and the passengers were all safe."

"All I could think about were the sharks we hear about all the time," Aideen said. "I was sick with dread. It's a miracle that no one was killed in the water."

"I believe you're right about that," Nora agreed.

The women combined their rations and made a pot of stirabout, which simmered over the fire, while Maeve prepared the pudding, covered the pan and set it to bake.

Most families had already finished their meals, and

here and there neighbors joined together with wooden flutes and fiddles to liven up the atmosphere.

"'I've traveled about a bit in me time,'" came a clear tenor voice. "'Of troubles I've seen a few. I found it far better in every clime to paddle me own canoe.'"

The ladies looked at each other and grinned.

A man with a deeper voice picked up the next verse. "'Me wants they are small. I care not at all. Me debts they are paid when due. I drive away strife from the ocean of life, and paddle me own canoe.'"

It was just the thing needed to change the mood after the death of Bridget Collins that morning and the emergency this evening. Maeve had never anticipated this much drama aboard ship.

"'I rise with the lark from daylight to dark, I do what I have to do. I'm careless in wealth, I've only me health to paddle me own canoe.'"

Someone got out their union pipes and joined the gaiety. The distinctive sound carried across the ocean, and Maeve was certain those remaining on the *Wellington* could hear the merriment.

The song changed to one less frolicking, but every bit as familiar and more sentimental. This time many voices joined in with the ballad. Even Bridget sang along. "'Tis the last rose of summer, left blooming alone. All her lovely companions are faded and gone.'"

Aideen joined in. "'No flower of her kindred, no rosebud is nigh, to reflect back her blushes, to give sigh for sigh.'"

The song continued, with other passengers picking up the familiar words and joining in.

The next song struck up and Maeve had to laugh. It was an exaggerated tale of a ship's demise, the lyrics listing millions of barrels and bricks among a multitude of supplies on the ill-fated ship. When it came to the last verse she joined in. "'We had sailed seven years when the measles broke out. Our ship lost its way in the fog. Then the whale of the crew was reduced down to two. Just myself and the captain's old dog.'"

The passengers wound up for the finale, singing loudly, and even Mrs. Kennedy joined in.

"'Then the ship struck a rock, O Lord what a shock, the boat was turned right over. Whirled nine times around, then the old dog was drowned. And the last of the *Irish Rover*. Whirled nine times around, then the old dog was drowned. I'm the last of the *Irish Rover*.'"

Laughter changed the somber mood that had prevailed since the poor girl's burial that morning. Around them merry conversations buzzed.

"We're a hardy people." Mrs. Kennedy wiped a tear from her eye. "To survive what we've been through and still have a zest for life."

They prayed together and shared their meal. A feeling of well-being and belonging settled over Maeve. There were many uncertainties ahead, yes, but the love of God and the assurance of His provision was a certainty. Already He'd given them new friends.

Chapter Nine

At daybreak the *Wellington* sent its own lifeboats, and crewmen on the *Annie McGee* filled theirs, and the process of returning all the passengers to their own vessel got underway.

The *Wellington*'s captain sent men back with bags of meal and a barrel of water to replenish provisions and as a sign of goodwill.

The process took a couple of hours, but once all the people had been returned, both ships unreefed their sails and let the wind catch them. Maeve had awakened early to witness the process and to enjoy seeing the ship set sail once again.

She made oatmeal for herself and her sisters and brewed a kettle of strong tea. Breakfast was ready when Bridget and Nora came above deck.

"Did you sleep?" Bridget asked.

"Aye. I don't believe I moved a muscle all the night through. I woke in the same position as I laid down."

Grace emitted a strong cry, and Maeve took her from Nora while Bridget went for milk.

"You're a hungry baby, you are. Do you want me to take her with me this morning?"

"If I need you to take her, I will bring her, but we should be fine."

Maeve brushed the baby's forehead with a kiss and handed her over. "I'm off to work, then."

She arrived at the dispensary just as Flynn was preparing to see Goldie to her cabin.

"Thank you for your kind attention, Miss Murphy," the woman told her.

"You're so welcome. Send for me if you need anything."

While the doctor was gone, Maeve put the dispensary in order, sterilized and organized the instruments. She changed all the linens on the cots and washed down every surface. Humming to herself, she sang and prayed softly as she worked. Her employment afforded her more quiet time than ordinarily available on this crowded ship, and she was grateful. By the time she got to her cabin at night, she was exhausted, and the lights were extinguished.

Cleaning the dispensary had become her quiet time, and she honored it as best she could. She was sure God understood the lack of privacy and honored her faithfulness.

Gavin McCorkle showed up with bleeding blisters on the palms of both hands. Though only eighteen years of age and lanky, he towered over her.

"Whatever have you done to put your hands in this condition?" she asked.

"One o' the mates by the name of Simon asked Dr. Gallagher if I'd be wantin' to apprentice. Seems he needed another lad. I'm not just a swabbie, neither. I'm a rigger."

The pride in his voice touched Maeve.

She gestured for him to sit and carried over a basin of water and a soapy sponge. "And what does a rigger do?"

"I inspect the rigging and report ropes and sails what need fixed."

"The task does sound important." She washed his hands and he hissed between his teeth. She got an uncomfortable feeling from his explanation. "Where do you do this inspecting?"

"Why, on the masts, o' course."

She'd observed the sailors and apprentices who climbed the masts like wiry monkeys, and her heart dropped every time. It sounded like a risky thing to do, especially for one so untested. "The doctor allowed you to take this position?"

"I don't recollect he knows about it just yet."

"Are they feeding you well?"

"Aye, more food than I can eat. Fish at every meal. The captain's wife gives us mackerel she's cured to take with us. As much as we like. I share with Emmett. He don't eat much."

"I don't know that it's a wise idea for an inexperienced young fellow like yourself to be swinging about on the sails." She pierced blisters that hadn't yet broken, dabbed them dry and applied ointment.

"I like me job, Miss Murphy. I'm earnin' money so we don't have to live in the alleys and beg food when we get to Boston."

"I don't believe Dr. Gallagher would let you live in the streets," she assured him. "And neither would I."

"You and Dr. Gallagher are the kindest people I ever did meet. The way this turned out was like God was makin' a way for us to get to America and have a new home."

"God didn't put Sean under that cart. That was that despicable Hegarty fellow."

"I know that, miss. But God used somethin' bad to change our future. A man still has to earn his own way."

She secured a bandage around both hands and looked him square in the face. The hairs on his chin were soft and as yet unshaved. He was a mere lad. But a lad with pride and integrity. She admired that about him. She wondered if she'd ever know how any of these boys fared once they landed. "You have to keep these bandages on and keep those areas clean, so they don't get infected."

"Aye, miss."

"Do you have a pair of gloves?"

He shook his head. "The other apprentices would laugh me right off the rigging."

He was a handsome young fellow, this one, with brown eyes that would someday set some lucky young girl's heart aflutter. He wasn't afraid to work, and he was determined to make a better life for himself and his brothers. The McCorkles' story paralleled that of the Murphy sisters in an uncanny manner.

She sent him on his way, and left the dispensary to have a word with the captain. She found Captain Conley on deck, his slouch cap shading his eyes and an ivory meerschaum stuck between his teeth, smoke curling upward. The area of beard and mustache around his mouth was stained from his habit.

"Gavin McCorkle is climbing the rigging, his first time on a ship," she told him.

"And a fine rigger, he is," Captain Conley replied.

"Is it your habit to place these young boys in dangerous positions?"

"Simon, my first mate, is the best instructor of the bunch," he assured her. "We've only had one accident in all my days as captain of this ship."

She studied him and noted no deception in his gaze.

"And the lad wants t' learn, Miss Murphy. He's an eager young fellow. 'Tis far safer to have the young ones up there than the others, I assure you. Simon wouldn't have picked him for the job if he hadn't known the lad was capable."

"I've treated his hands for blisters," she said.

He nodded sagely. "'Tis a common malady until their skin is seasoned."

The man was obviously convinced Gavin could handle himself. Without a doubt, hundreds had done the job before him—it just seemed more frightening when the person up there was of one's acquaintance. "I shall hold you responsible for his safety," she said at last. "I want him to sail into Boston Harbor whole and sound."

"As do I, Miss Murphy."

She reached to shake his hand, as though affirming their understanding, then turned and walked away.

Nora arrived at the dispensary midmorning. "I have cooking to do around the fire. Will this be a convenient time for you to take Grace?"

"This will be a fine time." Maeve accepted the improvised sling and adjusted it to fit her much smaller frame to hold the infant close against her, with her hands free. "Grace will be my little helper, won't you, *grah mo chee?*"

The baby blinked sleepily and then closed her eyes.

"She just ate," Nora said. "She should be good for an hour or two."

Flynn arrived a short time later. He barely gave Grace a glance and set about his work. Maeve explained Gavin's injuries and her talk with the captain. Flynn's quickly disguised amusement didn't escape notice.

The next patient to arrive was a gentleman wearing a pressed linen shirt and a jacket. He had a lanky frame and a face with craggy, yet aristocratic features. "Before I was delicate in health, I was a strapping man, would you believe?"

"Aye, I can tell you had all the lassies followin' you about, you did," Maeve teased. It amused Flynn how her brogue grew thicker when she jested or when she was provoked.

"I had eyes only for my Corabeth," the man told her. "She was an Irish beauty, she was. She had hair like yours." His eyes glistened and he took a moment to continue. "Gave me three fine sons, she did."

Maeve didn't want to ask about his sons and cause the man any more grief. Too many people had lost their loved ones, and she suspected this man had experienced loss.

"She and my Daniel, they died the same week," he told her. "Knowin' they are together was my only comfort."

Maeve nodded her understanding.

"Robbie and John ran off to America, they did. Found themselves wives and jobs. I'm goin' to meet my granddaughter. Don't let me die before I get there."

Maeve's heart went out to the man.

Flynn had led him to the table and listened to his heart. "You're not going to die on my watch, sir. I think you picked up a bit of a cold in that drizzle yesterday. Stay warm and drink a lot of fluids, and you'll be feeling fine in no time."

"How does his throat look?" Maeve asked.

Flynn asked their patient to open his mouth. "Somewhat red."

"I suspected as much from the sound of his voice. A wool sock filled with salt and heated on the bricks beside your fire will make that feel better." She went to a crock and scooped a portion of salt into a small bag. "This should be enough."

"That's just what my Corabeth used to do for our

boys," he said and accepted the salt with a smile. "Is that your baby there?"

Maeve glanced down and patted Grace's bottom through the sling. The baby still slept soundly. "The little one was found abandoned aboard ship. My sisters and I are caring for her temporarily. We call her Grace."

"Might I just touch her fair head?" he asked.

"Yes, of course." Maeve lifted the baby and adjusted her so the old man could better see her.

He touched her hair and rested a long finger against her cheek. At the sight of his spotted and wrinkled hands alongside Grace's pure fair skin, Maeve got tears in her eyes.

"I remember when my babies were this tiny," he said. "It's one of the many times I've seen God's hand as plain as day. So innocent and unblemished is a new baby. Sent straight from heaven to a mother's arms."

"Are you a poet, sir?"

He chuckled. "Hardly. A cobbler. You take care of that little one now."

Their patient left and Maeve closed the door behind him.

"You are good with people," Flynn told her.

She glanced at him.

"Exceptionally good."

"Thank you."

He raised an eyebrow. "Do you believe a sock filled with salt will cure him?"

She shrugged. "I don't know, but the treatment feels good, and it's familiar and comforting. I have found that sometimes comfort and confidence are the keys to healing."

"I thought as much."

"Did I do something wrong?"

"Not at all." He let his gaze fall to the sling she settled back into place. "Is the baby doing well?"

Maeve nodded. "Grace is a contented little dear."

"I didn't know you'd named her."

"Yes, that's what Nora calls her."

"Are you concerned your sister might get too attached?"

"I'm concerned we'll all get too attached. What do you think will happen when we arrive if no family is found and we never learn where she came from?"

"I have no idea."

"Do we have a hope of keeping her?"

"Do you want to keep her?"

"I don't think any of us want her to go to a foundling home. We do know something about little girls in this family."

"I'll put in a good word for you," he assured her. "But keep in mind that someone might eventually claim her."

"If they showed no care for her until then, that someone wouldn't deserve her."

He wanted to reach out and touch her hair...rest a hand upon her arm or her shoulder to reassure her. She never hid her feelings. She wasn't ashamed to show how much she cared about people. It was a quality that drew him in, made him want to be one of the people she loved and cared for so honestly and openly.

The thought caught him off guard. Everything about her unnerved him. She still studied the baby, so her long lashes were in sharp relief against her porcelain cheek. When she looked up, she pierced him with that guileless look he'd come to find so very attractive.

Every other woman looked at him with a predatory gleam or a glimmer of appeal. This one always met his eyes with honest concern or open friendliness, with nothing motivating her desire to speak with him, except her wish to ask an opinion—or express a concern. And in addition to her honesty and beauty, she was as bright as any student he'd ever known, with a natural instinct for making people feel safe and cared for.

The thought of her being hurt if the baby's parents claimed her disturbed him. "Remember, she has family somewhere," he warned.

"I remember," was all she said.

The following day was the Sabbath. The Murphy sisters dressed in their best dresses, which were still drab and plain in comparison to many of the other women's, and joined the others in the hold for prayers and singing.

There were two services for worshippers among the passengers—one for those who spoke only Gaelic and one for those who spoke English. While the sisters understood their native language, they had decided to join the English-speaking service in preparation for their new lives.

The men stood and the ladies seated themselves upon rows of trunks and small kegs. As Flynn entered the hold with Kathleen Boyd and her mother, Maeve followed her sisters and took a seat on the center aisle.

Quite naturally, the people separated themselves into another division as they gathered: the well-dressed, well-to-do passengers on one side and the working class on the other.

Maeve didn't miss the interaction as Kathleen spoke to Flynn and gave him a smile before seating herself on a keg as though it was a plush armchair in a grand parlor. With a self-satisfied expression, she arranged her voluminous skirts before scanning the nearby passengers as though they were her competition.

She didn't bother looking across the aisle at the poor faction.

A waving hand caught Maeve's attention, and she glanced over a row to see Sean McCorkle sitting with his brothers. Pleased to see him doing well, she gave him a warm smile.

Captain Conley strode to the front and opened the Bible, from which he read a chapter from the book of James. "'Every good gift and every perfect gift is from above and cometh down from the Father of lights, with Whom is no variableness, neither shadow of turning.'"

Maeve glanced at Nora. Baby Grace had grasped on to her index finger, and Nora looked upon her as though the act was unique. Nora met Maeve's gaze and smiled sheepishly. She turned her attention to the reading.

Maeve was having a little trouble concentrating, too, but it wasn't the baby distracting her. Her thoughts kept going back to Flynn arriving with Miss Boyd. Perhaps they'd met in the corridor, and their arrival together had been mere coincidence. It was no business of hers, but she had her finger on the pulse of these husband-hunting maidens aboard the *Annie McGee*.

Determinedly, she shook off her unkind thoughts. Hadn't she and her sisters discussed their need to find husbands only a few weeks before? Their situation wasn't that much different. Yes, all the female attention was laughable because of the young ladies' obvious flirtations, but she stood in no place to judge. However, a more straightforward approach might better serve them. Flynn deserved better than a woman who viewed him as a prize to be won.

The captain took a seat beside his missus. The gathering of worshippers observed several minutes of silent prayers.

In the silence, Grace sucked her fingers energetically, and Maeve smiled to herself.

A commotion interrupted the peace. Maeve looked

over her shoulder to locate the source. Mrs. Fitzwilliam, dressed in a royal-blue sateen dress and a feathered hat, stood and pulled her skirts aside. "There's an animal!" she shrieked. "I felt it against my skirts."

Chapter Ten

One of the sailor apprentices darted about the edge of the gathering, searching. Maeve imagined a rat and shuddered. She'd heard rodents got onboard ships and lived off the provisions, but as of yet she hadn't seen one of the critters.

A few of the women actually climbed atop the trunks and kegs in fright and another dashed from the room, hysterical.

A movement startled Maeve, and she had to overcome her hesitancy to look more closely. At the corner of a trunk, a black cat, with a white underbelly and white paws, peered from its hiding place.

Maeve stood and hurried the few rows back, passing Mrs. Fitzwilliam, who now stood in the aisle, fanning herself with a silk fan, and knelt to scoop up the frightened feline. "I think this may have been what you felt against your skirts."

"Surely there are rules prohibiting animals running wild aboard this vessel," the woman said in a scornful tone.

"Cats keep down the rodent population, ma'am," Captain Conley replied. "Thank you, Miss Murphy. Seems you're always rescuin' wee ones." He motioned to someone toward the front of the hold. "Roddy, take the cat above."

"Yessir." The young fellow hurried to do the captain's bidding. Maeve handed over the animal, and resumed her seat.

Men assisted the ladies in their awkward skirts back down to the floor.

Nora and Bridget were trying not to laugh when Maeve joined them. After that it was more difficult than ever to concentrate in the quiet, and the captain called the service to an end with a song.

Being the Sabbath, nearly everyone gathered around their fireplaces, and even the sailors were scarce that day, many taking coffee in the forecastle. The sisters donned their hats to protect their eyes and skin from the sun. There wasn't much of a breeze, so they made little progress sailing upon the bosom of the broad Atlantic.

Aideen and Mrs. Kennedy joined them at their fire, and Nora showed them how to bake a two-inch flat cake between two cast-iron skillets above the flames. Maeve had seen plenty of burnt cakes she suspected were raw in the middle, and listened to Nora's explanation for preventing a similarly poor outcome.

She plucked Baby Grace from the crate that had become her bed and held her in the crook of her arm, without the sling. The infant's eyes were open, but she squinted against the sunlight. Maeve adjusted herself so Grace was shadowed by her upper body. Grace still frowned, but she studied Maeve with her delicate mouth in an O.

"Did I see you with a bag of sewing?" Mrs. Kennedy asked Nora.

"Yes, I'm working on a few pieces for the baby."

"We would love to help you sew for the wee one," Mrs. Kennedy said. "It's the very least we can do to repay you for your kindness in sparing us from eating our own cooking."

The women laughed together. "You're learning," Nora told her.

"I *am* a sempstress," Aideen reminded her. "In fact, I have a trunk aboard with fabric and ribbon and lace. Most of it is special pieces I couldn't bear to leave behind. Do let me make Grace something lovely and feminine."

Until now the baby had worn pieces of Dr. Gallagher's shirt fashioned into makeshift clothing and a couple of hand-me-down gowns a generous passenger had offered.

"She could wear it the day we dock," Bridget said excitedly.

Nora's expression grew somber, and Maeve suspected it was because of her concern about Grace's fate once they were in Boston.

"We have time to make each of you a dress for that day," Aideen suggested.

"We could never accept such an extravagant offer," Nora said with a shake of her head.

Bridget's face fell. It was obvious she would have loved a new dress, something pretty and feminine, but she wouldn't argue with her older sister in front of the other women and embarrass all of them.

"My material and skill at sewing are the same as your preserved eggs and ability to cook," Aideen said softly. "It's all I have to offer."

Nora's face grew pink under the brim of her straw hat. The way Aideen had presented her case made it seem that Nora would be rebuffing her gift if she didn't accept. Nora glanced at Bridget, and the two exchanged a look. "I didn't mean to imply your gift wasn't special," Nora told her. "I was embarrassed that we don't have anything of equal value to offer."

"How did you ladies understand that verse in James this morning?" Maeve asked. "'Every good gift and every perfect gift is from above and cometh down from the Father of lights, with Whom is no variableness, neither shadow of turning.' I think James was saying that God doesn't change or choose favorites. His gifts are for everyone."

Nora gave her a perplexed look. "Did you just change the subject?"

"No. That verse was about gifts, was it not? All good gifts come from God. When we give out of love or kindness or compassion, those are good gifts."

Bridget had come up with a plan to erect a tent over the crate where Grace slept, so she'd be protected from the sun. She had cut a cast-off skirt and was hemming the edges. "No gift is more valuable than another as long as it's given in love. That's what I was thinking."

"Like the widow who gave her last mite," Aideen agreed. "And Jesus said she'd given more than the rich people who put many coins in the offering. The widow was poor, yet she gave all she had."

"So an egg and a dress are really of the same value," Mrs. Kennedy added.

Nora threw up her hands. "All right. You've all convinced me. It would be prideful to say no."

Bridget clapped her hands and gave Aideen a hug. "Oh, my! A new dress. I can hardly conceive of it, can you, Maeve?"

Maeve shook her head and placed Grace in the shaded bed. "'Tis a blessing indeed."

She couldn't remember ever having a dress that wasn't made over from one of her older sisters' or fashioned from coarsely woven wool. "I'm so thankful it's not raining like yesterday. We'd have had to spend another day below."

"They say it rains more in America," Aideen shared. "We might be surprised by the climate."

A group of children ran past, Emmett McCorkle dragging a rope with a stick attached to the end. The others tried to step on the stick. Sean brought up the rear with a barely discernable limp. The boys drew up short when they nearly ran into a family out for a stroll.

"Hello, Miss Murphy," a dark-haired man said with a bright smile.

Beside him, his wife, dressed in a lavender dress with lace inserts and cuffs, spoke to the three daughters accompanying them. "Greet Miss Murphy, girls."

"Hello, Miss Murphy," they chorused.

The youngest separated from the others and ran to stand before Bridget. She wore a dress made in a royal shade of purple, with contrasting white lace at the neck and wrists and a sash at her waist. "We saw fishes jumping in the water!"

"You did?" Bridget sounded interested. She turned to encompass those around the fireplace. "Mr. and Mrs. Atwater, these are my sisters, Nora and Maeve." She introduced Aideen and Mrs. Kennedy, as well. "Ladies, this is Mr. and Mrs. Atwater, Laurel, Hilary and Pamela."

Pamela was the one looking up at Bridget with a bright smile. The other two hung back and only spoke to appease their mother and at her urging. All three girls wore stiff-brimmed bonnets with satin ties, and their mother wore a broad-brimmed hat festooned with silk flowers and bright artificial cherries.

"Your mother hasn't joined you for your stroll?" Bridget asked Mr. Atwater.

"She's having tea on the foredeck. Enjoy your afternoon, ladies." Mr. Atwater tipped his bowler in a formal gesture and led his family on past.

"His mother is traveling with them," Bridget explained once they were out of earshot. "Her name is Audra, and frankly, she is more friendly than those two. Mr. Atwater's name is Beverly and she's Miriam. They're nice, don't get me wrong. It's just very plain that I'm the hired help."

"The young ladies are all pretty, with their father's dark hair," Aideen said.

"I do admire their hair," Bridget agreed. "Each day when I help them dress it, I long for tresses that stay within their bounds and don't defy pins or ribbons."

"You and your sister do have riotous curls," Aideen agreed. "But both of you have hair that is lovely. Yours is dark and lustrous, and Maeve's is bright and catches the sun."

"Thank you," Bridget told her with a grateful smile.

"Will you accompany us to our stateroom later?" Mrs. Kennedy asked. "We will look through trunks and select material for your dresses."

The sisters agreed.

"Tea sounded good when it was mentioned," Maeve said. "I believe I will put on a pan of water."

A squabble broke out a few cook fires away; three passengers argued over their ration of oatmeal. In these close quarters, it wasn't unusual to overhear the occasional quarrel.

"I'm so glad we have you for neighbors," Mrs. Kennedy said.

On their other side, a gentleman and his nephew kept to themselves. The Murphys spoke to them occasionally, but they weren't overly friendly. Another passenger had stopped to sit with them, and it was apparent they knew each other.

Mrs. Fitzwilliam and her manservant, Stillman, strolled past, with Stillman holding her parasol over her head. He gave Maeve an almost imperceptible nod, but Mrs. Fitzwilliam kept her gaze straight ahead.

The children ran up behind them and carefully maneuvered around the two adults.

"What's this game you're playing?" Mrs. Fitzwilliam called.

The boys halted and doffed their hats.

"It's tag, but with a stick of wood," Sean explained. "Me brother Emmett is the fastest boy on the ship, so he keeps the stick away from the rest of us. 'Specially me. I ain't as fast as I used to be."

"You're the young man who was injured on the dock, are you not?"

"Yes'm. I'm all better now. The doc and Miss Murphy took real good care o' me."

"Have you proper food and lodging?" the woman asked.

"Real good food," Sean replied. "What's lodging?"

"Your sleeping quarters," Stillman clarified.

"Oh, yes! We got real comfortable bunks. Ain't never had blankets and pillows afore. We like it here."

Mrs. Fitzwilliam's harsh expression softened. "See that you don't mow down adults strolling the deck now."

"No, ma'am." Sean stuck his hat back in place and the children clamored away. Mrs. Fitzwilliam and her manservant walked on past.

Seeing Sean playing with the other children blessed Maeve. She offered a silent prayer of thanks.

The ladies drank their tea, and Nora fed Grace. Bridget read a book while the others worked on Grace's underslip and dress, made from the embroidered front of one of the doctor's shirts.

"Dr. Gallagher's shirts are cut from fine linen and obviously well made," Aideen commented.

"One of the other ladies told me he's from an extremely well-to-do family," Mrs. Kennedy replied. "They own a home in England, as well as an estate in Galway. It's a mystery what he's doing here."

Aideen's attention shifted away, and her fingers grew still on her sewing. Maeve followed her gaze. A man in a wide-brimmed felt hat stood at the rail, a cheroot between his teeth, gazing out over the ocean. From the crow's-feet at the corners of his eyes, it was plain the cowboy squinted into the sun as a habit. Maeve had read of the men who herded cattle and horses across the American West, but she'd never seen one.

This man wore the hems of his trouser pants tucked into tall boots, and leather galluses crisscrossed his back. His mustache and sideburns would be the envy of all the young men in Castleville.

At a commotion farther down the deck, he turned his head to observe his surroundings. Spotting the women seated around their fire, he touched the brim of his hat.

Aideen blushed and fixed her attention on her needlework.

Maeve and Bridget exchanged a look, and the man took his time walking away.

"You're the doctor's assistant, aren't you?" the visitor beside them called to Maeve.

"I am," she replied, twisting her upper body to face their neighbors. "Maeve Murphy." She introduced the others.

"Michael Gibbon," he said. He didn't share their Irish brogue. "I've been visiting family in County Kirk and am on my way home."

"You're not Irish, then?" Maeve asked.

"English by birth," he replied. "But I've been in America for the past nearly twenty years."

Bridget finished the tent over the cradle and settled on a stool to join the conversation. "We've only met a few Americans so far," she told him. "We're headed for Faith Glen. Do you know it?"

"I know it well. My wife and I lived there until her death, and then I moved to Boston."

"I'm sorry for your loss," Maeve and Nora said at the same time.

"Thank you, ladies."

"Please tell us about Faith Glen," Bridget begged.

"It's a lovely little community," Mr. Gibbon replied. "The people are friendly. It's over an hour's ride from Boston, and I never tire of cresting that last hill and gazing down upon the village. There's a town square with spirea and lilac bushes that bloom in the spring. You first notice the white clapboard church facing the square. The General Store and Rosie's Boardinghouse sit on either side of it. If someone had painted the scene, he couldn't have done a better job of creating a welcoming atmosphere."

Maeve released a sigh of longing. "I cannot wait to see it," she breathed.

Nora spoke up. "Since you lived there, perhaps you know a man by the name of Laird O'Malley."

"I knew him, yes," Michael said.

The sisters all sat forward. "Tell us!" Bridget coaxed.

Michael searched each of their faces. "Was he someone important to you?"

Maeve's heart sank.

"Was?" Nora asked.

"I'm afraid he's been dead for several years," the man replied.

Maeve met Bridget's crestfallen expression. "Apparently, he deeded a house to our mother," she told the man. "We have the deed in our possession."

The man's face changed with recognition. "Your mother, you say?" He rubbed his knee as he continued. "There was always talk in the village about a woman Laird had loved and lost. He kept to himself and never got close to anyone that I know of. Lived in that cottage by the ocean and tended his garden. Roses, herbs, all manner of flowers and trellised vines. His garden drew a lot of attention."

He looked at the sisters one by one. "So, your mother was the woman he loved? She must have been a beauty."

"She was beautiful," Bridget agreed.

"Is the cottage still there?" Nora asked.

"Is it occupied?" Maeve asked.

"I couldn't say," Michael answered. "It's been several years since I was in Faith Glen, and I haven't kept in touch. You have the deed, you say?"

Nora nodded. "We've set our hopes on a place to live."

"Well, I hope for your sake it's still there. From what I remember, it was a charming little place."

"So Laird never married?" Bridget asked.

"No, no. He died alone."

Michael's news put a damper on their mood that evening.

"This was the risk we took," Nora told them later. "We had no way of confirming who Laird O'Malley was or if he still lived."

"We won't be able to ask him how he knew Mother," Bridget said.

"But we still have the deed," Maeve insisted. "Whether he's alive or dead, we have a legal document and a letter."

None of them mentioned the cottage might not remain.

"'Which of you by taking thought can add one cubit unto his stature?'" Aideen quoted. "You're here now."

"Aideen is right," Maeve said. "Worrying about it won't gain us anything except wrinkles. Between the sun and worry, we'll turn into old crones if we're not careful."

The other ladies laughed.

"Let's finish here and go select fabric."

Aideen and Mrs. Kennedy took the Murphy sisters to their stateroom and opened trunks filled with the most exquisite bolts of material any of the sisters had ever laid eyes upon.

With Aideen's help, Nora chose a vivid blue linen.

"Nothing fancy," Nora said.

"We're going to play up your tiny waist," Mrs. Kennedy told her. "The current fashion is perfect for you, with a fitted bodice."

"And a high neck," Nora insisted.

"Yes, of course. A high neck is daywear. And I think a paisley shawl with fringe will complement the dress. We can add a matching sash to a hat."

Maeve had difficulty even picturing her eldest sister in something so exquisite. She couldn't wait to see her in a dress worthy of her stately beauty.

"And now you," Aideen said to Bridget.

"With that dark auburn hair and those hazel-green eyes, she should wear green or gold," Mrs. Kennedy advised.

"I have the perfect thing!" Aideen announced and searched through stacks of rolled fabric. "Here!"

The fabric she chose was a striking green sateen. "We can add gold ruching and she can carry off ruffles and a crinoline," Mrs. Kennedy decided. "Perhaps even ribbon streamers at the elbows."

"It's beautiful." Bridget's eyes sparkled with delight.

Maeve hadn't seen her so happy for a long time. She and Nora looked at each other with tears in their eyes.

"I can't believe I'm going to have such a beautiful dress." Bridget touched the material in awe.

"And now *you,*" Mrs. Kennedy said to Maeve, pulling her forward. "You're too tiny for ruffles or pleats. We don't want to dress you like a Dresden doll. And your hair requires specific shades that don't clash."

"May I suggest something?" Aideen asked her aunt. She went to yet another trunk and opened it. The roll of fabric she removed took Maeve's breath away.

"It's French silk plaid," Aideen told her. "You're small enough to carry it off, where on a larger person we could only use it for trim or the interior of pleats. It's taffeta."

Maeve touched the orange, yellow, green and blue plaid reverently. "It's so beautiful, I don't know what to say."

"Simply say whether or not you like it."

"I like it very much."

"What would you say to trimming it with braid?" Mrs. Kennedy asked Aideen. The two women were completely caught up in their plans and held a discussion about the placement of the braid.

"And perhaps you could add one of your fancy-work collars," Aideen replied. "We'll need something for her hair that matches. Not a hat, because it would dwarf her, but a small headpiece. Lace and ribbon, I think."

"The maturity of the style will complement your petite stature," Mrs. Kennedy assured Maeve.

Maeve had often been mistaken for a girl, so wearing a dress that showed her off as a mature young woman would be a joy. The idea of fashionable new dresses was still so foreign, she had to get used to it.

She wondered what Flynn would think of her in a pretty dress, but captured that errant thought. He would certainly never look twice at her when he had the lovely and elegant Kathleen interested and available—and many other women besides. Women with money and social standing. Maeve was the hired help.

Why she even thought about him puzzled her. She hadn't come on this journey to snag a rich husband. Even had she wanted to, she didn't stand a chance.

They visited in the stateroom for another hour and eventually bade their friends good-night to go above deck and observe the luminous water in the dark. When the moon was bright, the ship seemed to glide through liquid fire. Maeve could watch it endlessly, but her sisters tired and went to their beds.

She strolled the deck, occasionally greeting one of the other passengers. Two women approached, walking the opposite direction, and in the gaslight below the chart house their forms and faces came into view. Mrs. Fitzwilliam and Kathleen's conversation halted when they spotted her.

"Good evening, ladies," Maeve said.

Kathleen leaned toward the other woman but didn't bother to lower her voice. "I can't normally say this, but the darkness improves that dress."

Mrs. Fitzwilliam said nothing, and they walked past as though Maeve hadn't spoken.

The women's rudeness and Kathleen's insult stung. Maeve swallowed the hurt, dismissed their insults and continued on. Finally, she stopped at the rail near their cooking area to enjoy the play of light on the water. Her thoughts traveled to Aideen's reaction to the cowboy and Michael Gibbon's description of their new home.

"Good evening, Maeve."

At the sultry deep voice she turned to discover her employer. The moon glimmered on his black hair.

"Good evening, Flynn."

Chapter Eleven

"Did you enjoy your Sabbath day?" Flynn asked.

"Indeed. Did you see many patients?"

"Only two who complained of fevers and stomach pain."

"What did you do for them?"

"I checked the water in their cabins and found it rancid, so I had fresh brought to them. I'm thankful the water supply is sufficient for the trip. And we'll be making a stop for fresh very soon. Some don't realize the harm contamination causes."

Maeve studied the moon. "We met a man from Faith Glen."

"Did you now. Did he tell you about your new home?"

"He told us Laird O'Malley has been dead for quite some time. He had no current information about the house, though when last he saw it, he said it was charming."

"Now you're concerned it might not be there or that your deed isn't binding."

She nodded.

"My offer stands, Maeve. I won't have you or your

sisters left without a proper home. I'll see that you're taken care of."

"Taking advantage of your charitable nature would be my last choice, but I do thank you and will remember in case we have no other option."

They stood in companionable silence for several minutes.

"How did you keep from laughing when that woman sprang from her seat in fear of the cat this morning?" he asked. "You went to her aid as though her indignant tirade was the most natural thing in the world."

She shrugged, but a grin inched up one side of her lips. "I don't know. I'm always the first to jump into a situation without thinking. It's a character flaw."

"I disagree. I think it's a charming quality and one I admire very much. Some of us sit on our hands deliberating until it's too late."

"You don't. You handle emergencies quite efficiently."

"Medical emergencies, yes. Others require more thought."

"There wasn't much to think about," she said. "It was just a cat."

"But no one else got up, in case it was indeed a rat."

"I saw the furry creature and knew it wasn't."

"You're far too modest."

"I'm just a simple girl, Flynn. I don't worry about ruining fancy clothes or getting my hands dirty. I just do whatever is needed at the time."

"Some people don't need fancy clothing to improve their beauty."

Flynn didn't know why he'd said that. He wasn't the sort to heap compliments upon young women or to use insincere flattery. But nothing he ever said to Maeve was insincere. She might wear plain clothing and have a few calluses on her hands, but she was far from a simple girl. She was an intriguing young woman whose beliefs and feelings ran deep.

He didn't know anyone he'd rather have working at his side...or anyone with whom he'd rather stand at the rail and watch the moon play upon the water.

"What I meant to say was you're not a simple girl, Maeve. Besides being kind and beautiful, you're bright and intelligent and quick-witted."

She didn't react for a moment, and he wondered if she would, but finally she raised her face to the heavens. "No one other than my mother and da ever told me I was beautiful."

"Your sisters take your appearance in stride, because they're both lovely, as well, and the rest of the world is jealous or threatened. If no young man has ever complimented you, then there's something wrong with the male population of Castleville."

She turned and looked up at him. Her wide eyes reflected the fiery dance of light on the ocean. He shouldn't have such tender feelings toward her, and he shouldn't let words like that trip from his tongue, but he did...and he had. His words were all perfectly true.

He did feel something for Maeve, however, and it was becoming more and more difficult to ignore that.

He leaned forward and pressed a kiss upon her soft lips, thinking only of her sweet countenance and how good her presence made him feel. His impulsiveness was completely out of character, but kissing her seemed like the right thing to do.

She didn't draw away, which pleased him and lent him a measure of confidence. He'd thought about kissing her for days now. It was a quandary why the idea toyed with him and wouldn't leave him alone. He had no intention of letting himself have feelings for anyone.

But he was drawn to test his imagination and confirm that reality never measured up.

Perhaps he just needed to do this and then he would be able to forget about it.

She gently rested her fingertips against the front of his shirt, catching him woefully off guard. Perhaps she'd simply needed to check her balance, so he gently grasped her upper arm and held her steady.

Now he doubted his foolish thinking: he wouldn't be able to forget about this. The memory of her kiss and her scent would be with him forever.

A breeze caught a strand of her hair and blew it across his cheek. The soft tress tickled his ear. He eased away, straightening, and stood upright, still holding her arm.

She reached for the rail, but didn't take her attention from his face. Raising her other hand, she placed her fingertips against her lips. "No one's ever done that before."

"Kissed you?"

She nodded.

He'd given Maeve her first kiss. Something inside his chest thrummed with tension. Was that his heart? Had he made a foolish mistake? Reaching for her hand, he took it in his grasp and caressed the back with his thumb. He didn't want this to adversely affect their working relationship. She stirred emotions he couldn't risk feeling. She was refreshingly open and honest. Without guile. And perhaps she was too naïve for her own good, he admitted to himself. But he didn't want to lose whatever this new feeling was that warmed his heart and added a buoyancy to his spirit that he hadn't known for a long, long time.

"I apologize if it was unseemly—or if you found it unpleasant," he said.

He suspected she blushed, but the darkness hid it if she did. She didn't pull her hand from his, instead she turned her face to the ocean. "It was not unpleasant."

The ocean air smelled better than he remembered, the breeze cool on his skin. His pulse had an unnatural rhythm that he now noticed. The warmth of her hand seeped into his being and gave him a hope he hadn't expected to know. He hadn't felt this way for a long time...maybe not ever....

Other feelings crowded these out, however. Guilt. Fear. Most especially fear. He had no business letting himself form any sort of attachment. It was wrong to start something he had no intention of following through with.

It wasn't fair to Maeve.

He released her hand and faced the rail, looking out across the display of light on the water for several silent minutes. Finally, he turned to her. "I apologize. That was inappropriate. I'm your employer, and it's wrong to place you in an uncomfortable position."

"It's all right, Flynn."

He'd told her to address him as such when there were no patients present. Why did his name on her lips suddenly sound too intimate? "No. No, it's not. Forgive me. I think I should see you safely to your cabin."

She raised her chin in a stubborn refusal. "I'm quite capable of seeing myself to my cabin when I'm ready."

"Very well. Good night, then." He headed for the ladder that led below deck.

Thoroughly confused, Maeve watched him go. After sharing such a tender moment, his abrupt change caught her off guard, even more so than the kiss.

The kiss.

She skimmed her fingertips across her lips in amazement. Nothing had prepared her for such sweet depth of emotion as she'd experienced when he'd kissed her. No wonder couples fell in love and courted and married. No wonder God had ordained a man and a woman to leave their parents and cleave only unto each other.

No wonder he'd come to his senses and hurried away.

The beautiful Kathleen was surely a more appropriate recipient for his romantic intentions.

She didn't regret having been kissed. She wouldn't. The experience was something of value she could tuck away. A couple of verses came to mind, and she said them aloud. "'Lay not up for yourselves treasures upon earth, where moth and rust doth corrupt, and where thieves break through and steal, but lay up for yourselves treasures in heaven, where neither moth nor rust doth corrupt, and where thieves do not break through nor steal.'"

She didn't own anything of value, and that was okay, because the Bible taught that material things were only temporary. Heavenly things were eternal, the things with value. Love, joy, peace—those were the real treasures.

The memory of Flynn's kiss would bring her joy, so she tucked it away. No one could take it from her.

The scent of fragrant tobacco reached her, and she glanced aside. Several feet away stood the cowboy, again at the rail with his cheroot. She'd heard about the wide-open spaces of America, the vast plains and unexplored wilderness. She supposed being cooped up on a ship was more difficult for some individuals than for others.

His presence brought her out of her reverie. She turned and quickly headed below deck.

Most of the women were already in their bunks. Maeve was thankful for the blessedly cool evening. The cabin often grew stuffy with so many people living and sleeping in it. Thankfully, everyone had agreed that all surfaces should be scrubbed twice a week, and their bedding laundered weekly.

Bridget had been holding Grace, but the baby fussed, so she quickly handed her to Nora, who loosened the infant's clothing and tried to make her more comfortable. A crying baby would not ingratiate them with their cabin mates. So far the others had been kind and understanding, but the sisters couldn't afford to push their tolerance.

Bridget left Nora on her lower bunk and climbed above to her own.

"'Rest tired eyes a while. Sweet is thy baby's smile. Angels are guarding and they watch o'er thee.'"

Nora's sweet voice as she sang the familiar lullaby with its lilting melody and trills on the syllables gave Maeve gooseflesh along her arms. Listening, she changed into her nightclothes.

"'Sleep, sleep, *grah mo chee,* here on your mama's knee. Angels are guarding, and they watch o'er thee.'"

The cabin grew still and silent; not even a rustle of bedclothes stirred as Nora continued her song. Maeve climbed up and stretched out upon her narrow bed. She had to consciously relax her muscles.

Maeve's mother had sung the tune to the three of them in their childhood years, and she suspected the tune was as sentimentally touching to the other women.

"'The birdeens sing a fluting song. They sing to thee the whole day long. Wee fairies dance o'er hill and dale for the very love of thee.'"

Maeve's throat tightened with bittersweet homesickness and the poignant reminder that they'd left behind everything familiar to risk this journey to a new land. Tears welled in her eyes.

"'Dream, Dream, *grah mo chee,* here on your mama's knee. Angels are guarding and they watch o'er thee, as you sleep may angels watch over and may they guard o'er thee.'"

After Nora sang another verse, she fell silent. The baby obviously slept now, for she was silent. The only sounds in the cabin were a few soft sniffles and a stifled sob. Maeve recognized Bridget's tiny hiccuping cry. She climbed out of her bunk and up to join Bridget on the narrow mattress. She'd shared a bed with her sisters their entire lives, and lying with Bridget now lent them both comfort. Maeve smoothed Bridget's hair down, so it wasn't in her face, and Bridget snuggled back against her.

Maeve tucked her arm around her sister and closed her eyes.

She could use a few of those angels watching over her, as well. And maybe a few more to help her guard her heart.

Chapter Twelve

The next day, the doctor acted as though nothing had happened the night before. In a way, Maeve was relieved. Things wouldn't be awkward between them if the incident was forgotten.

Odd how she thought of it as "the incident" now. As though she'd spilled tea on her skirt or had some other trivial mishap. But it was best left that way, so she focused on her work.

A sailor arrived around noon, a gash in the flesh of his palm, received while cutting open a fish. Flynn thoroughly cleaned it, much to the dismay of the cringing sailor, neatly placed six stitches in it and sent the man on his way.

"You should come above deck and watch the dolphins play," the bandaged sailor told Maeve on his way out the door. "Don't know when ye will see a sight like this again."

Flynn washed his hands. "Let's go. I'll carry up water and boil it, so we'll have a fresh supply."

Passengers stood gathered at the rail. Unable to see over their heads, Maeve found an opening to weave her way forward. Dolphins rolled in the water, and porpoises danced around the prow. The flying fish's aerial darts drew attention, as well.

Off to the west an island could be spotted, and a nearby Englishman mentioned they'd be stopping for water and to leave off a stowaway who'd been discovered.

Maeve heard sailors above and gazed up, finding Gavin on a mast. Her heart raced. Apparently, he looked down at the same time. "Top o' the mornin' to ye, Miss Murphy!" he called, and even from this distance, his broad smile was evident.

The other sailor in his company asked something of Gavin, and it appeared Gavin explained who she was. The sailor tipped his hat.

Maeve blushed and gave a friendly wave.

She took a stroll around the deck and spotted the captain's wife reeling in a net. She greeted the leathery-skinned woman.

"Good day to you." Martha Conley spilled the contents of the net into a wooden tub, picked out a baby shark and threw it overboard.

"Gavin McCorkle mentioned you provided him and the other sailors with fish."

"Cure mackerel several days a week, I do," she replied. "Help yourself to as many fresh as you'd like for your meals today."

"I couldn't take your food," Maeve said with a shake of her head.

"Nonsense. The ocean is filled with fish. Catching them gives an old woman something to do."

"That's very generous of you. Thank you."

Martha grabbed a scrap of canvas lying on the deck and rolled half a dozen mackerel into it. "Used to treat ills aboard ship, I did. Before we had a ship's doctor every voyage."

"You did? What medical experience do you have?"

"None to mention, save what I did here. Lost too many to sickness and fevers, we did. Those aren't days I'd want to live over again."

"I completely understand. I used to treat the people of my village, and all I had were herbs I collected and what little knowledge I'd learned from my mother and the midwives."

"Fine thing it was, Dr. Flynn workin' so hard to get the laws changed so there's a doctor aboard every ship now. He's a good man."

"He got laws changed?"

"Not single-handedly, but he used his influence and his money to get a better passenger act passed. This one requires enough sleeping space for each person, plenty of clean water and clean cabins and galleys. People don't die all the time as they used to. Not on our ship so much, but others, where the owners only cared about profit, not people."

Maeve could plainly see the doctor's involvement. Flynn was a man with deep moral principles and a commitment to healing.

"That man deserves a good turn," she added. "After losin' his wife and sweet baby, the way he did."

Maeve's heart skittered. *Wife? Baby?* She must have looked puzzled.

"Cholera, I think it was. Dreadful sickness. Heard tell that after they died, he quit practicin' and devoted himself to research. It was too late for his family, but I suppose in his mind, findin' ways to save others relieved the pain."

Maeve knew exactly what it was like to be unable to save the people she loved. For a man who had devoted his entire life to healing, she could only imagine his helplessness and self-blame.

"Thanks again for the fish, Mrs. Conley."

"Any time, dear. Say, will you and your sisters join us for supper tomorrow evenin'? The cap'n and I like to have guests join us."

"I would love to, and I will ask my sisters."

Maeve made her way to the galley where she passed along Mrs. Conley's invitation and asked Nora to store their fish until suppertime.

That night Bridget dined with the Atwater daughters, so Nora and Maeve fried the fish in a hot skillet and asked Aideen and Mrs. Kennedy to join them.

Nora had been given a small bag of potatoes, and they baked them at the edge of the fire.

"The sea air makes a person hungry, I've discovered," Aideen said. "I surely don't want to let out all my seams before we reach port, but it might be necessary."

The ladies laughed and enjoyed their meal.

Sean and Emmett McCorkle skidded to a stop in front of them.

"Hello," Maeve greeted them. "Have you eaten supper?"

"Yes'm," Sean replied. "We eat in the galley. Sometimes I see your sister there."

"This is Nora."

Sean glanced at the pile of bones on a tin plate. "I can throw those away for ye."

"Why, thank you, Sean." She handed him the plate.

Emmett ran right along beside him and returned like a shadow.

"Tell us what keeps you busy during these days aboard ship," Nora said to Emmett.

He lowered his gaze to the deck and attempted to slip behind Sean.

His older brother sidled away and pulled him forward. "He's been gettin' lessons with one of the families. Numbers and letters and the like."

"Why, that's wonderful," Nora told him.

"Sometimes I sit in, too, iffin' I ain't got no errands to do for the cap'n."

"Good for you. You need to know those things."

"Cap'n Conley says we'll be pullin' into a port tomorrow. Me an' me brothers are gonna go see a jungle!"

"A jungle, you say?"

"Don't worry. The cap'n is sendin' someone to look out for us."

"It's very good to know you won't be eaten by a wild animal."

Emmett's eyes widened.

"It ain't that kinda jungle," Sean said. "Just birds and monkeys an' the like. I hope they got coconuts. The doc told me coconuts was good to eat."

"I hope they do, too."

"Do you have any more jobs for us? We gotta get goin'."

"Can't think of anything right now."

"Okay. Well, 'bye."

The boys shot off, narrowly missing a collision with a couple out for a stroll.

Maeve exchanged a look with Nora, and they both grinned. Maeve prayed aloud that the McCorkles would find a good home once the ship landed. The other ladies agreed with resounding *amens*.

The following morning the *Annie McGee* sailed into a small harbor on a lush island. If they wanted to go on land, the passengers were instructed to venture ashore with a knowledgeable companion and were strongly advised to stay within sight of the ship at all times. They were warned that the ship would only be anchored for three hours, while casks of water were filled and loaded.

"Let's ask the doctor to be our companion," Bridget suggested while they prepared for the day, with the other women bustling around them in the crowded cabin.

Bridget took a faded pink bonnet from the large bandbox they'd carried aboard, the one that held all of their hats. "No one wears these coal scuttles any more," she said, brushing lint from the stiffened claret silk. At one time, it had been lovely headwear for a banker's wife. The woman had given it and a few others to their mother as payment for cleaning her house.

"It's a fine bonnet," Nora assured her. "Look how nicely that organza is pleated on the inside of the brim. It's a perfect frame for your pretty face."

"It was nice once," Bridget said. She traded it for a sized and wired straw bonnet with the same shape. "This one will be cooler. The crown is lined with cotton."

Nora took a similar one from the box and Maeve fished until she found the bonnet she preferred. She had replaced the frayed trim with green ribbon only last year. "No one will care which hats we wear."

She and Nora concurred that they should ask Flynn to accompany them, and Bridget went to find him.

He joined them wearing another of his white embroidered shirts and a handsome straw hat. He remarked about the wisdom they'd used in choosing hats to protect their heads and faces from the sun.

There was no dock, so those wishing to disembark waited in line for small rowboats to take them to the island.

What they found was a tiny fishing village, its brown-skinned inhabitants friendly and in the business of trade. Carts and wagons lined the dirt path from the shore to the rustic little community.

Each of the sisters had brought along a few coins from their wages. They purchased nuts, fruit and dates. Bridget bought a necklace made of carved ivory beads and wore it with her plain homespun skirt and blouse.

There were also prepared foods, native to the people of the island, but Flynn advised them not to eat the unfamiliar dishes, because the questionably prepared foods wouldn't sit well on their stomachs.

Flynn took time to delve into the undergrowth and pull from the earth a pouch full of roots he claimed had excellent medicinal qualities.

While her sisters looked at carvings, Maeve waited for Flynn at the edge of the junglelike area. He returned and showed her the tubers. She took one, brushed off black dirt, and sniffed it. She wrinkled her nose. "It has an unpleasant scent."

"I know." He grinned.

It was the first time she'd seen him smile, the first time they'd shared a private moment, since...the incident. Attractive dimples appeared on either side of his smile.

She recalled Mrs. Conley's account of the deaths of his wife and child. The information explained a lot. She should let the revelation go; his personal life was none of her business. But curiosity and compassion overcame wisdom.

"Martha Conley told me about your losses."

Her words took Flynn by surprise. He looked down into her eyes and read sympathy...compassion he couldn't handle. He knew exactly what she was referring to, and he didn't want to talk about it. "We should go wait for a boat to take us back."

"I know what it's like to lose people you've tried so desperately to save."

"Let's go find your sisters." He moved to walk away.

"Flynn."

She stopped him with a gentle hand on his shirt-sleeve. He could have easily moved on, but her touch held him. Her fingers were warm.

"I hadn't realized you'd been married."

He stood in place, but looked away, over her shoulder. Her eyes were too much right now.

"What was her name?"

His mouth was dry. "Johanna."

"And your child—a son or a daughter?"

"A son." The word pained him. His child's name was difficult to form on his tongue. His stomach dropped. "Jonathon."

He hadn't said it in years. Speaking his little boy's name made his blood pound in his ears.

"How old was he?"

She was relentless. "Barely three."

"I'm so sorry," she said softly, with as much emotion as one who truly understood would display. "You want to run from everyone who speaks of it."

He nodded.

"When someone tells you your wife and son are in a better place, you rage inside and think, 'No, *this* is where they belong. With me. They were robbed of their lives. *I* was robbed. This isn't better. It's not what God intended. It's *wrong*.'"

It was like she'd been in his head and heard all his unspoken sufferings. Slowly he let himself look at her. For such a tiny person, she packed a big wallop. His belly felt as though he'd been kicked by a horse.

"When someone tells you Johanna and Jonathon are at peace, you want to scream at them, because though it's true, it happened too soon. Eternal peace should come at the end of a lifetime, not when it did. Not too early."

The knot forming in Flynn's throat wouldn't go up or down. He swallowed in a futile effort. Anger surfaced, and it was directed at her for voicing those private thoughts—for knowing them, for speaking the names of his wife and son. Who did she think she was, this snip of a girl, to invade his private grief and insinuate her frighteningly accurate assessment of his feelings into his conscious mind?

"Just let it go," he said, his tone more forceful and his voice thicker with emotion than he'd intended.

She acquiesced with a single nod. "All right."

That was it? She'd flayed him open like one of Mrs. Conley's flopping mackerel and then decided evisceration was sufficient? If she knew that much about him, did she know he lived with the guilt of being unable to save them? Did she know what that felt like?

He couldn't ask.

She removed her fingers from his arm. "Just know you have a friend who understands. And cares."

He didn't want understanding, and he definitely didn't want caring. He was doing just fine being left alone. He didn't need anyone to dredge up feelings too painful to endure.

She moved ahead of him, back toward the island village. He forced his feet to move, but he walked as stiffly as a tin soldier.

Chapter Thirteen

They didn't speak much as they tended to patients that afternoon. Brief questions were met with brief answers. And it seemed as though there truly was no escaping the woman, because she was at the captain's overcrowded dinner table that evening.

The captain and his wife sat on either end, with Flynn between Kathleen and her mother, and all three Murphy sisters on the opposite side of the scarred plank table.

Captain Conley and Martha were down-to-earth, simple people. She enjoyed company and cooking for a variety of passengers. They didn't distinguish between social classes or they would never have asked Kathleen and Estelle to sit at the same table with the Murphys.

Flynn had never known a meal in this cabin to go severely wrong, so he hoped that would be the case this evening.

However, he could tell already that Kathleen wasn't happy with the guest list. She aligned her fork and spoon on the tabletop and gave Nora the once-over. "Where is that child you're always carrying?"

"Our friends are watching her this evening. Grace is an exceptionally good baby." She turned to Flynn.

"A generous passenger stopped me in passing today. 'I have a spare glass nursing bottle with a gum nipple,' she said. 'Would you be in want of it?' As you can imagine, I was delighted. 'I surely would,' said I. Grace has enjoyed two bottles of goat's milk since then."

"Well, that is thrilling news," Kathleen said.

"It's going to make my life so much easier," Nora continued with a smile, obviously not picking up on the sarcasm.

"Did you ladies go ashore?" Martha asked, including all the females in her query.

"We did." Bridget touched her necklace. "I bought this. Someone carved all these beads from ivory."

Mrs. Conley had probably seen a hundred ivory necklaces, but God bless her, she admired Bridget's. Flynn had always liked that down-to-earth woman. She got up and dished steaming stew from a black kettle into individual bowls.

"What have you made us this night?" the captain asked.

"Ballymaloe," his wife replied. A traditional Irish stew. "I bought lamb on the island." The fare smelled delicious.

She set a bowl in front of her husband and then before each guest. The captain didn't wait until everyone was served, just picked up his spoon and dug in.

Martha set a crusty loaf of bread directly on the table and tore off a hunk for herself before sitting.

The *ballymaloe* was filled with tender bits of lamb, onions, barley, parsnips and carrots and smelled exceptionally good.

The Murphy sisters picked up their spoons and tasted the stew appreciatively. "This is delicious, Mrs. Conley," Nora told their hostess. "What a treat to have vegetables, too."

"I bring enough to last the voyage, if used sparingly."

Kathleen and Estelle watched the others for a moment before dipping their spoons into the mixture. Kathleen tasted it. Her reaction amused Flynn. Accustomed to extravagant slices of braised meats and fancily prepared side dishes, this food was not the Boyds' usual fare. But there could be no objections to Martha's cooking, as they should have learned the last time.

In the past, Kathleen had been a good companion. They shared a history. Now, he questioned their friendship. He often enjoyed the opportunity to speak of familiar people and places in her company, but when others were around she showed a different side—this unbecoming superior side.

"Very tasty," Estelle said.

"Did you make any purchases?" Martha asked the others.

"I bought fruit," Maeve answered.

"I got Grace a gourd rattle," Nora said.

"We stayed onboard and sent a sailor to purchase shellfish." Kathleen took a sip of water. "There's nothing else of value to be found. Only cheap trinkets made by the natives."

The conversation fell away for a moment.

Bridget's spoon paused over her bowl, but she didn't look up.

"I gathered roots," Flynn mentioned. "A particular sort that are easy to find in the rich, dark soil on the islands and rarely found elsewhere."

Maeve placed her hands in her lap to address him. "I was wondering. Has anyone ever tried to take a few of those tubers and plant them in America? Transplant them."

Deep in thought, Flynn set down his fork. "I don't know. One of the researchers I studied under in England has a greenhouse where he grows hard-to-find species of herbs. Growing these roots may have been done, but if it has, I don't know of it."

Kathleen's sharp gaze moved from his face to Maeve's, where her eyes narrowed.

"Set aside two," Maeve told him. "And I'll try planting them in the garden we're expecting to have when we get to Faith Glen."

"Splendid idea." He reached for bread and tore off a piece.

Maeve resumed eating her meal.

"My dear," Kathleen said to her. "I'm so impressed with your frugality. The cut of your dress shows that it must be a least a decade old, yet you've so cleverly re-made it into a serviceable piece. And in such a practical color, too. Who could possibly spot a dusty hem on a skirt of such an earthy brown? Definitely the mark of a sensible nature."

Flynn glanced from Kathleen to Maeve, inwardly cringing.

"Besides, with that hair of yours, you've color aplenty in your appearance. You've no need for more eye-catching attire."

Bridget was the one who appeared incensed at Kathleen's backhanded compliments. Adding Maeve's naïve nature to the fact that she gave people the benefit of the doubt, Flynn suspected she didn't even realize she'd been insulted. He'd been angry with her all afternoon, but that emotion quickly faded as protective anger on her behalf changed his attitude.

Maeve almost lifted a self-conscious hand to her hair, but instead kept it restrained in her lap.

"There's a lot to be said for a sensible nature," the captain's wife said. "Some people set a lot more store by their hair or the cut of their dress than they do kindheartedness. Never read in the Bible that fancy clothing is a fruit of the Spirit, now, have you, cap'n?"

Captain Conley plainly intended to keep out of the conversation. He mumbled something unintelligible and stuffed a piece of bread in his mouth.

"I didn't wear my best dress, either," Kathleen said, though she was dressed in an elegant gown of deep bluc. "Why risk ruining nice things on this voyage? Tears and stains are inevitable."

Flynn wondered how Martha had planned this particular group of dinner guests and supposed she had invited the Murphy sisters after he and Kathleen had been invited. She may have forgotten who she'd already asked, but he suspected she rather enjoyed combining incongruent personalities and watching the outcomes.

"And you, dear," Kathleen said to Bridget. "I've noticed you on deck, and tonight you've done something different with your hair."

Bridget's face brightened. "Yes. One of our new friends helped me."

"Well, I admire your courage for trying."

Bridget's cheeks turned pink. Maeve turned and looked at Kathleen, as though a light had dawned and she'd recognized the intentional barbs delivered with each of the "compliments." She cast a frown on the dark-haired woman across the table.

"Faith Glen, you mentioned," Estelle Boyd asked, changing the subject. "Do you have family there?"

"No," Nora replied and didn't go further.

"We've inherited a cottage," Bridget supplied. "A lovely place near the ocean, with a garden."

According to Maeve, the sisters weren't sure about that, but Bridget wisely made a point of letting Kathleen believe they had a home once they arrived. He could only imagine her remarks if she knew the Murphys were uncertain of their future.

"Well, isn't that nice?" Estelle said.

Everyone finished their meal and Nora jumped up to help Martha remove the bowls and forks.

Maeve refilled the water glasses.

Accustomed to servants, Kathleen and Estelle remained seated.

Flynn recognized the heavy bowl of baked custard that Martha set on the table. Nora placed small dishes at each setting.

Maeve remained standing long enough to scoop out a serving for each person. Kathleen held up her palm to stop her from placing a bowl in front of her. "None for me, thank you."

Maeve set down the dish in the middle of the table and took her seat on the bench once again, near Martha at the end.

"You and your sisters are hardworking, mannerly young women," Martha told her. "Any young man who takes one of you for his wife will be fortunate."

The sisters looked only at their dessert dishes, and Maeve deliberately refused to lift her gaze. She dug into her custard.

Kathleen looked pointedly at the other women. "I wish I was as brave as the three of you. I go without desserts to fit into my dresses, and it's clear you don't give your figures a second thought."

Each of the Murphy sisters paused in enjoying their custard.

"Why, the bench doesn't even know a one of them is there," Martha said with a snort. "They're light as duck down. If anything, they could use some meat on their bones. Now your mother there, she likes a good custard, she does."

Having just finished her last bite, Estelle had been eyeing Kathleen's bowl. She dabbed her mouth with her handkerchief—the captain's wife didn't set the table with napkins—and gave Kathleen an apologetic glance.

"Thank you for another delicious meal, Mrs. Conley," Flynn told their hostess. "I've never eaten from your table when I didn't thoroughly enjoy the fare."

"Cookin' keeps me busy," she said.

"You told me fishing keeps you busy," Maeve said to her.

"Aye, fishin' and cookin'."

"I've offered her a house anywhere she pleases, but she's got the ocean in her blood as much as I." The captain fumbled on a nearby table and found his meerschaum, which he packed with tobacco and lit.

The fragrant scent curled around them.

"And I've told 'im a thousand times I'll live in a house when he does. We could raise a few sheep, keep a cow and have a little garden, mind you. But the old goat won't hear of it. I may as well be whistling jigs to a milestone."

It was obviously a conversation the couple revisited often.

"And you, Mrs. Boyd," Martha said to Estelle. "Where is it you have a mind to settle?"

"In Boston," the woman replied. "Our barrister has rented something for us, temporarily. Only until we're sure what the future holds for us, of course." She gave Flynn a pointed look. "Why don't the two of you have a walk on deck? It should be a lovely evening."

Times like this he got the distinct impression Kathleen's mother would have liked to see the two of them become more than friends. He'd come out and told her on more than one occasion that their relationship wasn't like that, but she didn't seem convinced. She probably made Kathleen crazy, too.

Maeve's blue-eyed glance followed him as he stood and pulled back Kathleen's chair. Her perusal disturbed him, as did most things about her, and he wasn't sure why. He gave her a hesitant smile, but she looked away.

He thanked their hostess once again and ushered Kathleen from the cabin.

Maeve and Bridget took a walk around the deck later, and she was thankful they didn't run into Flynn or Kathleen. They did discover an interesting sight when they reached Mrs. Fitzwilliam's fire, however. The woman and her hired man were not alone. Two children sat with them, apparently enjoying some sort of dessert from blue-and-white china bowls.

As the sisters drew closer, Maeve made out Sean and Emmett McCorkle keeping the woman company. Sean was chattering on about a school of porpoises he'd seen that day.

Mrs. Fitzwilliam didn't look their way or notice the Murphy sisters, so they walked on past.

"Mama used to talk about looking for the good in people," Maeve said. "Apparently, Mrs. Fitzwilliam has a side we haven't seen."

"Well, I don't believe Kathleen Boyd has a single redeeming quality, no matter what Mama said," her sister replied.

Maeve lay awake on her bunk that night, her mind in turmoil. Bridget had simmered over Kathleen's thinly veiled insults for the better part of an hour, but Maeve had simply tamped down her hurt. It was disturbing that another human being could be so unkind...and frightening that Flynn, a decent, honorable man didn't seem to recognize her glaring flaws.

Maeve wasn't worldly or experienced, but she recognized a wolf in sheep's clothing when she saw one. She liked to give people the benefit of the doubt but, as Bridget had predicted, she couldn't come up with any redeeming qualities to tag on the woman.

It had been apparent that Mrs. Boyd was pushing for Flynn to marry her daughter. At one time Maeve had believed the match was a wise one—they were from the same social class, moved in the same circles. But now…now she tried to picture the doctor cleaving to a woman so proud and haughty, and the imaginings made her feel sick.

She thought of what Flynn had been through, losing his family. He deserved someone kind.

"Lord," she prayed. "Give Flynn wisdom to make decisions. Send Your Spirit, the Comforter to heal his grieving heart. Your Word says You heal the brokenhearted and bind up their wounds, so Lord, I ask You to bind up Flynn's wounds of grief and guilt. Lord Jesus, be a healing balm to his heart and his mind. Show him You're holding him close and loving him. Take away the pain that's eating at him like a sickness. In the mighty name of Jesus, amen."

She rolled to her side and another thought came to her. She couldn't cast it aside. "And, Lord, I forgive Kathleen for being rude and haughty. She must be an awfully unhappy person to treat others so unkindly. Help Bridget be merciful. Help me be generous and kindhearted, Lord. Show Kathleen the truth of Your way, which is to love others. And if she's the wife You have planned for Flynn, please, please, *please* change her heart."

The cabin was stuffy that night. She threw off her sheet and tried to get comfortable.

"Are you all right, Maeve?" came the soft voice from the bed at the head of hers.

"Yes," she whispered. "Are you?"

"Yes," Bridget replied. "You're beautiful, you know. Inside and out, just like mother used to tell us."

"As are you," Maeve returned.

"Ssshh," came Nora's censure from below.

Maeve smiled and closed her eyes.

Chapter Fourteen

The following day they treated several patients for stomach complaints. "As many times as I tell people not to buy food from the islanders, they eat it anyway."

Flynn mixed peppermint oil with water and dosed it out most of the morning.

During a lull in the stream of patients, he said to Maeve, "I'd like to apologize for Kathleen's comments last night."

"It's not your place," she said.

"All the same, you and your sisters are gracious. Kathleen's barbs are uncalled for."

"She does have a tongue that would clip a hedge," Maeve replied. She should keep her questions and thoughts to herself. "Are you planning to marry again?"

He seemed surprised by her straightforward question. Would she never learn? After a moment he replied, "Why is everyone focused on getting me married?"

"Don't you want to marry?"

It was obvious that he struggled to reply. "It's the natural way of things, to marry, to make a home and a family," he said finally.

She paused in rolling a strip of bandage torn from a worn sheet. "You didn't really answer my question.

You merely stated a fact, like the sky is blue or cows give milk."

"Are you always this direct?"

"I guess so. My life hasn't been given over to small talk, and skirting around issues doesn't solve anything."

"And you're convinced I have problems to solve."

"You're avoiding your feelings. I'm praying for you," she answered. "I know God has a plan for you. The Bible says it's a plan for good and not for evil. He wants you to experience the fullness of life He offers. He's given us so much.

"It's hard to understand why things happen, why we lose our loved ones. There are a lot of things I can't explain. But I do know God wants only the best for us. He loves us."

He opened a palm in question. "How is it so easy for you to trust Him after all you've lived through?"

"Because He's the One who saw me through those things and brought me out on the other side. He's still bringing me through, with this move to a new land."

At that moment Gavin McCorkle showed up bleeding from a cut above his eye. He'd been hit by a padlock a fisherman had used as a weight on his fishing net.

"You can't barely see three feet before you," he told Maeve as Flynn cleaned the gash. "The fog is downright eerie, 'tis. But the fish are crowding each other out to get into our nets."

She hadn't been on deck yet. "Is Mrs. Conley up there with her net?"

"Aye. Has the biggest haul of all, she does. The cap'n's even helpin' her haul 'em in. We're near another island, but Cap'n Conley doesn't want to risk the reefs with such poor visibility."

"We took on plenty of fresh water already," Flynn agreed.

Flynn put in one suture to hold the cut closed.

A tremendous peal of thunder startled the three of them, and Maeve dropped the scissors she'd been holding. Her heart beat at an excessive rate.

Gavin jumped down from the table. "Orders are to double-reef the topsail if a storm comes upon us!"

He shot out the door.

Another roll of thunder encompassed them.

"I'm going topside to have a look," Flynn said.

Maeve set the supplies aside and followed him.

The fog Gavin had spoken of had lifted, but the sky had grown black as night. The day was as eerie as Gavin had declared. A violent gale arose as they stood near the ladder. Maeve held down her skirt hem, which threatened to fly upward.

Those who'd been at their cook fires extinguished them, gathered all their belongings and headed below deck for shelter. Sailors busied themselves securing sails and lines. Forked lightning zigzagged down from the heavens.

An angry storm at sea was a terrifying and majestic thing to see. Maeve would remember this sight all her days.

Rain descended in torrents, and they turned and climbed down the ladder as fast as they could. Flynn paused to maneuver a heavy door, one Maeve had never noticed before, over the opening.

"Be careful as you make your way to your berth," he told her. "Tell the others to tie themselves to their bunks for safety's sake. And stay calm."

One end of the ship rose as though on an angry billow, and Flynn caught her before she struck the wall. The next moment, the same end of the vessel plunged downward. "Here. I'll see you to your cabin."

He took her securely by the upper arm and led her

through the passageways until they reached her destination.

Cries of the terrified women greeted her upon entering. Untethered bandboxes and clothing lay strewn about the floor. Nora and Bridget had been waiting for her. Nora comforted the fussing baby. Bridget flung herself at Maeve. Her body trembled so forcefully, her teeth chattered.

"Dr. Gallagher said we must lash ourselves to our beds!" she said loud enough for the others to hear. "Do so quickly now and stay calm."

The females used sheets and blankets to tie themselves by their waists to the frames of their beds.

Successive peals of thunder drew shrieks, and the constant plunging of the ship had more than one woman losing the contents of her stomach.

Maeve's belly felt queasy, but she had a strong constitution and prayed her way through the fear.

The cabin grew stuffy, and the smell of vomit reeked throughout. Grace let out a tremulous wail and cried pitifully.

"Sing, why don't you, Nora?" Maeve called down.
"Now?"

"Yes. Everyone enjoyed your lullaby."

Nora cleared her throat. The first few notes were shaky. "'The primrose in the sheltered nook. The crystal stream the babbling brook. All these things God's hands have made for very love of thee.'"

The ship still rocked upon the ocean, but those who'd been crying quieted to listen.

"'Twilight and shadows fall. Peace to His children all. Angels are guarding and they watch o'er thee as you sleep. May angels watch over and may they guard o'er thee.'"

Grace had quieted, too. Perhaps Nora's voice had

comforted her when she'd begun to sing. At any rate, her song had brought a measure of comfort to the baby and their fellow passengers.

Soon after, the rocking of the brig lessened as the wind and waves abated. The sound of thunder moved off into the distance.

Still they waited to be sure the worst of the storm had passed. Half an hour later, Maeve loosened her bindings and hopped down. "Are all of you all right? Is anyone hurt?"

"I bumped my head on the bunk," an older woman said and rubbed the area.

"Let me have a look." Others were making their way out of their beds now and a few rolled up their soiled linens. Maeve probed the woman's skull. "You might have a headache, but you're fine."

She turned to the others. "No one will object to an additional wash day, so you may wash out your bedding, ladies. I'll ask a mate to string the lines as soon as the sky is clear." She turned to her sisters. "I'd better go straightaway to the dispensary in case anyone was hurt."

"I want to make sure the Atwater girls fared well," Bridget told her. She worked her hair into a braid and hurried off.

On deck, the leaden clouds had parted, and as though in defiance of the contending elements, the late-afternoon sun made an appearance.

The dark sodden deck shone in the light. Overhead, canvas sails snapped in the breeze as they were unfurled. Maeve should have gone below, but something held her in place. She felt as though she was waiting for something, though she wasn't sure what. She listened and waited.

Searching the sky, she was treated to a view of the

changing color and departing darkness. As the last remaining clouds scuttled out of view, the reason she'd lingered manifested itself, stretching wide across the sky.

The most magnificent rainbow she'd ever witnessed confirmed God's promise to the ages and His people. *Lo, I am with you always, even unto the end of the age,* she heard as plain as day.

A tear trailed down her cheek. Swiping it away, she smiled through blurred vision. God was good. His promises endured. He was going to see them to America safely. He would provide them with a home and security, and meet their needs. Anything less than solid trust and devotion was foolishness.

The affirmation of His enduring love buoyed her spirits. She caught herself wishing Flynn was here to see it, and then in a split second, she shot down the ladder and dashed along the corridor.

He'd arrived at the dispensary and was picking up the few supplies they'd abandoned when the storm hit.

"Come now!" she shouted.

He dropped something he held and ran after her. Up the ladder they scrambled, and came out on deck. "What's wrong?" he asked. "Who's injured?"

"No one. Look!"

A line creased his brow, but he shifted his attention to where she pointed. His expression softened.

Maeve said nothing. He'd as much as accused her of talking too much, of asking too many personal questions, and admittedly she was guilty of those things. So for once she held her tongue. She let God do the talking this time.

Again Maeve appreciated the majesty of the rainbow, but her interest was in Flynn's reaction. Emotions played across his finely chiseled face. His brows were as black as his hair, his nose straight and well-formed. He had a solid jaw and an expressive mouth. His eyes, fringed by black lashes, were dark and fathomless. When his face relaxed and lines of concern smoothed away, she realized what a handsome man he was.

Gradually, life resumed its natural rhythm around them. A few hardy souls came out and cleaned their cooking areas of debris. Riggers called to one another from above.

Huge birds flew overhead, as large as geese, pure white with jet black-tipped wings. Maeve supposed they were residents of the nearby island, which was now visible, but behind them.

Finally, Flynn turned to her and spoke: "Thank you."

She wasn't sure exactly what had taken place during that interlude, but she was glad she'd been prompted to go get him. She simply nodded.

"Let's get back to work," he said.

That evening they were treated to a splendid sunset, the colorful likes to which none other during their trip could compare. Bridget didn't join them for their evening meal, as she was dining with the Atwaters in the captain's cabin.

"I wish I had your fearlessness," Maeve said to Aideen, in a mocking singsong tone. "To stuff yourself on that mackerel and not care a whit."

Aideen, who had been told all about Kathleen's barbed compliments, chuckled and popped another bite in her mouth. She chewed with her eyes closed as though the smoked fish was smooth ambrosia.

"Maeve," Nora warned in her matronly, older-sister tone.

"Oh, I forgave her," Maeve told her. "I'm just going to laugh about it now. You know you want to laugh, too."

A tall man in a black suit approached them, and Maeve recognized him as the man who worked for Mrs. Fitzwilliam.

"My mistress asked that you accompany me to her stateroom," he said.

"Is she sick?"

"She is requesting your presence, miss. That's all I know."

Maeve set down her plate and brushed her hands together. "Well, let's go, then."

He led the way down the ladder and to a door on the opposite side of the lower level from where Maeve and her sisters slept. After rapping on the door, he opened it.

A set of mother-of-pearl inlaid folding screens shielded the room from view. She supposed it was a good solution to spare the woman's privacy when her servant was a man. It did set up a dramatic effect.

"Have you brought her, Stillman?" came a woman's voice from beyond.

"Yes, ma'am. Miss Murphy has arrived."

"Send her in."

"Mrs. Fitzwilliam will see you now." He gestured for her to proceed around the screen.

She had certainly met the most interesting people on this voyage. Maeve skirted the screens.

Lying atop a bed dressed with elegant satin draping and huge tasseled pillows was the woman who'd dressed her down the first day on the *Annie McGee*. She wore a silk dressing gown in a luscious shade of mauve and a pair of matching slippers with rhinestone embellishment.

"Are you feeling poorly, Mrs. Fitzwilliam?"

"I think I shall not make it through the night."

"Was it the storm? Perhaps some peppermint oil will settle your stomach. You had a rough go, I'd wager."

"It was not the storm, although that was an experience I do not wish to endure on any future occasion."

"What is it, then?"

"I fear it's my heart."

Chapter Fifteen

"I'd better send for Dr. Gallagher, then. I'm not a physician, you know."

"I don't want that man here."

"Why not? He's a fine surgeon."

"Because he looks like my dear departed Walter in his youth, and I couldn't bear for him to turn those eyes on me today of all days."

"But he's better equipped than I to treat a heart condition."

"I fear my heart is broken, and I doubt there's anything he can do about that."

The woman could add more drama to a conversation than even Bridget.

Maeve tugged an easy chair closer to the woman's bed. The contents of the bedside table were on the floor, apparently tossed there during the storm, so she knelt and set them back in place. Among jars and a leather-bound journal was a daguerrotype of a dashing, dark-haired man in a finely cut suit. A watch chain draped from inside his vest to a pocket, and he seemed to study the camera with a look of annoyance. Maeve placed it upright on the table.

Mrs. Fitzwilliam covered her face with a flowered

handkerchief. "I dream of him nearly every night. Mr. Fitzwilliam was industrious and always full of ideas. He could make even the drabbest day come to life. I never lived a dull moment in all our married years. We were going to travel abroad once he found an assistant he trusted with his business affairs. That just never seemed to happen, so our voyages were always business related."

Maeve settled on the chair and spoke softly. "You must miss him very much. When a person so full of life, like your husband, is gone, it sometimes feels as though a candle has been extinguished and the whole world is dreary without them."

Mrs. Fitzwilliam slowly tugged the handkerchief away from her eyes. She looked at Maeve. "That's it exactly. How do you know this?"

"That's how I felt when my mother went to glory. Even though we were poor and she and my father worked hard every day, she always found ways to make the most simple meal entertaining. She sang so beautifully, her voice could lift anyone's mood. Even in a work dress and apron she carried herself like a queen.

"My father adored her, and my sisters and I learned so much about life from her. For the longest time after she died it felt as though the spark had gone out of our family. But then, little by little, I would see things about my sister Bridget that reminded me of Mother. Or I'd hear Nora say something my mother said. Only today, as the boat was pitching and the thunder was crashing, Nora sang a lullaby in the same lilting voice as Mother.

"She left us a legacy of her beautiful spirit, her wisdom and her kindness. She's no longer of this earth, but she lives in our hearts."

Mrs. Fitzwilliam's eyes shimmered with tears that spilled over. She blotted her nose with the handkerchief.

"He does live on in my heart. And in my dreams. Sometimes they're so real, I wake up thinking he's still here and I will see his head on the pillow beside me.

"Sadly, we never had any children of our own. I was Walter's second wife, you see, and he had a daughter. He indulged her, much to my dismay. She grew into a selfish young woman without a lick of sense. Her offspring is a foolish spoiled snip of a girl, whom I was attempting to raise on my own after her mother left her in my care to chase after a French artist."

"So you do have some family?"

"I treated my husband's granddaughter as my own. I gave her everything a young girl could ask for—singing lessons, clothing, a parlor all her own in which to entertain her friends."

"Where is she now?"

Mrs. Fitzwilliam flattened a fleshy hand against her breast as though she was in pain. "The foolish child ran off six months ago. She met a ruffian of poor character, and when I refused to allow her to see him, she packed a bag and sailed off to Boston with him."

"So, you're going after her?"

"Of course I am. I can't let Mary fall to ruin when she has a perfectly good home and someone to care for her."

"Of course not. How old is Mary?"

"Eighteen now. Her birthday was only last month." She sniffled into her hankie. "I fear I'm losing my mind, Miss Murphy."

"Why do you say that?"

Mrs. Fitzwilliam finally roused herself upward to sit on the edge of the bed. "Have you ever glimpsed someone who looks so much like the person you lost that your heart catches? When you look more closely, it's not them at all."

"Aye," Maeve replied. "I could have sworn I saw my da on the dock when we were boarding, but it was just a silver-haired fellow in a homespun shirt. When he looked my way, he looked nothing like Da."

Mrs. Fitzwilliam nodded. "I used to think I spotted my Walter, too. And twice recently, I thought I saw Mary. Both times I glimpsed a girl with the same black hair, but when I looked again there was no one there. Do you think that means Mary is dead, like Walter?"

"No, of course not. You know better than that. She's on your mind is all."

"Does it mean I'll be placed in a sanitarium soon?"

"Certainly not. You've had a lot of concerns on your mind, is all. Sometimes our mind plays tricks on us. A woman in my village lost her baby at birth. Every night for months she awoke to the sound of a baby crying, until she was on the verge of hysteria."

"The poor woman."

"I'll be glad to help you find Mary when we get to Boston. I'll help in any way I can."

The older woman met her gaze directly. Her dark auburn hair had come loose from its fancy bun, and those blue eyes didn't appear quite as cold as they once had. "That's kind of you, Miss Murphy. Thank you."

"Call me Maeve."

"You may call me Elizabeth."

"Shall I help you dress your hair now?"

She pointed to a case on the floor. "My brush and comb are in there."

Maeve gathered the items and returned.

"How is the young boy faring? The one whose leg you saved?"

"Sean is quite well. He's running errands for the captain now. There are three McCorkle brothers. Seems they came up with a plan to escape a workhouse and board the ship. Things went awry when young Sean got hurt.

"Gavin is a rigger. I saw him overhead today. Little Emmett is caring for the sailors' chickens and goat. Mrs. Conley won't let them eat in the galley with the crew. She feeds those boys like kings, she does."

"Should they need anything—a place to stay, clothing…you come to me. Do you hear?"

"Yes, ma'am. I can't do this as intricately as you, but I can give you a serviceable bun. My sister Bridget could fashion it more stylishly."

"It will suffice, Maeve. Thank you." She gave her a sheepish look. "I just needed someone to talk to who could understand my distress. You seem like a kind and understanding person."

"We all need that. It's perfectly normal."

"I don't really have anyone, except Stillman. He was my husband's valet. Since Walter's been gone, he's been with me, as I didn't have the heart to let him go, but he is a man, after all."

"How are you feeling now?"

"Foolish."

Maeve ignored that. "I mean your chest. Any pain?"

"Nothing time won't heal."

"Very well." Maeve paused. She didn't want to leave without one last offer. Finally, she decided if it was rebuffed, she wouldn't care. "Would you care to join me and my sisters at our fire tomorrow evening and share a meal?"

The invitation seemed to toss the woman into a wave. She floundered for a moment, but then caught herself. "I would love to join you. Thank you for the invitation. I'm sure Stillman will appreciate a night off."

"All right. We'll see you then."

Her opinion of the woman had changed a hundred

percent. Immediately she recalled her prayer, asking for God's help in being generous and kindhearted. She'd directed that request toward her feelings about Kathleen, but quite obviously God thought she needed to treat everyone the same way.

She still didn't see herself inviting Kathleen to their fire any time soon, but stranger things had happened. She wasn't going to count anything out just yet.

Wait until her sisters learned who would be joining them the next evening.

Mrs. Fitzwilliam was an entertaining dinner companion. In her younger days, she'd traveled with her husband on business. She shared stories of India, Japan and even Africa.

"I am most likely the only person here who has ever ridden an elephant," she said at one point.

"I've ridden a donkey," Bridget said, and they shared a laugh that drew attention from their neighbors.

"*Everyone* has ridden a donkey," Maeve admonished her.

"I haven't," Mrs. Fitzwilliam proclaimed. And again they laughed heartily.

The Murphys had included Aideen and Mrs. Kennedy in their dinner plans and combined resources.

"The fish is exceptional," their guest said.

Everyone was growing weary of mackerel, but no one spoke of it. Plenty of fish was not a hardship in any way, shape or form. Their countrymen back home would love to haul in a catch like this and put it on the table for their families.

In a way Maeve felt bad for leaving so many people behind to fend for themselves, but on the other hand, she felt fortunate to have escaped the poverty and oppression.

Nora had outdone herself with a kettle of rice pudding.

Mrs. Kennedy was holding Baby Grace, so she asked Nora to save her a serving.

"I do so admire your courage for eating that pudding," Bridget said to Maeve. "You're so brave to blow yourself up like a puffer fish and not care a whit that your drab, ill-fitting dresses no longer fit."

"Bridget," Nora cautioned, but her voice had no true censure behind it. In fact, she quickly hid a grin.

Mrs. Fitzwilliam looked taken aback by Bridget's teasing, so Nora shared how a particularly rude passenger had behaved at the captain's table.

"Oh, dear," Maeve said to her oldest sister. "You haven't dressed for dinner. I'll make your excuses while you run along and change. Don't worry yourself if it's a rag. No one on this vessel has any fashion sense. They'll never know."

Nora did laugh at that.

"I am amazed at what some people consider a suitable dinner dress," Aideen told them, sipping her tea with her pinkie in the air. She turned to her aunt. "Why look at your hair! How generous of you to employ a blind maid."

They laughed over that, and even Mrs. Fitzwilliam got into the spirit, once she was convinced they weren't making sport of *her.* "I hope I never sounded like that," she said, turning a repentant gaze on Maeve. "I do apologize for anything unkind I said to you in the past."

"All is forgiven," Maeve assured her.

"But truly," Mrs. Fitzwilliam said to Maeve. "That's an interesting lace collar you're wearing. Did the mice get to it?"

Nora choked on her tea, and Bridget patted her on the back until she stopped coughing.

They were enjoying themselves so thoroughly, no one noticed the couple strolling nearby until they were practically on top of them.

"You ladies are certainly enjoying your evening," Flynn noted. "What is all this merriment about?"

Beside him stood Kathleen, her shiny dark hair in place, a paisley silk shawl wrapped around her shoulders.

"Nora did something incredible with this rice pudding," Maeve replied. "It seems we have enough to feed the crew. Would you care for some?"

Flynn glanced at Kathleen, and it was plain he wanted to accept. "That sounds nice," he said and led Kathleen forward.

The ladies scooted closer together to make room for two more. It wasn't a problem, since they had Aideen and her aunt's space to use. Maeve got a stool for Kathleen and sat on a mat.

Kathleen sat with her skirts tucked aside as though she didn't want to soil them by allowing them to touch one of the other women.

Nora placed a serving of rice pudding in a clean dish and handed it to Kathleen.

Everyone grew silent, waiting for her refusal.

The sound of the waves against the side of the ship was loud in the ensuing silence.

As though she sensed every eye upon her, the young woman glanced from person to person. Apparently refusing the offering in front of so many was too rude even for her, because she accepted the bowl and a spoon. "Thank you."

Flynn took his with a smile and tasted it. "Mmm. Indeed, this is the best rice pudding I've ever eaten in my life. And I'm partial to rice pudding."

"Evenin', Dr. Gallagher," their neighbors called over.

Flynn greeted them.

Kathleen took a bite.

"So what were you sharing such a hearty laugh over?" Flynn asked.

"Well…" Maeve studied the starlit sky.

"I'm afraid their amusement was at my expense," Mrs. Fitzwilliam said, surprising Maeve by coming to her rescue. "I was bragging about having ridden an elephant in India. They could not picture it. I wasn't quite as full-figured as I am now."

The baby fussed, and Nora got up.

"Let me," Bridget said. "I'll go." She grabbed a tin cup and headed across the deck in the moonlight.

Maeve took the baby from Mrs. Kennedy and changed her nappy.

"Where did she go for milk?" Kathleen asked.

"To milk the goat," Nora replied. "The sailors generously let us milk her whenever we need to, day or night."

"Why don't you just gather a whole bucket at once and save yourself the additional trouble?" she asked.

"Because it would be contaminated in the hours it was left exposed." Flynn's tone revealed his aggravation at the question.

Maeve stood and carried Grace over to their guests and extended her toward Kathleen. "You're welcome to hold her."

Kathleen just looked at Maeve with a blank expression, so Maeve placed Grace in her arms and stepped back.

The young woman looked as though someone had dropped a mud pie in her lap. She grimaced and held Grace as far from her as possible, without letting go. The baby fussed at the awkward position.

"Oh, here, like this." To Maeve's utter amazement, Flynn took the infant and nestled her into the crook of his arm. Grace immediately settled in and opened her eyes wide in the darkness.

"She's such a sweet little thing," Nora said.

"Still no idea how she came to be abandoned?" Mrs. Fitzwilliam asked.

Nora shook her head. "'Tis a mystery, it is."

"Quite obviously someone didn't want to get up and milk a goat three or four times a night," Kathleen remarked.

"Her own mother wouldn't have had to milk a goat," Maeve pointed out. "Nature takes care of that detail rather ingeniously."

"Oh." Kathleen pulled her shawl around her.

Bridget returned and Nora filled the glass nursing bottle.

"Do you wash it between feedings?" Flynn asked.

"Yes, doctor," Nora replied with a grin. "The nipple, too. Do you want to feed her?"

Flynn didn't reply for a moment, but then he nodded and took the bottle. Grace knew better than he what was required and latched on hungrily.

Seven women watched the only male in their midst, a tall broad-shouldered man, as he held and fed the tiny infant, a babe not even as long as his forearm. It was one of those moments that doesn't require comment, because it's so pure and beautiful on its own.

Maeve couldn't help wondering what he thought as he held Grace, truly acknowledging her for the first time, and not distancing himself. He must be thinking of his Jonathon, of the wife he loved and lost. He must be thinking how fleeting and fragile life is—and, in the face of a newborn baby, how beautiful.

Chapter Sixteen

When Grace was finished, Nora took the bottle. "Put her on your shoulder to work up a bubble now."

He did as instructed, propping Grace on his shoulder and patting her gently. She emitted a very unladylike sound and he chuckled. "Right on cue."

"I should take her to bed." Nora reached for the baby.

"Bridget and I will do the dishes," Maeve assured her.

Aideen got up. "I'll help."

"We should be going." Kathleen stood. "Thank you for your hospitality."

"You're quite welcome. It was our pleasure," Maeve said.

"Yes, do come back," Bridget added, as though they'd just had someone into their parlor for a tea party.

Flynn thanked them, as well, and the couple strolled away.

"That was interesting," Aideen remarked.

"I don't know what I'd have done if she'd refused the dessert," Maeve said.

They busied themselves with the dishes.

This week on the Sabbath, the boundaries in the hold were nearly obliterated. Aideen and Mrs. Kennedy, along with Elizabeth Fitzwilliam, sat with the Murphy sisters for Captain Conley's Bible reading and during silent prayer.

The McCorkle brothers sat directly behind them, and were the most boisterous singers in the room. When the service ended, Mrs. Fitzwilliam turned around and spoke to each lad.

After lunch, serious work began on the dresses. The Murphy sisters gathered in the other ladies' stateroom, where all the supplies were handy, and applied their efforts to cutting the fabric.

"I'm terrified of making a mistake," Nora said, the scissors trembling in her hand.

Mrs. Kennedy took the shears from her and all of them watched in fascination as a loud *snip snip snip* sounded and the fabric parted in perfect precision. Aideen wielded her own impressive pair of scissors to cut facing and bias strips.

"What about underclothing?" She glanced up. "Do you ladies have proper underslips and pantaloons? What about chemises?"

Nora's complexion turned pink. "No one will see our underclothing."

"It has nothing to do with who will see them and everything to do with how beautiful and self-confident you feel."

"And pantaloons will make me feel self-confident?" Maeve's eldest sister challenged.

"Yes," Aideen replied emphatically. "We shall fashion several sets, and you will not set foot on that gangplank without a proper ensemble beneath your dress."

Bridget smiled from ear to ear.

Nora acquiesced with a pretty shrug. "If you feel that strongly about it."

Maeve sat with Baby Grace in her lap and watched

her sisters with their new friends. "When we're living in Faith Glen, we shall travel to Boston to visit you. And you're welcome at our cottage any time."

"Oh, I would love that," Aideen told her. "I don't think I've ever had such pleasurable company."

They went on deck for a quick afternoon meal, and Maeve boiled water. "We were running low, so I purchased some lovely tea from one of the ladies I met."

"Thank you, Maeve," Nora said. "Afternoon tea sounds delightful."

Bridget agreed and added, "I do wish we had biscuits."

"Or those sweet little lemon cookies we once enjoyed at a wedding," Maeve added.

"You're making my mouth water." Mrs. Kennedy closed her eyes. "Let's pretend."

A scuffle broke out several fires away. The occasional argument was common, but this was beyond a verbal disagreement. The women sat in stunned silence as two men shouted and took punches at each other.

"Oh, my." Bridget rested a hand on her cheek.

One man chased the other across the deck, his boots making a loud racket on the planks. The man being chased carried a lumpy bag, and when he got to the side of the ship he paused, heaved it upward and threw it overboard.

Quite obviously incensed, the man in pursuit lunged forward with a loud growl. The sisters had seen the Donnelly brothers fistfight on rare occasion, but this didn't seem like a spat between rowdy brothers. Tight-fisted hits were met with grunts. They grappled to the deck, stood and circled each other with bent knees.

A flash of steel glimmered in the sunlight.

Both men stilled.

The first lunged.

The second slid to the planks, a crimson stain spreading across his shirt front.

The other, the one who'd thrown the bag overboard, wiped his bloodied dagger on the leg of the injured man, sheathed it and ran.

"After him!" someone shouted.

Already on her feet, Maeve shouted for someone to go for Dr. Gallagher, and darted to the bleeding passenger on the deck. She fell to her knees beside him.

The bearded man's eyes were already glassy. Blood trickled from the corner of his mouth. Still conscious, he rolled his eyes toward her. Attempting speech, he choked instead.

She tore open his shirt to find a deep wound that had obviously pierced vital organs. She tore off her shawl, rolled it and pressed the wad against the wound. She knew of nothing to do for him. He was rapidly bleeding to death. "If you need to make peace with God, I am believing this is your last chance."

He turned his head aside, spat and gasped, "Pray."

"You want me to pray with you?"

He nodded, grimacing so wide his bared teeth shone in the sunlight.

Heart racing now, Maeve leaned close to the dying man and asked God to forgive him of any trespasses and take him to glory.

He nodded as though agreeing with her prayer, but his eyelids fluttered.

"Henry!" A woman collapsed to her knees near his head. As though she didn't know what to do with her hands, she shook them before cradling his head in her lap. Sobs tore from her throat. "Why didn't you just let him go? You foolish, foolish man! Why couldn't you have stayed with me, Henry? Why? Why?" She shot her panicked gaze to Maeve's. "Why aren't you doing something for him?"

"I'm trying to stop the flow of blood, ma'am. I don't know what else to do. I'm not a doctor."

Henry's eyes fluttered shut and back open. He couldn't seem to focus on the woman.

"Don't you die on me, Henry! We're startin' a new life in Illinois. Don't you dare die. We've got five children to raise!"

Maeve's stomach clenched.

Henry's eyes closed and he emitted a deep ragged breath, then didn't draw another.

"*Henry!* Don't you die, Henry!"

Behind her, Maeve heard Bridget's sob and then Nora urging her away.

Finally, Flynn arrived and knelt beside Maeve. "What's happened?"

Relieved to see him, Maeve lifted her blood-soaked shawl to show him the stab wound in Henry's belly.

"Do something!" the woman shrieked. "Don't let him die!"

"Ma'am," Flynn said softly. "He didn't have a chance. This wound perforated too many of his organs. Even if I'd been here and immediately attempted surgery, I couldn't have saved him. He lost blood too fast."

She threw herself upon the dead man's chest and sobbed.

Maeve wanted to comfort her, but her hands were soaked with blood. She released the shawl, sat back on her knees and looked at the other faces in the gathered crowd, just now seeing how many people had watched that scenario unfold.

From behind her, Nora stepped around Flynn and knelt beside the woman. She draped an arm over her shoulder and spoke softly. "Come away now, *ma milis*.

I'll make you a cup of tea and you can lie down. Where are your children?"

The woman raised her head. Her expression registered shock, confusion. "Oh, dear God. The children." She looked at Nora then. "They're back near our fire."

Nora checked the crowd. "Does anyone know who this woman's children are?"

A woman stepped forward. "I do. Their fire is beside ours."

"Will you look after them, please? I'm going to take her to lie down."

"Take her to our rooms," Mrs. Kennedy offered. "It's quiet there. Private."

Once Nora had led away the grieving widow, Flynn ordered the nearby men to help him carry Henry's body to the prow, where a coffin would be made.

Maeve got up and stared at her hands, then her skirt, which was hopelessly stained. She was angry. Angry that something like this could happen in the middle of a day filled with sunshine and salt spray. On the Sabbath, no less. A hideous crime leaving a woman with five fatherless children to raise.

The crowd had dispersed. A couple of the apprentices carried buckets to the scene and poured water on the deck. The water diluted the thickening blood, which ran into the cracks between the planks.

"Blood is depressin' tough to remove from the deck," one of them said.

Maeve's skirt was ruined. Angrily, she reached for the button and ties in the back and stepped out of it. Not caring who saw, she wiped her hands on the wool, then used it to pick up her shawl before she stomped to the rail in her pantaloons. There, she flung the bloody clothing into the ocean.

Without a backward glance or a sideways look, she

marched to the ladder and ran to her cabin to wash and change.

Most of their mates had gone to the cabin, too. A few of them spoke to her, telling her she'd done all she could, most lamenting the fact that a man with a family had been struck down in the prime of life.

"They said that other fella stole their sack of provisions, he did, and Henry was simply goin' after what rightly belonged to 'im."

"'Tis a pity, it is."

"Poor woman. Five hungry mouths to feed and her man dead and gone. Can't help but wonder what will become of them now."

Maeve couldn't bear the talk. She picked up her Bible and made her way to the dispensary, where she could be alone. She poured more water into a basin and used Flynn's soap and brush to scrub her hands again, taking extra care to get under her nails.

The look in Henry's eyes as he lay dying was yet another picture of despair and hopelessness she would never erase from her memory. Her hands were clean, but she continued to scrub until her skin was red and irritated.

She poured more water and washed her arms and her face, as well. Finally, she dried her skin, and her motions slowed. The horror of what had happened caught up to her. The enormity of this voyage and their uncertain fates overwhelmed her.

She backed up to the wall for support. Her chest was tight and her lungs near to bursting. She tried to hold in the emotion, but her face crumpled and scalding tears ran down her cheeks. Sliding to the floor, she sat in a huddle with her knees drawn up, her face buried in her clean skirt, and cried great heaving sobs.

She'd never cried this hard or this much. She'd been

strong for her sisters and Da when Mother had died. She'd been strong yet again when Da had passed on. She'd been so resilient that sometimes she felt as though she must not have a tear in her.

But here they were, buckets of them, enough to soak her sleeve and the fabric over her knees. Blindly, she reached up to a drawer for a bandage rag on which to blow her nose and let herself simply breathe for several minutes.

Slow, even breaths.

If she felt this badly, how did Henry's poor widow feel? And his children? How young were they?

The door opened.

Please not a patient, Lord, she prayed. She'd thoughtlessly left the portal unlocked.

A clean, pressed white shirt in her peripheral vision assured her differently, however.

Flynn.

"Maeve?" he said, spotting her huddled on the floor and walking toward her. "What are you doing down there? Are you all right?" He drew up short at the sight of her. "Ah, Maeve."

"I'm fine," she said, but her stuffy voice and nose belied that proclamation. She could only imagine what her face and eyes looked like. And her nose.

He went to the basin of water she'd used, wetted a cloth and wrung out the excess water. "Place this over your face for a few minutes."

She obeyed and breathed through the damp cotton.

The cool cloth felt good on her skin, especially over her burning eyes.

He took one of her hands and splayed it open to examine it. "What have you done to yourself?"

After releasing her, he was gone for a moment and returned. With strong, warm fingers he rubbed glycerin into her raw skin. The massage felt better than she'd thought anything could. Her entire arm relaxed under his attention.

He let her shift that hand to hold the rag to her face and ministered to her other in the same way, applying the cool glycerin, massaging it into her flesh. Her other arm relaxed and tension gradually left her body.

Slowly peeling away the cloth, he dabbed glycerin with the pad of one finger under each eye.

He had another plan, because he went for more supplies and returned with peppermint oil. After he massaged a dab onto each of her temples, the oil spread coolness to her aching head, and the scent roused her flagging spirits.

Or perhaps it had been his tender care that had lifted her from despondency. She didn't feel as hopeless as she had only a short while ago.

He urged her to her feet and guided her to one of the chairs, then pulled another near and sat before her. "There was nothing you could have done differently. What I told his wife was the truth. His wound was fatal. You comforted him in his dying moments."

"I prayed for him. He asked me to."

"You did more than most people would have."

She nodded. "Perhaps. But knowing that doesn't change what happened or take away the futility I feel over one human being taking another's life. It's senseless."

"We're only people," he said. "We do everything we can, but we're not miracle workers."

She agreed.

"What would your da say if he was here?"

Puzzled, she looked at him. "My da?"

He nodded. "Was he a wise man?"

She didn't have to think too hard. The corner of her mouth quirked up. "He'd say, 'Maeve, me fine daughter, aimin' to cure the ails of this world is like hopin' to mind mice at a crossroads.'"

Flynn chuckled. "You must take after him, because it sounds just like something you would say. So he *was* a wise man."

"That he was."

She ran her fingers through hair that had fallen loose and tugged it away from her face. "It all rose up strong today, all the pain I've been pushing back and keeping inside and thinking I was over it."

"Maybe that's good."

"Maybe it is."

"You're the bravest woman I know."

She looked into his dark eyes. "No, I'm not."

"Yes. You jump right in and take a situation in hand. In fact, I'm a little bit concerned for you, since that seems to be your habit. I don't know what you'll get yourself mixed up in next."

"Well, I'm thinkin' about those fatherless children and Henry's widow. The Bible tells us to take care of widows and orphans."

He shook his head. "Here you are, not concerned about your own future, because you trust God has that in hand, but instead thinking how you can do something to improve their future?"

"Well…" She thought a minute. "Yes."

He laughed, and those dimples winked at her.

Without thought for consequences or propriety, she placed her palm against his warm cheek. The texture of his beard was pleasantly rough. "Thank you, Flynn."

"My pleasure." Quite spontaneously, he leaned forward and touched his lips to hers, a kiss that seemed as natural and pure as rain on a spring day.

Chapter Seventeen

It was a kiss of comfort, a bond of mutual understanding. This kiss showed care and compassion. Nothing more.

But if that was true, why did she feel as though she'd been swept overboard and caught up in a turbulent current? He threaded his fingers into her hair, and she longed to stand and have him wrap his arms around her.

Now she kissed him in return. Earnestly, without thought for anything as simple as comfort. She wanted to drown in his kiss.

The thrill of it was as amazing as last time…yet terrifying on the other hand. She feared she might burst into tears again, and that would never do. The beauty of it buoyed her and kept her on the chair when she might otherwise have toppled to the floor. Only one thing kept her from losing herself in his embrace.

Last time he'd apologized.

She inched away, and he released her.

"Will you be telling me you're sorry again?" She searched his dark mahogany-colored eyes. "I don't enjoy being someone's regret."

"I can't regret kissing you, Maeve."

"Are you not promised to your Miss Boyd?"

Something moved behind his eyes. Was that regret or surprise? "No, I'm not. Kathleen and I are friends."

"She and her mother speak differently. You and she seem so comfortable in each other's company. She doesn't see herself as your friend."

He frowned in confusion. "I've never let her think I'm interested in more. We have mutual friends, memories of our home. We talk and that's all."

"You feel nothing for her." It wasn't a question.

"Friendship, Maeve. Only friendship."

"You have never kissed her?"

"Not once," he assured her.

"Then these kisses of ours…perhaps they do mean something?"

The look in his eyes was definitely confusion. "I—I don't know what to say."

She stood on trembling legs and picked up her Bible from a counter. "You can't avoid your heart forever. Maybe if you faced your feelings you'd recognize what is it you want."

"Just because you run directly at a problem without forethought doesn't necessarily mean it's the only way."

This time she did think before she spoke. And she held what she really wanted to say in check. "I came seeking privacy. I'll be leaving now."

"You might want to stay away awhile longer. The council is deciding the fate of the man who stabbed Henry to death."

"The council?"

"Yes. Remember the group of men who were selected by their fellow passengers to mete out justice during the journey?"

"What about the captain?"

"He is like a judge. The council is comparable to a jury."

"What do you suppose they'll decide?"

"Murder is met with swift punishment in any country as well as on the sea."

She headed for the door.

He didn't try to stop her, but he followed.

On deck, passengers were gathered around the prow, much as they had the day Bridget Collins had been buried at sea. A man in a gray suit stood to pronounce the council's decision.

"We didn't deliberate long," he said. "And we've come to a unanimous decision. This man who refuses to give his name will be thrown overboard immediately."

A murmur went through the crowd. Maeve felt sick to her stomach. She'd lived in a peaceful little farming community her entire life. The most momentous events had been births and deaths by natural causes. She'd never before witnessed a murder or an execution. "Can't we take the man to Boston and give him a trial?" she called out.

"Massachusetts law wouldn't recognize a crime committed aboard ship," the speaker replied. "We're the judge and jury here."

"What of imprisonment?" she asked.

There were more murmurs from the gathering.

"Again there's the issue of who's responsible for his imprisonment."

Another member of the council spoke up. "And meanwhile would you have us feed the vile man from our own provisions? Why, he tried to steal Henry Begg's food right from his children's mouths. And when Henry called 'im out, he killed him. He showed Henry Begg no mercy, and he deserves none."

The man was hauled out into the open. Had an evil look about him he did, and a contemptuous glare. Sweat soaked his hair and ruddy face. His hands had been restrained behind his back, a rope tied about his shoulders and another at his feet.

"You have one last chance to state your name for the ship's record and to notify any family you may have," Captain Conley said.

The prisoner spat at him, but the captain was far enough away to avoid being hit.

Captain Conley opened his Bible and read a passage. The words didn't register with Maeve. He finished, closed his Bible and nodded at the mates who held the prisoner in place.

They hauled him up to the stern and balanced him there for a moment as wind whipped their hair.

Maeve's heart beat hard and painfully. She didn't want to watch, but she couldn't tear away her gaze. *Lord, take his soul.*

A sailor lashed out with a mighty shove, and the nameless man plunged headfirst into the waters below.

Her surroundings wavered in her vision. Maeve closed her eyes. Flynn grasped her by the shoulders and held her in place from behind. She hadn't realized she'd been swaying where she stood. At the sound of soft weeping, she opened her eyes and spotted Henry's wife surrounded by children of various heights and ages. The youngest was a chubby baby on her hip; the head of the eldest came to her shoulder. One small boy clung to her skirts, looking confused.

A moment later, the sound of bagpipes floated on the salt-laden air, adding another dimension to the event and stirring memories of home.

A plain pine box drilled with large holes was carried through the crowd and placed reverently upon the deck. *Now a funeral.*

"'So when this corruptible shall have put on incorruption, and this mortal shall have put on immortality,

then shall be brought to pass the saying that is written,'" Captain Conley read. "'Death is swallowed up in
victory. O death, where is thy sting? O grave, where is
thy victory? The sting of death is sin, and the strength
of sin is the law.'" He turned. "Come now, Mrs. Begg,
and say your last goodbyes to your husband."

She walked forward, still holding the toddler, and
reached toward the pine box with a trembling hand, but
then drew it back. The youngsters who were old enough
to understand what was happening, cried openly. She
ushered them away from the coffin and stood trembling.

Sailors in their best clothing worked two lengths of
rope around the box and hoisted it up and out over the
water. The bagpipes played a haunting melody, a familiar hymn, with which those standing in watch sang
along.

Maeve couldn't sing. Her throat had constricted.
She'd cried out every last tear earlier, so though her eyes
still burned and her nose stung, she had nothing left.

Once the sailors lowered the ropes, the pine box
pitched into the ocean.

Maeve couldn't allow herself to think of Henry's
body, just as she'd been unable to think of her father's.
At least Da's remains were on a lush hillside in his
beloved homeland and not buried under tons of water
and— She caught herself.

Henry Begg wasn't there in that fleshly vessel, she
reminded herself. He'd gone onto heaven to await his
family. Neither could she dwell on the poor Begg woman's shock and grief.

She went for a cup from their cooking area and
placed a few coins inside, then made the rounds of the
cook fires, asking her fellow passengers to share with
the unfortunate widow. The cup was brimming when
she delivered it to Mrs. Begg. "I know it's not much.

And it won't go far, but I shall pray for it to be multiplied."

The woman thanked her, and Maeve joined her sisters in Aideen and Mrs. Kennedy's stateroom.

Their previously lighthearted mood had vanished, and the ladies worked together with somber determination.

"It's easier on my eyes to do this in the sunlight," Aideen commented. She had picked up a basted bodice and begun stitching darts.

"Put it away for now," her aunt told her. "We can sew in the morning."

There was a rap at the door.

"Is Miss Murphy here?"

"There are *three* Miss Murphys here." Aideen grinned at Sean McCorkle.

"Miss Maeve," he specified.

Maeve walked to the door.

"The doc asked for you. There be a passenger havin' a baby, and he asked you to attend. I'll be showin' ye the way."

"Excuse me, ladies."

The others waved her on.

The passenger was one Maeve had only seen in passing, but had never spoken with. On seeing her, she'd wondered when this baby was due to arrive. Maeve introduced herself.

"Margret Madigan," the woman managed. It was obvious she'd waited until birth was close at hand to send for help. She had prepared sheets and blankets.

"Have you had other babies?" Maeve asked.

"Aye. Three previously. One didn't survive his first month. I had a poor supply of milk, I did."

"We'll not let that happen again," Maeve assured

her. "We have plenty of provisions and I'll see that you have a portion of goat's milk for yourself."

The woman grimaced and gripped the sheet on her bunk with white-knuckled fists. She or someone else had laid out folded flannel and provided two buckets of water.

"I'm going to wash in this one," Maeve told her. "And I want anyone who has any contact with you or the baby to do the same." She washed her already sore hands. "Are you feeling as though you have to push yet?"

"Aye," Margret replied.

"Is it all right if I have a look before you do that?"

"Let the whole crew have a gander if it moves this along any faster," Margret replied.

An older woman had remained in the cabin, and she and Maeve exchanged a look. The mature woman's eyes sparkled with amusement.

"Yours isn't a familiar accent," Maeve said as a distraction.

"Scottish," was Margret's brusque reply.

"Have you names selected, be this a lass or a laddie?"

"I hoped not to jinx the babe's fate," the woman replied.

Maeve wouldn't have another funeral this day if she could help it.

As the evening lengthened, Margret's efforts became more and more focused. The other woman bathed her perspiring face with cool cloths and spoke softly in a language Maeve couldn't understand. Her tone was soothing and encouraging.

Margret emitted a sharp cry and bore down.

"One or two more like that, and we'll see this baby's pretty face," Maeve told her. "There 'tis. And a curly head of hair, this wee babe has. Rest easy now for the next big push. This next one will do it."

Margret's next push expelled a good-size boy child into the world. Maeve quickly wiped his face and used her finger to clear his mouth. When he didn't cry, she turned his head down and swatted his bottom. "There you go, laddie. That's a fine healthy cry."

She handed the babe to the older woman, who cleaned him with the fresh water while Maeve attended to the new mother.

"He's a big one, he is," Maeve told her.

Margret didn't take her eyes from the baby, waiting until he was wrapped in flannel and placed in her arms.

She looked at his fingers and opened the wrap to examine his feet. She pressed her lips to his head and inhaled. Her eyes closed and a tear slid from under her lashes.

"Shall I go fetch your husband?" Maeve asked.

"My husband is waiting for us in Boston," she answered. "I thought I'd make it until we arrived, but this little fellow wasn't waiting."

"It's fitting somehow that after a fine man went to heaven today, another has just come into the world, don't you think?"

"I was down here all day, but I heard about the Begg fellow's untimely death," she answered. "I'd be devastated if I lost my husband."

"He's a handsome boy, Mrs. Madigan. Does he have a name now?"

"I have a son named after me father and a daughter named after me husband's mother. My father-in-law's name isn't fit for a child, so I'll not be givin' it to this boy."

"What is it?"

"His name was Urquhart."

Maeve had to agree the name might be a burden.

"What is your father's name?"

Maeve dried her hands. "His name was Jack. He was a fine, tall handsome man, with a heart as big as the sky."

"Jack is a very good name. Jack Madigan has a pleasant ring to it, does it not?"

"Aye."

"My husband will like it, as well. Actually he'd like anything that wasn't Urquhart."

Maeve laughed. "Let's get you into some dry clothing. You must be hungry now. I'm going to get you a meal and a cup of milk. Drink plenty of water, too. We took on a fresh supply."

"I wish I could repay you," Margret said, allowing Maeve to hand the infant to the other woman in order to help her change.

"Your smile and that healthy little fellow are sufficient reward. Dr. Gallagher pays me to assist him, you know. He will come listen to Jack's heart and look him over."

"Thank you."

Maeve tucked her into her bunk and handed the baby back to her. "Rest now."

"God bless ye, Miss Murphy."

Flynn got the message Sean delivered from Maeve, and immediately went to examine the newborn. Mrs. Madigan's strapping baby boy was as big as Baby Grace, yet two weeks younger. Flynn took the baby from her, laid him on a top bunk and listened to his rapidly beating heart. After looking him over from head to foot, he pronounced him healthy and gave him back to his mother.

The woman had already eaten and had something to drink, as evidenced by the dishes on the nearby floor. "Maeve took good care of you, I see."

"An excellent midwife, she is," Mrs. Madigan agreed. "And a fine young woman."

He could well imagine. As efficient and full of compassion as Maeve had proven herself, she was surely a blessing in assisting babies into the world.

"I named him Jack. That was Miss Murphy's da's name."

"I like it."

Leaving baby and mother behind, Flynn went on deck and stood at the rail, looking out across the obsidian ocean. The moon was obliterated by clouds tonight, so the water was black and fathomless.

It had been an exhausting and depressing day. Images danced in his mind. One of the most haunting had been the look on Maeve's face and her condition when he'd found her alone in the dispensary. The most thought-provoking had been her questions.

Her optimism and cheerful attitude had previously never waned in any situation, therefore her obvious devastation had been difficult to observe. She was feisty and painfully straightforward. So much so that she made him look inside himself and see things he didn't want to expose or admit.

He was looking now, and he didn't like what he saw.

He had much to consider as far as his feelings were concerned. Grief, regret and guilt weren't easy to face. Nor was his attraction to Maeve.

But consider he must.

Chapter Eighteen

Maeve had been right to confront him. He had no business kissing her without making his intentions clear. He wasn't a man who toyed with others' feelings.

He'd told himself he was an honorable man, a widower still working his way past grief and unwilling to bring any more complicated feelings into the equation. But perhaps he should have given more thought to the feelings and expectations others had for *him*.

According to Maeve, Kathleen had led her to believe there was more between them than there was.

Thinking over the barbed words that had spilled from her lips as she had insulted the Murphy sisters, he guessed she wasn't too proper or genteel to deliberately slur her fellow passengers, no matter how she disguised her claws—or to spread rumors about a romantic relationship that did not exist outside of her own mind.

And this was the woman he called a friend? Try as he might, he couldn't think of one thing other than their long-time acquaintance that made her a friend. Her background explained a lot about her general sense of entitlement, but it couldn't forgive her for being unkind.

Now Maeve…there was a woman who'd be a good friend. But he didn't think of her in that way. He thought of her differently. Reverently. Kindly. Warmly. He thought of kissing her.

And if he was perfectly honest with himself, he wanted to think of being able to open up and love someone again. He just didn't know how.

It had been a long time since he'd let himself love anyone—even God. He was rusty at praying.

But Maeve's example inspired him. Perhaps opening his heart to the Lord could be the first step in opening his life to a chance at happiness again.

"Lord, I'm thankful You haven't forgotten me, even though I've neglected You. I have to admit I spent a lot of time wondering where You were and why You didn't care."

He swallowed hard. "But You do care. It's evidenced all around me. If You sent Maeve to shake me up and open my eyes to my self-pity, then help me not resent that. Or her.

"If You sent her to point out my glaring flaws, then I thank You. I could use wisdom to make decisions and to let myself heal. I'd appreciate Your showing me the changes I need to make and where to go from here.

"Sometimes I feel as though my future is as black and bottomless as this body of water. I can see into it no better than I can see the ocean's floor."

A cloud parted just enough to let a glimmer of moonlight reflect off the water's surface. He studied the heavens. How many times had he crossed the Atlantic now? Six times? Maybe eight? And he'd never taken time to simply stand here and behold a night sky laden with stars. Tonight they were hidden, and he wondered about the irony.

He remembered the captain's reading over Henry that day, and the scripture returned to him. "O death, where is thy sting? O grave, where is thy victory?"

Because of God's mercy and redeeming grace, death was only cessation of life upon this earth. His Johanna...his Jonathon were inhabitants of an eternal kingdom. He'd always believed that. He knew the truth in his heart, but he had never had the courage to release them. He'd suffered their deaths every moment of each day since they'd been gone. "Come unto me, ye who labor and are heavy laden, and I will give you rest."

That rest had to mean peace. Had to mean laying aside those things he'd carried like sacks of boulders until the burden crippled him.

Quite plainly now he saw that he must release those he loved in order to have any kind of peace in his heart. He wanted that rest.

His heart thumped. He'd avoided thoughts of them for so long that allowing himself to remember them was frightening. He'd hidden that part of his past—that part of *him* away—and he didn't know if he could change.

Johanna first.

He let himself remember her sweet face, surrounded by silky, fair hair. She'd been tall and slim and carried herself with grace and dignity. She'd been raised in a wealthy family and trained to run a household and servants, but she'd been generous and accepting. She had been devoted to him and their child.

She would want him to be content. To move on.

And his boy.

Jonathon had possessed fair hair like his mother, but his eyes had been hazel—brown one moment, green the next. He'd been a fun-loving, active little fellow who'd run to his da at the end of the day. Flynn's arms ached with overwhelming emptiness. This was why he hadn't let himself think of them...why he guarded his thoughts so jealously.

"Into Your care I give them, Lord Jesus." He almost choked on the words, but he spoke them anyway. "Thank You for providing a way for them to dwell with You until we're together again."

He sagged against the side and held himself upright with his fingers gripping the rail. "Lord, please give me good memories to sustain me, and erase the images that bring such unbearable pain."

Waves lapped against the side of the ship.

He'd been running from this for so long.

Words resonated in his heart—clear and unmistakable. *Be still and know that I am God.*

In other words, stop running from the memories. He needed to let them overtake him. Anything less was a disservice to what he and Johanna had shared, and a betrayal to his son.

He searched for a good memory, and it came to him. A day at a fair. Jonathon had loved the pony rides and begged to ride again and again. Flynn had patiently walked beside him in a field with a figure-eight path worn into it.

The sun had warmed Johanna's hair to rich gold that day. He'd purchased her a comb with ribbon streamers, and she'd worn it in her gilded tresses. They had shared laughter...and created memories.

Memories to last a lifetime, he realized now. *His* lifetime.

Nothing could take those away from him, but he'd thrown them away. He took them back now, tucked them safely into his heart. "Thank You, Lord. Thank You for the time we had together and the memories we created."

A stiff breeze ruffled his hair and buffeted clouds away from the moon. A handful of stars winked at him.

There was something he needed to do. It was too late tonight, but tomorrow he had to speak with Kathleen.

* * *

Things were quiet at the dispensary when Flynn told Maeve he would be gone for a while and went in search of the Boyds.

Estelle was in their stateroom, but she told him Kathleen had gone above for fresh air. "You've never come in search of my daughter before," she said with a curious tone. "Is everything all right?"

"I want a word with her," was his only reply.

Long, purposeful strides carried him along the starboard deck until he spotted her in a lavender dress and a hat with a matching ribbon trailing down her back.

What surprised him was the man standing beside her.

A wide-brimmed hat shaded his eyes from the sun, and he wore a plain shirt and trousers, which were tucked into tooled leather boots with inch-and-a-half heels. Flynn had met Western men on his travels, and had on more than one occasion listened to stories of Indian wars and cattle drives. Some of these men were ranchers, who owned huge parcels of land and raised horses for the army.

At his approach, Kathleen spotted him and stepped slightly away from the cowboy. "Flynn! What a pleasant surprise to see you on deck this morning."

"I do seem to indulge my passion for work most of the time." He extended a hand toward her companion. "Flynn Gallagher."

The man had strong work-roughened hands. "Judd Norton. Pleasure to make your acquaintance. The ship's doctor, if I'm rememberin' correctly."

"Yes, sir."

"Mr. Norton purchased horses from somewhere near County Galway," she told Flynn. "Waterford, wasn't it? Now he's on his way home."

"Heard of a gentleman who was sellin' his stable of

Irish draft horses," he told Flynn. "They're excellent cross-country animals and economical to keep. It didn't take me long to figure out I wanted 'em, so I boarded a ship. I'm gonna breed 'em with my Spanish mares. I have high hopes for excellent riding horses."

"Where are you from?"

"I have a spread in the Nebraska Territory."

Flynn thought a moment. "Quite a distance to travel before you ever got to the ocean."

The man agreed. "I'd never been that far east b'fore. I admit I'm hankerin' for wide-open spaces that don't include waves or sharks."

"Were you looking for me?" Kathleen asked, turning the conversation.

"I don't want to interrupt your visit."

"Not at all," the American said. "I spend a lot of time right here and appreciate anyone who takes pity on my boredom. Miss Boyd made my mornin' pass more quickly." He touched the brim of his hat, but didn't remove it. "Miss. Nice to meet you, doc."

He sauntered away.

"What brings you out here?" Kathleen asked.

"Would you like to sit or are you comfortable standing?"

"I'm quite comfortable, thank you."

He took a place beside her, but not too close. He'd had a lot of time overnight to think about how he would say this. There'd be no wrapping what he had to say in sugar. "I've been self-evaluating. This trip has given me a lot to think about and stirred up some things that have lain buried."

"What makes this trip different?" she asked.

"I'm not certain," he answered, but he was pretty sure Maeve was the difference. She hadn't allowed him to hide.

"And what have you been thinking of that makes you look so serious?"

"How long have we known each other?"

A surprised look came over her face. "Fifteen, sixteen years, perhaps."

"You're aware, I'm sure, that our parents formed an alliance at some point. They were hoping to take my mind off Johanna and Jonathon and spoke to me of marrying you."

Her dark eyes widened. The subject of his marriage and the family he'd lost had always been off-limits. "You've never before spoken their names in my presence."

"I deliberately put them from my thoughts. It hurt too much to think of them. I've devoted myself to research."

"And legal dealings to do with immigrant ships," she agreed. "No one could blame you for that."

"The more I buried those feelings, the less sensitive I became to everything around me. I'm only beginning to see what I've done." He glanced at the water and back at her. "I've determined I shall change that behavior now."

"I do hope that's good news, Flynn. Are you ready for a change in your life? What did you promise your parents when they inquired?"

"I told them you and I were only friends and nothing more. I told them there could never be more between us. Kathleen, I apologize for being insensitive and not realizing you might have thought there was hope for marriage."

She seemed to absorb his words. "I believed you only needed time. I suspect you're about to tell me something entirely different."

Her tone held a surprising edge.

He nodded. "I'm sorry if this pains you, but there will never be more between us."

This would be the time to tell her she was special

and desirable and another man would be lucky to earn her favor, but the words wouldn't come. Eventually she would make some man's life a living nightmare. Flynn was fortunate it wouldn't be him.

"Mother and I left everything behind," she told him. "She sold our property and a home that had been in our family for three generations to follow you to America."

"I had nothing to do with that. I've actually spent a very small portion of time in America and most of my time in Edinburgh. I never encouraged you to sell your property."

"You never encouraged me on any count."

"Thank you for seeing that." She knew. She wasn't a fool. "Your mother wanted to leave Ireland ever since your father died, did she not? I still don't know where I'm going to settle."

"But you have a home in Boston."

"It's a convenient place to stay between trips. You're still welcome to use it until you find somewhere to live."

"How generous of you."

"It was never my intention to lead you on." She was probably expecting him to say they would remain friends, but he didn't see that happening. He didn't want to be friends with someone who could treat others so unkindly.

"This is for the best," she told him. "I can see that."

He nodded, though he didn't understand.

She gathered her voluminous skirt that dragged on the deck without whatever feminine frippery she couldn't wear aboard ship and headed away from him, her posture stiff.

"The fortunate thing about this," she said pausing in her exit, "is how utterly forgettable you will be."

Chapter Nineteen

That morning, for the first time during a voyage he regretted leaving the sunshine behind to go below. Flynn felt as though a weight had been lifted from his shoulders. The reason for his ease was more than setting the record straight with Kathleen. Last night he'd faced his pain and allowed God to begin a healing process. Like any healing, it might take time, but he'd sought the Great Physician, and His power and love were unfailing.

He wanted to tell Maeve all that had taken place, but their last conversation had left things between them uncomfortable, and all morning she'd been cool.

At noon he took a stroll along the port side and discovered Martha Conley casting a net over the side of the ship.

"Would you miss the sea if the captain were to agree to settle down on land?" he asked her.

"Not for a minute. I do this to keep my sanity and feel productive. Rather be tendin' a garden, I would. I've eaten enough fish to last all me live long days. Green things, that's what I long for."

"But you've come along with him all these years."

"The sea's his mistress," she told him. "He loves her and I love him, so here I be."

The next person he spotted was a man sitting at an easel. The fellow wore a paint-spattered smock and a wide-brimmed straw hat. Fully expecting to find a seascape, Flynn approached the painting.

Instead, the man was painting a portrait of a woman. Glancing about, Flynn had spotted no one posing who looked like this person. "Who is she?" he asked.

"Her name is Sharon."

"An Irish lass?"

"Romanian. A traveler."

Flynn had heard of the clans that roamed the countrysides of Europe. The artist's voice held regret.

"But you're headed for America."

"I'm not her kind. Travelers don't marry outside their own people."

"And you paint her from memory."

He shrugged. "It's a knack I possess. But she is an indelible image on my heart."

"It's a wonderful painting. She's a beautiful young woman. I thought I would see a painting of the sea on your easel."

"My stateroom is full of them. B-19. Please come select one."

"I'll buy one from you."

"I need only paint and canvas to exist, so they're not expensive."

"Later this evening, perhaps."

Back in the dispensary, Emmett McCorkle was standing not far from the door.

"Young Emmett waited for you," Maeve told him. "I offered to help, but he wouldn't even tell me what brought him."

"Well, why don't we go into the other room back here, and you can tell me what brings you down here on such a fine day."

He ushered the boy into the room and closed the door. A few minutes later, he returned for water, rags and a scalpel.

"May I be of assistance?" she asked.

"It's a personal matter," he replied. "Go on upside for air. We won't be long."

A moment later Emmett cried out. Maeve left the dispensary. She found Aideen and Mrs. Kennedy at their fire and joined them for a cup of tea.

"A woman inquired about you only a few minutes ago," Aideen told her. "She mentioned the number of her stateroom and asked you to call on her."

"Was it an emergency? Why didn't she come to the dispensary?"

"I have no idea. She didn't say."

"Thank you for the tea. I needed the refreshment."

She made her way to the stateroom Aideen had mentioned and rapped on the door. A woman opened it and invited her in with a smile.

"What can I do for you?"

"We're fine, Miss Murphy. I have noticed you from time to time. My daughter and I beg you to take a few things off our hands."

"I'm not sure I understand."

"Come this way." The room was sectioned off with freestanding folding screens, and behind them were trunks and hatboxes and chests of every size and shape. "I'm sorry," the woman said. "I haven't even introduced myself. I'm Beth Mooney, and this is my daughter, Clara."

Clara was probably about twelve or thirteen, with sleek dark hair and an olive complexion.

Beth urged Maeve forward. "Clara has undergone a growth period recently, and though we've packed all these dresses and underthings, it's obvious she will no longer be able to wear them once we arrive. It seems she will need practically a whole new wardrobe."

Maeve still hadn't figured out what Clara's exceeding height had to do with her. "I'm afraid I don't understand what it is you want from me."

"We were hoping you would try on a sampling and see if you might get wear out of them. They're well made and still quite fashionable."

Now Maeve understood. The Mooney woman wanted to pass along clothing from her daughter and thought Maeve would be a suitable size to inherit. "Oh. I see."

"Here's what we'll do," Beth told her. "The screens adjust like so, and you just step behind there and try on something. This one is nice." She stuffed a voluminous green dress into Maeve's arms. "Go ahead. I'll unfasten your buttons for you. Don't be shy."

Maeve reluctantly tried on the emerald dress. It was fashioned with pleats in the skirt and lace at the neck and each wrist. Never had she worn fabric so elegant or fine.

Beth urged her to come stand before their full-length mirror and fastened the back closed. She plucked the large pins from Maeve's hair and the ringlets sprang free and draped her shoulders. Though the style was definitely suitable for a younger girl, the vivid garment enhanced her hair and skin.

"I had no idea this color would be suited to you, but it's striking."

Maeve couldn't disagree. "I could never accept such a generous offer," she said with a shake of her head. "The things are too nice to give away."

"Give them away I will. I'll offer them to charity once we land if you don't want them."

"I'm afraid I don't have room to store them. We share our cabin with several women."

"Take a few now and leave the rest here until we land. There's a pretty dressing gown and a nightdress Clara just discovered have grown too short, as well. Surely you can use those."

"It's generous of you. Thank you."

The woman made a stack and offered to carry more for her, but Maeve assured her a few items were plenty for now.

"Well, you come get them if you want something else before we dock."

Maeve carried the clothing to her cabin. Mrs. Mooney had noticed her. Noticed her shoddy clothing? Noticed her small stature? While she was thankful and the woman had been generous and thoughtful, it stung to know others perceived her as needy.

She hung the dresses on the hooks near their bunks and folded the nightclothes into the trunk she shared with her sisters. She could hear Bridget now, exclaiming over the clothing.

She met Emmett in the companionway, walking rather stiffly for one so young and agile. The lad had filled out and the sun had kissed his skin and encouraged freckles. He looked far healthier than he had the first time she'd laid eyes on him. He ducked around a corner and was gone before she could speak.

The doctor was sterilizing a scalpel when she entered.

"Beautiful day, isn't it?" he said.

"Lovely."

"The laddie had a boil thrice the size of a Norse silver penny on his backside," he explained. "I doubt the boy has been able to sit for a week. Finally told his brother, and Gavin made him come to me."

"That explains why he wouldn't let me 'ave a look."

"No lad wants to show a pretty lady his bum," he agreed with a grin.

She wiped down the counters.

"It's a good day when no one is sick aboard a ship this size," he said.

"I was thinking about visiting a few people," she told him. "If I have your permission, that is. I am wondering how Goldie is getting along and if she needs any additional ointments for those burns."

"Why don't I do that while you call on Henry's wife and Mrs. Madigan and her baby? That way we'll both be attending patients and will finish up twice as quickly. It would be nice to enjoy the weather on deck this afternoon. And I'd like to talk with you."

"Very well. I'll be on my way."

"Meet me under the forecastle when you've finished."

Henry Begg's widow and her five children shared a cabin with one other woman who had several children and her mother traveling with her.

"Is your daily allotment sufficient for your growing children?" Maeve asked.

The woman nodded. "Our countrymen have shared with us, as well."

It was common, just as when Maeve's father had died, for neighbors to share their own provisions.

"And you?" she asked the widow. "Are you eating? Sleeping?"

"Don't have much of an appetite, but I want to sleep all the time."

Maeve stayed and talked with her awhile longer. "Take the little ones for walks on deck," she told Mrs. Begg. "They need the exercise and the fresh air will help you."

The visit with Margret Madigan was far easier.

Maeve found the mother and her little ones seated at their fire. She and the baby were flourishing, and her two other children, though small, were good company for her and adored their new brother, Jack.

Flynn waited for her where he'd indicated. "The day was too nice to spend the entire time below deck."

His new attitude surprised her. "You're different today."

"You're absolutely right. I am." He guided her on a leisurely stroll. "I left a note on the door of the dispensary. In case there's an emergency, everyone will know we can be found up here."

Maeve had stopped for a bonnet before stepping up into the sun again. It shaded her face, but she couldn't bring herself to tie it under her chin, so she let the ribbons dangle. A gathering at the rail caught her attention and she joined them to see what was of interest.

The top fins of two enormous whales could be seen cutting through the surface of the water. "I've seen whales from a distance, while standing on the cliffs above the village, but never this close or from this vantage point. They are magnificent."

"I've never been to Castleville," he told her. "What's it like?"

Together they moved away from the others and walked a little farther. "The shoreline below the cliffs is trimmed with golden sands and rocky outcroppings. When we were children, we used to walk an hour or more to make our way to the bottom. We felt safe because the Donnelly brothers, Scully and Vaughan, came with us. Adventurous and strong boys, they were. There are caves to the north, but Da warned us of the dangers, and we never dared explore them."

"Your childhood sounds happy."

"We didn't have much, but we didn't realize it.

Things were good before the famine. Before the sicknesses came."

"They get snow in America," he told her. "Have you ever seen snow?"

"No, never. Da saw snow in the mountains as a lad."

"There are extremes of weather, because the ocean isn't absorbing heat. So winter is cold and summer is hot. Once it snowed when I was in the city. It's pretty, but it's also an inconvenience. Shopowners must remove it from in front of their doors, and it makes the streets more difficult to travel. You and your sisters will need coats and winter boots."

"I don't know that I'll like that."

He chuckled. "We Irishmen are indeed spoiled by ideal weather."

"What was it like to grow up rich?"

No one had ever asked him that before. He had to think about it. "Like you, I knew nothing different. Not until I was older and understood the struggles of those going hungry after the blight and farmers losing their homes. For us the blight was inconvenient, but not a major problem. We simply ate more fowl and lamb. For others it was life and death."

"And on top of the hunger came disease," Maeve said.

"Money didn't draw a line there," he told her. "My father is a surgeon. I went to the finest school in England to become a physician. We had no tools or medicine to fight cholera or relapsing fever. No one was spared."

She agreed and nodded her understanding.

He rested a hand on her shoulder and led her to the side of the ship, where he dropped his hand and studied her. "You spoke to me as no one ever has, when you suggested I should face my feelings."

"I shouldn't have—"

"Yes, you should have." He was nervous to tell her what he'd done. He took a deep breath.

Chapter Twenty

"Last night God showed me some things. Plain as day. I can't deny His guidance."

Maeve glanced across the water and then back at his face, waiting patiently for him to continue. He'd never started a conversation like this before—not one that included God. Her curiosity was piqued.

"You are perceptive, and you were right. I'd been hiding from my feelings. I had buried every emotion that remotely reminded me of my former life—all the memories, the bad and the good, as well."

"You were simply protecting yourself. It's understandable. It's human nature to shield a wound."

"But I was missing so much by denying even the pain. I couldn't bear to live with it, so I never let myself think about it. I still have to deal with feeling as though I failed my wife and son…but I'm no longer ignoring the guilt, so now I can finally learn how to deal with it."

She understood the regret. There was always the question of whether or not she could have done something differently that would have changed the outcome for others. She lived with the burden of having let them down, even though she knew she'd done all she knew to do. How much worse must it be for him—a man who studied and had the finest medicine and equipment at hand—to helplessly stand by and lose the two people he loved most in all the world?

"I do understand," she assured him. "Truly I do. But there's no known cause and no cure for cholera, Flynn. You are not responsible for letting them die."

"The cause is so *close* to being discovered," he said. "I know with certainty the spread has something to do with drinking water or waste or other contamination. I have funded all my own research. I searched for a partner to join me, but was unsuccessful. My efforts are too late for Johanna and Jonathon, of course, but not for future victims."

"Perhaps you'll have more of an impact in America and your colleagues will listen. Is there as much cholera in America?"

"New York experienced outbreaks in the early thirties and late forties. Most say the '32 epidemic spread from London. New York was and is squeezed into overcrowded wards by an influx of immigrants."

"What about Ontario and Quebec City? I've heard many people left County Galway bound for northern areas."

"The worst of the coffin ships landed there," he told her. "They developed quarantine stations on an island, anchored ships and kept passengers secluded until health officers allowed them into the country. Hundreds and hundreds died right on the ships."

"Those are the ship's conditions you devoted yourself to improving."

"Something needed to be done. The only businesses flourishing along the coast were coffin makers and undertakers. Now if shipowners don't comply and still overcrowd or don't supply adequate clean water, they are fined so heavily they can't continue to operate."

"And you know that the death of your wife and child are no more your fault than those of all the other people, while your measures meant that untold lives have been *saved*."

"I know. But I have trouble accepting that I'm a physician and I was helpless to save them."

"I understand, Flynn. I felt helpless, too, when my neighbors grew sick and died. When my own father caught influenza and didn't recover. Nothing I did made any difference. I thought if I'd had more knowledge, if I'd had better medicines, they wouldn't have suffered the way they did. They would still be alive and life wouldn't have had to change. I have longed for those days before the blight, before death came knocking at every door in our village."

He nodded his understanding. "We have so much in common, Maeve. But you didn't shut yourself off as I did. God showed me plain as day what I'd been doing by not letting myself remember my wife and child. Last night I welcomed the memories."

"I'm happy for you."

"There's more."

She studied him curiously. What more could there be? His realization and vow to change was monumental. She waited.

"When I left the dispensary this morning, I sought out Miss Boyd."

"Kathleen?"

"Yes."

"To share all this with her? I suppose that was fitting."

"I only touched on these things. She wouldn't have understood."

Before she could digest his words, a sweeping breeze caught her bonnet, and sailed it up into the air and dropped it in the ocean. Maeve reached up to her tousled hair and belted out a surprised laugh.

She and Flynn watched her bonnet drift on the current, growing farther and farther away.

She laughed again as it finally sank into oblivion. "A fitting demise for the old girl," she sputtered and pealed out yet another burst of laughter.

Flynn wore an expression of complete confusion. "What's so funny? You're not upset?"

She took the pins from her hair and let it fall about her shoulders and catch in the wind. "No, I'm not upset. It was at least ten years out of date and secondhand to boot."

His dark gaze took in her wild hair. "I don't think another woman exists who would laugh if her bonnet was carried off and dropped into the Atlantic."

"Life's too short to mope about headwear."

He'd been wearing half a smile, but it disappeared with his next words. "I spoke with Kathleen about her mistaken beliefs."

Chapter Twenty-One

"I told Kathleen I'd never had feelings for her."

Maeve stared at him. "You told her that?"

"Not in those precise words, but yes."

She pushed her hair away from her face and looked out at the ocean. Why had he told her this? In a short time they'd developed a relationship that completely puzzled her. Theirs was a relationship unlike any that she'd ever had with a family member or even a friend. She was comfortable talking to him about experiences and even many of her feelings—things she'd never told anyone before. She found herself wanting to know more about him. He'd confided a careful measure with her, but there was much more below the surface.

Talking about Kathleen seemed different somehow. Maeve had assumed he was fond of the woman—that he intended to marry her. Apparently, that wasn't the case.

Maeve collected her thoughts. What exactly had she prayed? She'd asked for Flynn's grief and guilt to be lifted and for Kathleen to see the truth. She'd meant the truth about God's love for her and how He wanted her to treat others, but maybe Flynn seeing the truth about Kathleen was an answered prayer, too. *You're an amazing God.*

"How do you feel today?"

"Relieved. Unburdened."

"Well, then, I'm pleased for you."

"I'm more than pleased, Maeve. I'm relieved and thankful—and actually anticipating any more changes God wants me to make. I'm able to remember my wife and our life together. I can think about my son now, and, even though it's painful, it's no longer more than I can bear."

His revelations were a lot to take in. She went over everything he'd told her, absorbing these changes in his attitude.

After a minute he asked, "I didn't even ask you how Mrs. Begg and Mrs. Madigan are."

Maeve explained how her visits had gone. "And your call on Goldie?"

"I found her at her fire. She's done a fine job keeping her dressings and bandages clean. She probably has several more weeks of healing, but as long as she's as diligent as she has been, she'll heal well. I warned her she may have discoloration, even once the skin renews itself."

"I doubt she'll care about that, as fortunate as she is to have not been more seriously burned."

"Now that I've had occasion to speak with her when she's not suffering, I've seen what a positive and spirited woman she is. Her husband is attentive, and I don't think that's just because of this accident."

"I saw that, too. Remember how he didn't want to leave her side for an instant?"

"I suppose we should return and see if anyone's left messages. I want to make a fresh cotton paste for Goldie and leave it with her."

Maeve accompanied him to the dispensary, and they resumed their tasks.

That evening, Aideen and Mrs. Kennedy had dinner with the captain, so the sisters cooked their supper and ate together with only the three of them gathered at the fire.

"This is a change," Bridget remarked.

"I enjoy having the other ladies with us, but sometimes being alone is nice, too." Nora uncovered the skillet cake she'd made. "I'll let this cool."

Maeve told them about the woman who'd given her her daughter's clothing that day.

"I wish the dresses would fit me," Bridget said. "I would dearly love so many new pieces of clothing. I'm perfectly green with envy."

"You're not envious," Nora cautioned, like a mother.

"All right, I'm not envious. But I do wish someone my size would grow out of her clothing."

"Why, you've always received my outgrown clothing," Nora told her, feigning a serious expression.

"You know that's not what I mean, and your dresses weren't new when they fit *you*," she lamented.

"You never had anyone to impress anyway," Maeve teased her. "Vaughan Donnelly always thought you were beautiful, even barefoot and dressed in Nora's hand-me-downs."

"Vaughan Donnelly was a toad," Bridget returned. Maeve laughed.

"He helped Da mend our roof last year," Nora reminded her. "And he and Scully dug Da's grave, if you'll remember."

Bridget ate the last of the stirabout. "Maeve speaks of him as though he was a romantic interest. Nothing could be more ridiculous. He married someone else, if you'll recall."

"I merely pointed out that you've always been beautiful, even without expensive dresses."

Bridget gave her a sidelong look that revealed her skepticism. "I might just wear those new dresses of yours anyway, even if the hems come to me knees and the cuffs bark me elbows."

"I'm not that much shorter than you! You're exaggerating."

"I'll be a leader in fashion when the ship docks. Soon all the American women will want skirts to their knees, so their knickers show."

"Bridget Murphy," Nora admonished. "Don't be vulgar."

Maeve and Bridget exchanged a mischievous look.

"Did I mention the dresses look like something a twelve-year-old would wear? They might suit your maturity level, after all."

Bridget couldn't hold back her amusement at that remark, and the two of them giggled like schoolgirls.

"Honestly, sister," Maeve told her. "You may find some underpinnings that will suit you, but I dare say most will be too small. You're welcome to whatever you want, however. You can even use the fabric if it strikes your fancy."

"Some day I shall have a closet full of beautiful clothing," Bridget told them. "Why, I won't wear the same dress twice in a month."

"I need a new bonnet," Maeve told them and shared her tale.

"I believe we should toss all of them overboard before we get to Boston," Bridget said.

Maeve sliced the flat cake that Nora had rested on the bricks to cool and prepared her next words. "Dr. Gallagher is not interested in marrying Kathleen Boyd."

Now she had her sisters' attention. "How do you know?" Nora asked.

"He told me so today. Last night I told him she had

indicated their relationship was more serious, and this morning he told her there was no future for the two of them."

"I had assumed they had an understanding," Nora said. "I guess none of us realized it was one-sided."

"How did she take it? Did he say?"

"He didn't give details, no."

Bridget got a gleam in her eye. She picked up a slice of cake and leaned forward. "Maeve, I dare say he's sweet on you. It makes perfect sense now."

"That's impossible."

"Of course it isn't. It's plain he admires you. He seeks your opinion and relies on you."

"That's merely part of our doctor-assistant relationship."

"Tell me he hasn't shared with you more than talk of poultices and warts."

Maeve's cheeks grew warm. "There have been no warts that I know of."

"You two discuss more than rashes and coughs, now. Admit it's true."

She shrugged. "It's true."

"Aha!" Bridget took a bite of her cake. "This is a tasty sweet, Nora. Thank you." She enjoyed her slice and brushed her fingers clean before returning her attention to Maeve. "Once the man saw you beside Miss Boyd, Maeve, his decision wasn't difficult to make."

"It wasn't like that at all."

"No, how was it, then?"

Maeve picked up their dishes. "God revealed some things to him."

"Of course He did. And one of those things was that you'd be a far more suitable wife than Miss Boyd."

"That's quite an assumption," Nora piped up. "But I

have seen the way the man looks at you, Maeve. There may still be some things God hasn't revealed to him."

"Do you really think he likes me in that way?"

"I've only seen him with you when Miss Boyd was there, as well, so I can't really say. But I did observe that he didn't look at her the same way he looked at you."

"He's from a family of physicians," Maeve said. "They own homes in three different countries. He's been to university and studied in England. He's met fascinating people. I'm only a simple farm girl who grew up barefoot and dirt-poor. What could a man like him possibly ever see in me?"

"The same things we see," Nora told her. "A generous, compassionate, gifted and beautiful woman who has a lot of love to give."

Maeve explained then how Flynn had lost his family and blamed himself for so long.

"And it took a simple farm girl who grew up barefoot and dirt-poor to show him he needn't blame himself." Nora stored away their cooking utensils.

Maeve smiled. "Perhaps."

Bridget released a sigh. "It's ever so exciting. A shipboard romance."

"Don't be putting the cart before the donkey," Maeve warned her.

"If you're to be marrying into the Gallagher family, you'd best be removing donkeys from your vocabulary."

Maeve picked up the bonnet Bridget had discarded. She waved it above her head. "Stop with your matchmaking or I will pitch this over the side of the ship."

"No, you won't. You're far too practical."

"Watch me."

"If you think I care, you're mistaken."

Maeve stood and marched away.

From behind she heard her sister leap to her feet, so

she ran. Upon reaching the railing, she threw the bonnet as high as she could.

A minute later it was a blot on the surface of the glistening water.

Standing with both hands on the rail, Bridget leaned forward. "I wish it had been daylight, so I could have appreciated the sight of it swooping out over the waves. Perhaps a dolphin has it now."

"And is taking it home to his dolphin wife."

They laughed together.

"We can do Nora's tomorrow." Maeve's tone was impish.

"We cannot."

"Well, we can't afford to lose any more of ours or we'll burn in the sun."

"You're so right. Nora's 'tis."

Maeve barely slept for thinking of Flynn and her sisters' disclosures about the way he looked at her. Considering him in a romantic way had been forbidden these past weeks. He was her employer. She'd believed he was courting another woman.

He would remain her employer for only another ten days or so. And now she was aware he had never been courting another woman. Kathleen Boyd was not his sweetheart.

Maeve had been a fine one to point out to him how he'd buried his own thoughts and feelings. She had pretended no interest in him whatsoever, while a deeply buried longing wished he would look at her twice.

He was a marvel. Handsome, mannerly, educated. He'd traveled the world and learned more than twenty Castleville villagers put together would ever know. He challenged her thinking. His nearness took her breath away, and sometimes, at the mere thought of him, butterflies fluttered in her belly.

She hadn't dreamed she had a chance with a man as fine and smart as Flynn Gallagher. What could he possibly ever see in her? Nora had suggested he found her compassion, gifts and beauty appealing. She didn't see herself like that, but he himself had said she was beautiful.

Maybe there was hope. *Show me the way, Lord. Make it plain enough for a simple girl like me to see.*

As the night drew out, she considered the married couples she'd known and tried to think of ways the pairs were different and yet compatible. Her parents' relationship had always seemed ideal, but now that was in question, due to the curious letter from Laird O'Malley.

The gentleman who'd come to the dispensary with a cold and who had been on his way to visit sons in America had spoken reverently of his wife. Maeve remembered her name because of the way he'd said it. *Corabeth.*

Would a man ever say her name like that? Would Flynn?

She thought of the big McHugh man's devotion to Goldie. She'd guess they shared a similar background, however. His dedication to his wife had been endearing.

Mrs. Fitzwilliam had been married to a man of her own station, too. A person could go mad from this kind of back-and-forth thinking. Maeve deliberately closed her eyes and forced herself to focus on something else. She thought of Grace and wondered how things would turn out when they landed. She thought of Mrs. Conley and her desire to settle on land and grow a garden. There was another devoted couple…

It was a long night.

Chapter Twenty-Two

Maeve was up before any of the others in their cabin. She washed in tepid water and wet her hair to control it. After gathering it in the most severe braid she could muster, she fastened it on the back of her head. A look in Bridget's hand mirror showed her that it looked nothing like Kathleen's sleek dark style.

After examining each of the dresses she'd hung the previous day, she selected one she thought would fit the best. The underskirt was a whole new experience, and she had to wear one of the hand-me-down chemises because of the dress's square neckline.

"Bridget," she whispered. "Wake up and fasten the back of this dress for me, please."

Her sister blinked at her. "What day is it?"

"Thursday. Now please come help."

Bridget wiped her eyes and climbed down from her bunk. She blinked at her sister. "Oh, my. It's not so bad."

Maeve presented her back.

The dress fit pretty well, with the exception of the bodice. There hadn't been as much of Clara Mooney to stuff into this portion. Maeve wasn't twelve, quite obviously.

But she exhaled and waited for Bridget to fasten the hooks.

"I expect you'll not be takin' a deep breath today," her sister whispered from behind.

"But it looks pretty, does it not?"

"Aye. It looks lovely, it does."

Nora roused and left Grace asleep on her bunk to stretch and dress.

Others were waking now, too.

"I'll go start our fire for breakfast," Maeve offered. "Shall I put on a pot of oatmeal?"

"Aye, that would be nice, *ma milis.*" Several lamps had been lit, and Nora got a better look. "Look at you, Maeve Eileen Murphy. You're a heartbreaker to be sure."

Maeve escaped the cabin and made her way on deck.

First thing that morning, Flynn was summoned to the Boyds' stateroom.

"She refused to let me send for you." Estelle Boyd rinsed a cloth in a basin of cool water and placed it on Kathleen's forehead. "She's been feverish all night. Today, when she started vomiting, I told her I was sending for you and that was that."

Flynn might have thought her illness was feigned, as it had been the last time—if she'd come seeking him. But the fact that she hadn't wanted him calling on her today convinced him she was truly ill.

"Fever and vomiting," he said. "Other symptoms?"

"I ache all over," she told him. He'd never seen her without her hair fashioned in a stylish knot. Her face was pale. She wore a dressing gown and was lying on her bed with a sheet over her. Her mother had placed a bucket on the floor beside her. "I can't bear to roll over. My back and hips hurt severely."

"Have you done anything to injure your back?"

"Nothing. It's not that kind of pain."

He tested her pulse and listened to her heart. There hadn't been any cases of influenza aboard, but her symptoms pointed to it as a definite possibility. "Are you eating and drinking?"

"Mother brings me small meals, and I eat a few bites, but since yesterday nothing stays down."

"I'll go make you a tincture for the vomiting, and I'll check on you every few hours."

"It's not necessary to check on me."

"Actually it is. I'm the ship's doctor, and you're quite ill."

Kathleen waved him away.

Since he'd been called away from the dispensary so early, he hadn't yet seen Maeve. Entering his work area, he drew up short at the sight of the diminutive woman wearing a plain apron over a fancy pleated dress with puffed sleeves. She'd fastened her hair so tightly upon her head, the only curls visible were the little corkscrews that framed her face.

"Maeve?"

"I saw your note," she said, turning. "There has only been one patient, and it was a sailor with a scrape I cleaned and bandaged. Reeked of smoked fish, he did. I wouldn't be surprised if you could still smell it in here."

"You've never worn such a lovely gown before. Is there a special occasion?"

Pleased that he'd noticed, her face grew warm with embarrassment. "Nothing at all. I simply wanted to wear something different."

She was pretty no matter what she wore, but this color enhanced her skin and the blue of her eyes. He missed her usual tumble of corkscrews, however. Her unruly hair was part of her charm. "You look beautiful."

Forcing his thoughts back to his patient, he explained about Kathleen's condition and set about making a tincture to help her stomach ailment.

He returned to see the young woman several times. Her symptoms only worsened as the day progressed. Her condition concerned him, because he didn't have a diagnosis that satisfied him.

"Will you accompany me to Kathleen's stateroom?" he asked Maeve that afternoon. "You've seen a lot of influenza. I wouldn't mind a second opinion."

She gave him a wide-eyed stare. "*My* opinion?"

"Don't depreciate your medical knowledge, Maeve. You have an instinctive sense about these things."

She was obviously reluctant to go with him, but she agreed. She removed her apron, and the parts of the dress he hadn't before seen came into view. A large square neckline trimmed with lace drew attention to her lovely face. Another woman would have worn a jeweled necklace in that open area—an emerald most likely— but Maeve was the jewel. She didn't need adornment. He couldn't allow his gaze to linger or move any lower.

She glanced down. "Is there something wrong with my dress?"

"Not a thing."

He grabbed his leather bag and ushered her out of the dispensary.

"Why have you brought *her?*" Kathleen asked immediately.

"Miss Murphy is my assistant. You know that."

"I don't want her touching me. Poor people carry disease."

Maeve, a shining beacon of grace under duress, showed no reaction to Kathleen's caustic remark. She merely set Flynn's bag on the foot of the bed and opened it. Her composure and dignity made her all the more beautiful.

There wasn't a dress in all the world that could lend that much poise to Kathleen's character.

"I shouldn't need to point this out to you." His tone was stern, but matter-of-fact. "You're the one lying there sweating, and Maeve is the one who's perfectly healthy, yet risking her own safety to be here."

Her dark eyes flashed, and it was obvious Kathleen loathed lying there in her unglamorous and ineffectual state. "Ladies don't sweat, and there's no need to be vulgar."

He held his tongue. Why had he ever considered himself friends with this person? "Describe your symptoms this afternoon, please."

"I told you all that this morning."

"Tell me again now."

Exasperated, she tucked the sheet under her arms. "I'm feverish. My stomach is reeling. And now your boorish behavior has given me a headache."

"She didn't have a headache earlier," he said to Maeve. Turning to address Mrs. Boyd, he asked, "Have you been on deck at all or eaten today? One of us will stay here with Kathleen so you may have an hour to yourself."

The older woman's expression showed deep concern, but also appreciation for the opportunity to leave the stateroom. "That's very considerate of you, Flynn. I shall go stretch my limbs and have something to eat."

"I'll stay with her if you need to return to the dispensary," Maeve offered.

Maeve was kinder than necessary, kinder than Kathleen deserved, and her stature grew more and more in his esteem. Kathleen treated her poorly, yet she was willing to sit by her sickbed.

"You're not leaving *her* here with me," Kathleen said, though her voice was weak.

"I am."

"Look at her. She's wearing a day dress a ten-year-old would wear to tea with her mother."

At that point Estelle interrupted her daughter. Her face had turned bright red, and Flynn recognized her high color as stemming from Kathleen's rudeness. "Mind your tongue, Kathleen!" Estelle said to her daughter, and her tone displayed her indignation. "The doctor and Miss Murphy are here to help you. Don't be ungracious. It's unbecoming of a lady."

Too ill for further argument, Kathleen closed her eyes and ignored them. Again Mrs. Boyd thanked them for the respite. She left the stateroom.

"Go ahead, doctor," Maeve told him. "I'll come get you if her symptoms change."

With a nod, he left her with the patient.

As the day passed, Flynn sutured a sailor's head, removed another's splinter and checked a child's eyes and lungs after he'd been dangerously close to smoke erupting from his family's cooking fire.

The first mate had discovered a sailor unconscious in one of the supply compartments, and Flynn had declared him inebriated and in need of several hours' sleep.

When the day grew late, he again joined Maeve in Kathleen's stateroom, and she reported the young woman's condition the same. "She's been quiet, sleeping mostly."

One at a time he raised Kathleen's lids and looked at her eyes. She roused only momentarily. Through the sheet, he palpated her abdomen.

Kathleen grunted in pain and swatted his hands away, then turned her face aside and slept again.

"I'll come back later this evening," he told Estelle.

"Thank you for your attention, Miss Murphy." Her mouth was pinched as though she wished she didn't owe either of them thanks, but she'd said the words nonetheless.

Maeve handed her a book. He assumed Estelle had lent it to her. "I'll bring you breakfast in the morning, so you won't have to cook for yourself."

Estelle couldn't meet Maeve's eyes. After an awkward moment, she extended the book. "Please keep it. You can finish it at your leisure."

Maeve accepted the gift. "Thank you. I don't have any books of my own, except my Bible, of course, so I shall treasure this one. I can't wait to see how it ends, but I'll be disappointed once the story's over. I can always read it again, though, can't I? A book is a gift that keeps giving."

Flynn thought Estelle was going to cry. He wanted to himself. He thought of the extensive libraries in two of his family's homes. They owned duplicates of many books so there were the same editions wherever they were staying and they didn't have to move them.

A good many of the immigrants he'd encountered couldn't even read, but Maeve and her sisters did have that benefit. He imagined a life where every penny and effort was spent on daily survival. The Murphy sisters were women of character.

Estelle had quite obviously been affected by Maeve's gratitude over such a simple offering, as well. She composed her features and returned to sit at her daughter's side.

Kathleen had slept during the entire exchange, so they left without disturbing her.

"Did you feel anything in her abdomen?" Maeve asked once they were in the companionway.

"Perhaps some swelling in the area of her liver. Her pain is disturbing," he said. "So many things could be causing the fever."

"What are you thinking?"

"I don't want to guess. There are a lot of things it could be."

"Such as?"

"Yellow fever. But she didn't go ashore at the island, and it's unlikely she caught it at sea."

"But not impossible."

"I don't think so."

She didn't know much about yellow fever, but she knew it was most often fatal. "What else?"

"Puerperal fever is contagious between women who have given birth, doctors and midwives. Since no one else has the same symptoms, it can't be that."

That one was unfamiliar to her.

"And there's jaundice, but I don't know how she'd have picked it up."

"And again there haven't been any other cases, and she didn't go ashore at the island."

"It's puzzling to be sure. We will know for certain if the whites of her eyes turn yellow."

"Or her skin," she added. "But either way, there's little we can do but wait. In the meantime, why don't you come join me and my sisters for our supper?" she asked.

"Thank you. I'd like that." He followed her up the ladder and across the deck.

Chapter Twenty-Three

Bridget grinned from ear to ear when she saw the doctor accompanying Maeve. "However did we get so fortunate this evening?"

"Maeve generously invited me to join you. I often eat in the galley, but any time I receive an offer to dine with someone at their fire, I accept."

"We're pleased to share our supper with you," Nora told him. "Sit now and join us. Don't wait for Maeve to light in one place. She'll be flittin' about for a while yet."

"Kathleen Boyd has taken ill," Maeve told them. "It's quite serious, so we must include her in our prayers this evening."

"But of course we will. Is there anything we can do?" Nora asked.

"Perhaps one of you could make her some gruel like Maeve made for Sean. She's not keeping down food."

"Aye, that will give her strength," Nora replied. "I'd be happy to do that." She removed the sling that held the baby. "She's just falling asleep. Would you mind?"

Her request caught Flynn off guard. He'd been self-conscious the last time he'd held Grace, with Kathleen eyeing him. He reached for the baby. It was a warm evening, almost balmy, so she was draped in a piece of lightweight flannel.

Her tiny mouth made sucking motions, and she cracked her eyes open and squinted, as though wanting to see who now held her. The hand that wasn't tucked against his chest waved and trembled, so he took it gently in his grasp and stroked her tiny arm with his thumb. Her eyes closed once again.

Through his shirt, her rhythmic breathing was calming. He understood the sisters' concern for one so tiny and helpless. He hadn't allowed himself to dwell on the situation before, because looking at her had stabbed him with such painful memories. Now he thought of his Jonathon. The dark-haired infant had been as loved and coddled as this one. He'd been a happy, chubby little fellow. He'd never had a day of want in his short life. He'd been accepted and loved. Adored.

Every child deserved to be wanted and loved. Every child deserved a chance to not simply survive, but to thrive.

His heart ached with loss.

He had so many wonderful memories. He closed his eyes and saw the first time he'd laid eyes upon his tiny child. He remembered holding him while fearful of breaking him. He thought of Jonathon lying on the bed between him and Johanna as they admired his sleeping profile. His wife had been happy. So proud and content. He'd loved her immeasurably.

"Are you all right, Flynn?"

He looked up into Maeve's questioning blue eyes. "I am now. I was remembering my Jonathon when he was this small. He had dark hair with a touch of curl. I used to smooth it down, but Johanna would coax it back up atop his head. We laughed about that."

The sisters had paused in their chores to listen.

"What month was Jonathon born?" Bridget asked.

"April."

"A spring baby. How special and appropriate. Grace is a June baby, don't we think?"

"Definitely," he answered. "She was brand-new when your sister found her."

Aideen and Mrs. Kennedy joined them then. "Are we interrupting?"

"Of course not," Nora told Aideen. "The doctor has joined us for supper, and I'm making Miss Boyd a gruel. She's taken ill."

"That's unfortunate," Mrs. Kennedy said. "Is there anything we can do?"

"We could take turns checking on her tomorrow," Bridget suggested. "I understand Maeve sat with her most of the day today. Most likely you missed your assistant at your side attending patients, doctor."

"That's generous, but until I'm certain exactly what she has contracted, it's better if we don't expose a lot of people to her."

"Of course," Bridget replied. "That's wise."

Mrs. Kennedy offered their bag of daily provisions. "It's rice tonight. I know how to prepare it now. May I?"

Maeve opened their own sack. "I doubt you'll hear a one of us decline that offer. While Nora is making the gruel, I'll mix together batter for a flat cake."

Bridget offered a small wrapped bundle. "Mr. Atwater's mother gave me raisins today. Can you use them in the flat cake?"

Flynn was impressed with how they pooled their supplies and came up with a meal. No one seemed out of sorts that they didn't have a table and chairs or fancy plates. If they'd have preferred a steaming roast with vegetables, no one spoke of it.

"You are the most contented lot of people with whom

I've ever spent time." He looked from one face to the next. "You share what you have. And you're happy to do it. I can't in a hundred years picture my sisters—or my mother—preparing their meal from the ship's allotment and happily doing all this work."

"We never prepared a meal before we came aboard," Aideen admitted. "Neither of us knew the first thing about lighting a fire or cooking. The Murphys have shown us all we know."

"And bright students you are," Nora praised.

"To be honest, Dr. Gallagher," Bridget said. "Our daily provision is more food than we had in two or three days at home. It had been that way for the past couple of years. We are grateful to have this much and more than happy to share."

"I am humbled to be included." His speech was husky with emotion.

Eventually the rice finished cooking. Maeve had added onions and bits of fried mackerel to make a tasty meal.

Nora prayed, including a petition for Kathleen's healing and Flynn's wisdom in knowing how to treat her. She took Grace from Flynn, so he could eat.

"I almost made a big mistake," Flynn told them.

"What was that?" Bridget asked.

"I nearly allowed grief and discouragement to consume me. It was easy to avoid the things that hurt. I focused all my thoughts and energy on external conditions. Everything that meant something to me had been lost."

The ladies gave him their full attention.

He didn't know why he'd chosen to say this now. He had carried nearly three years of unacknowledged pain bottled up inside. Maybe it needed to come out.

Maybe he recognized their compassion and knew they would understand.

"Everyone deals with grief in their own way," Nora said.

"Continuing as I was would have led to a colossal ruination of my life and peace of mind."

Bridget and Aideen didn't raise their gazes from their tin plates. Nora and Maeve exchanged a look.

Mrs. Kennedy spoke up. "I was married to a wonderful God-fearing man who was taken from this earth before his time, Doctor. I understand the hopelessness that comes with the cessation of all the dreams you shared with that person. The anguish is difficult to live with. You feel alone in the world, as if no one understands or really cares."

He studied her, thoughtfully. He'd never spoken so openly with anyone, except Maeve. It felt good to talk with the others. "You do share my experience, ma'am. If you don't mind my asking, what does that loss feel like now?"

Mrs. Kennedy appeared thoughtful for a moment. "I still think of my husband often, but sometimes it's as though that part of my life didn't really happen."

"I don't want that to happen. What I mean is, I've just recovered the memories. I don't want to lose them."

"You won't lose them, young man. But they will fade. I never had another opportunity to marry. I think I would have felt more productive and fulfilled if I had. Instead, I have remained a widow to this day."

"Perhaps you'll meet someone in Boston," Bridget said.

Mrs. Kennedy only laughed. "And perhaps a gull will come flying overheard wearing your bonnet."

Her jest lightened the mood and they all shared a hearty laugh.

"Maeve threw Bridget's bonnet overboard," Aideen told him.

He chuckled. "I should have liked to have seen that. The demise of Maeve's own bonnet brought her much merriment."

"We've plans to toss one of Nora's. You are invited."

"The two of you can fling your own headwear in the ocean if you like, but leave mine be," their older sister warned. "I will still need protection from the elements when I arrive in Boston."

"Speaking of arrival in Boston," Aideen said. "We are ready for final fittings on your dresses before we add the trim and do the hems."

"I can't wait!" Bridget turned to him. "We're making dresses. Beautiful dresses! Each of us will have a new one the day we dock. Our generous friends have provided everything—the fabric and trim, ribbon and thread. And each dress is unique."

"Suited to each sister appropriately," Aideen added.

"That will be a sight to behold," he told them. "The young men of Boston will be falling over each other to carry your bags and assist you wherever you want to go."

Bridget laughed, but it was plain she was delighted with his teasing prediction and flattery. "Do you really suppose so?"

"Indeed I do. Not that a one of you needs a beautiful dress to win a man's heart. Your natural beauty is more than sufficient."

"I would never have considered you a man to take risks," Nora told him.

"Risks?" he asked.

"Seems, it does, you've risked life and limb a time or two to dangle from the parapet at Blarney Castle and kiss Mr. McCarthy's stone."

The others had a good laugh over her teasing remark.

"As a matter of fact, never have I kissed the Blarney Stone." He feigned an indignant frown and pressed a hand to his shirt front. "Everythin' I say comes straight from me heart."

The women did share a hearty laugh over his affected brogue. Because his speech was always so proper, it made his teasing all the more humorous.

Maeve sliced the flat cake into equal portions and passed a piece to each. She'd sensed his eyes on her more than once that day. As soon as she'd gotten to the dispensary that morning, she'd felt foolish for wearing this dress. His appreciative gaze had relieved her discomfort—until Kathleen had pointed out the dress was made for a much younger person.

Maeve had no idea how one could tell—except that the bodice fit so tightly—but she supposed someone who knew about fashion would know. Neither Aideen nor Mrs. Kennedy had remarked.

Truth be told, she was having difficulty breathing and couldn't wait to change for the night. It had been worth the discomfort to hear Flynn's praise, however.

She reached for the empty pan, but Bridget brushed away her hand. "I'll do these dishes. I played games and read with the Atwater girls all day while you worked, so you go for a walk and enjoy the night air."

Maeve straightened. She wasn't going to argue with that.

"Will you join me for a walk around the deck?" Flynn asked.

Aideen extended a shawl, and Maeve accepted it. "That sounds nice."

As they passed fires, more than one person greeted the doctor.

"Will you call on Kathleen yet again tonight?" she asked.

"Yes, I want to check on her once more." They walked at a leisurely pace. "I'm missing something, and I can't figure out what it is. I have diligently sought out any others with the same symptoms. There are none. A contagious disease takes three or four days from the time of contact to reveal itself."

"Then it's not contagious."

"We can't be sure."

"Her mother's fine, she is."

He sighed. "I know. Yes, I know. It's completely frustrating."

A streak of lightning zigzagged across the distant sky. A moment later thunder sounded in the distance.

"Not another storm, I pray," she breathed.

"It's miles away." He rested his arm on her shoulder and drew her close. "And the wind isn't blowing it this direction. Are you afraid of storms?"

She liked his nearness. "We never had many to speak of at home, but no. I simply don't like the idea of being stuck in a cabin below with others who are frightened."

"Perfectly understandable." They stopped at the rail and gazed out across the water, and he dropped his arm to her waist. "My Johanna didn't like thunderstorms. And she was deathly afraid of spiders."

"She wouldn't have liked to clean some of the places I've cleaned, then. How did she feel about pigs? We had one neighbor who kept two pigs and left them to wander in and out of her house through the open door."

"Johanna wasn't a farm girl. She would probably have run them out."

"I tried that when I was there for the birth of one of her children. The pigs just laid down in the doorway and wouldn't budge."

"Were they young pigs?"

"At one time, but not by the weekend I was there."

"Johanna had a cat. A white one, with long silky fur. Even after Jonathon's birth, she would let him jump up and lie on her lap, and she'd stroke his head.

"She used to plan dinner parties down to the last detail. Four courses followed by coffee and dessert in the sitting room. She played the pianoforte for the guests. What a picture that was."

Maeve understood that all this was new to him. Remembering his wife, thinking of his child. She'd encouraged him to lift the cloak he'd kept over his past and let himself feel, and he was doing it.

"Once I married her, I never expected to find myself alone again." His voice held a wistfulness and regret she'd never heard before. "I didn't expect to be sailing across the Atlantic again and again. I don't know how I got here."

"Escaping, most likely. Running away."

"What a coward I've been."

She edged away so she could look into his face. "Not a coward, Flynn. You turned your pain into worthwhile endeavors. Look at all the good you've done. Your efforts to improve ship conditions everywhere are saving hundreds of lives every day."

"I didn't do it alone."

"Why don't you stop and give yourself a little credit, instead of considering your work part of your punishment?"

Without replying, he speared her with a censuring look.

"You've allowed yourself very few comforts," she pointed out. "Compared to the life you're used to, these ships are barren. I dare say you wouldn't be eating what you ate tonight if you were at home."

"I no longer have a home."

"What about your house in County Galway?"

"I signed the deed over to the nuns. It's now a found-ling home."

"That was a generous thing to do. Another worth-while gift."

"It was also cowardly. I never had to face the rooms where my son spent his few short years of life."

"Part of your punishment," she guessed.

"My son deserved to live."

"Yes, he did."

"I should have spent the rest of my life with Johanna, watching him grow up and become a man."

"Yes," she agreed.

She'd been foolish to imagine Flynn had any true in-terest in her. He'd had the love of his life and lost her. Maeve was no society wife. She didn't know the first thing about dinner parties. She was a simple foolish girl.

"It's time I took myself off to bed, 'tis."

Chapter Twenty-Four

Maeve hurried away to the cabin. Her sisters had arrived ahead of her and were already changed.

"Please help me out of this dreadful dress," she said to Bridget.

"You looked so pretty. The doctor couldn't take his eyes off you."

"You're reading too much into things," she warned her sister. "He's still very much in love with his wife."

Sleep eluded her yet another night. Maeve gave up trying to sleep, dressed in her familiar plain attire, went for fresh water and made her way to Mrs. Boyd's stateroom.

"I'm glad to see you." Estelle ushered her in. "She hasn't been fully alert since yesterday."

"Have you been making her drink water?"

"Yes. She doesn't wake, but she'll drink for me."

"We'll use the remainder of that bucket to bathe her now and this fresh one is for drinkin', 'tis."

Estelle helped Maeve bathe her daughter, preserving her modesty with a sheet as they cooled one area at a time. Maeve understood Estelle's desperation only too well. As morning neared, she told the woman to lie on the cot they'd had set up to get some rest and promised she'd remain by Kathleen's side.

Picking up a small Bible, she turned the lamp higher and read through the Psalms. She'd always found it interesting how David's life had often been turbulent. He'd made big mistakes and he'd fled from Saul's army to hide from the man's jealous wrath, but he'd always turned to God in every situation. Some of his writings were desperate pleas and others love songs to his God.

She skipped through more familiar verses to one she'd read less times. *O give thanks unto the Lord; for He is good: because His mercy endureth for ever,* the verses said in repetition.

Were those words repeated so many times so that simple people like her would get the point or because they were written as a song? She read them over several times, imagining how David would have sung them.

It is better to trust in the Lord than to put confidence in man. Or in princes, the next verse said.

It was surely better, then, to put her trust in the Lord, rather than her own knowledge or in any other person. She called on the Lord in distress, too. Many times.

She read down farther, then went back to the beginning and softly read the whole verse aloud to Kathleen. "Kathleen," she said once she'd read it all. "The Lord is your strength and your salvation. You shall live and not die. You and I both will declare the works of the Lord and praise Him. He hears us, and He's our salvation. We rejoice in this day and we are glad in it. God is good, and His mercy endures forever."

Mrs. Boyd sniffled from her cot, and Maeve supposed she had overheard her.

It didn't matter how Kathleen had treated her. Maeve was called to be at her side, to minister to her and pray over her, and so she would.

Sometime later, she must have fallen asleep in the chair, for a soft tap at the door startled her awake.

Flynn entered the unlocked door and joined her. "How is she doing?"

"The same."

"How long have you been here?"

"I couldn't sleep."

Estelle rose from the cot and straightened her hair. "She's been here half the night."

"What baffles me," Flynn said. "Is that no one else aboard the ship has these symptoms. It's as though she's been in contact with someone or something that no one else has. Which is highly improbable."

"The two of you eat the same food," he said to Estelle. "Share meals."

Estelle nodded. "Even when we eat with the captain and Mrs. Conley, everyone has the same fare."

Maeve thought back to the evening she and her sisters had dined at the captain's table along with Kathleen and Estelle. That evening had come to mind more than once, but she'd deliberately worked to set aside the memory of Kathleen's rude behavior.

Bridget had been so proud of her ivory bead necklace.

Mrs. Conley had purchased lamb on the island, and they'd all eaten it with no ill effects.

Maeve had purchased fruit and shared it with her sisters.

They kept going back to the fact that Kathleen hadn't even gone ashore. What was it she'd said? She searched her memory. Something to the effect that she and Estelle had remained onboard as though setting foot on the island was beneath her. *There's nothing else of value to be found,* she'd said. *Only cheap trinkets made by the natives.*

Nothing else?

Her memory screamed Kathleen's words and Maeve grabbed Flynn's sleeve.

He looked to her.

"She said she sent a sailor to purchase shellfish."

He glanced at Estelle, who nodded. "She loves oysters. I don't know where she got that affinity, because I certainly don't share it. She bought fresh oysters as well as smoked, because they last longer."

"When did she last eat them?"

Estelle shrugged. "Several days ago."

"That's it," he said to Maeve and looked at Kathleen's eyes. "The whites are a little yellow today."

"What does that mean?" Estelle asked.

"It means her liver is struggling to handle the contamination."

"What can we do?" Maeve asked.

"Fluid in and fluid out is her best hope."

"She drinks for us," Maeve told him.

"Good. Make her drink as much as you can. A cup every ten minutes. Maybe more of that gruel for her blood."

"I'll make it."

Estelle sat on the chair Maeve had vacated and sobbed into her hands. "I can't lose her. She's all I have in the whole world." She looked up at Flynn. "Please save her."

Maeve's heart dipped, not so much at the plea, but at how she knew Flynn would feel about it. He'd dealt with so much guilt already, and he was a man upon whom responsibilities weighed heavily.

Quickly, before he could react or reply, Maeve picked up Estelle's own Bible and opened it to Psalm 118. She ran her finger down the page and then showed the verses to Estelle. "'It is better to trust in the Lord than to put confidence in man,'" she read. "'It is better to trust in the Lord than to put confidence in princes.' We do what we can do, but we're only human. Place your trust in God now, and look to Him."

Estelle nodded tearfully. "Yes. Yes, I will."

Maeve stopped Flynn with a hand on his arm. "May I speak with you for a moment?"

"Of course."

"You are smarter by far than I am. I certainly would never want to step on your toes or elevate myself."

"Say what you like, Maeve. Do you have an idea?"

"You're now convinced this is jaundice."

He nodded. "It's the only diagnosis that makes sense."

"The mariners along our coast sometimes came in contact with Chinese sailors. My mother learned that the Chinese treated jaundice with licorice or ginger tea."

He thought a moment. "Licorice being a liver detoxifier."

"And the ginger tea helps with the nausea and vomiting."

"I'll send Sean and Emmett to ask all the passengers if anyone's brought licorice aboard. I have ginger root. It's definitely worth a try. Good suggestion."

Maeve headed on deck to prepare the gruel.

She remained with Kathleen and Estelle the rest of the day, following Flynn's directions while he attended to his regular duties and stopped by every chance he got.

Maeve napped briefly on the cot that afternoon. When she awoke, she sent Estelle to sit with her sisters for supper on deck and fed Kathleen strong ginger tea.

She glanced at Kathleen's comb and knew how hopeless the tool would be in trying to tame her hair. She had a wide-toothed comb her father had carved her years ago, and it was the only thing she could work through her curls. She worked her fingers through the mass and bound it in a fat braid. Then she washed her face with the soap Estelle had left out for her.

The lather was emollient and had an exotic smell she didn't recognize. No wonder Estelle's skin was so lovely and unwrinkled.

Flynn showed up a short time later. "You smell like coconut."

"What's coconut?"

"It's a large hard-shelled hairy nut found in the tropics. Inside is milk and white meat. The milk is used for hair and skin products, or for cooking, and the fleshy part for cooking and baking."

"I believe I'd like to try a coconut."

"I should have found you some on the island. The scent suits you."

"It does?"

"Yes. Natural, fresh. A perfume would never do you justice." He leaned over her and inhaled.

His nearness was disturbing, as always.

Without intending to, she leaned into him and rested against his warm strength, her cheek to his chest. She closed her eyes, and the moment seemed so natural and right. He had his own scent, too, one she'd noticed many times—sandalwood and pressed linen.

His arm came around her. "You had a long night, followed by a trying day."

His voice rumbled under her ear.

"I wanted to be here."

"I'll stay with her tonight, so you can go sleep in your own bunk."

Maeve could have remained that way forever. In his arms she felt safe. It was a feeling she hadn't known for much of her life, a security she hadn't felt since she'd been a wee child.

She felt drained and tired. It would be nice to let someone else carry the load for a while.

That thought roused her back to her senses and she drew away. She'd only just told Estelle to put her confidence in God, not a man. God was carrying her load, and that was that.

At a sound, they both turned.

Kathleen moaned and turned her head on the pillow.

"Kathleen?" All business, Flynn hurried to her side. He touched the backs of his fingers to her forehead.

She blinked up at him. "Flynn?"

Chapter Twenty-Five

Kathleen stared at him. "Flynn, what are you doing in my dream?"

"You've been quite sick," he told her. "We're doing our best to help you get better."

"Oh, Maeve!" she said, noticing her and greeting her as though she was a long lost friend. "I knew you'd come. There's a package on the foyer table for you."

"All right. Well, I'll just get it, then." She met Flynn's gaze with raised eyebrows. "While you're awake, I have some water for you."

"Will you ask Abigail to bring tea?"

"If you'd like tea, I'll make you a pot."

"That would be lovely."

Maeve helped her drink a cup of water. Kathleen settled back on the bed and closed her eyes.

"I'll take a few minutes to go make tea and stretch my legs."

Her sisters already had tea brewed, so she poured a container full for Kathleen.

"Your gracious sisters shared their supper and prayed with me," Estelle told her.

"You'll be happy to know your daughter spoke to me only a few minutes ago."

"She did! What did she say?"

"It wasn't so much what she said as the fact that she roused and recognized Dr. Gallagher and me."

"Well, glory be!" Estelle said. "I'm taking this as a good sign."

"As am I," Maeve agreed.

The breeze on deck was balmy that evening. Maeve turned her face into it and inhaled the salty sea air.

"What is that scent?" Bridget got up and leaned over Maeve to sniff her hair, then her cheek. "Why it's you."

"It's coconut," she replied. "Mrs. Boyd let me use her soap."

"I've never smelled anything like it," Bridget said. "What kind of nut has so much fragrance?"

"It's a very large nut, actually," Estelle explained. "That grows on a palm tree."

Maeve smiled and left them to return to Kathleen.

She slept in her own cabin that night, and while the room was still crowded and stuffy, she at least had her own space and several uninterrupted hours to rest.

Sean McCorkle was waiting for her outside her cabin door when she emerged. His skin had darkened from sun, and his face had filled out. He looked positively healthy. "Sean! Good morning."

"Mornin' to you, Miss Murphy. The captain be wantin' Dr. Gallagher to call on the missus. She be feelin' poorly, she is. I couldn't find the doctor."

"He attended a patient through the night, he did. I'll go tell him right now. Thank you."

Sean darted away.

She took time to start their fire and make oatmeal and tea, which she carried below deck in a shallow crate.

Kathleen was awake when she arrived at the stateroom. Flynn appeared tired, as expected. She relayed the news about Martha Conley, so he gathered his bag and left.

"I've brought breakfast," she said and rested the crate on a trunk. "Enough for you, too, Mrs. Boyd."

After spooning oatmeal into a dish, she carried it to Kathleen. "Are you able to feed yourself today?"

The other young woman accepted the bowl. "I believe I am."

Maeve prepared Estelle a bowl and then sat with her own.

"Mother told me how long you stayed with me," Kathleen said.

"You were alarmingly sick for a few days. Your mother was exhausted from worry and from caring for you."

"I owe you both a debt of gratitude."

"You owe me nothing," Maeve assured her.

"You can be indebted to me," Estelle said to her daughter. "The fright took ten years off my life. I think I developed a wrinkle, as well." She touched a pinkie to the corner of her eye. "Perhaps two."

Her remarks amused Maeve. "Does the doctor believe the danger has passed?"

"Her eyes aren't yellow today," Estelle replied.

Kathleen straightened the covers over her lap. "That must have been highly unbecoming."

After they'd finished their breakfast and their tea, Maeve helped Kathleen wash and dress. Kathleen tried to offer Maeve a pair of silver filigree combs for her hair, but Maeve wouldn't accept them.

"I should like to repay you for your kindness," she said, and her expression was sincere. "Please take them. If you won't wear them, give them to one of your sisters."

Bridget would love to have the lovely combs. That suggestion convinced her. "Thank you."

She slipped them into her apron pocket.

"Flynn said I might take Kathleen on deck for fresh air this afternoon, if she's feeling up to it." Estelle's relief was plain. "I'm remembering what you said and the Psalm about declaring the works of the Lord. I put my confidence in Him, and my daughter is recovered. God deserves the glory for this."

Maeve met Estelle's eyes and smiled for the first time in days. "His mercy endures forever."

Tears formed in Estelle's eyes.

Flynn wasn't in the dispensary and there were no notes, so Maeve headed for the captain's cabin and knocked. Flynn's voice called out to enter and she found Martha Conley on her bed, the captain pacing the cramped space. "Got sick last night, she did."

Maeve joined Flynn beside Martha's bed.

"Hello, dear," Martha told her. "Sorry to be a bother."

"You're not a bother, now. I came to see if I could help. Does she have a fever?"

"A mild one."

"'Er heart is beatin' too fast, 'tis," the captain said from behind them. "I've driven the poor woman to her grave."

Flynn ignored him. "She has a headache and is dizzy."

"Fell down twice, she did," the captain said.

Maeve touched Martha's cheek, then rolled back her sleeve. "Her skin is hot and dry."

"What did you do yesterday, Mrs. Conley?" Flynn asked.

"Hauled in the biggest nets of fish you ever did see. Even had nice big crabs in the catch, I did."

"I'd wager you didn't drink much the entire time, and might not have even worn a hat."

"My hat blew overboard, and I couldn't be bothered to go for another while the fishin' was good."

Flynn stood. "I'm going to leave Maeve to assist you. You got too much sun, and didn't take in enough water. If you aren't cooled off, it could be dangerous." He turned to Maeve. "Get her cool. Remove constrictive clothing, keep her skin wet, simulating perspiration. Fan her. And make her drink water. Lots and lots of water."

"I am so glad you travel with plenty of clean water," she said to the captain.

"'Ave no choice with this doctor aboard. Is she going to be all right?"

"She should be fine. Let's go and let Maeve take care of her now."

"You snap out of it, you 'ear, Martha?" her husband called to her. "I'll not 'ave you passin' on b'fore I've bought you a 'ouse with a garden."

"Is this what it took to get me house?" she asked.

"Fool woman, fishin' all day in the blisterin' sun." He followed Flynn out the door.

"I don't know how you've remained at sea all these years." Maeve helped Martha out of her wrap. "Tell me where to find you some loose underclothes. Here? I've only been onboard these few weeks, and I can't wait to get on solid land. I can't think of a good enough reason to bring me back to the ocean."

"If you had a man who had the sea in his blood, you would follow 'im wherever he took you, you would. 'Tis only my affection for my husband that keeps me here. I fish to keep me sanity—and to be useful."

By evening, Mrs. Conley's temperature had gone down, and she was feeling much better. Maeve cooked for the captain and his missus and left them alone together.

* * *

The following day was the Sabbath, and Flynn insisted Maeve attend services with her sisters. The captain read from his Bible, and Martha sat upon a trunk in the first row as usual. Maeve thought he gave her tender looks now and then. She smiled to herself, remembering the crusty remarks that didn't begin to hide his concern.

After the service, Mrs. Fitzwilliam took Maeve's arm and led her aside. "I have truly lost my right mind."

"What's wrong?"

"I imagined I saw her again. I dream of young Mary at night, and then this morning I glimpsed her as I made my way here."

"A lot of young girls have black hair," Maeve told her. "Didn't you say she has black hair?"

"She does."

"And she's on your mind, so it's only natural that you'd associate another girl's appearance with your granddaughter's. I told you I used to think I saw Da in the village. Once I swore I saw him in the field, and when I looked back, there was nothin' there. Our minds play tricks on us. Do you know how to sew?"

Mrs. Fitzwilliam seemed surprised by the question. "I do needlework, yes."

"Join us for our noon meal today. We are putting the finishing touches to dresses my sisters and I will wear when we dock."

"Are you sure it will be all right with your sisters?"

"Goodness, yes."

"I don't want to be a burden. I'm just a lonely old woman, Miss Murphy."

"You're not a burden, and the way to alleviate loneliness is to make friends and volunteer your services."

She joined the sisters, along with Aideen and Mrs.

Kennedy, for a meal of crab lobscouse, the crab and vegetables provided by Mrs. Conley.

"This is quite good," Aideen said. "But my mouth is watering for fried chicken."

"A slice of beef," Mrs. Fitzwilliam added.

"A lovely guinea fowl." Nora rolled her eyes comically.

"A real cake," Mrs. Kennedy suggested. "With frosting."

"Strawberries," Bridget contributed.

Maeve tested the biscuits. "'Tis quite a feast you've dreamed up. I'm only glad that I don't have to wash all the pots and pans."

The dishes only took a few minutes to wash and clear away. Nora laid out sheets to create a clean workspace. Now that the dresses had been put together, they took up a lot more space.

Mrs. Kennedy enlisted Mrs. Fitzwilliam's help with the hats, and the two of them struck up a conversation.

Judd Norton, the cowboy from the place called Nebraska Territory, stopped to extend a greeting. Nora invited him to sit, and he thumbed back his hat and joined them.

"Those are interesting boots, Mr. Norton," Bridget observed.

"They're for riding. Pointed toes make it easy to get feet in the stirrups and the underslung heels hold 'em there. 'Course I'm not wearin' my spurs onboard the ship. Riders wear spurs with blunt rowels to prod their horses."

"They're so fancy," Bridget said. "I don't imagine everyone has such a fancy pair of boots."

"No. These are my Sunday boots. I have a pair o' stovepipes I wear on the ranch. Good pair o' boots costs a man half a month's wages."

"I suppose your hat is practical, too," Mrs. Kennedy said. Being a hat maker, she would take notice.

"Yes, ma'am. The brim shades the eyes o' course. Keeps my head cool. Protects my neck from rain and snow. Why, a good hat will protect you from thorns and low-hangin' branches, carry water or grain, fan fires—and last for years.

"You can tell a man by his hat. A plainsman is different from a sou'wester. Mexicans wear a sombrero, sometimes even made of straw."

"Will we see many men wearing this sort of clothing in Boston?" Aideen asked.

"Not likely, miss. City fellas wear fancy coats and boots. Beaver hats."

"Beaver?" she asked, with raised brows.

Judd chuckled. "Trappers sell all sorts of furs for clothing. Beaver is popular because it's sleek and repels water."

"I've only just learned about all the rain and snow," Maeve told him. "Do you see snow in Nebraska Territory?"

"Snow piles so high we tie ropes from the house to the barns and privy so we don't get lost and freeze to death."

"Methinks you joined the good doctor on his trip to kiss the Blarney Stone," Nora told him, with a teasing grin. "That's a tall tale."

"I assure you, miss, it's the truth. In America we call what you're talkin' about spinnin' a yarn, but snow isn't a yarn, I guarantee you. An unexpected blizzard will freeze cattle where they're huddled along a fence line."

"Are all the parts of the country like that?"

"Down in the Southwest, it is dry as a bone, nothin' but cactus and rocks as far as the eye can see."

"And what of Boston, Mr. Norton?" Aideen asked.

"I've only visited in fair weather," he told her. "Where in Ireland did you live?"

She told him where she'd been born and raised.

"Don't reckon you'll find weather as nice or land as green in Massachusetts. But you will find opportunities. Ladies own millin'ry shops and boardin' houses."

"My aunt and I hope to buy a small establishment," she told him. "We've brought supplies to get us started and once we're settled, we'll order more."

"If Boston has too much competition, you might want to consider cities farther west for that sort of shop. Might even be more profitable."

"How does one travel west?"

"Rails are bein' laid to major cities every day. Horses and wagons are leavin' all the time."

"I suppose if we've endured a trip across the Atlantic, a few more miles won't kill us."

The conversation had narrowed down to the two of them: Aideen and the cowboy. Maeve couldn't help noticing the inflection in Aideen's voice or the way Judd cast her an engaging smile. Maeve's own heart fluttered at their sweet exchange.

She met Bridget's gaze. She and her sister shared silent recognition.

"I should be movin' on," Judd said several minutes later. "Don't want to wear out my welcome. I might want to come back another time. I do enjoy the company."

Aideen's struggle with her expression was clear as day.

Bridget jumped up. "Aideen and I will keep you company on your stroll, if you don't mind."

"I wouldn't mind at all."

Bridget reached for Aideen's hand and pulled her to her feet. They'd only taken a few steps, when she stopped. "I almost forgot. It's my turn to get milk for

Grace." She raised a hand and let it drop. "You two go on. I'll catch up with you later."

Judd touched the brim of his hat and extended his elbow for Aideen to take his arm.

Bridget sat back down with a self-satisfied smile and picked up the length of ribbon she'd been assigned to stud with seed pearls for her hat.

"Bridget Murphy." Nora's voice held that caution-ary tone Maeve knew only too well. "You had better go milk that goat now. No daughter of Jack Murphy will be found tellin' an outright lie—especially not on the Sabbath!"

None of the others raised their gaze, and Maeve had a difficult time to keep from laughing.

Bridget unwrapped a clean tin cup and marched away.

"We'll have a little milk for our tea," Nora said once she was out of earshot.

The others laughed then.

Some time later, Mrs. Fitzwilliam thanked them and departed. Not long after the cowboy had returned Ai-deen, they were folding up their sewing because of the impending darkness when Flynn joined them.

"How do the passengers fare this day?" Maeve asked him.

"Quite well. Kathleen is much improved. You saw Mrs. Conley at service, of course. I treated a few sail-ors with minor injuries." He glanced at the others, then back. "Why don't we go talk shop somewhere else, so the others won't be bored with our conversation? We can walk."

Maeve excused herself to join him, and they took a leisurely stroll. The passengers' fireplaces they passed provided scenes of merriment, domestic chores and the occasional squabble.

They came upon Mrs. Fitzwilliam and Stillman at her fire. To Maeve's surprise and delight, all three McCorkle brothers sat with them, obviously enjoying biscuits.

"Please join us! It will be a nice change to host the two of you at our fire," Mrs. Fitzwilliam said.

Stillman held out a tin plate of biscuits and they each took one.

"Young Gavin here is the same age as my Mary," the woman told them. "Here he is working and making something of himself. Why, even Sean and Emmett run errands for the captain. They have no family, did you know that?"

"We did," Flynn replied.

"I'll be buying a home when we reach Boston," she said. "I have Stillman here, of course, but young helpers would be a benefit. I would like to offer you young men a place to live. I'm a lonely old woman, and I'd be happy to have your company."

Sean looked at Gavin.

His shaggy-haired older brother appeared thoughtful. "I could work and pay you rent, I could."

"We'll work something out," the woman said.

"We can help take care o' you, like Stillman does," Gavin added.

"I'd be more than glad to pay for your help," she answered.

"We don't want no pay," Gavin insisted. "The Lord says a person should just do good without expectin' nothin'."

"An' you remind us of our granny what used to make us soup and bread when we was little."

Elizabeth Fitzwilliam dabbed the corners of her eyes.

Flynn experienced an unfamiliar glow of hope. He'd taken Sean aboard and given the three of them jobs to prevent them from suffering the fate of stowaways, so he'd felt responsible for their welfare and had been concerned about what would become of them once they landed.

The McCorkles had gone from being orphaned and homeless to having the promise of a good life. There were still a lot of things that could go wrong. The Irish were not welcome in many areas of America. It pained him to think any of these people could be turned away or spoken down to, but he wasn't going to dwell on negative possibilities.

He considered whether or not he should give them a warning, but in the end, he didn't want to discourage them. He'd already mentioned it to Maeve.

"I'll visit whenever I have an opportunity to be in Boston," Maeve told them.

Flynn didn't want to think about what he'd be doing after they landed this time. He'd had plenty of opportunity to think about the things Maeve had said to him. He wanted to deny that he'd been punishing himself by coming on these voyages.

Surviving the elements and risking contagion was like defying the fact that he'd been spared when Johanna and Jonathon had both died.

Doing without and being alone were his punishment for letting his wife and son die.

But since Maeve had forced him to recognize he wasn't to blame, he could say he'd done his time aboard the ships. The laws were in place. He could step back and be confident immigrants were safer than they had ever been. Death counts were considerably lower than ever before.

Was his work done, then?

His self-sacrifice had filled his months and occupied his thinking. What would he do if not this? Go to

Edinburgh and become one of the scientists who were so involved with their research that reality blurred in the background?

Emmett showed Maeve a small wooden figure of a whale. He explained how one of the sailors had carved it for him. Maeve admired it appreciatively.

She was good with children of all ages. She fed and changed Baby Grace as though it was the most natural thing in the world. And she interacted with Emmett in a manner that drew out the shy boy and encouraged him to speak. She was efficient and compassionate in everything she did. Maeve would make a fine mother one day. A fine wife. Some man would be fortunate to marry her.

Chapter Twenty-Six

Flynn and Maeve thanked their hostess and resumed their walk. Before they'd gone very far, they came upon Mrs. Conley and the captain, seated on wooden folding chairs, admiring the sky.

"How are you feeling this evening?" Flynn asked Martha.

"My head has finally stopped throbbin'," she answered. "I learned my lesson. I'll not be fishin' the entire day without proper headwear or plenty of water."

"I've learned me lesson, as well," the captain said. "I was mighty fearful of losin' her, I was. 'Tis not a proper home or occupation for a woman, bein' aboard a ship all her livelong days. Loyal to the end, this one is, but I'll not be carryin' her back out to sea, unless o' course she wants her house and garden to be in Ireland."

"You're buying her a house?" Maeve asked, with delight in her voice.

"And settlin' down to till the ground and weed the vegetables in her garden. This shall be my final voyage as cap'n."

Maeve knelt down near Martha's chair. "Where do you want to live?"

"Ireland is no longer the land of my youth. The landlords have starved our people and burned them out so they can become richer. People like us can't farm a piece of land without the tyrants takin' the crops." She shook her head sadly. "No, we'll be findin' us a place in America."

"They say Faith Glen is a lot like the villages back home," Maeve told her. "Perhaps you'd like to live there."

"Wherever we are, ye can be certain that we will keep in touch, we will, Maeve Murphy."

Maeve stood and self-consciously blinked back tears. "I've become attached to so many during this journey. Parting will be as difficult as leaving home was. I feel as though I've known the two of you a lifetime. I shall miss you."

"You're a sweet girl, you are." Martha reached for Maeve's hand and squeezed it.

"This is likely the last Sabbath before we reach Boston Harbor," Captain Conley told her. "Checked charts this morning, I did. We've had a good tailwind."

"I'll be glad to arrive, but after making so many friends, it will be bittersweet."

By the time they'd made it all the way around the deck a couple of times, the night sky was dark and stars winked at them.

"I thought of something when Mrs. Conley was so ill," Flynn said at last. "Before I realized what was wrong with her."

"Thought of what?"

"I thought about her wish for a home. If she hadn't sought help—or if we hadn't been able to bring down her body temperature and she had died—the captain would have had to live with his regrets. The rest of his days he'd have been sorry he put off buying her a house until it was too late. It's easy to let things go."

"I suppose it is."

"I admire you, Maeve. You sometimes act before thinking, but you always act. You say the things that are on your mind. You tell people what you want them to know before it's too late."

"Sometimes there aren't second chances," she told him. "It's no shame to confess your feelings."

"Not everyone's as brave as you."

"I'm not brave."

"You are."

She looked at him. "Is there anything you might regret not saying or doing if you don't do it before we dock?"

"There is."

Her heart fluttered. "Can you take care of it right now?"

"I'm not sure." He cleared his throat nervously and looked away.

Maeve experienced disappointment. She didn't know what she wanted him to say or do, and she'd resigned herself to the fact that he was still in love with his late wife, but there were things left unsaid between them.

"I would regret never kissing you again."

The knowledge brought her joy—and disappointment at the same time. She, too, would regret parting ways. He would take a piece of her heart with him.

"Well, I've said what I was thinking. But I don't know that I feel any better for it."

"Likely you won't feel better until you've actually done it." She took a bold step forward.

Flynn didn't waste any time. He leaned forward until his warm lips covered hers in a soft, hesitant kiss. She hadn't known kisses could send shivers along her spine or take her breath away, but this one did. The moment felt right, but it was dizzying at the same time. She grasped the front of his shirt and clung to the fabric to keep from falling.

He wouldn't have let her fall, however. He flattened his wide hands across the small of her back and gently held her in place.

She'd given a lot of thought to their previous kisses, surely more thought than was appropriate. When she'd remembered, she'd wondered if their kisses had really been so good or if her memory had blown them out of proportion.

Her memories were not inflated.

Kissing Flynn made her feel feminine...and wanted...and *disappointed*. Disappointed because this was something she could get used to, but she wouldn't have the chance. Disappointed because she'd only just discovered her feelings for him, and their time was drawing to a close.

She released his shirt. He straightened, but kept his palms against her back. Maeve took the initiative to move away, just as she'd taken the initiative to welcome the kiss, and he dropped his hands away.

The night air felt cooler than it had only minutes before. A chill ran across her shoulders and down her arms.

Was he thinking of his beloved wife? Perhaps he compared the way she'd made him feel. Maeve couldn't bear to fall short of his memories.

Something leaped in the water beyond the side of the ship, bringing them out of their reverie. Maeve turned toward the sound. "It's late," she said finally.

"Will you please let me walk you to your cabin?"

"Yes, of course."

He took her hand and led her toward the ladder. She led the way along the narrow companionway. "Rest well, Maeve."

"And you."

Even with all the troubles she'd had at home, Maeve had never had as much trouble sleeping as she had aboard the *Annie McGee*. Her problem was Flynn Gallagher, of course.

Chapter Twenty-Seven

Maeve had let herself fall in love with the handsome doctor. Even though she'd known from the beginning that she wasn't the sort a man like him could love, the inevitable had happened. From only the few mentions he'd made of his wife, it was obvious the woman had a similar background to his and had come from a well-to-do family.

Johanna had probably gone all the way through a fancy school and had read stacks and stacks of books, about which the two of them conversed at length. Most likely, Johanna had been able to entertain guests with ease and knew all about fashion and good manners. She'd been the perfect wife for a man of his position.

No wonder he'd had to bury those feelings so deeply. Losing one's true love had to be the worst heartache of all.

As she would soon learn.

Considering Maeve had known from the first time she'd met him that they were not destined to become a couple, she questioned her wisdom in letting her feelings rule. There was a proverb that said wisdom was better than rubies. Another said, "Happy is the man who findeth wisdom." She wanted to be wise. She wasn't a foolish girl.

Though she did act impetuously, it was true. She spoke before thinking and acted on instinct. It must only stand to reason then that she would fall in love headfirst and only recognize her mistake in retrospect.

She wanted to be loved by Flynn. She wanted him to care for her as deeply as he had his wife. She wanted him to want her for his wife.

What would a wise person do right now?

Sleep, of course, but she was finding that impossible.

There were only a few days until the *Annie McGee* docked in Boston Harbor. She rerouted her thoughts. She was a strong person. She could capture those wayward musings. Would she see any of the passengers who had come aboard that first week after they'd departed Ireland? The ones who'd fled the *Wellington* after a frightening fire on deck? Perhaps one of them might recognize her.

More likely they'd recognize Flynn.

Where would Captain and Mrs. Conley settle down? Maeve imagined all the years they'd been married, all the years Martha had traveled the ocean with her husband because she hadn't wanted to be apart from him. Even if she'd had a house and remained behind, she would have been lonely with him at sea.

Maeve's thoughts traveled to her mother and Laird O'Malley. Her whole life she'd believed her parents enjoyed a fairy-tale love. Now she questioned if it had been as perfect as she'd imagined. It could still be true. Apparently, her mother had chosen between two men, if the letter was a true indication, and had chosen Jack Murphy for a good reason. Love?

Praying for wisdom and sleep, she closed her eyes.

Only a few more days.

* * *

Flynn deliberately grew standoffish, placing much-needed distance between himself and Maeve. She made him look at too many things. She forced him to look inside himself.

All his past months of service she called self-punishment. What was he punishing himself for? She'd pegged it: he'd blamed himself for living when Johanna and Jonathon had died. He never even got sick.

In those early days he'd wished he'd died. Living was too painful. Remembering them was torture. It hadn't taken long until the house tormented him with memories.

He'd sold it.

People tried to comfort him, talk about his wife and child.

He'd fled from them.

His father assured him the practice would be a comfort, that family would help him come to terms with his devastating losses.

He'd quit and gone to England.

Instead of practicing medicine he'd taken up a cause that consumed his thoughts, his time, his energy. He'd lost himself in research.

He'd lost himself.

Maeve Murphy, with her unassuming grace and unaffected generosity had made a crack in the wall of his fortress. And then she'd planted her dainty foot in that crevice and brought the whole thing crashing down around him.

She made something happen that he'd deliberately protected against: he'd felt pain.

But along with pain, he felt other things.

Baby Grace inspired the same tender, protective feelings Sean had brought about—the same feelings he thought he'd lost. Watching the trio of Murphys care for her resurrected stirrings of compassion.

The love between Maeve and her sisters made him admire them and long for something similar...long to be a part of it. They made him feel longing.

Maeve's unwavering faith in God both shamed and motivated him. Something came into play that hadn't been active for a long time—hope. If she could have that peace of mind and spirit, maybe he could, too.

When Maeve spoke of his work, he felt accomplishment. When he taught her something and she used the knowledge effectively, he experienced pride. When he learned from her—lessons like the most simple and basic principles of love—he felt humility.

Sorting through all that, he came to a hard-fought conclusion: as much as all that confused and pained him—as long as it had been—he liked feeling.

Feeling made him feel human.

Captain Conley passed the news that they would sail into Boston Harbor in two days. The relief that swept through the passengers was tangible. People sang and played union pipes on deck at all hours of the day. They hadn't had any illnesses or accidents for two days, so Maeve helped Flynn take inventory of the remaining supplies and wrap glass bottles for storage.

"We have most everything accomplished here," he told her. "Go join your sisters and friends and enjoy the day. If I need you, I'll send for you."

Kathleen was about and walking, and she and Estelle stopped by their fireplace. Bridget was helping the Atwaters pack, but Nora and Maeve were seated with Grace on her crate.

"We've brought each of you a little parting gift." Estelle opened the brocade bag she carried. "There are two bars for each of you—Bridget, too."

Maeve accepted the paper-wrapped rectangles. The scent reached her nose, and she knew immediately what lay within the wrap. "Face soap? Oh, ladies, this is so generous."

She placed a bar right under her nose and inhaled the lovely coconut fragrance.

"Thank you," Nora said. "Bridget will be grateful, as well."

"We just wanted you to know how much we appreciated your generosity."

Kathleen had been silent throughout the exchange. Her mother glanced at her expectantly. Finally, the dark-haired young woman looked at Maeve. "Perhaps when you visit Boston, you will come for tea."

"It will be nice to have so many friends in Boston," Maeve replied.

Once they'd moved on, Nora held the soap to her nose. "I shall save mine for special occasions."

"Not I." Maeve grinned. "I'm going to use it every day until it's gone." She folded all the bars together and tucked them in their basket. "My fingers are still sore from the last of our sewing. I don't know how Aideen does it day in and day out."

"She doesn't prick herself every few minutes."

Maeve chuckled. "At least all the finishing touches are done and the dresses are ready. I'm going to feel like a princess."

The afternoon passed uneventfully. Bridget had taken it upon herself to invite Judd Norton to join them that night, so the cowboy sat at their fire and shared their lobscouse. "No offense to your fine cookin' ladies, but I am sorely missin' roast and ham. Even a buffalo steak would be a nice change right about now. The first place I go when we land will be to a restaurant with meat and gravy on the menu."

"I've seen drawings of buffalo," Aideen told him.

A visitor paused, taking them all by surprise. It was the gentleman who sat at his easel and painted each day. "Good evening, ladies. Gentleman. I hope I'm not intruding."

"Not at all. Please join us."

"I won't be staying, thank you. I simply wanted to present this to you."

He turned the canvas around so they could see what he'd painted. Maeve's heart stopped.

It was a likeness of her and her two sisters in profile. He'd painted them in stair-step fashion, with the sky and the ocean meeting in the background, and the three of them looking out across the vast Atlantic with wistful expressions.

Her heart beat again. Maeve studied the detail he'd given their hair, the turn of each mouth and the depth of their eyes. He'd captured how she felt about their voyage so instinctively and with such passion. In each face in the painting could be seen anticipation, uncertainty...hope.

A tear edged from the outer corner of her eye and she wiped it away. "It's absolutely breathtaking. I can feel the life in these people. In *us*."

Nora drew her gaze away to focus on the artist. "How did you do this? We never posed for you. At least I didn't."

"Neither did I."

"You were here every day, and you are fascinating subjects. And I have a knack for remembering details."

"An uncanny knack," Bridget agreed.

Maeve experienced regret. "We have nothing to offer you."

"There's nothing I need. If you enjoy it, that will be gift enough for me."

He was tall, so Maeve had difficulty giving him a hug, but he leaned forward to accommodate her.

"Oh, my goodness," she said when he was gone. "What an incredible gift."

"We shall hang it in the cottage." Bridget couldn't stop admiring the painting.

The instruments had all tuned up again, and men, women and children gathered to sing and dance. Bridget tugged Nora's hand and beckoned Maeve and Aideen. "Let's join them!"

Cuddling Grace, Nora followed, and their little group joined the bigger gathering. It was a lively tune, and the sisters joined the singing. "'As I got down to Turra market, Turra market for to fee. I fell in with a wealthy farmer, the barnyards of Delgaty. A linten addie toorin addie, linten addie toorin ae. Linten lowrin lowrin lowrin, the barnyards of Delgaty.'"

Judd grinned at the nonsensical lyrics, but he tapped his foot and clapped.

"'He promised me the one best horse that e'er I set my eyes upon. When I got to the barnyards, there was nothing there but skin and bone.'"

Maeve spotted the McCorkle boys with Mrs. Fitzwilliam, and they appeared to be having a jolly time. The brothers had all put on weight and looked clean and healthy. She hoped she got to see what became of them.

Her gaze found Flynn. He stood beside Margret Madigan and her children, and he was holding the baby in the crook of his arm.

Aideen laughed and clapped and finally grabbed Judd's hand and pulled him toward the throng of foot-stomping dancers.

"I don't know how to dance a jig," he balked.

"There's nothing to it. You just move your feet."

Maeve had to laugh, because he looked so out of place among the immigrants in his hat and fancy boots.

Seeing Flynn disturbed her. As much as she wanted to put him out of her mind, he was always there. She leaned into Nora. "I have to check on something."

Quickly, she moved away from the crowd of merry-makers, pausing only to check that their fire had died down to glowing embers, and moved along to the far end of the ship, where she could be alone.

The stars had chosen this night to mockingly shine brightly and wink in the vast sky. It should have been the best night of the trip. She wanted to experience closure. She wanted to move forward into this new life with no regrets.

Help me, Lord.

"Maeve?"

His voice startled her. She turned. "Did you finish the packing?"

Flynn stood close and rested one hand on the side. "I don't want to talk about packing or patients, Maeve."

"Oh. All right. Is something else on your mind?"

"Aye. The same thing that's been on my mind ever since this voyage began."

"What's that?"

"You."

"I didn't mean to trouble ye."

"Trouble me is all you've done. Challenged me. Frightened me. I don't believe you've spared me a thing."

"Whatever have I done?" His words disturbed her now.

"You're just you, and that's enough. More than enough. You made me look at myself. You're perceptive, and you never missed a chance to point our my self-defeating actions."

Maeve winced. "Mother always did say I had a tendency to lay things out in plain sight. I'm sorry if I overstepped. I meant no offense."

"Your plain truths were just what I needed. I was running away. From myself, from things I was too cowardly to deal with. I thought if I kept busy enough I'd never have to face things that were painful. It doesn't work that way."

"And now you can talk about your wife and son," she supplied.

"Yes. And say their names. I hadn't even spoken their names in years, Maeve."

"You will always have the memories of your time together."

"And I've let them go. Released them into God's care. I know they've been there all along, but on my part, I wasn't letting go. It seemed a betrayal."

"I understand."

"I realized something else, too. For me death was always defeat. Death meant I hadn't been successful at my job. But I've been able to accept that death is a natural part of life, as odd as that sounds."

"It doesn't sound odd at all."

"You're satisfied your loved ones are in a good place, waiting for you. Our years here on earth are but a blink of an eye to God. We'll join them soon. Death isn't the end of life, but the beginning of life eternal. That gives me comfort."

Maeve blinked back the sting of tears. "As it does me."

"I'm finished with this shipboard life. I need a purpose again. I'm ready to move on."

"Meaning you won't be sailing again soon?"

"I hope not to sail for a long time. I want a home. A family."

Her stomach lurched. He had told her he wasn't interested in Kathleen.

"What's your deepest desire, Maeve?"

She'd only recently admitted it to herself. The wish was still fragile. "Not so different from everyone else's, I expect."

"Won't you tell me?"

She shook her head.

"Tell me," he coaxed.

She took a deep breath. She'd made a fool of herself before, what was once more? "I want to be loved. Wholeheartedly. Unselfishly. I want a love that knows no boundaries. A love that age only deepens. And I want it while I'm young."

"Your wish is easy to fulfill. In fact, it's already done."

In the background the music and gaiety was a contrast to their serious conversation. "How can that be?"

He reached for her hands. She hadn't realized how chilled hers were until the warmth and strength of his captured them.

"Because I already love you. I fell in love with you when you saved Sean's life and insisted he let you scrub him and wash his hair. I fell in love with the way your brogue is exaggerated when you're arguing a point or when you're put out. I love your bravery and the way you challenge my thinking. I love how you do what's right—what comes straight from your heart—without compromise or question."

Maeve was listening, but her mind was catching up with her ears.

"I love how your hair curls around your ears when you've tried so hard to tame it. I love the twinkle in your eyes when you're amused. I love that you sing a little off-key."

"I don't."

"You do, but it's endearing. I love how you can talk to anyone and how you really, really care about them. I love how real you are, Maeve. How touchingly, beautifully real you are. You don't possess a single affected trait. Not one.

"My hair's too red."

"It's the perfect color to me."

"I'm too small."

"You're the perfect size for me."

She took a breath and released it. "I'm a poor farm girl with one good dress, and it was a gift I haven't even worn yet."

"There's only one thing that could be a problem."

"What is it?"

"I'll not ask you to marry me if you don't think you could love me in return. I wouldn't want—"

She reached up and placed her fingertips over his lips.

"I don't foresee a problem, Dr. Gallagher. But before I say it, I have one more question."

"Amssmms-bfft."

She removed her fingers from his lips. "What?"

"Ask anything you like."

"Are you able to love me as much as you loved Johanna?"

"I don't deny I loved her. But God and I had a long talk. I actually listened this time. I released her and Jonathon. I will always remember them and love them, but I'm still alive and I want to live the rest of my life loving you. I promise I'll make you a good husband, and you'll never want for anything."

"I don't want to be spoiled."

"It could never happen."

"Do you think you might stop talking long enough to kiss me and see if this still feels right?"

Flynn scooped her against him. She wrapped arms around his neck so tightly her toes lifted off the ground. She kissed him back.

And it still felt right.

Epilogue

Maeve felt like a princess in her taffeta day dress. Aideen had been right about the exquisite French silk plaid in shades of orange, yellow, green and blue being striking on her small frame. Even her underclothing was made of quality fabric and lay smooth beneath the dress. Since her headpiece had become a wedding veil, Mrs. Kennedy had added a ruffled piece of ecru lace to her tiny hat accented with yellow silk flowers made to look like wild iris. The hat smartly covered one side of Maeve's forehead.

Martha Conley had done the honors of placing the hat and veil upon Maeve's head, because tradition called for a happily married woman to do that task.

Maeve wasn't much for superstition, but she loved the traditions of her homeland. The fact that sun shone on her now was thought by some to bring good fortune. She preferred to believe God had brought a bright day to assure her He was present and blessing their union.

Her sisters took her breath away in their new dresses, as well. Bridget's emerald-green sateen showed off her lovely hair and sparkling eyes. Nora stood regally tall and elegant in vivid blue linen. Grace wore a gown fashioned from one of Flynn's embroidered white shirts and trimmed with lace and pink ribbon. Nora had even managed to get a tiny bow to stay in her wispy auburn hair.

Nearly every passenger had gathered on the foredeck to witness the occasion. Maeve's gaze took in the Atwaters, Goldie McHugh with her husband and children, as well as Kathleen and her mother. She gave Mrs. Fitzwilliam and the McCorkle brothers a warm smile.

"You're the most beautiful woman ever to cross the Atlantic." Flynn's voice made gooseflesh rise on her arms. His dark eyes made a million promises, and her heart swelled.

The captain stood before them, looking resplendent in a dark blue uniform with his beard neatly trimmed and his hair cut. Beside him Martha dabbed her eyes. "I'm so pleased that the last wedding the cap'n performs is yours."

Gulls and pelicans flew overhead in profusion. The *Annie McGee* now sailed only a few miles from Boston Harbor, the entire coastline in view. Butterflies set up a wild flutter in Maeve's stomach.

She reached for Flynn's hand.

"Are you ready?" he asked.

She turned and looked up into his handsome face, and everything else faded into the background. This was the most important day of her life. The day that united her with Flynn Gallagher for life, a day they would tell their children about…a day to rejoice and be glad in.

"I'm ready."

* * * * *

Renee Ryan grew up in a Florida beach town where she learned to surf, sort of. With a degree from FSU, she explored career opportunities at a Florida theme park and a modeling agency and even taught high school economics. She currently lives with her husband in Nebraska, and many have mistaken their overweight cat for a small bear. You may contact Renee at reneeryan.com, on Facebook or on Twitter, @reneeryanbooks.

MISTAKEN BRIDE

Renee Ryan

And now abideth faith, hope, charity, these three;
but the greatest of these is charity.
—*1 Corinthians* 13:13

To Harlequin Love Inspired editors Emily Rodmell
and Elizabeth Mazer. Thank you for your hard work
and unceasing efforts in editing this book.
I'm in your debt. Your suggestions made the story
much stronger. It was a joy working with you both!

Chapter One

Boston Harbor, July 1850

To Bridget Murphy's way of thinking the voyage to America was more than a thrilling journey across the vast Atlantic Ocean. It was the beginning of a new life. For her and her two sisters. But especially for her.

From the moment she'd boarded the *Annie McGee,* Bridget was simply Bridget, the soft-spoken Irish lass earning her way to America as a stand-in nanny for the Atwater family.

No more humiliation hanging over her head. No more whispers trailing in her wake. The past had finally become *the past*.

And now the wait was over. Today she would begin her new life in earnest. Endless possibilities awaited her in her new country—her new home.

Bridget leaned over the ship's railing for her first glimpse of America, the ribbon streamers at her elbows billowed in the breeze. A gasp of delight flew past her lips, not only because she felt very smart in her new green sateen dress, but at the sight that met her gaze. Chaos, utter and complete chaos, met her gaze. The air vibrated with seagull shrieks, calls for carriages, laughter and commands.

Caught up in the madness, she took a moment and simply watched the activity below. Passengers disembarked the ship with hurried steps. Workmen staggered under the weight of their cargo. Carts full of wares were scattered everywhere. Children darted headlong past the lopsided piles.

Although she recognized many of the people already on the docks, none noticed her.

More the better.

A sudden movement in the distance caught her attention. She narrowed her eyes. A man, alone, worked his way through the crowd with methodical grace. His tall, lithe form stopped every few moments to speak with one of the passengers. There was something about him…

Something that tugged at her very core.

She couldn't tear her gaze away.

He moved with the kind of steps only a man confident in his own worth could pull off. Bridget placed her hand on her forehead to shade her eyes from the sun and continued watching him. He had broad shoulders, long legs and lean hips. Even though she couldn't see him clearly from this distance, she knew his eyes would be a vivid, piercing blue. The kind of color that turned silver in the light.

A little shocked at herself, at the fact that she was admiring a man when her heart was still so tender, she tried to pull back, to duck out of sight. But she found herself leaning forward ever so slightly.

As if sensing her eyes on him, he looked straight in her direction.

Her breath caught in her throat and she pulled back

from the rail. Surely he hadn't seen her watching him. The distance was far too great.

Torn between embarrassment and a sudden wish to see the man up close, to discover if his eyes were truly the color of the sky, she hesitated a moment longer. She'd tarried long enough.

Joining the rest of her fellow passengers, she hurried across the ship's main deck. She'd told the Atwater siblings farewell earlier this morning. Pamela, the youngest, had been the saddest over their parting. Well, besides Bridget. Laurel and Hilary had been too busy arguing over a treasured bonnet to care overmuch that they'd never see their temporary nanny again.

Bridget sighed to herself. The journey hadn't been long enough to win over the older two girls. If only—

No. No more regrets. No more *if only*. Bridget was finished trying to fix the unfixable. Never again would she dwell on things she couldn't change.

Increasing her pace, her boot heels struck the weathered planks in perfect rhythm with the rapid beating of her heart.

She'd lost sight of her older sister, Nora. No matter. Nora, being Nora, had prepared for this very contingency and had set up a common meeting place near the gangplank.

Not wishing to hear yet another lecture on setting priorities and keeping to timetables, Bridget increased her pace. She resisted the urge to look over the railing at the wharf below. Was *he* still there? Winding his way through the thick knots of people and cargo, looking for someone in particular? Someone special?

Who? she wondered.

Without breaking stride, Bridget tossed a jaunty wave at the widow Mrs. Fitzwilliam, who had befriended the Murphy sisters on the journey. With her was her attendant Stillman and the three McCorkle brothers Mrs. Fitzwilliam had taken in as her wards. Good-hearted, gracious souls, getting to know them all had been a real blessing. Already running late, Bridget did not stop to speak to them.

Then again...

She'd already fallen behind. What would be the harm in saying one more goodbye to her new friend and those darling boys?

Just as she changed direction, a throng of passengers surged from behind, shoving her back on course at an even greater speed. She would have to catch up with Mrs. Fitzwilliam and the boys later.

Nearing her destination, Bridget wrenched free of the crowd and slid into another small, unoccupied spot along the ship's railing. At the precise location she'd been told.

Nora was nowhere in sight.

More relieved than annoyed, Bridget took a deep, steadying breath. And promptly wrinkled her nose in chagrin.

Throughout the month-long journey across the Atlantic, she had created vivid pictures of America in her mind. She had *not* accounted for the smell.

She raised a gloved hand to her mouth. One moment passed. Two. On the third she drew in another tentative gulp of air. Her eyes immediately filled with water. The stench was truly, truly awful. A mixture of rotting fish, animal sweat, burnt tar and something else entirely— garbage, perhaps?

Another jostle from behind and Nora wiggled in beside her.

"There you are," Nora said, familiar frustration in her tone. "You weren't here earlier."

Bridget ignored the gentle reprimand and smiled at

Aideen

her sister. She, too, wore her new dress, a gift from fellow passengers Ardeen Nolan and her aunt, Mrs. Kennedy. "Don't fuss, Nora. I only just arrived."

"Well, that explains it, then."

With her dark chestnut hair parted in the middle and contained in a tight bun, Nora should look severe. Instead, she positively glowed. Perhaps it was the vivid blue of her new gown. Or the paisley shawl. Or perhaps Nora glowed for an entirely different reason.

They had arrived safely in America and had added a new member to their small family.

Smiling, Bridget lowered her gaze to the squirming infant clutched possessively in her sister's arms. "I see no one has come forward to claim baby Grace."

Nora's pretty blue eyes narrowed to tiny slits. "Not a single person."

Bridget bit her lip to keep from stating the obvious—that Grace had likely been left behind for good. She'd suggested it before, but Nora refused to believe it. Sometimes Nora was the wisest person she knew, and sometimes surprisingly naive. Baby Grace had been abandoned days after her birth. Nora had found her shortly after the start of their journey, and had cared for her ever since.

"I suppose she'll have to make do with us for the time being." And Bridget wasn't completely sorry for it, either. The baby had become a part of both their lives, Nora's more than hers, even if only on a temporary basis. Grace wasn't really theirs, no matter how much they wished it to be so, but for now, they were all she had.

Nora looked out in the distance, her eyes taking on a troubled look. "I'm sure there's been a mistake." She lowered her gaze to the child in her arms. "Who could abandon such a precious little girl?"

Who, indeed?

In Bridget's estimation anyone who walked away from their own baby didn't know the first thing about love. Every child deserved to be loved. Even the difficult ones.

Familiar stirrings of regret filled her. She had so wanted to turn all three Atwater girls into friends, as much as charges. She'd almost succeeded. With a little more time…

She was doing it again. Trying to change the unchangeable.

"We'll have to report her situation to the American authorities as soon as possible," Nora said only half-heartedly.

It was, of course, the right thing to do.

Though Grace's mother had left her behind, there may well be other family with a claim.

"I suppose we must." Bridget reached out and touched the baby's flawless cheek. Large blue eyes stared back at her. "She's really quite beautiful, isn't she?"

"She's perfect."

Bridget couldn't argue with that bit of truth. All children were a gift straight from the Lord. One day Bridget wanted at least five tiny blessings for herself.

A space opened up along the gangplank and she started forward, then stopped and looked back at Nora. "Are we to meet Maeve here or on the docks below?"

"Below," she said. "Flynn had a few last-minute details he needed to address before he could leave the ship. Maeve chose to stay behind with him."

Of course she had. Bridget's younger sister adored her new husband, as did they all. The ship's doctor was now a part of their family. Best of all, Maeve's shipboard romance had restored Bridget's faith in the possibility of finding love again for herself.

Love. Romance. Marriage.

Were they still possible for her at the age of four and twenty? Had she missed her chance when Daniel had decided he didn't want to marry her?

She ignored the pang in her heart and reminded herself anything was possible with God. Despite the thirteen years between their ages, Flynn Gallagher was a perfect match for Maeve. Their union was a blessing and a testimony to the power of love.

Finished feeling sorry for herself, Bridget tossed her shoulders back and stepped away from the railing. "Right, then. Here we go."

Without looking back, she moved onto the gangplank. For once Nora allowed her to take the lead.

All the planning, prayer and gathering of meager funds had brought them to this glorious day. The moment Bridget's feet touched the wooden dock, her legs wobbled beneath her and her breath caught in her throat. "Oh, Nora, we're finally in America. Isn't it wonderful?"

"Breathtaking." Nora made a face. "As long as you cover your nose."

Bridget waved a dismissive hand. Nothing was going to ruin this moment for her. Not even the awful smells. Besides, Boston wasn't their final destination. Once they gathered their few belongings, Flynn would hire a carriage to take them to the small town of Faith Glen.

Faith Glen. The name had a nice Irish ring to it.

Heart slamming against her ribs, Bridget turned in a slow circle. She wavered a bit, not yet used to the feel of the docks beneath her. There were so many sights to take in, so much noise to filter through her mind. The shouts and laughter mingled together from every corner of the wharf.

A stiff breeze kicked up, tugging several tendrils free

from their pins. Bridget shoved at her loose hair, which was quickly becoming an untidy mess. It seemed the wind always won the battle against her best efforts to tame her unruly curls.

She waved at her new friends, Ardeen and her aunt. They returned the gesture but didn't approach, too intent on finding their luggage. The two had been so kind to Bridget and her sisters. Ardeen wasn't particularly young, but was attractive and fashionable. Mrs. Kennedy was shorter and a little fuller figured. Both were single and appeared out of their depth amidst the chaos on the wharf. Bridget should help.

"Watch yourself," came a shout from behind her.

With only seconds to spare Bridget dashed out of the way of a cart careening by. Undaunted by the near-miss, she cut a glance to the other end of the wharf but couldn't find Ardeen and Mrs. Kennedy.

People of every age, size and station milled about. Caught up in the excitement, Bridget gravitated to a location out of the main thoroughfare. All she wanted to do was watch, listen and learn the many secrets of her new homeland.

"Stay focused, Bridget." Nora placed a light touch to her arm. "We still need to locate our luggage before we rendezvous with Maeve and Flynn." Her tone was pure Nora—brisk, efficient and more than a little impatient.

Nora was in her sensible mood. Best to move out of the way and let her take charge.

"Why don't you give Grace to me?" Bridget reached out her arms to the wiggling bundle. "I'll take her out of the hot sun while you search for our luggage."

Nora hesitated.

"If I stand over there—" Bridget cocked her head toward a spot directly behind her "—I'll be able to watch for Maeve and Flynn."

"That's not a bad plan." Slowly, with more than a little reluctance, Nora handed over the baby. "But stay put," she ordered, her warning gaze proving she knew there was a good chance Bridget might not do as commanded. "I won't be long."

Bridget had no doubt. "Run along, Nora. Grace will be quite fine with me."

That seemed to mollify her and she scurried off at a quick pace.

With the infant nestled safely against her, Bridget moved into the shadow cast by the ship's hull and continued watching the activity around her.

As though sensing all was well, the baby promptly fell asleep in her arms.

Equally content, Bridget sighed. The starkly handsome ship rocked in the brackish water behind her. Caged in the dark pool, the enormous structure swayed its lofty head in impatience. The groan of the rigging sounded like an angry mutter of protest against its current confinement.

Bridget had felt that same way back in Ireland. At least in the end. But she and her sisters would soon claim a home of their own, their first, the one deeded to their mother years ago. It was the discovery of that long-hidden deed that had spurred the sisters to set out for America. Now, she couldn't wait to see where their journey led.

So many possibilities lay ahead. Her mind wanted to wander. She let it.

Far too little time passed before Bridget caught sight of Maeve disembarking with her new husband. They hadn't seen Bridget yet. Arms linked, leaning into one another, the newlyweds moved as a single unit. Flynn's dark head bent over Maeve's lighter one. He whispered something in her ear. They both laughed, and the sound reached all the way to where Bridget stood with Grace.

Did they know how happy they appeared to outsiders?

Something hard knotted in Bridget's stomach and she looked away as a familiar sense of loss filled her.

No. She would not give Daniel McGrath such power. It had been a year since he'd left her heartbroken and humiliated. Nothing was going to ruin this day for her, especially not bad memories of the one man who'd disappointed her.

For I will turn their mourning into joy...

Letting the Scripture sink in, Bridget decided to wait a moment longer before she approached Maeve and her husband.

Just as she was ready to step out of the shadows, a movement caught her eye.

Something was coming toward her. No, some*one*— weaving through the thick crowd with purpose.

Bridget struggled to moderate her breathing, even as she craned her neck to see over the bobbing heads.

One blink, two and she saw him. The same man she'd watched from the ship's main deck.

The sound of her heartbeat echoed in her ears.

How could a stranger affect her so?

He was a full hundred feet away and Bridget still couldn't make out his features, yet she couldn't look away. She knew—*she knew*—he was different. Special. And just like earlier, she was inexplicably drawn to him, fascinated, perhaps even bewildered.

A shiver of anticipation skittered up her spine and she instinctively leaned forward. Toward him. Her eyes narrowed for a better look.

He wore a dark frock coat over lighter-colored trousers and carried what looked like a soft-crowned brown hat in his right hand. By his dress alone she knew he was no average dock worker. Or weary traveler.

He had to be a businessman. An American businessman?

In spite of the impeccable clothing and dark hair cut in a very modern style, a shocking air of raw masculinity resonated out of him.

He surveyed his surroundings with meticulous care, checking faces only. Occasionally he would stop and ask a question of someone, shake his head, then continue his search.

She still couldn't see the color of his eyes, but he seemed to be looking for someone in particular.

Grace? Was he here to claim Grace?

No, that couldn't be right. The baby had been born on the journey over. This man had not been on the ship, she would have remembered him. He couldn't possibly know of the child's existence. Could he?

Her body reacted with an odd sensation and she tightened her hold on Grace. The baby wriggled in her sleep but didn't awaken.

Bridget lowered a soothing kiss to the child's forehead, even as she kept her gaze locked on the stranger.

Meeting such a person on her first day in America could be a dangerous prospect, especially if he was here to seize Grace.

If only Bridget could see his eyes, she would know more about the man's intentions and his character.

Look at me, she silently ordered.

As though hearing her call, his head turned in her direction. It was only then that Bridget realized several people were pointing at her.

Her? Or Grace?

Oh, Lord, please no. No...

Despite her desperation, or perhaps because of it,

the moment her gaze met the stranger's Bridget lost her ability to breathe. She couldn't look away, didn't *want* to look away. The man's eyes were indeed blue, a liquid silver-blue, and filled with a fathomless pool of blank emotion, except for a flicker of...what? What was it she saw in that instant? Hurt? Loneliness?

For that brief instant, she felt an undeniable pull. She reached out her hand, as if she could soothe him from this distance.

He gave one hard blink and the moment passed.

Her throat clenched.

He was coming her way.

And looking very determined.

She almost considered melting deeper into the shadows, but if Grace belonged to him, Bridget couldn't deny him his right. She had to trust he would be good to her.

She took a step forward. Toward him.

He took one slow deliberate step, as well.

Feeling a bit light-headed, Bridget sighed.

Grace gurgled.

The stranger took another step forward.

Bridget sighed again. Really, this odd reaction to a total stranger was beyond ridiculous. She didn't know this man. Or his intentions. She should slip back into the safety of the shadows.

She almost did just that, thinking it the wisest course of action. Except one of Bridget's flaws was that she never retreated from a dare. And, *oh, my,* the man's intense blue eyes held quite the dare.

Chapter Two

William Black stood in muted astonishment. *That hair.* Wild and glorious, the sight of those untamed curls refusing to obey their pins drew him yet another step forward.

Was this woman his future bride, the one he'd sent for all those months ago?

Surely not. Yet several people had pointed at her when he'd mentioned her name—Bridget—and then given her ordinary description of brown hair and dark eyes.

There had to be some mistake. There was nothing ordinary about the woman. She was a blend of the unexpected and the extraordinary, a beautiful female impossible to overlook. In short, everything he avoided in a woman.

As if to mock him, a beam of sunlight escaped like a finger through a crack in the clouds, landing directly on her, bathing her in golden brilliance. Under the bold light of midday she looked delicate, inviting, almost ethereal.

What if this was *his* Bridget?

He'd paid for her passage and promised to marry her, promised to make her a much-needed part of his family. He couldn't go back on his word, regardless of his current misgivings. Duty and honor were the principles that guided his life, all that a man had left when everything else was stripped away.

Will swallowed, remembering what had driven him to acquire an Irish mail-order bride in the first place. Irish women were supposed to be honest, hardworking and proper.

No proper woman had hair like that.

Whoever she was, the beauty staring back at him was perfectly unsuitable to become the mother of his three-year-old twins.

Not after the pain Fanny had put them through this past year and a half.

For a dangerous moment Will's mind fled back in time. To the day when he'd been fool enough to think he could make his marriage work. When he'd thought love was enough to conquer every obstacle thrown their way.

He knew better now. He would never marry for love again. His children deserved stability. And his poor mother deserved relief from the physical demands of caring for a pair of toddlers, no matter how well-behaved.

If this woman with her wild hair and commanding eyes was the one with which he'd corresponded, then Will would honor his promise. As he would any other business transaction. But what would become of his family then?

Mind made up, he continued forward, then stopped, frowned, dropped his gaze. The woman was holding a baby in her arms.

The letter hadn't mentioned a child. Had his intended lied to him? A burning throb knotted in his throat. Was she using him to—

He cut off the rest of his thoughts. He was jumping to conclusions before he'd even met her. The baby might not be hers. And there was still no proof this was indeed his bride.

Will owed it to his children to find out for sure, before he brought the woman into his home and his life. As much as he wanted stability for the twins he would not condemn them to living with a woman of loose morals. Not again. Not *ever* again.

Closing the distance, he forced a smile on his lips and put as much charm into his voice as possible. "Are you Bridget?"

"I...well, yes." Her lovely Irish lilt washed over him and brought an odd sensation of comfort. "Yes, I am Bridget."

An echo of a smile trembled on her lips and Will found himself responding in kind.

Despite his first impression, this woman with her radiant smile and soft expression looked the picture of innocence. A bolt of yearning struck him out of nowhere.

Will ruthlessly suppressed the unwelcome sensation. He didn't want, or need, a wife for his own sake.

"Hello, Bridget. I'm Will," he said without feeling. "Your future husband."

Her future...*what?* Her...her...husband?

The boldly spoken words echoed around in Bridget's mind, yet she couldn't make sense of them. She must have misunderstood the stranger—no, not a stranger anymore. Will, his name was Will.

Bridget shook her head free of her jumbled thoughts and tried to focus on the relevant matter at hand. He wasn't here to claim Grace.

Relief made her legs go weak. But then confusion took hold. Surely this man, this...his name was Will.

Surely *Will* hadn't just referred to himself as her future husband.

It was really quite absurd to think that he had.

So Bridget waited for him to continue, or rather to explain himself in greater detail.

He remained completely, perfectly silent.

When the moment stretched into the uncomfortable, she swallowed several times and then opened her mouth to respond.

To her horror, nothing came out.

She snapped her mouth closed.

And still, Will held to his silence, with only a hint of impatience in his stance.

All Bridget could do was blink up at him in return. He towered over her by at least six inches. The breadth of his shoulders and the powerful muscles beneath his finely cut jacket indicated a man familiar with physical labor.

Bridget should be afraid of him.

She was not.

She was, however, rendered speechless. Still.

"I... I..." The rest of what she'd meant to say sputtered out in a gurgle. She swallowed and tried again. "I'm sorry, I must have heard you incorrectly, you said you were my, my—"

"Future husband."

Oh, my. His deep, raspy voice skimmed over her. A warm, curious sense of inevitability pulled her a step closer to him. Foot poised in midair, she stopped herself before she took another. "That is quite impossible. You have mistaken me for someone else."

His gaze instantly dropped to the baby in her arms and his eyebrows slammed together. Bridget could practically hear the thoughts running through his mind. She braced for the unavoidable questions, trying to decide how best to answer them when they came. She was no stranger to uncomfortable questions.

Will surprised her by skirting the issue of baby Grace altogether. "You are Bridget, are you not?"

"I am, yes." She cleared her throat, comprehending his mistake if he did not. "But I am not *your* Bridget."

His frown deepened. Something dark and turbulent flashed in his eyes.

As she recognized the shift in his mood, it occurred to her once again that she should be afraid of the man. *Why am I not more frightened?*

They were surrounded by hundreds of people, yes, any of whom would come to her rescue if she screamed for help. But that wasn't the reason for her lack of fear. It was Will himself. Or rather, his eyes. They were a deep, liquid blue so compelling and beautiful and yet so—very—bleak.

Bridget felt the familiar quickening of compassion in her heart. Something had made this man sad.

The realization brought an unexpected yearning. She'd never been able to turn away from a person in need. Daniel had considered her sympathy for the wounded and disadvantaged her greatest flaw. Bridget considered it her greatest strength. Their difference of opinion had been enough to cause a permanent rift, one that had ultimately torn them apart and brought her profound unhappiness over the past year.

Although she couldn't explain why, her desire to help this man, this stranger, was different than any other time before. Stronger.

Personal.

Had the Lord brought Will to her for a reason?

No. This entire meeting was a mistake. She didn't know him. And he didn't know her, regardless of what he seemed to think.

Baby Grace chose that moment to wiggle in her sleep and then cry out in frustration. Bridget had been holding on too tightly.

Loosening her grip, she took a step back. Away from Will. Away from whatever it was drawing her to him.

The shadows cast by the ship enveloped her, bringing instant relief from the heat of the day.

"I'm sorry," she said again, wishing she could be of more help but knowing it was best to walk away.

His face turned impassive, but she recognized the desperation that lay just below the surface. He wasn't going to walk away from her. Not yet. Not until he was certain she wasn't the woman he'd come searching for.

Oddly enough, Bridget wasn't surprised by his determination. Will was not a man who accepted defeat easily. She wasn't sure how she knew that about him. She just *knew*.

How was it she understood more about his stranger than she had Daniel, a man she'd known all her life and had been willing to marry?

"Perhaps this will spark your memory." Will reached inside his coat and retrieved what looked like a letter. He unfolded the worn parchment and thrust it toward her.

Rearranging the sleeping baby in her arms, Bridget took the letter. The handwriting with its soft, looping scroll clearly belonged to a female.

A female that was not her.

Nevertheless she read each word slowly, carefully, and soon realized she was holding an acceptance letter. The woman had agreed to become this man's bride. Not just any bride, his *mail-order* bride.

Bridget tried not to gasp aloud. She'd heard of such things. The potato famine had left many families destitute, eager to latch on to any lifeline, even if it meant marrying a stranger and moving far from home. But as she looked at Will from beneath her lowered lashes she decided he didn't seem the type who needed to pay a woman to marry him. He was too handsome, too inherently confident, too...masculine.

Women should be lining up to become his wife.

Yet he'd sent all the way to Ireland for a bride.

Hands shaking, Bridget turned over the letter and skimmed to the bottom. The signature read Bridget *Collins*.

He did, indeed, have the wrong woman. Sorrow settled inside her heart. The sensation made her feel as though she'd lost something important, life-changing.

She sighed.

Without meeting Will's gaze directly, Bridget returned the letter to him. "I was right. You have the wrong woman." Her voice wasn't quite steady, even to her own ears. "My name isn't Bridget Collins. It's Bridget Murphy."

For a long, tense moment he looked taken aback by her words. He swallowed once, twice and again, each time harder than the first.

"You did not write this letter?"

"I'm sorry, no." Why she felt the need to apologize, she couldn't say. But he seemed truly shocked by the news and she wanted to make everything better. If only she knew how.

"I see." He glanced down at the baby. Understanding dawned in his eyes. "You are already married."

"No. I am not. I—"

"Forgive me." He took a step back. A very large step, the gesture confirming her worst fears. He thought Grace was hers and she'd had the child out of wedlock.

"The baby isn't mine," she said in a halting voice.

"Of course not." He turned to go.

"No. Wait." She reached out a hand to his retreating back then quickly curled it around the baby once more. "Please."

He swung back around to face her, a question in his eyes.

Although she knew she would never see him again, she couldn't bear him thinking ill of her. "This is baby Grace," she said past the lump in her throat. "I'm holding her for my sister."

It was the truth, if not entirely accurate. The situation was far too complicated to explain in a few succinct sentences.

"I understand."

Did he? Oh, his words were kind enough, but in the next instant he gave her a formal nod of his head. The gesture was cool, polite and an obvious dismissal. Yet he didn't leave right away. He just stood there staring at her.

"I'm sorry I couldn't be of more help." She meant every word.

"As am I."

Once again he turned to go. This time he stopped himself before he took the next step. "Might I ask you one last question?"

"Yes, of course."

"Do you know Bridget Collins?"

She searched her brain, reviewing all the women and girls she'd met on board the *Annie McGee* named Bridget. It was a common enough name, so much so she counted four off the top of her head. None of them had the last name Collins, though, not that she remembered. Then again, she hadn't known most of her fellow passengers' full names.

Collins. The name triggered a memory, one Bridget couldn't quite grasp. There was a Collins family back in

Castleville and there were several daughters among the eight children. Had there been a Bridget among them?

Yes, that must be why the name sounded familiar. "I'm afraid I don't remember meeting your Bridget aboard ship."

"Pity."

It was, indeed.

"Thank you for your understanding, Bridget, I mean, Miss Murphy." He shoved his hat onto his head. "I apologize for disturbing you and the child."

A heartbeat later he was gone, disappearing into the crowd to continue the search for his bride.

Feeling oddly lost without his company, Bridget watched him weave through the maze of people and piles of luggage along the wharf. He moved with masculine elegance, the fluid motion proving he was a man used to controlling his body, confident in who he was and exceedingly comfortable in his own skin.

It was a very attractive, heady combination of traits. Just watching him made her feel very feminine.

In spite of the awkwardness of their meeting, Bridget had liked him. Even now as she watched him search for his bride, concentrating only on the faces of women near her same age, she felt a pull of—something. Something strong and lingering and very, very pleasant. Attraction?

Maybe.

Or perhaps the sensation was simple curiosity. Yes, that must be it. She couldn't possibly find this man attractive when she knew the potential for heartache. Her sisters claimed she was a romantic, but that did not make her naive. Giving in to *curiosity,* she wondered what possible scenario would induce a man like Will to seek out a mail-order bride, a man with undeniable breeding, wealth and good looks.

Before she could contemplate the matter further, Nora returned.

"I found our luggage," she said, a wee bit breathless, her eyes shining. "It's on the other side of the gangplank, about a hundred yards down."

When Bridget merely blinked at her, Nora indicated the spot with a jerk of her head.

Realizing she was expected to respond, Bridget nodded.

Eyebrows pulling together, Nora made an impatient sound deep in her throat. "What's wrong with you? You don't seem yourself."

"I… It's…nothing. I'm simply preoccupied." That was true enough. "There are so many new things to see and hear, to feel, to comprehend. My head is spinning."

"It's all very exciting." Nora reached out her arms. "I'll take Grace now."

Bridget handed over the baby without argument.

Hoping for one last glimpse of Will, she lifted onto her toes and caught sight of another familiar set of faces heading straight for them.

Head held high, marching along in all her regal glory, Mrs. Fitzwilliam led her new charges through the bustling wharf. The three McCorkle brothers following in her wake watched the activity around them with wide eyes. Although it had taken Bridget a while to warm up to the imperious widow, the boys had been a different matter. From the moment Bridget had met them, they'd inspired her sympathy *and* her faith. She was pleased to see them find a happy ending with Mrs. Fitzwilliam as their foster mother.

As was her custom, the older woman had chosen to wear a dress designed in the latest fashion. The pale blue silk, adorned with delicate lace and ribbon trim, was undeniably beautiful but couldn't possibly be comfortable in the midday heat.

The widow didn't seem to notice. She looked cool, elegant, her dark auburn hair contained in a beaded snood that would have been more fitting for a ballroom. Bridget wondered briefly where her attendant Stillman had gone. Perhaps to hire a carriage?

"Well, hello, my dear Murphy sisters." Mrs. Fitzwilliam drew to a stop, her nose in the air, eyes cast downward. "I see you still have that precious baby with you." She reached out and caressed Grace's cheek with a loving, gentle touch. "Such a beautiful child."

Nora accepted the compliment with genuine pride in her eyes, as though the baby was her own. "I couldn't agree more."

Nodding her approval, Mrs. Fitzwilliam continued studying Grace's sweet face. "My stepgranddaughter Mary had the same coloring."

At the mention of the girl, a sad, faraway look entered Mrs. Fitzwilliam's eyes. The widow's quest to find her missing relative had led her to make this trip to America. The rebellious Mary had run off with her boyfriend, Thomas. The lack of any contact from the girl, not a single letter, had left Mrs. Fitzwilliam quite concerned, enough to seek the help of a professional.

"Will you be meeting with a detective soon?" Bridget asked, unable to hold her tongue in light of the distress she saw in the woman's gaze.

"As soon as possible. Oh, yes indeed. As *soon* as possible."

"You will keep us informed?" Nora asked.

Never taking her eyes off the baby, she gave one firm nod. "You may count on it."

After touching Grace's cheek one final time, Mrs. Fitzwilliam turned her attention back to Bridget.

"Enough with all this gloom." She shook her head as if to wipe away the remains of any negative thoughts swirling around. "Now tell me, my dear girl, are you prepared to claim your new home today?"

"Oh, aye," Bridget answered, all but cradling her reticule against her waist as snugly as Nora held the infant. "You will come visit us once we're settled, yes?" She made eye contact with each of the McCorkle boys. "The invitation includes you three, as well."

"Thank you," Gavin, the oldest of the brothers, answered for all of them. "We would enjoy that very much, Miss Bridget."

"Then it's agreed." Bridget punctuated her statement with a smile.

Gavin smiled back. Tall and lanky, at just eighteen he was on the cusp of manhood and took his role as big brother seriously. Emmett and Sean were considerably younger than him, eight and ten years old respectively. Despite the age difference there was no mistaking the three belonged to one another. All had the same reddish blond hair, pleasing features and big blue eyes.

They were a little rough around the edges, but they were good boys with big hearts. Back in Ireland they'd nearly starved to death in a workhouse.

"…and once Stillman hires the carriage the five of us will head to my home here in Boston." Mrs. Fitzwilliam's voice broke into Bridget's thoughts. "After I meet with the detective and determine my next step concerning Mary, we will make the trip to Faith Glen." She spoke as if the four of them were already a family.

Who would have thought the haughty woman of weeks ago would turn out to be so—sweet. Bridget felt her smile widening. The widow was doing a wonderful thing, taking in the boys and raising them as if they were her own kin.

Although Gavin had done his best to provide for his younger brothers, he wasn't educated and had had no job prospects in America. The McCorkles had taken a large risk when they'd set out to stow away on the *Annie McGee*. The Lord had protected them when things hadn't worked out as planned. Their leap of faith had ultimately brought them a kind, if somewhat stern, benefactor in Mrs. Fitzwilliam.

God was good. And now the lonely widow had a family of her own.

Would Will's story end so happily?

Rising to her toes, Bridget caught his attention just as he left another group of women. At the questioning lift of her eyebrows he shook his head in the negative.

Bridget lowered back onto her heels and sighed.

"Bridget Murphy." Mrs. Fitzwilliam's tone held a considerable amount of reproach. "Were you flirting with that man?"

Flirting? "No, of course not."

"And yet, I wonder. I saw you speaking with him earlier, without the benefit of a chaperone in sight." The widow's eyes had turned a hard, dark blue, reminding Bridget of the imposing woman they'd first met on the ship weeks ago.

Refusing to be intimidated—after all, she'd done nothing wrong—Bridget raised her chin in the air. "Yes, I spoke with him earlier. But I assure you, Mrs. Fitzwilliam, nothing unseemly occurred between us." The words tumbled out of her mouth. "He mistook me for his bride."

She realized she'd spoken too plainly the moment Mrs. Fitzwilliam's eyes narrowed.

"That man thought you were his bride?"

Nora gasped at the implication. But before she could speak, Mrs. Fitzwilliam sniffed loudly, her disapproval evident in the unladylike sound. The gesture reminded Bridget that the woman had always adhered to a strict moral code of conduct.

A wave of heat rose in Bridget's face. She glanced at Nora, noted her widened gaze, then hastened to explain. "It wasn't unseemly, but rather a simple mistake. He thought I was his *mail-order* bride. Her name is Bridget, as well. And aside from sharing her name, apparently I fit the woman's description, too."

After a moment of consideration—a long, tense moment where Bridget fought the urge to continue defending herself—Mrs. Fitzwilliam conceded the fact with a short nod of her head. "I suppose that could happen."

She sounded as skeptical as she looked. But Bridget had other concerns besides earning Mrs. Fitzwilliam's approval on the matter. "He still hasn't found her," she said more to herself than the rest of the party.

As if to prove her point, Will approached another group of passengers disembarking from the *Annie McGee*. After a brief conversation, he walked away empty-handed. Again.

"Wait a minute." Nora swung into Bridget's line of vision, her face full of concern. "Did you say the man's bride has similar features as you?"

"Yes."

"Don't you remember, Bridget?" Nora said. "The terrible accident when the girl fell from the forecastle onto the deck."

"I…" Bridget closed her eyes and thought back. A young girl with dark hair had fallen to her death. There was some confusion over her identity. In fact, Flynn had feared the dead girl was Bridget at first, and had gone to inform Maeve of the terrible accident. They'd all been happily surprised when Bridget had joined them in the middle of his story.

"Yes, oh, my stars, *yes,*" Nora said with more conviction than before, her voice breaking into Bridget's thoughts. Nora gasped as though remembering the moment when they'd thought Bridget was dead. "It was all so horrible."

Bridget remembered now. The girl had died early in the voyage. Maeve, acting in the role of Flynn's medical assistant by then, had been upset over the entire matter, especially when they hadn't been able to identify her conclusively. Bridget wasn't even sure they knew her identity still, not without doubts, but she did remember hearing someone say that she was called Bridget.

"Oh, dear." Could this be the reason why Will hadn't located his bride yet? Because she was dead?

The crowds had thinned out and, still, he continued searching for his bride. To no avail.

Bridget couldn't bear to watch any longer. She had to tell him what she knew. Or at least what she *thought* she knew. She and Nora could be wrong. But if they were correct, if Will's bride had died during the sea voyage over, someone needed to tell him. And that someone should be her, not some stranger who wouldn't take care with their words.

Bridget bid a hasty farewell to Mrs. Fitzwilliam and the boys, then set out.

"Bridget," Nora called after her. "Where are you going?"

"I must tell him about the accident." She tossed the words over her shoulder, her mind made up, her feet moving quickly.

"Bridget, it's really none of your concern."

Oh, but it was. It had become her concern the moment Will had introduced himself to her.

Chapter Three

William caught sight of Bridget Murphy hurrying toward him at an alarming speed. Still reeling from his earlier encounter with the young woman, he noted two things about her as she approached. She no longer held a baby in her arms and she had a very determined look on her face.

Oddly enough, the fierce expression made her more appealing, not less. For a brief moment he experienced a wave of regret that she wasn't *his* Bridget. She was truly beautiful, if he looked past the unruliness of her hair. She had a smooth, oval face, a gently bowed mouth and hazel eyes, more green than brown, a color so rich and intricate he could stare at them for hours and still come away fascinated.

But her hair gave him pause, that glorious, untamed hair that refused to obey its pins. The silky strands snapping in the wind gave her a spirited look that Will found dangerously appealing. He hadn't been this attracted to a woman in—never. He'd *never* met a woman that made his blood rush and his brain spin out of control. Not even Fanny.

It was a very good thing this particular Bridget was not his bride after all.

Swerving around a group of her fellow passengers, the woman skidded to a stop directly in front of him.

She was breathing hard and blinking rapidly.

Something had upset her greatly.

"I have news for you, sir, I…" She let her words trail off and her brows pulled together in a frown.

No woman should look that attractive while frowning.

"I just realized," she said in that soft Irish lilt that left him feeling warm and comforted, like the melted chocolate his mill workers turned into hard cakes. "I don't know your full name."

He blinked again. "It's William. William Black." He paused. "But, please, call me Will. Considering the circumstances of our first meeting anything else would seem too formal."

She digested his words a moment, watching him closely as she did, and then gave him one firm nod. "And you may call me Bridget."

He smiled his agreement.

After another moment passed, she took a deep, shuddering breath, opened her mouth to speak again but stopped herself just as quickly.

Will continued looking into her eyes, those beautiful, gut-wrenching eyes that were fully green in the sunlight with only a few flecks of gold woven throughout. There was no subterfuge in her gaze, no secretive games being played. Or rather, none that he could decipher.

Despite knowing he should keep up his guard, despite her beauty, he sensed this was a woman he could trust. An illusion he didn't dare give in to, for the sake of his children if not for himself. They needed stability and a mother. No matter what his personal feelings were on the matter the job was already filled. Will was firmly committed to following through with his promise.

He cleared his throat. "You said you have news for me?"

"Yes." She worried her bottom lip between her teeth. "I'm afraid it concerns your bride."

By her manner alone he knew he wasn't going to like what she had to say. "Go on."

"There was a young woman on board who bore my same description, one I had forgotten about until my sister reminded me. Her name was Bridget, and she had dark hair and eyes and…" Her words trailed off again. He could feel the misery rolling off her in waves.

Now he knew for certain he wasn't going to like what she had to say. Nevertheless he pressed her to continue. "And?"

"*And…*" She sighed. "The Bridget I'm speaking of died on the crossing over."

Dead? His future bride was dead?

His gut rolled at the news.

No. Not dead. Not possible. The words refused to register in his brain. And yet he found himself asking, "How did she die?"

"From what I remember, although I didn't see the accident myself, she lost her footing and fell from the forecastle to the deck." She touched his arm with tentative fingers then quickly pulled back when he lowered his gaze. "She did not survive the fall."

Will shook his head, the news sinking in slowly, painfully, but far too clearly. "When did this happen?"

She cocked her head at a curious angle, as though unsure why he'd asked the question. "It was a few days into the journey."

His worst fear confirmed. His bride had fallen to her death on board the ship, *after* she'd left the safety of her homeland.

All his careful planning, all the research he'd done to

avoid making another mistake, and for what? Another woman was dead because of him.

Bridget watched a complicated array of emotions cross Will's face. He was no longer stoic, or unreadable. He was distressed. Visibly so.

That terrible look of despair, that awful pain in his eyes. She'd done that to him.

Her heart constricted with sympathy. It wasn't in her to watch such suffering. She desperately wanted to erase the worry from his eyes.

"I'm sorry, Will, I mean… Mr. Black," she corrected, knowing it was best to keep their relationship formal, at least at the moment. "I'm very sorry."

He blinked down at her, his eyes unfocused, as though he'd forgotten she was still standing beside him. In the next instant his troubled gaze darted up the gangplank, then across the wharf, then back to her again. "Are you certain the woman was Bridget Collins?"

"I… No." A moment of doubt whipped through her. "No, I'm not certain at all. From what I understand there was some initial confusion over her identity. She looked enough like me for the ship's doctor to believe it was me that had died." *Oh, please, Lord, please, let me be wrong. For this man's sake.*

"Then you will excuse me?" He looked over his shoulder, heaved a hard pull of air into his lungs. "I must check with the ship's officials to determine if this unfortunate news is, indeed, true."

Of course he would want to verify the information she'd just given him. "I think that's a very wise idea. I could very well be incorrect." *Oh, please, please.*

"Let us hope that you are." His words were abrupt, but not unkind. More distracted than anything else.

He gave her a brief, formal bow. "Good day, Bridget."

"Good day. And—" she placed her fingertips on his arm once again "—Godspeed in your search for your bride."

He stared at her hand for a breathless moment. Then, shrugging away from her, he left without another word.

Not at all offended by his abrupt departure—well, only a little—Bridget watched him work his way toward a small, official-looking building that was most likely the shipping office. Even in his distress, William Black paced through the wharf with those same fluid, masculine, ground-eating strides she'd noticed earlier.

Her heart heavy with the distress of bearing such devastating news, Bridget continued staring after him until he disappeared inside the building. She might have sighed a few times in the process.

What would Will do if his bride was the young woman who had died aboard ship? Why did it matter so much to her? Why did she sense there was more to his story, something tragic that made this news so much worse?

Caught up in her troubling thoughts, she didn't notice Nora's approach until a firm hand gripped her shoulder. She nearly jumped out of her boots. Spinning around, she glared at her sister. "Nora! You scared me half to death."

"So sorry." She didn't look remorseful in the least. "But I did call your name three times. You didn't answer."

"My mind was otherwise engaged."

"I figured as much." She hitched her chin in the direction of the building. "How did he take the news?"

"Not well." Bridget sighed. "Not well at all."

"I don't suppose anyone in his situation would."

"No." She lowered her gaze and noted that Nora's arms were empty. Completely empty. Terrible possibilities filled her mind. A wordless cry lodged in her throat. "Where's Grace?"

"Maeve has her. The two of them are sitting with our luggage while Flynn is over by the street hiring a carriage. Come, Bridget." Nora tugged on her arm. "Our new home is waiting."

Their new home. She'd almost forgotten why she was here in America. And no wonder. Her excitement had been dampened by the unfortunate incident with William Black. Or rather, Will, as he'd first introduced himself and then later asked her to call him. Proper or not, she would forever think of him as *Will*.

Again she wondered why he had sent all the way to Ireland for a bride. What was the rest of his story? *And what will he do if his bride is dead?*

Bridget wished there was more she could do to help the man, and perhaps there was. An idea began formulating in her brain, one that might not bring Will the good news he hoped for but at least would give him accurate information. As her dear mother used to say, it was always easier to plan once you had all the facts.

With that in mind, Bridget hurried ahead of Nora, eyeing the pile of luggage where her sister Maeve waited with baby Grace cradled in her arms.

Was someone out there missing the tiny infant? If that was so, why hadn't she, or perhaps even he, come forward to claim the child? What terrible event had occurred to warrant abandoning a newborn in the ship's galley?

They may never find a definitive answer.

And Bridget had another pressing matter to address, one she hoped would bring Will certainty if not relief.

As she stopped in front of her youngest sister, Bridget couldn't help but notice how good Maeve and Grace looked together, how natural.

Maeve had left her hair falling in loose curls down her back. Like Bridget and Nora, she wore her new dress, as well. Hers was a French plaid, the orange, yellow and green setting off her coloring. Her rich strawberry-blond hair had turned a soft ginger in the sunlight and she looked as pretty as a picture as she smiled down at the baby.

Maeve would make a wonderful mother, evidenced by the careful attention she showed Grace now. Bridget once again experienced a pang of regret. Had Daniel wanted to marry her, had he followed through with his promise, she could be holding her own baby right now.

Bridget didn't take the time to linger over the thought. "Maeve, where's your husband?" Impatience made her voice just short of shrill. "I need Flynn at once."

"What's the rush?" Maeve's eyes widened. "Has someone been hurt?"

"No, nothing like that." Bridget shook her head decisively. "But I need Flynn's help right now."

"Whatever for?" Maeve's eyes narrowed in confusion.

Holding on to the last thread of her patience, Bridget quickly explained Will's situation. Nora added what she thought she remembered about the girl who'd fallen from the forecastle. Between the two of them they laid out the sequence of events as best they could recall.

When they finished Maeve's gaze turned thoughtful, then sad. From that look alone, Bridget knew her sister remembered the day the girl in question had died. Maeve never forgot a patient, nor did Flynn for that matter, but this one's death was especially heartbreaking.

"Do you remember her?" Bridget asked, trying her best to keep her voice steady. "Did you ever discover her name? Was she Bridget? Bridget Collins?"

Maeve's eyes misted slightly, a small switch in mood, easily missed if Bridget hadn't been looking. "As the ship's doctor, and custodian of all the medical records on board, Flynn would be the one to ask."

Bridget wasn't fooled by her sister's evasive words. Maeve knew the answer, but wasn't saying anything more.

"Please, Maeve. It's important. Will has been searching for his bride all morning, wondering why he can't find her. Wouldn't it be best for him to know the truth, whatever it is, even if it's bad news?"

"You know I can't give you that information, Bridget." An apology settled in Maeve's eyes. "I was only an assistant in the infirmary. You'll have to ask Flynn."

"Ask me what?"

Bridget swung around at the sound of the familiar deep voice, her gaze landing squarely on Maeve's new husband, Dr. Flynn Gallagher. Or rather, her gaze landed on Dr. Flynn Gallagher's black cravat.

The man was taller than any of the Murphy sisters, even Nora. He was muscular and lean like William Black, just as handsome and so in love with his new wife that he reflexively looked to Maeve for the answer to his question as though she was the only one in their tiny group.

Maeve nodded to Bridget. "Go on," she urged. "Tell him what you just told me."

Practically shaking with impatience, Bridget went through the story again, faster this time and without waiting for Nora's input. Just as she drew to the end of the tale she caught sight of Will exiting the building he'd entered only a few moments before. Head down, jaw firm, he approached yet another group of passengers.

He must have been unsuccessful in the shipping office.

"There." She pointed to Will. "That's him, the man approaching that small cluster of people."

Her hand moved instinctively in his direction, aching to soothe away his worries. She started out.

"No, Bridget." Flynn stopped her with a gentle hand on her arm. "You've done your duty. Let me handle the rest."

"But—"

"I insist you stay here with your sisters." He shared a look with his wife, one that seemed to communicate a message only the two of them understood.

Maeve quickly stood, handed the baby to Nora and then drew alongside her husband. Side by side they made a dazzling pair.

"It'll be all right, Bridget." Maeve touched her arm and smiled. "Flynn will handle the matter with great care, like he always does."

Flynn dropped a tender kiss to Maeve's forehead. "I'll be back shortly."

He left them to stare after his retreating back.

Bridget had always considered herself an obedient woman, one who usually adhered to the Christian precepts of ideal female behavior. Her manners were impeccable, as well. Consequently she shocked even herself when she trotted after Flynn, all the while ignoring Maeve's cries to leave the matter alone, that it didn't concern her. The same words Nora had used earlier.

She knew it didn't concern her. And yet, somehow, after all that had happened, it did.

She picked up her pace.

With determination on her side, and the element of surprise, she bypassed Flynn at the last possible moment and approached Will first.

As though sensing her standing behind him, he turned to face her at the very same moment she spoke his name.

He seemed stunned to see her again. "Bridget?"

Breathless from her rapid trek across the docks, her words came out in a jumbled rush. "I have brought someone to help you find your bride, or at least give you more information."

The look in his blue, blue eyes plainly said: *What are you talking about?*

"The ship's doctor," she said in reply, her heart pounding with the force of her urgency. "I have come to introduce you."

She didn't have time to explain further before Flynn closed the distance between them.

Will lifted his gaze from her to Flynn then thrust out his hand. "William Black."

With his characteristic professional manner, Flynn took the offered hand. "Flynn Gallagher, the doctor in charge of the infirmary on the *Annie McGee*."

Will wasted no time getting to the point. "Do you know what happened to Bridget Collins on the voyage over?"

The ensuing silence pressed in on them all. Will looked so concerned, so in need of kindness. Bridget almost went to him and wrapped her arms around him.

"I believe I can enlighten you." Flynn's expression was that of a man about to give the most terrible news of all.

Will must have understood what was about to come because he asked, "Is she…dead?"

"I'm afraid that she—" Flynn cut off the rest of his words and looked down at Bridget. He frowned at her briefly then returned his attention to Will. "Perhaps we should continue this conversation aboard the *Annie McGee*. Just the two of us."

Bridget opened her mouth to object, but Flynn stopped her with a look. "My dear Bridget," he said, his voice filled with equal parts authority and understanding. "You must wait with your sisters while I escort Mr. Black to the infirmary."

And with that one sentence her *dear* brother-in-law had revealed his intentions. He had no plans of allowing her to accompany them any further. Perhaps, like Maeve and Nora, he didn't think the matter was any of her business.

Did Will agree? She glanced into his vivid expression and discovered her answer. He didn't want her in the infirmary with him, either.

Horrified to feel the sting of tears, she lowered her gaze and concentrated blindly on the wooden dock below her feet. She knew the matter was none of her business, and yet...

And yet...

They were all correct. She had no right to insinuate herself into a stranger's private affairs. She should have realized that sooner. Her concern had made her act impulsively, perhaps even rudely. She'd meddled, something so unlike her that her cheeks began to flame.

Clenching her fingers into the material of her skirt, she forced a pleasant smile onto her lips. "I will tell Maeve where you are."

"No." Flynn's voice stopped her from leaving. "On second thought, please have my wife join Mr. Black and me in the infirmary."

Hard as she tried to remain calm, Bridget cast him a dark look. Why would Flynn allow his wife to accompany him on this errand and not her?

He answered her unspoken question aloud. "Your

sister was my assistant, Bridget. As such, she was in charge of keeping the medical records in order. Maeve will know precisely where to look for the information Mr. Black needs."

How could Bridget possibly argue with that bit of logic? "Of course." She released her death grip on her skirt. "I will tell her to find you at once."

Before she turned to go, Will covered her hand with the reassuring pressure of his own. "Thank you, Bridget." He squeezed gently. "Thank you for your help and…*thank you.*"

For a moment she stared down at his fingers wrapped around her own, wondering why she experienced that mystifying feeling again, the one where puzzle pieces seemed to be fitting together perfectly. "Oh, Will, you are quite welcome."

He released her hand.

This time when she turned to go, neither man stopped her. As she made her way back across the docks, for good this time, Bridget only looked back in Will's direction once. All right, twice. She only looked back twice.

Chapter Four

As it turned out, Flynn and Maeve did not accompany them to Faith Glen. The last Bridget saw of the pair were their retreating backs as they climbed the gangplank, with William Black following closely behind. Maeve had told Nora and Bridget to go on without them and Nora, efficient to a fault, had them on the road in no time at all.

If Bridget was truthful with herself she'd admit she wasn't completely sorry Maeve and Flynn weren't making the trip to the new town just yet. Since Flynn had a house in Boston, she knew they would be just fine on their own. Better than fine. Although Bridget would miss her sister dreadfully, the newlyweds needed time alone.

That left Bridget and Nora the task of claiming the house bequeathed to their mother. Her stomach rolled at the thought, at the possibility all may not turn out as they hoped. The rocking of the carriage added to her queasiness.

Swallowing back her nausea, she focused on the scenery passing by. The countryside was very green, the gently rolling hills much like the ones they'd left back in Ireland. The lingering sound and smell of the ocean was familiar, as well.

A sense of homecoming filled her.

She caught Nora's eye.

Her sister smiled. "I've directed the driver to stop at the Sheriff's Office before we head to the house."

"I suppose it's for the best." She tried not to sigh again. She'd done quite enough of that for one day. "I assume you plan to publicly announce Grace is in our care?"

"It's the right thing to do, Bridget. She's not ours."

"She feels like ours."

"Yes, she does." Nora's eyes filled with tears. She lowered her head and whispered, *"Grá mo chroí."* *Sweetheart* in Gaelic.

The baby's little eyelids fluttered open and she yawned. Nora was already rummaging in her bag. A few seconds later and Grace suckled a bottle of milk in noisy contentment.

Leaning her head against the cushions behind her, Nora breathed out deeply.

"Tired?" Bridget asked.

"A bit. But excited, too." She straightened. "We should probably show the deed to the sheriff while we're there. If nothing else, he'll be able to direct us to the house."

Or take it away from them. "Oh, Nora. What if the deed isn't legal?"

The horrible scenario was possible. Laird O'Malley, a former suitor of their mother's, had left for America years ago. He'd been heartbroken their mother hadn't wanted to marry him, but not enough that he'd lost hope she would one day change her mind.

He'd built her a house in Faith Glen and had put the deed of ownership in her name. The wording had made it possible for Colleen Murphy's daughters to inherit the property.

Or so they were all counting on.

But what if they were wrong? What if the property wasn't theirs for the taking? This entire trip to America had hinged on that promise.

As though sensing where her mind had gone, Nora nudged Bridget's foot with the toe of her boot. "You leave the worrying to me, Bridget Murphy. I had the document verified in Ireland. Everything will work out fine."

"Who are you trying to convince? Me or you?"

Nora patently ignored the question. "We'll stop at the Sheriff's Office, report Grace's situation and then head to our new home."

Their new home. What a wonderful, exciting, terrifying prospect. But what if the deed wasn't legal, or if the house had been torn down?

Faith. All she needed was a little more faith.

Stiffening her spine, Bridget turned her attention back to the passing scenery. The road ran parallel to a small, fast-moving river. If she closed her eyes she could envision walking the high banks, dipping her toes in the fresh, cool water. There was a man by her side. A tall man with dark hair and blue eyes the color of the midday sky. The haunted look was gone from his expression and...

Bridget quickly snapped open her eyes. William Black was not the man of her dreams. He couldn't be. There was no man in her dreams—not after what Daniel had done. And even if, sometime in the future, she let herself trust a man enough to consider love and marriage—well, surely Will wouldn't be the man at her side. For all she knew he'd sorted out the situation with his missing bride and was at this very moment escorting the woman to his home in Boston.

She paused midthought, realizing it would do her no good to dwell on a man she would never see again.

Determined to put William Black out of her mind, her gaze landed on a sizable building, a mill of some sort. The large wheel churning in the river filled the moment with the happy, trickling sound of rushing water. The scent wafting in the air was nothing she'd ever smelled before, a heavy, almost sweet aroma.

Delighted, Bridget leaned out the carriage window. A few moments later they crested a hill and a small village came into view. The large green-and-white wooden sign in the shape of a rectangle identified the town as Faith Glen.

The main feature of the town was a tidy village square. A white clapboard church dominated all the other buildings. A general store sat on one side of the church and on the other was—Bridget squinted to read the sign hooked to the porch ceiling—Rose's Boardinghouse.

On the opposite side of the square was the Sheriff's Office. The bars on the windows gave it away, as did the fact that the structure had been built out of stone. Not brick or wood like the other buildings in town, but solid stone.

"We're nearly there," Bridget said.

Nora pulled the bottle from Grace's mouth and gently swung the child to her shoulder. When the carriage drew to a stop Bridget scrambled out of the carriage ahead of her sister.

The driver, an older man with thinning hair and a thick, handlebar mustache, had already released the ropes securing their trunks and was fast at work unloading their belongings.

Bridget rushed forward. "What are you doing? We haven't reached our final destination yet."

"This is as far as I go, miss." His gruff voice had a Scottish burr underneath the words. And a hint of meanness.

"But Dr. Gallagher paid you to take us to our new home."

"He paid me enough to get you to the town," he corrected. "Not a foot more."

That was a bold-faced lie. Bridget knew Flynn would never leave them stranded like this.

"It's all right, Bridget," Nora said, exiting the carriage with sure steps. "We'll ask the sheriff for assistance once our business is complete."

Bridget relented, a little, but only because the driver was already in his seat and spurring his horses forward.

"Well, now." A deep, masculine voice drifted over her. "What have we here?"

Heart lodged in her throat, Bridget swung around to face a tall man with kind eyes. Blond-haired, blue-eyed, the man looked to be of Nordic descent. The tin star pinned to his chest told her she was staring at the sheriff of Faith Glen.

He was very handsome, in a rugged, earthy sort of way, and Bridget immediately noticed how Nora stood frozen in place, eyes blinking rapidly as she stared at him.

Bridget's sentiments exactly. In the next few minutes they would either lose Grace or their new home, perhaps both, or—God willing—take the next step in claiming a new life for themselves in America.

When Bridget and Nora continued staring at him, neither making a move to speak, the man smiled warmly. "I'm Cameron Long. The sheriff of Faith Glen." His gaze lingered a moment longer on Nora than Bridget. "What brings you two lovely women to our fair town?"

When Nora remained surprisingly silent under the

sheriff's scrutiny, Bridget stepped forward. "My name is Bridget Murphy and this is my sister Nora. We've just arrived from Ireland—"

Grace let out an earsplitting wail. Bridget smiled. "And *that* healthy-lunged child is Grace. One of the reasons we've come here today."

He glanced briefly at the bundle in Nora's arms, then proceeded to ignore Grace. "You've come to Faith Glen because of a baby?"

"No." Nora found her voice at last. "We came to *you* because of a baby."

His eyes widened ever-so-slightly. "Me?"

"You are the sheriff of Faith Glen?" Nora looked pointedly at his badge. "Are you not?"

Instead of being offended by the haughty tone, Cameron Long appeared amused. "I am, indeed."

His lips quirked at an attractive, lopsided angle, making him look even more handsome than before.

And if Bridget wasn't mistaken, she heard Nora's breath hitch in her throat. Interesting. But unsurprisingly, her sister recovered quickly and explained how they'd found the baby in the ship's galley. "When no one came to claim her, we realized the child had been abandoned. And we," Nora said as she smiled at Bridget, "plan to care for her until someone comes forward to claim her."

"Commendable, to be sure," he said, his eyes again holding Nora's a beat too long. "But that doesn't explain why you've brought the baby to me. Why not report her situation to the authorities in Boston?"

"Can you not do that for us?" Nora asked.

"Of course I can." He stuffed his hands in his pockets. "But that doesn't explain why you are *here,* in Faith Glen."

Nora turned to Bridget. "Show him the deed."

She dutifully reached inside her reticule and retrieved the precious document that had led them to America.

The sheriff accepted the deed and Bridget held her breath. After what seemed an endless eternity, he raised his head. "Who is Colleen Murphy?"

"Our mother," Nora answered. "She died ten years ago."

He considered her response a moment then redirected his gaze to the document once again.

"Is the deed legal or not?" Nora demanded, her patience evidently reaching its end.

"It would appear so."

"Well, then." She plucked the paper out of his hand, relief softening the tight lines around her mouth. "If you would be so kind as to direct us to our home we would be ever grateful."

"I'm afraid I can't do that."

Bridget gasped. "But you said the deed was legal."

"I said it *appears* to be legal." He ran a hand through his hair. "Unfortunately, there's no way of knowing for certain until we check your document against the official copy in the County Clerk's Office."

Bridget's heart sank. "But we were told the deed was all we needed to claim the property."

"That may be true in Ireland, but not in the state of Massachusetts. Every land deal requires two copies of the transaction." He spoke with genuine remorse, as though he understood how important this was to them.

"Two copies." Bridget pushed the words past a very tense jaw. No one had warned them of this possibility.

"The law originated back in the early colonial days," he explained. "When fraud was at a premium."

Nora rose to her full height. "We did not travel all this way to commit fraud."

"Didn't say that you had." He lifted his broad shoulders in a gesture surprisingly elegant for such a big man. "Nevertheless the law requires that the original deed be compared against the copy, the one that is kept in—"

"The County Clerk's Office," Nora finished for him. "And where is this…office?"

"In Dedham, about eight miles due north."

Bridget glanced at the afternoon sky in frustration. Even if they left now, there wouldn't be enough time to travel eight miles north and back again before the sun set.

"What are we going to do?" she whispered.

The question had been rhetorical, but the sheriff answered her anyway. "You will be able to verify the deed come Monday morning. I'll escort you there myself."

It was a gallant offer, but Monday was three days away.

"It's just a formality," he promised, his voice full of encouragement, his smile wide.

"Will you at least show us the house?" Bridget asked.

Not quite meeting her gaze, he shook his head no. "I would suggest you wait until we've verified ownership."

He wasn't telling them something, something important about the house. "But we only wish to see the property."

"Not today."

And with those concise words, spoken in the brief, decisive tone of a determined lawman, Bridget accepted the reality of the situation at last. She would have to put her dreams on hold for another three days. Three… more…days.

Early the next morning Will entered his private study with a heavy heart and a mind full of turmoil. Regret played with his composure as he lowered himself into the chair behind his desk and closed his hand in a tight fist. Bridget Collins had, indeed, fallen to her death. And now he was in possession of the girl's luggage, the undeniable proof of her identity.

Closing his eyes, he sucked in a harsh breath. He'd been responsible for the woman, having taken on the cost of her passage and ensuring the details of her trip were in order. Yet he'd failed her. And, in the process, his children, as well. His sad, motherless children.

Will swallowed back the hard ache rising in his throat. He was in no better position than before he'd decided to acquire a mail-order bride. Acquire. What a miserable way to put it, as though finding a wife was a matter of walking over to the general store and pointing to the woman he liked best. *There. That one, I want that one to be my wife.*

He should have known better.

Yet what other choice had there been? His aging mother was doing her best with the children. But the physical demands were taking their toll.

Running a hand through his hair, Will looked out the bay of windows on his right. The sun was making its grand entrance for the day, spreading tentative, golden fingers through the hazy dawn. A kaleidoscope of moving shadows flickered across the floor at his feet, creating an eerie accompaniment to his somber mood.

Pulling out the ledger he'd brought home with him from the mill, Will went to work. Despite the early hour, the air already felt hot and sticky and promised to turn unbearable once the sun was fully in the sky. He'd made the right decision to close the mill for the next two days. Grinding cocoa beans and turning them into blocks of chocolate was hot work on any given day. Deadly during a heat wave like this one.

Will was proud of the fact that the Huntley-Black Mill had a reputation for treating its workers well. He employed most of the residents of Faith Glen, including many of the Irish immigrants unable to find work elsewhere.

An unexpected image materialized in his head of the pretty Irish lass he'd met yesterday on the docks in Boston. Bridget Murphy had been beautiful and compassionate. But not his. *His* Bridget was dead.

"Forgive me," he whispered, rubbing his forehead with his palm. The gesture did nothing to relieve the ache growing stronger behind his eyes.

He had to find someone to care for his children, a stable woman who wouldn't leave them when boredom struck and then show up again when the round of parties ceased to amuse her. In other words, a woman nothing like their mother. At least in death Fanny had finally offered her children the consistency she'd denied them in life.

But her loss had still come at a cost to both Olivia and Caleb. They were far too subdued for their age. Will had never wanted perfect children in his home. He wanted *happy* children.

A tentative knock sounded at the door. He set down the quill and called out, "It's open."

The door creaked on its hinges and soon a head full of white-silver hair poked through the tiny opening.

"Well," his mother said with a smile. "You're up early."

"No earlier than usual."

"I suppose not." She stepped deeper into the room, looking especially tired this morning with the dull light emphasizing the purple shadows under her eyes.

He'd intended to bring home his new bride last night, one who would take the burden off his mother and love his children as much as he did. A beautiful woman with wild, dark hair, mesmerizing green eyes, a soft Irish lilt and…

Wrong woman, Will. You're thinking about the wrong woman.

He slammed the ledger shut. No more work today. Not for him, *or* his mother.

Rising, he shoved the chair out of his way and then circled around his desk. Everything in him softened as he caught sight of two small heads peeking out from behind his mother's skirts.

He might have vowed never to love another woman after Fanny, but Olivia and Caleb were a different matter altogether. His love for his twins grew daily, his heart nearly bursting with emotion at times like this.

If only he could figure out a way to let them know they were allowed to be happy, playful. Even noisy and messy sometimes. He feared they followed too closely after his own sober, saddened behavior, and wished he knew how to bring some joy into their lives. And his own.

"I see we have more early risers." He bent low enough to look into both children's eyes. "Good morning, Olivia, Caleb."

They each gave him a wobbly smile in return. Will hated these moments, when he couldn't read his own children's moods. Their three-year-old thoughts were impossible to decipher behind those solemn masks.

Nevertheless, he forged ahead. "Did you sleep well?"

"Yes, sir," they answered in unison, their words filled with that polite tone he dreaded most.

Hoping to alleviate their shyness, Will opened his arms in silent appeal and went for the direct approach. "Can I have a morning hug?"

Caleb toed the ornate rug at his feet, his eyes huge and luminous. Olivia's mouth slowly quirked into a sweet, tentative grin. A heartbeat later she rushed forward and flung her spindly arms around Will's neck.

His throat tightened.

With Olivia tucked in close, he reached out and ruffled Caleb's hair. The little boy lifted his chin, the look so full of adoration Will found himself struggling for his next breath. These two beautiful, perfect children were the best thing he'd done in his thirty years of life. He would not fail them.

Letting go of his shyness, Caleb launched himself into the air and landed on top of his sister, tumbling all three of them to the ground. Will shifted midair to soften the children's fall. In the next moment the sweetest sound of all filled the air. Laughter. His children were laughing.

Will levered himself onto an elbow. Peace filled him as he watched his smiling, happy children. But he knew the moment wouldn't last long. Far too soon they would grow somber again. His poor, innocent children had faced too much sorrow in their short lives, and here was the sad result. Even if they wanted to continue their moment of playfulness, they simply didn't know how.

He couldn't bear it. Not today. "What do you say we go on an outing, just the three of us?" Even Will was surprised at the words that had come out of his mouth. But then again, why *not* go on an outing? Maybe all three of them could use a lesson in having fun.

Both children froze, their mouths gaping open at him. Caleb was the first to speak. "Truly?"

Will confirmed it with a nod. "Truly."

"Where?" the little boy asked. "Where will we go?"

"Well…" For a moment his mind went blank. He hadn't thought that far ahead.

Olivia scrambled onto his lap. "Can we go to the store?" she asked with a hopeful smile.

The store? He'd had something a little more exciting in mind. Say, fishing. He hadn't gone fishing in years. Maybe even a decade, before his father had died. "I was thinking about taking you down to the river to try some fishing."

"Oh." Olivia clasped her hands together and her tiny shoulders heaved with the force of her disappointment.

Not the reaction he'd hoped for. "You don't want to go fishing, sweetheart?"

"I'll go with you, Papa." Caleb wiggled onto Will's lap.

"Well, I suppose I could, too, if…" Olivia turned her big blue eyes in his direction, "I can get a new dolly first."

Now her earlier suggestion to go to the store made sense. His daughter was mad about dolls.

"I think a new dolly is a definite possibility." He wrapped his arms around the children, pulling each of them close against his chest. "And perhaps a toy ship for Caleb."

Caleb gasped. "Truly?"

"Truly." Will squeezed both sets of shoulders. "Now go get dressed and then we'll leave."

They sped out of the room, Caleb leading the way. Will smiled after them, pleased by their excitement. They so rarely showed enthusiasm since their mother left.

He clenched his jaw against a jolt of ugly emotion. He tried not to give in to his anger, anger he could just as easily turn inward. Fanny might have started this, with her selfish abandonment of her family, but Will hadn't done enough to rectify the situation.

That changed today.

Chapter Five

Two. More. Days. Bridget thought she might go mad from the wait. She didn't know what to do with herself. Rose of Rose's Boardinghouse was friendly enough. She'd offered Bridget and Nora a place to stay until they discovered if Laird's house was theirs free and clear. But sitting in someone else's front parlor and sharing tea with a roomful of strangers, many also from Ireland, wasn't how Bridget wanted to spend her first full day in America.

The decor didn't help matters. The room was too ornate, the wallpaper too bold, the furniture too fragile. Taking tea in here, where she was afraid she might spill and ruin the brocade upholstery was—well, not something she wished to endure.

She decided to take a walk instead. She needed to be alone. To think. To plan. And, God forgive her, to worry. With their money running low, she and Nora would have to find jobs soon. But how many prospects were available in a town this size? Surely not many.

With nothing but her depressing thoughts to keep her company, Bridget allowed herself a moment to wallow as she made her way down the boardinghouse stairs.

Five steps out she'd remembered God's faithful promise: *Never will I leave you; never will I forsake you.*

It was a good reminder. So she handed her concerns to the Lord as best she could and made her way around the tidy square. Birds sang a happy tune, the smell of fresh grass and wildflowers wafted on the air, children laughed in the distance. A horse whinnied.

Her heart was already feeling lighter. Oh, the worry was still there, working into a hard knot in the pit of her stomach, but she was able to shove it aside momentarily and focus on her new home.

What treasures awaited her here? Bridget couldn't wait to find out. She quickened her steps, and stopped at the small building on the opposite side of the church.

The general store wasn't much to look at from the outside, but it beckoned her forward all the same. Once she pushed through the door, the pleasant smell of spices and lavender filled her nose. The aroma was followed by the scent of grain and oats and—she sniffed—licorice.

There were no other customers that she could tell, only astonishing amounts of merchandise. Bridget swept her gaze across barrels of dry goods, past the sacks of flour and shelves filled with kitchen utensils, canned goods and so much more. The store seemed to have every item imaginable for sale. She noted a counter that not only had jars filled with colorful candy but all sorts of children's toys. One whole row was dedicated to an array of dolls.

Delighted, Bridget decided to start there and work her way through the rest of the store at her leisure.

Her feet slowed, hesitated, then stopped altogether. She wasn't alone in the store after all. Two small children studied the shelves of toys in complete silence. They had their backs to Bridget and were huddled close together, hands joined, bodies pressed side by side. By their size, Bridget decided they were somewhere between three and four years old.

A range of emotions sped through her, concern foremost. Their little bodies were unnaturally still as they stared upward.

Why weren't they fidgeting? Or looking for trouble? Or reaching for the toys they wanted?

Why did they seem so solemn?

The urge to gather them close and comfort them surprised Bridget, especially since she hadn't yet seen either of their faces to determine if her impressions were correct. They could simply be well-behaved children.

Where were their parents?

She looked over her shoulder. Nobody else seemed to be in the store. Concern took hold.

But then the little girl angled her head and reached up to pull one of the dolls free. Her hand fell short of its goal. The little boy whispered something in her ear then attempted to help her, but his arm was too short, as well.

Bridget couldn't stand back and watch any longer. She approached the two with slow, careful steps.

"Hello." She plucked a doll from the shelf, one with a porcelain face behind a cloud of silvery-blond hair and clothed in a lovely, pale blue dress trimmed with white. "Is this what you wanted?"

The child's eyes widened. She didn't move right away, as if afraid to touch the doll, but then she reached out and skimmed a fingertip along the sleeve.

While she carefully inspected the doll's clothing, the boy watched. Bridget took the opportunity to study both children. They had the same color hair, a soft ginger, the same striking features and the same arresting blue eyes. These two were clearly related to one another.

No, not just related. Their similar size and nearly identical features, if a bit more delicate on the girl than the boy, indicated they were twins. They were as darling and as sad as she'd suspected.

The look in their eyes captured her sympathy. This time the feeling was so strong she nearly pulled them into a comforting hug. She didn't, of course. Such a bold move might scare them.

Yet as Bridget continued looking at them she realized they reminded her of someone, someone she couldn't quite place in her mind.

She stretched the doll closer to the child. "I'm sure it'll be all right if you hold her awhile."

The girl's gaze darted over her shoulder then back again. Finally she reached out and took the doll.

At the same moment the boy took a step to his left, away from Bridget. She gave him an encouraging smile but didn't make a move in his direction.

Shifting from one foot to another, he blinked at her with large, round eyes.

Bridget lowered to her knees and placed her hands flat on her thighs. "My name is Bridget." She kept her voice soft, her tone gentle. "What's yours?"

She directed the question at both children, but the little girl chose to answer.

"I'm Olivia." She tugged on the doll's dress with tentative fingers. "And that's my brother, Caleb."

"Well, Olivia and Caleb, it's a pleasure to meet you."

"You talk funny," Caleb said, scuffing his foot back and forth on the floor in a nervous gesture.

Bridget hid a smile at the bold statement. She loved the honesty in children, how they spoke the first thing that came into their minds. There was never any doubt as to what they meant, or how they felt.

She thought of Daniel, how he'd hurt her with his change of mind and mean accusations and...

This wasn't the time to think on such things.

"Well, Caleb," she began, still smiling, "I suppose I talk funny because I'm not from around here. I just arrived in America yesterday."

"You did?"

"Oh, yes, I came over from Ireland."

His little eyes rounded even more. "Where's that?"

"All the way across the ocean." She made a grand gesture with her arm, sweeping it in a wide arc. "I sailed on a large boat, a ship called the *Annie McGee* and I—"

The front door swept open with a bang, sufficiently cutting off the rest of her words.

"Caleb, Olivia." A deep, masculine voice rang out from the front of the store. "Where are you?" There was a note of worry in the voice.

Both children's faces brightened, but they made no move to run toward the man, as Bridget would have expected. Had they come to the store without permission?

That hardly seemed likely, given their timid natures.

Well, whatever the situation, Bridget would not leave them to face their fate alone.

Reaching out, she waited for one child then the other to place their hands in hers. Only then did she rise to her full height and turn the three of them toward the front of the store as a single unit.

After the briefest of hesitations, both Olivia and then Caleb leaned in against her legs. Their tiny weight brought such a sense of completion Bridget lost her ability to breathe for a brief moment.

She'd always loved children, but this—this feeling of rightness, of being in the perfect place at the ideal time was entirely new. And thrilling, as though she'd finally come home.

"Children!" The man's hint of worry was now full of unmistakable fear.

Yet all Bridget could think was that she knew that voice, had heard it before.

A thousand thoughts collided together in her mind. And then, as if this meeting had been destined from the beginning of time, planned by the Lord Himself, Bridget's mind grasped on to a single word swirling above the jumble in her head: *him*.

She could feel his approach, in the reverberation of his heels striking the wooden floor, each step filled with grave purpose.

He was heading her way.

But she couldn't see him yet.

And, thankfully, he couldn't see her. She needed a moment to prepare.

When the rich, masculine voice called for the children a third time, Bridget forced herself to reply. "Over here, on your right, by the toys."

The footsteps quickened.

She breathed in deeply and tightened her hold on the children. They responded in kind.

Half a heartbeat passed. And then...

He came into view. The one person Bridget hadn't been able to get out of her mind since arriving in America. William Black.

The moment his gaze connected with hers he came to a dead stop. Surprise registered in his eyes first. Then confusion. Followed by something she couldn't begin to decipher.

For several more seconds he stared at her, unmoving, not speaking.

Bridget was stuck in a similar state of shock.

Before either had a chance to recover, Olivia yanked her hand free of Bridget's and lunged forward, her doll raised in the air. "Papa, Papa. Look what I found."

* * *

Olivia's excited words barely registered in Will's mind. He struggled to moderate his breathing and calm his thoughts. But no matter how hard he tried to focus, he couldn't fully accept that he was staring into the mesmerizing eyes of Bridget Murphy.

She was here. In Faith Glen's general store.

Holding his son's hand.

Will's stomach performed a slow, unexpected roll. Was that confusion spinning around in his gut? A sense of foreboding? Nervousness, perhaps?

"Papa. *Papa.*" Olivia tugged on his pant leg. "I'm talking to you."

Will lowered his gaze. A tiny frown creased the soft skin between Olivia's slim brows.

Sometimes, he thought with a burst of affection, his daughter could be such a serious little creature.

In an effort to calm his child's worry, or whatever had put that look on her face, he smoothed his hand over her hair. "What have you found, my darling? Show me."

"A dolly." She thrust the toy higher, a slow grin spreading across her lips. "I couldn't reach her at first. The nice lady helped me get her down from the shelf."

The nice lady. Did his daughter mean Bridget? Bridget Murphy?

Will looked up again. This time he felt an actual impact when his eyes met Bridget's. Under her soft gaze something unexpected awakened deep within him, as though a part of him had been half asleep, poised and waiting to come alive until this precise moment.

Bridget smiled. The feeling dug deeper.

"Hello, Will."

He managed a short nod. "Bridget." He could think of nothing more to say.

Needing a moment, he dropped his chin and gazed

at his son. Will had never seen Caleb that at ease with a stranger. In fact, the boy was holding Bridget's hand with unmistakable confidence, as though he'd been doing so all his life.

"I see you've met my children." Will spoke past the lump in his throat.

"I have." Her gaze went blank a moment and then understanding filled her expression. The look said she'd put several missing pieces of the puzzle together in her mind. "Well, that explains it."

"Explains what, precisely?"

"Their eyes." Her voice softened. "They have your eyes."

How often had he heard that before? Too many times to count. But spoken in Bridget's soft Irish lilt, the compliment seemed to take on new meaning.

Olivia tugged on his pant leg again. "I like her, Papa."

He did, too. God help him, he liked her, too. Perhaps a bit too much. He'd been down this road before, to devastating results. Had he learned nothing from his mistakes?

Will swallowed back a wave of unease.

Unaware of his discomfort, Olivia skipped back to Bridget and took hold of her free hand.

A brief moment of silence passed. The three stood there, looking back at him with smiles on their faces. Bridget and his children looked comfortable together, happy, as if they were a family.

The sight nearly brought him to his knees.

There was no denying that Bridget Murphy, in her simple muslin dress and hair confined in a neat bun, looked the picture of a happy young mother spending the day with her children. An illusion, of course. A trick of the eye.

Again Will wondered why the woman was here in Faith Glen.

Perhaps her appearance on the scene, at this particular moment in time, was no accident, but a part of God's plan for all of them.

Is she our answer, Lord?

There was an easy way to find out. But not in front of the children. "Caleb, Olivia, have you picked out your toys yet?"

Olivia studied the blond-haired doll in her hand, looked up at Bridget, then shook her head decidedly. "I don't like this dolly anymore. I want one with brown hair—" she pointed up to Bridget "—like hers."

Although surprised, Will couldn't blame his daughter for her change in preference. Bridget had the loveliest head of hair he'd ever seen. He was sorry for the perfectly neat bun, sorrier than he should be. "Then go on and pick out a different one."

Olivia skipped off.

Caleb, however, wasn't budging from Bridget's side. He had that stubborn look on his face, the one Will knew all too well. The boy was staying put.

Before Will could decide how best to pry his son loose, Miss Murphy provided a solution of her own. "Caleb, I think I would very much enjoy a miniature boat to remind me of my trip across the ocean. Would you go pick one out for me?"

It was all the encouragement the boy needed. He rushed toward the display of toys with a promise to find her the very best one in the store.

Will's heart twisted in his chest. He hadn't seen his son that enthusiastic in a long time, maybe never.

He turned back to Bridget. She watched the children with a soft smile playing on her lips. She was really quite beautiful when she smiled like that.

The thought put Will immediately on guard.

The woman could be hiding a selfish heart behind that pleasant look. Or she could be exactly what she seemed, a lovely Irish lass worthy of his trust.

He was desperate enough to hope for the latter.

"When we met yesterday," he began, keeping his voice even, "I hadn't realized your final destination was Faith Glen."

She turned to look at him. "Nor I, you."

"You are staying with relatives?" He didn't recall any Murphys in town, but Bridget could have family living here under a different name, perhaps on her mother's side.

"No." She shook her head. "My sister and I are renting a room at Rose's Boardinghouse."

Although that didn't explain *why* she was in Faith Glen, Will nodded his understanding. "I see."

Her features suddenly shifted with concern and her cheeks turned a becoming pink. "Oh, you must think me terribly callous. I haven't yet asked you, what did you find out about your fiancée?" She touched his arm, the gesture full of compassion. "Please, tell me I was wrong about Miss Collins and that she is here in Faith Glen with you now."

As if hoping to find the woman in the store, she looked over his shoulder and scanned the immediate area behind him.

Will shoved back the despair that tried to rise within him. "Unfortunately the woman who died in the accident aboard ship was by all indications my intended." He had her baggage in his possession to prove it.

"Oh, Will." Her hand tightened on his arm. "I'm sorry for your loss."

He believed her, believed the sadness in her tone and the sympathy in her touch. Something in him, some need he hadn't known was there, wanted to rest inside all that gentle concern. If only for a moment.

He didn't dare. This wasn't about him. It had never been about him.

"Thank you for your condolences." His voice sounded as stiff as he felt. He hadn't met Bridget Collins. Her death was surreal to him. But that didn't mean he didn't feel sadness and guilt. Especially guilt.

Bridget must have sensed his shift in mood because her hand fell gently to her side. "Do your children know their new mother is de—" She cut herself off before finishing the word. "I mean, do they know Miss Collins is…gone?"

"No." He shook his head. "I thought it best not to tell them anything about her until she arrived, in case something happened on the journey over."

And something had happened, the worst possible something. Had Will not sent for Miss Collins, had he not insisted she come immediately, she might not have been in the wrong spot at the wrong time. She might still be alive today.

Forgive me, Lord, for putting the innocent woman in danger.

"Keeping your bride a secret until she arrived." Bridget's expression turned thoughtful. "That was rather wise of you."

Wise? No. He'd merely been protecting his children from the possibility of another disappointment. "Olivia and Caleb have endured enough broken promises in their short lives. I won't be responsible for adding another."

He hadn't meant to speak that plainly, regretted doing so the moment he noticed the change that came over Bridget. It was subtle, of course, and could mean anything, but she was no longer smiling.

"Would you say, then, that you are a man of your word?" She asked the question in an odd voice.

It was clear his answer mattered to her but he couldn't fathom why. "Yes. A man's word is his most valuable commodity in this life."

"I agree." Everything in her seemed to soften then, her eyes, her shoulders, even her smile. "What will you do now that you know the truth about your intended?"

He answered without hesitation. "Find another bride."

"I see."

She fell silent. As did Will. He could tell Bridget wasn't finished, though, by the way she studied him with her brows pulled together in a thoughtful expression. When she did speak again she seemed to choose her words with care. "Perhaps you should consider hiring a nanny, at least until you are able to find another bride."

"I've considered that option, but no." He gave one, decisive shake of his head. "I don't want my children getting used to someone who will eventually leave them like…" He let his words trail off.

No matter how comfortable he felt around Bridget, there were some subjects he couldn't share with her. Or anyone, for that matter. Only his mother knew the full truth behind Fanny's tragic death.

"Won't you at least consider me for the position? I have experience. Your children and I already get along. It would be a great honor to—"

"No." His tone indicated the discussion was over. His children already adored Bridget. If she took a position in his home, then changed her mind, where would that leave Olivia and Caleb? Hurt. Confused. Devastated.

The possibility of another upheaval in the twins' short lives wasn't worth the risk.

"I have considerable background as a nanny," Bridget continued. "And I could use the job. I would be willing to start immediately."

"I said no."

Her eyes widened at the vehemence in his tone. He hadn't meant to answer so abruptly, or so harshly, but he didn't want to get anyone's hopes up, not even his own.

Bridget glanced over at Olivia and Caleb. "I don't understand why you won't consider my suggestion."

"I know. And I'm sorry." But not sorry enough to explain himself further, his secret shame was his to bear alone.

Bridget might be willing to care for his children, now, but she had no real obligation to any of them. She could suddenly change her mind. Perhaps even meet a man one day and wish to become his wife.

Although...

What if Will made a different offer than the one she'd suggested? What if he supplied her with a more permanent position in his home, one that would solve the problem of losing her to another man?

"Bridget Murphy." He captured her hand in his and held on tight. "Would you consider becoming my wife?"

Chapter Six

His wife?

William Black was asking her to marry him? With only the benefit of a two-day acquaintance? This wasn't the first time Bridget had found herself rendered speechless by this man. She doubted it would be the last.

There was more to his story. Something terrible had happened, something that had left him feeling as though he had no other choice but to hire a bride.

What Bridget didn't understand was why a man like William Black, one with many obvious qualities to recommend him, would settle only for a wife and nothing else? He had to be holding part of the story back beyond the explanation he'd already given concerning his children.

The children. Poor little Olivia and Caleb. They were so sad, so lonely.

What sort of trauma had they endured? Perhaps the trouble had something to do with their mother, as did Will's refusal to consider anything but a wife. Bridget could practically feel the tension rolling off him as he waited for her answer.

"Oh, Will. Surely, you can't be serious."

"But I am."

Bridget opened her mouth to decline his offer, politely as possible, but he spoke over her. "You said you needed a job. What I'm offering is a much more permanent solution. I don't see the problem."

Where to start?

She stared at him, stunned by his words, but even more by the realization that part of her wanted to accept his proposal. "There are considerable problems with your request, but the first one that comes to mind is that we don't know one another."

"Most couples don't know one another on their wedding day." The way he said the words—with a clenched jaw and narrowed eyes—Bridget had to wonder what had happened in his first marriage to make him so cynical, so jaded.

Not that she didn't agree with him, at least in part. Her experience with Daniel had taught her that many men and women walked down the aisle with half their story hidden.

What had she really known of her fiancé? Not enough to predict that last, hurtful conversation with him.

A hot tingle of shame tried to steal her breath. She swallowed the sensation away.

"You said you weren't married when we met yesterday," he pointed out.

Will's tone as much as his words had her lifting her head to meet his gaze. "Yes, that's what I said."

"Has that changed?" he asked.

"No." She actually felt a smile tug at her lips. "My marital status has not changed in a day."

"Then I don't see the dilemma." He lifted a single eyebrow. "Our marriage would be a formal arrangement only, if that is what concerns you."

As though realizing he'd said quite enough, he clamped his mouth shut and waited for Bridget to speak.

Again Bridget had no idea how to respond. He offered a marriage of convenience, one in name only, as if there were no real difference between a nanny and a wife other than an exchange of vows in front of God and a handful of witnesses.

Sadly enough, had he presented his proposal in a more romantic manner, had there been hope of something more between them, at least in the future, Bridget might have been tempted to accept his offer.

Unlike Daniel, Will was a man of his word. Or so he claimed. She leaned toward believing him. She even trusted he would never hurt her intentionally. After all, his actions spoke for themselves. He'd withheld the news of his future bride from his children in case something happened. Which, of course, something had.

Bridget knew firsthand the pain that came from broken promises, the disappointment and humiliation. Will had wisely spared his children.

There was no doubt he loved Olivia and Caleb. And they adored him in return. All three of them needed someone to bring joy into their lives.

Bridget wanted to be that person. She wanted to erase those haunted expressions in their eyes, the look that never seemed to go away. But she would *not* do so as Will's wife. Ever since Daniel had left her at the altar—literally—she had promised herself only the greatest of love would induce her into matrimony. Surely she wasn't ready for that kind of love yet. Not with her heart still healing. And definitely not with a man who wanted a marriage in name only.

No. No matter how much she wanted to help this family, she could not accept Will's offer of marriage.

"I'm sorry." The words were hard to say. Bridget was not one to turn away people in need, especially children. "I simply cannot become your wife."

His jaw clenched tight. So tight, in fact, that she could see the pulse ticking in his neck.

Wanting to soothe him, Bridget reached out and touched his arm. A jolt of awareness took hold. She quickly dropped her hand. "If you ever change your mind, I would still consider a position in your home as the children's nanny."

"No." He shook his head, his mouth a grim slash. "I won't have them grow to love you if you don't plan to stay permanently."

She had to appreciate his conviction, even if she didn't completely understand what motivated his decision. "Then I'm afraid we are at an impasse."

"So it would seem."

Bridget lowered her head again. What terrible pain had Will and his children suffered that made him want a marriage in name only? Why was he so bent on taking a wife that he would settle for nothing less?

She had no idea how to continue this strange, intimate discussion.

Thankfully, Olivia stepped into the conversational void. "Look, look, Miss Bridget, I found another dolly. And she has hair just like yours. See?"

"Well, isn't that something?" Bridget fingered the doll's pretty lavender dress, the same color as her own, then ran a hand down the brown curls that were a close match, as well.

Will reached out to the doll just as Caleb swerved past him and skidded to a stop inches short of colliding into Bridget's legs. "I found it, Miss Bridget. I found the perfect boat for you."

Smiling at the little boy's eagerness, she focused on Caleb next. In his tiny hand he held an exact eight-inch replica of the ship she'd disembarked only yesterday. The toy was made out of wood and string and had re-

markably accurate detail, all the way down to the individual sails.

"Why, Caleb, that looks just like the *Annie McGee.*"

He turned it over in his hand. "Truly?"

"Oh, yes. Look. Right here—" she pointed to a spot
on the ship "—those small round white dots are windows. On a ship they're called portholes."

"Portholes," he repeated, chewing on the word a moment before turning the boat around to face her. "What's
this called?"

"The wheelhouse. And this is…" She thought for a
moment, decided to go simple. "The main deck."

"More," he demanded. "Show me more."

Like most boys his age, Caleb Black had an eager,
inquisitive mind. He would be a joy to teach, if only his
father would give her a chance. For the next few moments Bridget busied herself explaining various points
of interest on the toy.

Caleb stayed alert throughout. Olivia, however,
watched them with dwindling interest, the doll cradled
in her arms pulling her attention away quite effectively.

As each moment passed, Bridget experienced a pang
of regret. Both children were utterly charming, even
in their reserve. Sensing their father's eyes on her, she
turned and noted the disappointment radiating out of
him, a feeling she shared.

Oh, Lord, if only…

No, there could be no *if only* in this situation. Bridget
would not wed William Black, no matter how much
she liked his children. Marrying a man like him, with
his desire for a wife in name only, could only end in
heartache for her. And for his children, as well. Possibly even for Will.

She glanced at him. His posture said it all. He'd finally accepted defeat. "Children, we should be on our way. Tell Miss Bridget goodbye."

In unison they swung to face him. Caleb spoke for them both. "But we were just starting to have fun."

"We need to check on Nene before we head out to the river."

"Nene?" Bridget asked before she could stop herself. She usually wasn't quite so curious, but this man had asked her to become his wife. Didn't that give her certain rights?

"Nene is my mother," Will said, his tone full of quiet gravity. "Caleb gave her the name when he first started speaking."

Confused, Bridget cocked her head. "I don't understand."

"Her given name is Naomi Esther Black. She usually goes by Esther but Caleb must have heard her full name and tried to say it and—"

"Nene was what came out."

"Precisely."

A moment of understanding passed between them. And then, William Black smiled. He actually *smiled*. The gesture revealed a hidden dimple in his left cheek and Bridget's heart stuttered. She'd never met a more handsome man. For a moment she considered accepting his offer of marriage right there on the spot.

She kept her mouth firmly shut.

Farewells were said far too quickly, purchases were made for the twins, and with more sorrow than she would have expected Bridget watched the Black family troop out of the store.

At the last moment Olivia looked over her shoulder. Bridget waved. The child returned the gesture.

And then...

They were gone.

They need me. The realization slammed through her so plainly Bridget stumbled back a step. It took every ounce of willpower not to chase after them and accept Will's proposal.

Instead she took a large pull of air and went to introduce herself to the store owner.

A quarter of an hour later Bridget made her way back to the boardinghouse, her heart troubled. Hattie James, the sole proprietress of Faith Glen's general store, had been a kind, if somewhat severe older woman with iron-gray hair, weathered features and an infectious laugh. Bridget had liked the woman well enough, but her mind had been too full of William Black and his children to engage in a lengthy conversation.

If Will would just give in and accept Bridget's help, on *her* terms, maybe those children of his would smile more often.

Lord, surely something can be done.

No solution came to her, not even when she squeezed her eyes shut and prayed harder.

Head down, she rounded the last corner to the boardinghouse and nearly collided into Cameron Long.

"Oh." She reared back, nearly losing her balance. "Pardon me, Sheriff."

"My fault." Although he appeared to be leaving he changed direction and joined her on the boardinghouse's walkway, matching her step for step as they commandeered the stairs together.

Bridget couldn't help but wonder what business had brought him here on a Saturday.

Then she caught sight of Nora's face. Her sister looked very pleased with herself, happy even. Perhaps the sheriff had told her the house was theirs and they could move in right away. There was no need to travel to the County Clerk's Office after all.

For the first time since arriving in Faith Glen, Bridget let excitement settle over her. Her feet barely hit the porch as she hurried to Nora's side.

"You've had news about the house."

"Sadly, no." Nora shook her head, her gaze sweeping past Bridget a moment to land on the sheriff. She lowered her eyelashes.

"Oh." Bridget tried not to pout like an unhappy child who hadn't gotten her way.

To her surprise, when Nora lifted her head she was still smiling. "Now don't look so down, dear sister. Sheriff Long has brought other news almost as exciting."

What could possibly be as exciting as finding out they owned Laird O'Malley's house? Bridget looked from the sheriff to Nora and back again.

Neither seemed willing to take the lead in the conversation now that the subject had been broached.

"Well?" she prompted. "Won't someone tell me the news?"

"Cameron has agreed to hire one of us to cook and clean for him and his deputy on a regular basis."

Cameron was it? Nora was on a first-name basis with the sheriff already? How...intriguing.

And completely beside the point.

Bridget smoothed her hands down her skirt, unsure why she wasn't more pleased by this new bit of information. Perhaps she was still sad over the situation with Will and his children. If matters had gone her way Bridget would be bearing good news, as well.

Nevertheless with their money draining away faster than expected due to their boardinghouse stay, this job offer was a blessing, an answer to prayer. "That's very kind of you, Sheriff."

"Not so kind." He shrugged off her compliment, looking oddly embarrassed. "More like selfish. My deputy and I have been sharing the duties these past few years, to disastrous results. It's a wonder one of us hasn't killed the other."

He smiled, as though he'd told a rather funny joke.

Bridget couldn't help but smile back.

"The duties would include cleaning the living quarters and jail cells, as well as feeding any prisoners that might spend the night behind bars. Of course that's a rare occurrence," he said when Nora gasped. "There's a no-saloon ordinance and a strong Christian presence in Faith Glen. We're a peaceful community."

Bridget had already come to that conclusion after her walk this morning. But she was happy to hear her assumptions confirmed from the sheriff's own mouth.

"I'll pay a fair salary." The number he mentioned was more than fair. "But the hours will be long, sunrise to sunset."

"That's only to be expected," Bridget said, chewing on the information.

As wonderful as the offer was she had one main concern: the sweet bundle sleeping peacefully in the bassinet beside Nora.

If Will decided to change his mind and hired Bridget as his children's nanny—*oh, please, Lord*—she wasn't sure the offer would include Grace, as well. And even if it did, Nora would never give up the child for any great length of time. She'd grown uncommonly attached.

Under the circumstances it was best to make certain the matter was settled before her sister's first day of work. "Would Nora be able to bring baby Grace with her?"

The sheriff stared at her as though he didn't understand the question.

Nora looked at her with the same glazed expression in her eyes.

Bridget glanced from one to the other, wondering at their odd reaction to a simple question. Was she missing something? Had she struck some unknown point of contention between them?

Seconds ticked by. Neither Nora nor Sheriff Long would look at one another. Or Bridget for that matter.

What had happened while she'd been at the general store?

"Nora?"

Her sister moved a small step away from the sheriff, enough to make her point without appearing rude. "I was thinking you would take the job."

"Me?" Bridget didn't bother hiding her surprise. "But you're the better cook."

"You are competent, as well."

Competent, yes, while Nora was exceptional. The sheriff and his deputy deserved the best cook possible. After all, they were the reason this peaceful community was, well, peaceful.

"Bridget, we have to consider what's best for the baby. Considering all she's been through, Grace—"

"Can come with you during the day," Cameron Long said, putting an end to the rest of Nora's argument.

Before either could change their minds, Bridget spoke first. "Then it's settled. Nora will start Tuesday." The day after they met with the county clerk and discovered the truth about Laird's house—*their* house.

"That'll be fine." The sheriff stuffed his hat on his head. "I'll see you both bright and early Monday morning."

He turned and started down the steps.

Bridget called after his retreating back. "Sheriff, wait."

He paused, but didn't turn around right away.

"Won't you consider showing us the house today?"

At that bold statement he turned slowly around, his movements precise, his expression hidden under his hat.

"There's a lot of day left," she persisted, deciding she had little to lose at this point. "Surely, there would be no harm in us taking a brief look at the house."

For a moment he seemed to debate silently with himself. Bridget shared a look with Nora. Neither dared break the silence, in case the man was using the time to rethink his earlier decision.

"Ordinarily I would agree with you." He thrust out a heavy sigh. "But there's an elderly couple in residence who've been acting as caretakers for the past seven years. For all intents and purposes, Laird's house is their home now. They have no place else to go."

Bridget gasped at the implication she heard in his words, finally understanding the man's reticence and yet offended all the same. "We would never throw an elderly couple off our property."

The Murphy sisters knew better than most what it meant to be tossed off land they'd considered their home. In their case, back in Ireland, it had been simply because the landlord decided to offer the tiny piece of property to his own kin. To suggest they would do the same was woefully incorrect.

"You go too far, Sheriff Long," Nora added, returning to the formal address as if to make a point. "We would certainly allow this couple to stay on as long as they wish, indefinitely if need be."

"That's good to know." He seemed relieved, even as his gaze darted from Nora to Bridget and back again.

"But I still recommend you verify ownership before you undertake the half-mile journey to the house."

As was true the first time they'd had this conversation, Bridget sensed the sheriff was withholding information, something more than this business with the elderly caretakers, something to do with the house itself.

A sliver of panic sliced through her. Nora must have had a similar reaction because she straightened her spine even further. "What are you hiding from us, Sheriff?"

He bristled at her tone, or perhaps the overly formal use of his title. "Now don't go getting all high and mighty on me, Nora Murphy. I'm only trying to save you both added grief. At the moment the house isn't, shall we say, presentable."

Bridget didn't like the sound of that. How bad could it be? Apparently bad enough that he felt the need to warn them.

She refused to be daunted. They'd survived the potato famine and being thrown off the land they'd called home all their lives. They could handle a house not quite presentable, especially if it was *their* house.

"Sheriff Long, please," Bridget pleaded. "We would like to see the house and decide for ourselves what sort of condition it is in."

"I see I cannot dissuade either of you." He whipped off his hat and speared his fingers through his hair. "If you insist—"

"We do."

"Then I'll take you over tomorrow, after the church service has let out."

Bridget clasped her hands together, her spirits lifting by the second. "That would be lovely."

"Yes," Nora agreed, her shoulders relaxing ever-so-slightly. "Yes, it would."

"If I were you—" he crammed his hat back on his head "—I'd hold off your excitement until you see the place."

With that simple warning Bridget knew, knew for sure, that there was something dreadfully wrong with the house. And yet, her excitement remained. If the elderly caretakers still lived there, then the structure was at least habitable.

At the moment that was good enough for her.

Chapter Seven

Will strode along the lane with two cautiously excited children in tow. His sad, despondent twins of mere hours before had lightened somehow. The solemness from before wasn't entirely gone, but now it seemed to be mingled with hope. All because of a short visit to the general store and a fortuitous meeting with a beautiful young woman.

Relief, joy, disappointment…he hadn't known it was possible to experience this many conflicting emotions all at once. Uncomfortable with the sensation, he shoved every unwanted feeling aside and focused on his children. His *happy* children, he noted.

Olivia was walking sedately, but she was smiling broadly, her new doll clutched desperately against her heart. Caleb's expression was more serious, but he darted around her, bobbing his ship in the air as though the tiny boat rode a series of invisible waves. The toy was identical to the one he'd found for Bridget.

Neither child appeared to notice the suffocating, thick heat. They were too contented.

Will wiped at the sweat on his brow and looked back over his shoulder, wondering where the pretty Irish lass was now.

Bridget Murphy had accomplished a task no one had been able to do in over a year. She'd made his children smile with genuine pleasure on their faces.

Was it any wonder he'd asked her to marry him?

He'd acted rashly, he knew, and contemplated his own behavior with a slice of concern now that he had a moment to think clearly. The instant his eyes had landed on Bridget at the store he'd discovered the pull of attraction between them was still there, stronger than before, tugging at a hidden place deep within him that had whispered: *she's the one you've been searching for.*

His throat tightened with emotion. There was no denying she was beautiful, soft-spoken and outwardly kind. But Fanny had been all of those things when he'd first met her, too. In his wife's case, the facade of a sweet, untouched innocent had been a lie. Consequently she'd taught him never to trust a first impression, or a second or even a third.

Like Fanny, Bridget could be hiding unseemly qualities below that pretty, engaging surface of hers.

His steps faltered.

When had he become so cynical, so jaded? Had he missed all the signs of a good, honest, trustworthy woman because he'd been expecting to find a dishonest one?

Unhappy with all this introspection—Will hated introspection—he drew in a deep, slow, steadying breath and swerved around a branch on the pathway.

Stick to his original plan; that was what he must do. All he really needed in a wife was a woman who would be good to his children.

Bridget has been that, and more.

Will shoved aside the thought. She had refused his proposal and that was the end of the matter. He would start his search for another bride first thing Monday morning.

For now he would enjoy the day with his children.

After rounding the final corner to their home, the twins raced up the stairs leading to the front door. Caleb rushed ahead of Olivia.

"Nene! Come see what Papa bought me." The little boy shouted in a high-pitched, excited voice, his words tumbling over one another. "It's a ship. And Olivia has her very own dolly with brown hair. Brown hair!"

"Well, honestly, I've never heard so much yelling in all my life." Will's mother entered the hallway, her feet shuffling slowly across the wooden floor in the way she did when her hip was bothering her. "What's all this excitement about?"

Shutting the door with a soft click, Will turned and studied his mother more closely. She appeared tired, more so than she had earlier, even with the added rest he'd provided her this morning.

He started to ask her how she was feeling, when Olivia skirted past him.

"Look, Nene." Her words flowed just as quickly out of her mouth as her brother's had. "Look at my new dolly. Isn't she pretty?"

The little girl planted a tender kiss on the porcelain cheek then thrust the doll in the air toward her grandmother.

Will's mother made a grand show of studying the toy carefully. "Oh, my, yes. She's very pretty. I especially like her long, curly, *brown* hair."

The color choice was significant. Until today, Olivia had chosen only blonde dolls for her private collection. It was clear Bridget Murphy had made an impression on his daughter. Will wasn't sure how he felt about that.

"She's not as pretty as Miss Bridget," Olivia added as she fingered the doll's hair. "But close."

"Miss Bridget? As in, Bridget..." His mother swept her shocked gaze up to Will. "Collins? Was there some mistake, and she's still ali—"

"No." Will gave a brief but fierce shake of his head, the gesture a silent warning to hold back the rest of her questions until they were alone. "The twins met Bridget Murphy."

He put considerable emphasis on the last name, willing his mother to understand that the woman the twins had met today was not the same one he'd intended to wed.

"You met *another* Bridget?" Her voice sounded incredulous.

Will lifted a shoulder. "It's a common Irish name."

"Is it?"

Will nodded, trying not to react to the reservation he saw in his mother's eyes. From the start Esther Black had been privy to every aspect of his search for a mail-order bride. She hadn't entirely approved, she'd made that clear enough, but after what Fanny had put them all through she'd understood.

Or so she'd claimed.

When he'd come home alone the night before, she had been full of sympathy, accepting his brief, pained explanation without pressing for details.

"Am I to assume that this Bridget... *Murphy* lives here in Faith Glen?" She angled her head at a curious tilt.

"It would appear so." Will looked everywhere but directly in his mother's gaze.

"I have never heard of her," she said.

"That's because she arrived on the *Annie McGee* just yesterday."

"The *Annie McGee?*" She obviously recognized the name. "How very…interesting."

It was a mistake, Will knew, to look straight into his mother's eyes, but he did so anyway. If only to prove he had nothing to hide. Which, of course, he didn't. The fact that he'd met a young woman named Bridget, who'd traveled to America on the very boat his intended bride had boarded, was simply a strange, unexpected coincidence.

Nothing more.

"William Black." She planted a fist on her hip. "You mean to tell me—"

"Yes, mother." He cut her off midsentence. "The children and I met a woman named Bridget in the general store this afternoon. And, yes, she traveled to America from Ireland on—" he gritted his teeth *"—The. Annie. McGee."*

She considered him a moment. "But she is not the woman you—"

"She is not." He didn't explain any further, not with Olivia and Caleb staring at him with large, rounded eyes and poised ears.

His mother must have noticed the children's interest because all she said was, *"Well."*

His sentiments exactly.

He hoped that was the end of the matter. He should have known better.

"And what, may I ask, brought this other Bridget to Faith Glen?"

"I don't know." As soon as the words left his mouth, Will was reminded again that he'd acted rashly today, dangerously so. He'd proposed marriage to a woman he hardly knew and hadn't bothered to acquire the most basic particulars of her life. Such as why she'd traveled all the way across the Atlantic only to land in Faith Glen, Massachusetts.

Was her presence a coincidence, as he'd thought earlier? Or God's providence?

He didn't know.

One thing was for certain. He should have asked Bridget about herself. Not because it would have been the polite thing to do—although that was certainly part of it—but because whatever had led her to settle in their small town might have given him a clue to her character.

She might be harboring a bitter secret, or running from a terrible scandal, though he doubted either scenario. The woman hadn't shown any signs of deceit. And he knew them all.

Suddenly Will was seized with a desire to learn every detail about Bridget Murphy, small and large. He wanted to know her hopes, her dreams. What she liked to do for fun. The titles of her favorite books. Did she have a strong faith in God? Did she trust the Lord to guide her daily path? Would she—

He cut off the rest of his thoughts, reminding himself Bridget's life was none of his concern. He had more important matters in which to attend, like finding a woman to care for his children on a permanent basis. A woman willing to accept a marriage in name only.

That didn't mean he couldn't assuage his curiosity about Bridget Murphy. As the largest employer in the area, he liked to know all the citizens of his community.

Faith Glen was a small town. It wouldn't be hard to locate her again, even easier to discover what had brought her to America in the first place.

He knew exactly where to start.

Cameron Long, the local sheriff and a good friend of Will's, made it his business to meet all the newcomers in town. After church tomorrow, Will would make a trip to the jailhouse. And find out exactly what sort of woman Bridget Murphy was under that sweet, pleasant exterior.

The next morning Bridget eyed Faith Glen's only church from the bottom of the perfectly measured steps. Situated directly across the town square from the jailhouse, the white clapboard structure with its tall steeple and thin iron cross on top rose majestically under the clear azure sky.

The building practically glowed beneath the sun's warm rays, beckoning Bridget forward. She climbed the first stair without hesitation, her gaze darting from left to right, right to left. Rows of square windows lined both sides of the wide double doors. Sunlight polished the glass into clear, sparkling diamonds.

Cradling a sleeping baby Grace in her arms, Nora matched her step for step. It was a shame Flynn and Maeve had sent their regrets and wouldn't be able to make a trip to Faith Glen for a few more days. Bridget understood why. Flynn's home was close by in Boston, yes, but they were newlyweds. They deserved time alone, just the two of them, while Bridget and Nora needed to get on with their own lives here in Faith Glen.

The moment they entered the church all heads turned in their direction. Although the attention was unnerving, Bridget had expected this blatant interest. She and Nora were strangers in town. But that wouldn't be true for long. Bridget would work hard at making friends here. Not only because she liked meeting new people, but because Faith Glen was her home now.

The Lord had guided them here, had protected them throughout the journey across the ocean. Bridget had to trust all would turn out well, if not exactly as they had planned.

She lifted up a silent prayer for courage, moved deeper into the building and set out down the center aisle ahead of Nora. Refusing to be intimidated by the undisguised curiosity, Bridget smiled at several individuals along the way. Thankfully all returned the gesture.

We're a peaceful community. The sheriff's words echoed in her mind, providing the courage she'd prayed for moments before.

Still smiling, Bridget took another step and stopped as two tiny voices shouted her name in unison.

"Miss Bridget," they squealed in unified delight. "Over here. Look, we're over here."

Turning her head slightly to her right, she caught sight of Caleb and Olivia Black two pews up. Dressed in their Sunday best, their hair combed and eyes shining, they waved in her direction.

Bridget waved back and then took note of the only other occupant in their pew. The children's father. William Black. Or rather, Will. His gaze locked with hers and for a moment everything stopped.

Bridget blinked, her mouth opened then closed. The man's eyes were as remarkable as she remembered, the color still the same pure blue as a cloudless sky.

Holding her steady in his gaze, he smiled.

Something deep within her, some part of her that had been filled with tension since boarding the *Annie McGee* simply...let...go. Her shoulders relaxed. Her face warmed.

She quickly looked away.

"Miss Bridget," Caleb said her name in a hissed "whisper" that was nearly as loud as a shout. "Come sit with us."

"I take it you know those children?" Nora's surprise was evident in her tone.

"I met them in the general store when I went for a

walk yesterday." Bridget didn't expand. Not now, not here. Someone could overhear and come to the wrong conclusion.

"That man sitting beside them," Nora said in a hushed whisper. "He looks familiar."

"It's William Black, from the docks in Boston. Remember, he was looking for his…bride."

Nora's eyes narrowed. "He's smiling at you."

"At *us*," Bridget corrected her. "He's smiling at us."

"Well, then." Nora readjusted her hold on Grace. "I say it's time for a proper introduction."

"Of course." Bridget continued to the pew where the Black family sat.

"Hello," she began. "Isn't this is a happy coincidence?"

She smiled at the children first then looked up at Will. He'd already risen to his feet and was staring at her with such a compelling gaze her breath hitched in her throat.

"Bridget. I mean…" Will cleared his throat and glanced at Nora. "Miss Murphy. It's a pleasure to see you again."

"And you, as well." She swallowed back her expanding nerves. "This is my sister Nora. Nora, this is William Black and his children, Olivia and Caleb."

"Oh!" Olivia gasped in delight when she caught sight of the bundle in Nora's arms. "You have a baby, too. Mine's sleeping." She rocked her dolly back and forth to prove her point.

"Mine is, too." Nora laughed softly. "Her name is Grace."

"I named my baby Bridget." Olivia's face practically glowed as she turned to smile at her doll's namesake.

Bridget's heart filled with warmth and affection.

Nora shot a look in her direction, the lift of a single

eyebrow indicating that explanations would be in order once they were alone.

Bridget suppressed a sigh, knowing full well she was in for another lecture, one that would surely include a list of the various complications that could arise when a person kept secrets from their older sister.

"Please, ladies, won't you join us for the service."

The invitation came from Will. There was a look of urgency in his eyes Bridget had missed earlier. A gasp worked its way up her throat and stalled. Had something happened since they'd last seen one another?

"We'd be delighted to join you," Nora answered for them both.

There was a moment of jostling and organizing and arguing among the children over who would stand next to Bridget. In the end neither did so. Olivia ended up beside Nora. Caleb settled on Will's right, while Bridget ended up on his left in the middle of the pew.

Olivia proceeded to pay homage to Grace while Caleb plopped onto the floor with his toy boat in hand. Will opened a hymnal, shifting until Bridget could see the page, as well.

As if on cue, the first strains of organ music wafted through the air. Although Will concentrated on the book in his hand, Bridget could feel his attention solely on her, as if he had something important he needed to say to her. She briefly wondered what had happened and why she wasn't more uncomfortable standing this close to him. He smelled of soap and pine. She took a deep breath, leaned in closer and promptly began singing the selected hymn.

Peace enveloped her.

The song rolled off Will's tongue in a clear, perfectly pitched baritone. Bridget's voice joined with his in flawless harmony, as though they'd been singing together all their lives.

Against her best efforts to stay focused on the song, her thoughts turned fanciful. She imagined her and Will, together, sharing their love of music with their children. Five of them, to be exact. Olivia, Caleb, another set of twins, both of them girls, a smaller boy. They would...they would...

She shook away the image, shocked at the direction of her thoughts. Had she learned nothing in the past year? She needed to guard her heart, to hold a portion of herself back, or she'd risk another heartache.

Out of the corner of her eye she glanced at Will, only to discover he was watching her in the same covert manner. Despite the tension she felt in him, something quite nice passed between them, a feeling that instilled utter contentment.

She swallowed a flash of misgiving and kept singing.

Halfway through the second hymn another person joined them in the pew, a man, his lean, muscular frame sending everyone a few steps to their right. Bridget couldn't fully see the newcomer around Nora's hat. But from her sister's quick intake of air she had a good idea who the man might be.

Sheriff Cameron Long had joined them. Bridget hadn't pegged him for the churchgoing type. She suspected Nora was the reason for his appearance, and that her sister was secretly pleased by this turn of events. Of course she would never admit to such a thing to Bridget. Maybe not even to herself.

The singing came to an end. There was another round of jostling for position. This time Caleb landed on Bridget's lap, his little cheek pressed against her shoulder. Olivia climbed over the lot of them until she settled in an identical position in her father's arms.

Bridget and Will shared a smile over his children's heads. She had to breathe in hard to gather a proper amount of air in her lungs. Truly, William Black should smile more often.

As the preacher made his way to the pulpit, Will leaned forward and inclined his head toward the additional member of their tiny group. "Cam, nice to see you here this morning." There was a hint of irony in his voice.

The sheriff grinned. "Never say never."

There was no more time for conversation before the preacher took his place. He was exactly what Bridget would have expected of an American pastor. Tall, scare-crow-thin, with gray, thinning hair, he was an ordinary-looking fellow with somewhat angular features.

His voice was surprisingly pleasant. Low, soft and compelling. Within moments Bridget found herself riveted by his every word.

When he quoted Hebrews 11:1, she sat up straighter. She'd memorized the verse back in Ireland and had recited it to herself throughout the sea voyage.

Now faith is the substance of things hoped for, the evidence of things not seen, she repeated in her mind.

She listened intently to the rest of the sermon. When making a particular point, the preacher would lower his voice. The entire congregation leaned forward, hungry for whatever bit of wisdom he was about to impart. The whole experience was quite dramatic.

Bridget slipped a quick glance in Will's direction. He appeared to be listening as intently as everyone else. It comforted her to know he took the sermon seriously.

Olivia, far too young to pay attention, spent the time quietly grooming her doll's hair. She twisted the strands into a long, messy braid that would surely end up in

Chapter Eight

Seconds ticked by and Bridget wondered why Will wasn't speaking.

Get on with it, she nearly shouted at him. Perhaps he was waiting until the children were out of earshot. With that in mind, she made eye contact with Nora, gave a meaningful look at the twins and then angled her head in Will's direction.

Understanding the silent message, Nora steered Olivia and Caleb farther down the aisle, toward Cameron Long. Shoulders tense, lips flattened, he politely gave the twins his undivided attention. The poor man looked slightly uncomfortable, but he was making a gallant effort at hiding his reaction.

With the children occupied, Bridget turned back to Will.

The look of urgency was back in his eyes. "Will?"

"Something has occurred since we spoke yesterday, something that makes it imperative I reopen our previous discussion."

Not sure what she heard in his tone—worry, apprehension, despair?—she braided her fingers together and told herself not to panic, not to jump to conclusions. Patience was the key in situations such as these.

"You see, my mother, she has…" His words trailed off and for an instant he looked slightly helpless.

Bridget gasped. "Is she hurt? Has she been injured?"

"Nothing like that."

"Praise God."

"Yes." He blinked. "But I'm afraid she is not entirely well, either. I'm no doctor but if I had to give a diagnosis I'd say she's suffering from a case of exhaustion."

His concerned expression told Bridget what she'd already determined for herself. This man cared deeply for his family.

"My mother missed church today," he continued, his eyes filling with world-weariness. "It's the first time since my father passed."

"Oh, Will. I am sorry." Bridget reached out to him, but realizing where they were she dropped her hand before she made contact with his arm. "Has she seen a doctor?"

He shook his head. "Not yet."

An idea formulated in her mind. "I could ask Flynn to examine your mother. He is very good, very kind. He would know what to do for her."

His eyes narrowed. "Who is Flynn?"

"Flynn Gallagher," she said. When the name still didn't seem to register, she added, "The ship's doctor you met in Boston. He is my brother-in-law."

Will looked down at her with a thoughtful expression, as if he were untangling several details in his mind. "The woman who'd accompanied us in the infirmary," he said. "She is your…sister?"

"Yes, her name is Maeve."

"Maeve." He digested this a moment, then nodded. "Right, I remember now."

Bridget waited for him to continue.

"I…" He shoved a hand through his hair. "My mother

is stubborn. She doesn't want to admit she isn't well. But if she is not better soon, I will insist she see a doctor."

Bridget wanted to push the matter, wanted to do whatever she could to help, but she'd interfered enough. This wasn't her family, or her concern. At least that's what everyone kept telling her.

Nevertheless she wasn't one to walk away from anyone in need. And by the look of concern on Will's face the man was clearly in need.

"If it is agreeable with you," she began, "I would like to inform Flynn of the situation. Perhaps he could give advice without having to meet your mother."

Letting out a breath that wasn't entirely steady, he inclined his head. "Perhaps. In the meantime—" he cleared his throat blinked once, twice "—I find it necessary to do what I can to relieve my mother's daily burden."

"That is perfectly understandable," Bridget agreed.

He cleared his throat again. "Would you reconsider the offer I made to you yesterday?"

Bridget shook her head. "I'm sorry, no."

He paused, one beat, two. On the third he blew out a slow breath of air then nodded in resignation. Despite his hesitation, her answer didn't seem to surprise him. "Would you consider becoming—" he grimaced "—my children's nanny?"

At last. *At last,* Bridget thought. The man was willing to make a compromise. He was putting aside his own preferences for his mother's sake. That said a lot about his character, as well as his love for his mother.

Bridget wanted to help him. She wanted to honor this man's leap of faith with one of her own. They could work out the particulars in time.

Then what was stopping her? Why wasn't she saying yes?

* * *

Will did not like the look of indecision he saw on Bridget's face. Nor was he overly fond of the way she continued to hold to her silence long after he'd relented and asked her to become his children's nanny instead of his wife.

The arrangement had been her idea. Why wasn't she agreeing on the spot?

Finally, she broke her silence. "I'm not sure I understand. I thought you wanted a more permanent solution."

"I do. But with my mother's current health situation I don't have time to send away for another bride. I see how you are with my children, and they with you." He swallowed. "They haven't had much to smile about in the past year. But with you they seem quite…happy." He had to believe that was a good sign.

"And you'd be willing to risk me leaving them, sometime in the future, whenever that might be?"

What other choice did he have? His mother had looked beyond exhausted this morning, more than usual. At this rate he feared she wouldn't last the months it would take him to make arrangements for another mail-order bride. If she wasn't better in a few days he would send for the doctor.

"Yes, Bridget," he said her name with conviction, knowing he could no longer jeopardize his mother's health. "I am willing to take that risk."

She fell silent again, pressing her mouth into a flat line of concentration. Her gaze landed on the twins and a sigh slipped past her tight lips. "I do adore them."

Although he already knew that, hearing her say the words brought a wave of relief. "Then you will become their nanny?"

"On one condition."

He would give her whatever she wanted. Money. Gratitude. "Anything."

"I will accept the position only on a trial basis."

"A trial basis?" He didn't like the sound of that.

"Yes." She nodded her head firmly, as though she'd made up her mind and that was the end of the discussion. "You will allow me to work for you for one full week. At the end of that time we will reevaluate the situation, before the children become overly attached."

It was a solid enough plan, except for one major flaw. The twins were already half in love with the woman. One week in her company would probably send them over the edge. They would end up devastated if she left them, even after only a week.

The answer to the problem was simple. He would give Bridget no cause to leave them. "Agreed."

She smiled and his heart picked up speed, making him feel as though he were running a race with no end in sight.

"Can you begin tomorrow?"

She opened her mouth to respond, then shut it just as quickly. "Wait here a moment."

He gave her retreating back a nod.

She hurried out of the pew and approached her sister, pulling her slightly away from Cam and the children. The two women whispered together for several moments. Will took the opportunity to study Bridget in greater detail. She'd donned the same dress she'd worn the first day they met, a striking concoction with ruffles and gold ribbon streamers at the elbows. She'd pinned her hair on top of her head and, as always, several long tendrils had already escaped.

Her hair really was quite glorious. It was no wonder Olivia had chosen a doll with the same color.

Unaware of his inspection, Bridget called Cam over

next. Her sister returned to the twins. More whispering ensued. Cam nodded a few times, then touched her arm and smiled reassuringly.

Seeing the ease in which the two conversed, something dark and ugly swept through Will. With their heads bent close together, Cam and Bridget looked completely in tune with one another.

An ugly memory surfaced. Will remembered the way Fanny had been with other men, one in particular. He remembered her outrageous flirting, the way she'd—

No. Will stopped his train of thought abruptly. Bridget was not Fanny. Cam was not that other man. All signs pointed to the fact that the pretty Irish immigrant was a woman of integrity. Although, she was rather friendly with Cam. And they were both unattached.

Perhaps a one-week trial was a good idea, after all. Will could use the time to ferret out Bridget's true intentions. If she turned out to be just like Fanny, he would send her packing.

If she was nothing like his dead wife, then he would…he would…

See what came next.

He narrowed his eyes, wondering what was taking so long. What was she discussing so secretively with Cam?

Bridget eventually stepped away from the other man, spoke to Olivia and Caleb a moment then approached Will once again.

"Yes." She gave him a winning smile. "I can start tomorrow morning."

Relief spread through him, the emotion so strong it threw him back a step. He swallowed, hard, and focused on calming his raging pulse before speaking again. "Excellent." He rattled off his address.

She smiled.

"And where are you living?" At her lifted eyebrow,

he explained, "I ask so I can make arrangements to pick you up in the morning."

"Not to worry." She looked over her shoulder, her smile still firmly in place. "Sheriff Long has agreed to drop me off on his way out of town."

The dark emotion he'd suppressed earlier spread through Will again. *One week,* he reminded himself. He had one full week to discover if Bridget Murphy was a woman he could trust around his children. "Then it's settled."

"Lovely." She clasped her hands tightly together.

Unable to stop himself, he touched her braided fingers. "Thank you, Bridget."

"You're welcome, Will." She held his gaze a moment. "Do you wish to tell the children about our arrangement, or may I?"

He hadn't thought that far ahead. He was still trying to process the fact that this woman would be in his home, everyday, helping to raise his children. Not as their mother, he reminded himself, but as their nanny. "You may do the honors."

Her eyes brightened and before two complete heartbeats passed she was stooping in front of Caleb and Olivia. After a brief conversation, the children squealed in delight and then launched themselves into Bridget's outstretched arms. Laughing, she hugged them tightly to her.

In that moment Will knew he'd made the right decision—for his children.

But what about for himself? Had he just made the biggest mistake of his life, hiring a woman he knew so little about? Or would this turn out to be the best decision he'd ever made?

At this point only the Lord knew for sure.

* * *

William Black left with his children soon after the hugging and smiling and laughing subsided, with the understandable excuse that he needed to check on his mother. Bridget watched their departure, tossing waves to the children and then staring after them long past the time they'd disappeared around the corner.

"The twins are darling," Nora said from behind her.

"Yes, they are."

Coming around to face her, Nora studied her.

Bridget knew that look in her sister's eyes. "Speak, Nora. Just say whatever it is you have on your mind."

"All right. I will. Are you certain you want to work for William Black? He seems rather…severe."

Severe? Yes, perhaps he was. But today Bridget had gained a bit more insight into what drove the man. Not only did he love his family, his concern for them took precedence over his own preferences.

A wistful ache pulsed through her. What would it be like to have a man care for her so completely, so sacrificially? Daniel had always been more concerned with appearances than Bridget herself. Why hadn't she realized that sooner?

"If Will seems severe," she said in his defense, "it's because he's worried about his children." She decided to keep his mother's health crisis to herself for now. At least until she consulted Flynn. "I want this job, Nora. Truly, I do."

Her sister didn't appear entirely convinced. "If you are certain."

"I am." Bridget quickly changed the subject. "Oh, Nora, just think. We're to get our first glimpse of our new home this afternoon."

The house was theirs, she told herself firmly. She

wouldn't allow herself to think otherwise. Determining the legality of the deed was only a formality.

Smiling at last, Nora ran the tip of her finger over Grace's cheek. The baby cooed softly in return. "It's all rather exciting, isn't it?"

"Oh, aye, it is."

They made their way down the church steps just as Cameron Long broke away from a young couple and ambled toward them.

"Well, ladies. I'm at your disposal for the rest of the day." He swept the hat off his head and bowed grandly. The gentlemanly gesture encompassed both of them, but his eyes kept straying to Nora. "Do you want to head to the house now, or later this afternoon?"

"Now," they chimed as one.

"Right, then." His lips curved in a lopsided grin. "Follow me."

He guided them toward a rickety wagon with an empty flatbed in the back. He apologized for the rustic accommodations, explaining that the three of them would have to share the lone seat up front. "It might be a bit cramped," he warned.

"It'll be fine," Bridget said for them both, not wanting to give him any reason to change his mind.

Once they were settled on the hard seat, Nora and baby Grace first, then Bridget, the sheriff rounded the wagon and climbed on board, as well. A series of creaks and groans met the additional weight. Shifting forward, he released the brake. A flick of his wrist and they were off.

"If you ladies don't mind," he said, "I need to stop by the jail before we head out of town."

The request sent a wave of impatience sweeping through Bridget, one she firmly clapped into submission. What was one more delay at this point in their journey?

Thankfully the trek around the square took no time at all.

"Hey, Ben," the sheriff called as he drew the wagon to a halt, gruff affection in his voice. "Get out here, you old coot, and meet Faith Glen's newest residents."

"I'm coming. I'm coming." The door to the jailhouse swung open and an older gentleman sauntered onto the planked sidewalk. He had a pleasant, ruddy complexion, a full shock of white hair and wore a badge clipped to his chest.

Bridget guessed him to be in his late sixties and immediately noted how his dark brown eyes gleamed with mischief and good humor.

"Don't tell me these lovely young women are the Murphy sisters." He spoke with a pleasant, if somewhat thick Irish accent. The familiar brogue reminded Bridget of home.

Nostalgia tried to overwhelm her, a sensation that felt as bittersweet as it did unexpected. Oh, how she missed the people of Castleville and the comfort that came from relationships built over a lifetime.

Refusing to allow her melancholy to ruin this special day, Bridget blinked away the memories and forced a smile on her face. This was not a time for looking back, but for focusing on what lay ahead.

"Ben." Cameron Long jumped to the ground and slapped the man on the back. "Meet Nora and Bridget Murphy. Ladies, this is Ben MacDuff, the former sheriff of Faith Glen and now my acting deputy."

Without waiting for any of them to respond, he disappeared around the corner of the building with a cryptic explanation of needing to gather a few things.

While he was gone, Nora introduced Grace to the

deputy sheriff. As he admired the baby, Bridget said to his bent head, "Deputy MacDuff, I was wondering—"

"Now let's get something straight right now, young lady. I don't answer to no formal title." He winked at her, the gesture taking away the sting of his words. "Everyone calls me Ben."

"Oh, well, then, Ben." She winked at him in return. "Did you know Laird O'Malley?"

"Know him?" He yanked off his hat and slapped his thigh with the brim. "Yeah, I knew him. Met him the day he arrived here from Ireland. I was the town sheriff back then."

"Will you tell us about him?" Nora asked.

Ben shrugged. "Not much to tell. He kept mostly to himself. Guess he weren't the type for interacting with others, if you know what I mean."

Bridget's heart sank. Laird O'Malley had been a recluse. Had he been so in love with their mother, so heartbroken she hadn't returned his feelings that he'd shut himself off from the world? Or had that just been his nature? Either way...

"How sad," she whispered.

Ben shrugged again. "It was what it was."

Cameron Long returned with a large basket in his arms, the contents covered with a colorless muslin cloth. He loaded the basket in the flatbed then strode toward his deputy with ground-eating strides. "You're in charge while I'm gone."

"I figured as much." Eyeing Nora and Bridget, he said, "Now don't you two go worrying about that old house. You're in good hands with Cameron. The boy will sort this out for you in good time."

A chill slid down Bridget's spine. What, exactly, did *the boy* have to sort out? The confusion over the deed?

Or was Ben referring to something else, something more specific to the house itself?

Before she could voice her questions the sheriff released the brake, picked up the reins and they were on their way again.

Bridget waved to Ben over her shoulder.

Silence filled the majority of the ride through town. They eventually turned off the main road and began winding their way down a path overgrown with underbrush and scrub. As the wagon bumped along the lane their horse's tail idly swished at the flies swarming around his flanks.

Bridget fanned herself with her hand, her pitiful efforts useless in the rising midday heat. There was no breeze. Yet despite the hot, still air, birds chirped a happy tune from their perches in the towering trees up above. The smell of grass mingled with the fragrant flowers in bloom.

An idyllic scene, to be sure. Yet Bridget could find no joy in the moment. Not only was the heavy underbrush growing thicker with each step the horse took, her nerves were winning the battle over her attempt to remain hopeful.

No. Bridget refused to allow her apprehension to get the best of her. Whatever they found at the end of the lane, she would consider it an additional blessing among the many they'd already received since leaving Ireland.

A month ago they'd faced destitution. But now Maeve was married to a good, honorable man. Bridget and Nora had acquired jobs perfectly suited to their talents. The Lord had guided their path every step of the way.

Her optimism firmly in place, Bridget held her breath with eager anticipation. The wagon rounded a small bend and...

"Oh, my," she gasped, shaking her head blindly. The house, the very reason for their journey to America was…it was…

A disaster.

Chapter Nine

Oh, my. Oh, my. Oh, my. The words continued echoing in Bridget's mind, making coherent thought impossible.

She shaded her eyes from the sun and took in what amounted to years of neglect. The roof sagged, leaning dangerously off-center and slightly to the right. Loose shingles hung haphazardly in places. The paint, once white but now a faded gray, was peeling off in various places, giving the entire structure a chaotic, patchwork feel.

They had traveled all the way from Ireland with so much hope in their hearts for—this?

A disaster, she repeated to herself. The house was a complete and utter disaster.

Speechless, Bridget drew in a shaky breath and lifted up a silent prayer. It seemed better than crying.

Drawing her bottom lip between her teeth, she looked to her right, saw a garden overrun with weeds. There was a rickety old bench sitting under a large shade tree that had a sign tacked to its trunk. The sign read—she leaned forward—Colleen's Garden. Bridget blinked back tears. Laird O'Malley had planted a flower garden for their mother. How—sweet.

Off to her left she spotted a structure that looked like

a barn, a barn that had seen better days a decade ago. A scrawny cow grazed on a patch of grass nearby and a few chickens scratched in the dirt.

As the wagon slowed to a stop Bridget took her first look at the rich, black soil beneath the wheels and smiled for the first time since arriving. The fertile dirt would produce food abundantly, with a bit of hard work on their part. Bridget was not afraid of hard work. Neither was Nora.

"This isn't so bad," she said aloud, warming to the burst of ideas swimming in her head now. A bit of paint, a few new shingles, a lot of weeding and they would have a fine home to call their own.

"Not bad?" Nora swung her wide-eyed gaze in her direction. "It's impossible."

"I did warn you," Sheriff Long said under his breath as he set the brake and hopped to the ground.

Ignoring him, Bridget scrambled down as well and grabbed a handful of the black dirt. "Look at this soil, Nora. It'll grow whatever we plant."

Nora made a face, her unhappy expression indicating she was not feeling nearly as hopeful as Bridget.

Undaunted, Bridget turned her gaze to the house. "We'll give it a good cleaning, weed that garden over there then take stock of what repairs need addressing first." She shaded her eyes again. "We'll take this one step at a time. Isn't that what you always say, Nora? One step at a time?"

"Yes, Bridget, that's what I always say." Nora studied the dilapidated structure. "The house must have been truly lovely at one time."

"And it will be again," Bridget said, remembering the sermon from this morning, the part about trusting their greatest burdens to the Lord. Yes, that's exactly what they would do in this situation. "Faith, Nora. We just need a little faith."

"And a lot of elbow grease," she mumbled.

Bridget laughed. "Precisely. One step at a time, dear sister. Now come." She reached for Grace so Nora could climb down from the wagon. "Let's go inside and introduce ourselves to the Coulters."

She handed back the baby and started off.

"Wait." The sheriff's voice stopped her midstep. While she'd been busy convincing Nora all was well, he'd retrieved the basket from the bed of the wagon and had rounded back to the front once again. "Let me lead the way."

The stoop wasn't much, just a few steps on a raised slab. Nevertheless the sheriff tested each stair before he motioned for them to follow. They trooped up the steps single file, Nora and Grace bringing up the rear.

"Agnes?" he called out, shifting his load so he could tap on the door frame. "You home?"

A small, thin voice responded to his question. "Come on in, Cameron. I'm back in the kitchen."

He elbowed past the door and then held it open with his shoulder so Bridget and Nora could enter ahead of him.

Once inside Bridget came to the unfortunate realization that the interior had been equally neglected. The walls were stark, with chipped paint their only adornment. The carpets were threadbare, holes literally worn in places.

The furniture, what little there was, also sported holes in the tattered upholstery. At least the room was clean, not a dust mite in sight. That said something about the Coulters. They might be elderly, and probably didn't have many resources, but they were doing their best.

The sheriff led them through the sparse room, steering them toward the back of the house. Impressions slid over one another. Faded paint, broken furniture, torn rugs, there was little to recommend the place.

And yet Bridget saw the possibilities.

The rooms were clean and spacious, the windows positioned to allow the light in but not the summer heat. Laird O'Malley had thought through the design with an eye for functionality. Paint, a bit of pretty wallpaper and a few new pieces of furniture would do wonders.

They ended their short jaunt in a spacious kitchen. Shoving past Bridget, Nora laughed in delight and made straight for the large black iron stove. Bridget understood her sister's pleasure. They'd only had a fireplace in their home in Ireland.

Glancing around the room, Bridget's gaze landed on a frail-looking woman sitting at a sizable table in the middle of the room. Her fingers slowly shelled beans. She looked painfully thin and wore a dress as threadbare as the rugs in the front room. Lines spiked around her pursed lips, giving her a look of suppressed pain.

Bridget smiled gently. "You must be Agnes Coulter."

"That's me," came the uneven reply. She didn't make any move to stand.

Still smiling, Bridget sat down in one of the empty chairs next to her. "I'm Bridget Murphy and that's my sister Nora. The baby she's carrying is Grace."

"Murphy." The woman's eyes lit with recognition, and something else. Wariness, perhaps? "Would that mean you're Colleen's daughters?"

"Well, yes. Yes, we are." Bridget reached out and touched the woman's bony hand, the skin practically translucent over the thin purple veins running across the knuckles. "You know about our mother?"

She focused on her bowl of beans. "Laird spoke of her often, especially in the end."

Bridget squeezed her hand gently. "Then you must know about the deed he sent her."

She nodded. "You've come to claim the house."

"Yes—" she gentled her voice even further "—but since we both have jobs in town we'll need your help running the place."

A deep clearing of a throat preceded an elderly man's entrance. He shuffled into the room, his gait sporting a decided limp. His hair was a wild white cloud around his face. His eyes were a rheumy blue.

"So," he began, his narrowed eyes landing on first Nora and the baby then Bridget. "You've finally come to push us out."

"No." Bridget jumped to her feet. "On the contrary, we want you to stay on as before. We need you to help us care for the house."

While we care for you, she wanted to add but knew by the mutinous look in his eyes she would insult him if she did. She'd met many like him in Ireland, men who had endured the potato famine and had come away proud and humbled, the kind who would rather die by their own effort than live on someone else's charity.

"Please," Nora added. "We want you to live in this house with us and carry on as before. Nothing need change."

"Nothing," Bridget reiterated. "Except you'll have two extra pairs of hands to put this place back to rights."

"I warn you," he said, then drew in a shuddering breath. "There's a lot of heavy work ahead."

Bridget heard the hoarseness in his grizzled voice, the pride behind his words. He was obviously ashamed the house had gotten away from him. She wanted to ease his worry, to help him see they weren't here to

judge him or his efforts. "We've lived through famine and drought. We aren't afraid of hard times or hard work."

Arms folded over his chest, he assessed her then Nora then Bridget again with a noncommittal aloofness. Despite his gruff exterior, Bridget saw a good man who took pride in his work, one who took his role of caretaker seriously. "You will stay on, won't you?" she asked.

"I suppose."

"Splendid."

Cameron Long, silent throughout this exchange, stepped forward and set the basket in his arms on the table with a loud thump. "I brought you some things, Agnes."

The woman bristled, the bowl of beans in her lap bobbling. "You know we don't need your charity."

"Who said this is charity?" He gave her one of his big, friendly smiles. "You'll pay me back when you're able."

The comment solidified what Bridget already knew about Cameron Long. He was a kind, down-to-earth man with a generous heart.

Agnes's eyes filled with unshed tears. "You're a good boy," she said, patting his hand.

He dropped a kiss on the top of her head. "Anything for my favorite girl."

"Oh, honestly," she shoved at him with a surprising burst of energy. Setting aside her bowl, she rummaged through the contents, her smile wobbling. "Coffee, flour, sugar, eggs." She looked up at her husband, then quickly thrust her hand back into the basket. "A cured ham."

Nora took charge, wordlessly handing Grace over

to Bridget. "Let me put these supplies away and fix us all something to eat."

While she went to work, Bridget took baby Grace and sat back at the table. "That cow outside, is she a milk cow by chance?"

Agnes nodded. "She is."

Bridget caught Nora's eye and smiled. Fresh milk would be readily available for the baby. It was another blessing to add to their list.

With that matter solved Bridget proceeded to entertain everyone with tales from their trip across the Atlantic. She told them about the widow Mrs. Fitzwilliam, her search for her missing stepgranddaughter and, of course, the McCorkle brothers. She highlighted how Maeve's quick thinking had saved little Emmett's life. Halfway through the story, the sheriff cut her off. "You mean to say, the other two boys stowed away on the ship?"

His expression reminded Bridget he was a lawman first, a friend second. "Yes," she said carefully. "Flynn, the ship's doctor, had taken Emmett on board before they could come forward. They had to follow or be left behind. And besides, they couldn't let their brother sail to America without them."

She didn't add that the boys' original intent had been to stow away together, all three of them, before the injury changed their plans. Best not to get anyone in trouble. "Once Dr. Gallagher found out about the other two boys, he put them to work around the ship so they could earn their passage."

The sheriff lifted a single eyebrow. "That was certainly resourceful of Dr. Gallagher."

"Kindhearted, too." Bridget rose, hoping to end the conversation there. She should probably set the table, but wasn't sure what to do with Grace.

Agnes offered the perfect solution. "May I hold her?"

"Of course." Bridget surrendered the baby then went to help Nora.

Once the meal was served, and everyone was sitting at the table, conversation flowed easily. Talk turned to a local mill, the Huntley-something-or-other. Bridget hadn't caught the full name. Assuming they were speaking about the mill she'd seen on her way into town, she asked, "What sort of mill is it?"

"A chocolate mill," Agnes said, her eyes gleaming. "It's been in the area for nearly seventy-five years, begun by one of Faith Glen's founders, Reginald Black."

She straightened at the name. "Black? Any relation to William Black?"

"Absolutely," the sheriff said. "Your new employer owns the largest mill in the area. He ships his chocolate cakes all over the world, the kind used for baking."

James joined the conversation, his hard voice of earlier softened now. "The Huntley-Black chocolate also makes the best warm cocoa I've ever tasted."

Bridget digested this new information. She wasn't surprised to discover Will was a successful business owner. Even in his desperation to find a mother for his children, he'd had an air of confidence that indicated a man used to being in charge.

Which begged the question: Why had he chosen to send all the way to Ireland for a bride? What had driven him to settle for a marriage in name only instead of seeking a love match?

The sensible voice in her head warned her to reconsider working for William Black. There were too many unanswered questions surrounding him.

Her heart told her he needed her help. Bridget knew she would go with her heart, as always.

Decision made, she spent the rest of their visit getting to know her future housemates better.

Too excited to sleep, Bridget clambered out of bed early the next morning. Night had yet to surrender fully to dawn. Shadows still flickered across the floor at her bare feet.

She loved this time of the morning, when everything seemed possible. By the afternoon she and Nora would have their answer about the deed. A formality, she reminded herself. Nothing more. There would be work ahead of them, *hard* work, and she looked forward to every aching muscle.

Dressing quickly, she chose serviceability over style. She would be spending her day with two three-year-olds. That meant short attention spans on their part, exhaustion on hers and flat-out good fun for them all.

Bridget did not attest to the common notion that children should be kept inside and out of mischief. Children, in her mind, should be children. She remembered her own youth, how she and her sisters had spent hours fishing and digging for buried treasure with the Donnelly boys.

With impatience making her fingers fumble, she managed to lace up her boots after only two tries. She then twisted her hair into a single braid down her back and after a quick breakfast, rushed out of the house.

Nora was already waiting for her on the porch, leaning against the wall as she fed Grace.

"Am I late?" Bridget asked, skidding to a stop then hopping on one foot to regain her balance.

"Actually, you're early."

Relieved, she sank onto the top step. "We have a big day ahead of us."

"Our very own new beginning," Nora added.

"You scared?" she asked over her shoulder, smiling.

"A little. But excited, too."

"Scared and excited, that describes how I'm feeling perfectly."

Bridget closed her eyes and lifted up a silent prayer of thanksgiving. God had brought them here safely. He'd blessed Maeve with a doting husband, and had provided both Bridget and Nora with a means to earn money. They would eventually restore the house Laird O'Malley had built for their mother. In the process they would provide a safe home for James and Agnes Coulter, as well as themselves.

Thank You, Lord, she whispered in her mind. *May Your blessings continue. I pray You use me as Your instrument to tend to the children in my care.*

She opened her eyes just as Cameron Long drew his rickety wagon to a halt in front of the boardinghouse.

"You ladies look especially lovely this morning." He included Bridget in the quick sweep of his gaze, but his eyes lingered on Nora, as they seemed to do often.

Bridget hid a smile behind her hand. Her sister did look especially pretty this morning. Her dark hair gleamed in the early-morning sun, the soft light shooting gold threads through the rich brown. She'd wrapped Grace in a blue swaddling blanket, the softer tone a nice contrast to her darker dress.

After making it clear they were to call him Cam or Cameron, not sheriff, the short trek to Will's house was made in companionable silence. By the time *Cameron* reined in his horse, Bridget was blinking up in wonder at the most beautiful house she had ever seen.

There were rows of windows on three full stories. The first and second floors were identical to one another. Each had five sets of windows and shutters. The top level could possibly be an attic? Or maybe a loft?

It was a large home, meant for a large family, a dream manifested in brick and mortar and seventy-five-year-old wood.

Suddenly overcome with a moment of sorrow, Bridget had to look away. She feared something dreadful had stolen the happiness William Black and his children deserved.

Unaware of her change in mood, Cameron helped her to the ground with a smile. Just as she steadied herself the front door flung open and a pair of loud squeals erupted in the air.

"Miss Bridget!"

Two tiny blurs bulleted down the walkway. Little Olivia stopped short of running into Bridget. Caleb, on the other hand, slammed into her legs, nearly toppling them both.

Cameron steadied Bridget with a hand on her arm. She steadied Caleb in the same manner.

Disaster avoided.

She smiled her thanks to the tall man then focused her attention on her new charges. Their faces were full of joy and they practically bounced in place.

"We've been up for hours," Caleb said.

"Hours and hours," Olivia added.

Heart in her throat, Bridget laid a hand on both their heads, ruffled the matching light auburn hair, and then sighed. She was completely and utterly doomed. Her affection for these two children was quickly outdistancing her ability to remember she'd agreed to work for Will only on a trial basis.

Who had she been kidding with that stipulation? She was here to stay.

Cameron's voice broke through her thoughts. "Your sister and I will be gone most of the day." He climbed back into the wagon, acknowledged the man striding down the walkway with a hitch of his chin, then turned back to Bridget. "Ben will be at the jail all day. Let him know if you need anything in our absence."

"I'll be fine," she assured them both.

Fighting to contain a surge of anxiety as the wagon rolled away, Bridget offered up a silent prayer that all would go well at the County Clerk's Office.

"Miss Bridget." Olivia tugged on her skirt, her shoulders rocking back and forth in a little girl dance. "What are we going to do today? Tell me. Tell me."

"Oh, we're going to do lots of things."

"Like what?" Caleb demanded eagerly.

Bridget leaned over and placed her hands on her knees. "You'll have to wait and see."

"All right, children. Don't crowd your new nanny." Will's voice slid over her like a cool splash of water.

Feeling her cheeks warm in response, Bridget raised her gaze to his. "Hello, Will."

"Hello." He stared into her eyes a moment, and then—finally—he smiled.

The sky tilted, the ground shifted beneath her feet, her equilibrium shattered. With very little effort William Black could hook her heart just as thoroughly as his children had.

She'd never felt this drawn to a man. Not even Daniel had been able to steal her breath so completely.

Still holding her gaze, Will took her arm. "Come, Bridget." His eyes said things she had no idea how to interpret. "Come and meet my mother."

She looked up toward the house, only just now noticing an older woman standing in the doorway, her smile wide and full of welcome. A beautiful woman despite her advancing years, Esther Black wore a light pink dress with a lace collar and matching cuffs. The pretty, soft color set off her white hair and blue, blue eyes.

A lovely woman, to be sure, but there was no mistaking the exhaustion in her gaze and the tight lines of fatigue around her mouth.

I was right to come here and serve this family.

Chapter Ten

Hand pressed lightly on her arm, Will directed Bridget toward his house, his chest rising and falling in perfect rhythm with his heartbeat. As impossible as it would seem, the woman was more stunning than he remembered.

Her smile had nearly knocked him off his feet. And when their glances had met, then melded, there had been a tangible impact in his gut, the kind that made him think of things he had no right thinking, like maybe Bridget could become more than his children's nanny.

And…

She wasn't his, he reminded himself sternly. The woman was Olivia and Caleb's temporary nanny, here on a trial basis.

One week. Will had one full week to determine if he could trust her in his home and with his children.

The twins, their excitement still in full force, rushed ahead of them then flanked their grandmother. All three smiles were larger than Will had seen in months.

Bridget had better not break their hearts. *Or mine.*

The thought made Will scowl. "Mother." His voice came out gruffer than he'd intended. "I'd like you to meet Bridget Murphy." He turned to the woman by his side. "Bridget, this is my mother, Esther Black."

Bridget favored his mother with a smile that Will wanted for himself.

He looked quickly away.

"It's a pleasure to meet you, Mrs. Black." Bridget's soft lilting accent washed over him. Surely no woman with a voice like that could be dishonest.

"Welcome, Bridget." Taking the children's hands in hers, his mother stepped backward. "We're very pleased to have you in our home."

Already running late and suddenly needing vast amounts of air, Will gathered the papers and ledgers he'd left in the entryway. "Mother, I'll leave you to help Bridget settle in this morning."

"Of course." She walked toward him and then pecked him on the cheek. "What time will you be home tonight?"

"Early enough to escort Bridget to the boarding-house."

"Oh," Bridget said. "I'm sure that won't be necessary. Cameron said this was a peaceful town. Surely I could walk the short distance."

Will felt an odd pang at her words. Whether from her casual reference to Cam or her refusal of his offer, he couldn't say.

"Nevertheless." He held her gaze, warning her that the subject was not up for discussion. "I will walk you home this evening. No matter how peaceful our community might be, I won't have you on the streets alone."

She studied him a moment, a glint of pleasure in her eyes. "That is very good of you."

Deciding the matter was settled, he kissed both the children, nodded to his mother and Bridget then left the house as the rest of his family tugged the new nanny into the next room.

One of the last things he heard was the woman's delighted gasp. "You have a piano."

His mother's inevitable response came next. "Do you play, dear?"

"I haven't had the pleasure in a while, not since—"

Not wanting to hear the rest of Bridget's answer, Will shut the door behind him with a decided snap. Fanny had played the piano exceptionally well. Her talent had been one of the things that had drawn him to her. He'd wrongfully equated her love of music with a depth of character that had not been there.

He'd been disappointed to discover she'd played to win favor and for no other reason. Music in his childhood home had been for joy, yes, but was also a way to worship the Lord.

Fanny hadn't wanted anything to do with God, or with Will, as it turned out. After the birth of the twins he'd hoped she'd change her mind, on both counts.

He'd been deluding himself, on both counts.

Fanny had continued avoiding church. She'd craved the life she'd left behind in Boston, and had sought it out as soon as the children were weaned. Wishing to see her happy, Will had encouraged her to visit her friends. He'd counted on her missing the children, possibly even him.

Instead her day trips had grown longer, turning into weeks. Then she had…

He shook the rest of his thoughts away and steered his carriage the final rise to the mill.

In the end Fanny had taught him a very valuable lesson. Never again would he be fooled by a pretty face. *Never again.*

* * *

Bridget folded her arms across her waist, leaned a shoulder against the wall and watched her new charges nap peacefully in their beds. They looked sweetly innocent in their sleep, their little faces relaxed and carefree. A soft, rhythmic snore slipped out of Caleb while Olivia mumbled something incoherent then snuggled deeper under her blanket.

Bridget smiled with pleasure. The twins were completely worn out, as children should be after a day of vigorous activity.

The hours had flown by this morning and she was ever grateful. With Caleb and Olivia occupying most of her time, and nearly all of her thoughts, she'd found little opportunity to fret over what Nora and Cameron might—or might not—discover at the County Clerk's Office.

Just as well. Bridget had learned long ago that no matter how much she worried about a situation, the outcome never changed. *Fear not.* Wasn't that most common command in the Bible? Didn't the Lord promise to feed and care for His flock, always?

With that in mind, Bridget focused on the sleeping children once again.

Like most three-year-olds, Olivia and Caleb had active, inquisitive minds and were ready to play any game she suggested. But unlike other children their age, there were moments when they possessed an unnatural reserve. It was as if they feared upsetting Bridget. But why? If only she knew the reason behind their restraint.

She needed more information and, sensing their mother's death was at the heart of the problem, decided to start by finding out what had really happened to the woman.

Satisfied the children were resting peacefully,

Bridget pulled the door shut and went in search of Esther Black. The housekeeper told her she could find the older woman in the front parlor.

Bridget stopped in the doorway and waited a moment, watching Esther pour tea into a cup. She looked rested from her own nap, which was exactly what Bridget had hoped. One of her goals had been to relieve this kind woman's burden, and it appeared she was making progress. Bridget would still consult Flynn, but for now she stepped into the parlor.

"The children are asleep," she said.

Esther looked up, smiled and then signaled her to take the empty seat across from her. "Join me, please."

Once Bridget was settled, Esther set a teacup in front of her. "I know I've said this countless times since you arrived this morning, but I'm going to say it again. You are a blessing to us, Bridget Murphy, a true blessing."

Bridget felt her cheeks warm. "Oh, Esther, I've had a wonderful day. The children are utterly charming." A burst of longing shot through her, reminding her how desperately she wanted children of her own. "I'm quite taken with them."

"And there's no denying they adore you, as well." Esther busied herself pouring tea into both cups. She seemed relaxed, but from the furrow on her brow Bridget sensed she had something more to say, perhaps something concerning the children's mother? Dare she hope it would be this easy to gather the information she wanted?

"I understand," Esther began, "that you traveled to America on the same ship as Will's intended."

Surprised and slightly uncomfortable at the direction of conversation, Bridget clasped her hands tightly together in her lap. "Well, yes, I did."

"Did you know her, then?" Esther kept her eyes on

the tea service. "Would she have been a good mother to the children?"

Something in the other woman's manner, the way she kept her gaze slightly averted, led Bridget to believe Will's mother hadn't been in full agreement with his decision to "hire" a bride.

It would have been nice to have alleviated Esther's concerns, to have informed her that the woman with which Will had corresponded was worthy of him and the children. Unfortunately Bridget couldn't say for sure. "I'm afraid I never met her."

Esther fell silent, evidently taking a moment to process the information. When she continued looking down at the table, Bridget decided to ease the tension in the air and shift the conversation back to the children.

"The twins are very sweet, but they often seem…a bit…" she searched for the proper word "…subdued."

"It's been a hard year for them."

To hear her concerns spoken aloud, in that sad tone, well, her stomach twisted in sorrow.

"I'm sorry." She reached out to touch Esther's hand and squeezed gently. "For all of you."

Acknowledging her sympathy with a slight incline of her head, Esther pulled her hand free and then scooted a plate of scones in Bridget's direction.

She ignored the pretty pastries. "I assume the children's mother died a year ago?"

"That's correct."

Bridget waited for her to say more but, yet again, Esther didn't give any further details. Instead she made a grand show of buttering a fresh scone and handing it to Bridget.

Accepting the pastry out of politeness more than hunger, she took a bite. As the buttery goodness melted on her tongue, she wondered all the more what had happened to Will's wife. Something tragic? Heartbreaking, perhaps? "The children never mention their mother."

"They don't remember her."

How odd, Bridget thought. Although Olivia and Caleb were young, not yet four, most children their age had memories from when they were much younger.

Should she continue questioning Will's mother? No, Bridget decided. She'd pried enough for one day. Time would reveal the answers she needed.

"Esther, would it be acceptable if I played the piano for the children when they wake from their nap? Maybe I could teach them a song?"

She peered over her shoulder into the other room as she spoke. The gleaming instrument was the finest she'd ever seen. Bridget desperately wanted to test the keys and determine for herself if the sound matched the piano's exquisite beauty. She loved music and would enjoy sharing her fondness with the children.

Esther's gaze shifted to the piano. After a moment of silent contemplation, she gave one firm nod. "I think teaching the children to sing a song is a grand idea."

With such an enthusiastic answer it was a wonder the woman had taken so long to consider her response. What had been behind her initial hesitation? Bridget wondered.

She wouldn't ask. She'd been nosy enough for one day. Tomorrow morning she would take the children outside to enjoy the fresh air. But today, oh, today, there would be music in this house.

Smiling in satisfaction, Bridget leaned back in her chair and took another bite of her scone.

With his paperwork complete, Will decided to check on the day's production. As he made his way to the main floor of the mill, he reflected over all he and his ancestors had accomplished in seventy-five years. When his grandfather had founded the company he'd been an educated man, a doctor by trade, with absolutely no desire to practice medicine. Upon meeting an Irish immigrant, Liam Huntley, a man who'd been an expert in making chocolate, Reginald Black had struck upon the idea of a chocolate mill.

Within a few years the mill became a phenomenal success, even surviving the American Revolution when cocoa beans had been difficult to acquire.

Will's father had inherited the business upon Reginald's death. Will had taken over ten years later. In his hands Huntley-Black chocolate was now available all across the country. In order to meet the increasing demand, Will had moved the business to this larger facility five years ago, right after his marriage to Fanny. The conversion had demanded long, sixteen-hour days.

Perhaps Fanny had felt neglected and that was the reason she'd strayed. Perhaps she'd missed her friends and family, as she'd claimed. Or perhaps she'd simply been bored and that had led to her poor decisions.

Will would never know for sure why his wife had sought another man's affections. Even now, at the thought of the resulting tragedy, anger and guilt burned deep.

Looking back, he wasn't sure he'd fought hard enough to bring Fanny home. When he'd finally gone to fetch her he'd been too late. Why hadn't he sought her out sooner?

What did that say about *his* character?

Will shook away his unsettling thoughts with a swift jerk of his head and focused on his surroundings once more. Still in the grips of a dangerous heat wave, the day had grown uncommonly hot, the interior of the building twice as sweltering.

But despite the heat, the atmosphere inside the mill was congenial. Noise and chatter filled the air, mingling with the sound of grinding millstones crushing the newest shipment of cocoa beans into powder. Farther down the line the powder was heated into a thick syrup. Still farther down, workers poured the syrup into molds to make hard cakes that would eventually be sold under the name Black's Best Chocolate.

Although the cakes were used for baking or grated into hot milk to make a sweetened beverage, Will was working with his best chocolatiers to create a new product that would contain a higher sugar content. His children, both lovers of sweets, were his inspiration.

At the thought of Caleb and Olivia, Will's mind wandered to their new nanny. Bridget Murphy. Had she been sent to them straight from heaven?

Will shut his eyes momentarily and prayed. *Lord, let it be so.*

Focusing once more on his surroundings, he looked around the main floor of operation. The men and women were hard at work. He employed most of the Irish immigrants who lived in the area and liked to think he treated them fairly. But chocolate making was hot, grueling work, especially in the midst of a heat wave.

Combing a hand through his sweat-dampened hair, he went in search of his foreman, a middle-aged man with strong arms and a ready smile. "Joe. A word."

"Mr. Black." Joe stepped away from the millstone and greeted him with his no-nonsense tone and sharp manner. "Any news on the shipment of my nuts?" Joe always called cocoa beans nuts.

"The ship left South America on schedule. If the weather holds it will arrive in Boston Harbor sometime next week."

Wiping the sweat from his brow with a muscled forearm, Joe let out a relieved puff of air. "Not a moment too soon."

Will silently agreed. Business was so good they were running out of Joe's *nuts* at an alarming rate. "How we doing for today's production?"

"Ahead of schedule."

As Will expected. Joseph Ferguson was an excellent, efficient foreman who managed to inspire his workers to new heights of excellence.

Nodding his approval, Will pulled out his watch and checked the time. Four in the afternoon. Early still, but not alarmingly so. "Let's call it a day. Send everyone home."

Knowing better than to second-guess the decision, Joe made the announcement.

A loud cheer rose up from the workers.

"Joe, you go on home, too." He clapped the shorter man on the back. "Enjoy your family." Advice Will planned to take himself.

"You got it, boss."

Several workers thanked him personally as he made his way back to his office to retrieve his papers and other belongings. He thanked them in return for their continued hard work.

His gratitude was genuine. Many of the residents of Faith Glen thought of the Irish immigrants as intruders, outsiders. Will saw them as honest, honorable, hard-working people, which had been the primary reason he'd sent to Ireland for a bride.

A cold, ruthless wave of guilt spread through him. Bridget Collins deserved better than what he'd provided her. She'd suffered a terrible ending, death at sea, all because she'd been looking for the better life he'd promised to provide her in America.

Even as he thought of his bride with sadness, his

mind steered toward another female immigrant, the one who'd kindly stepped in, if only temporarily, to assist Will and his family while he determined what to do next.

He wondered what Bridget and the children were up to this very minute. Were they playing, laughing, having a good time together?

He quickened his pace, eager to hurry home and see for himself.

Less than a half hour later, Will stood frozen on the front steps just outside his house, struck immobile by the music wafting past the open windows. Then he noticed the sounds of laughter, and high-pitched, childish joy. He'd forgotten those sounds. For a moment he simply closed his eyes and allowed the music to wash over him.

Then more unwanted memories slammed into him, the kind he'd suppressed for a full year but seemed to be coming at him at an alarming rate these days. When he'd met Fanny at a dinner party in Boston she'd been playing a piano. The owner of a shipping company Will commissioned to import his cocoa beans had invited him to his home, under the guise of discussing business. But Richard Osmond had had another agenda in mind. He'd wanted Will to meet his daughter, Fanny.

Will had been smitten from the start. Fanny had been beautiful, talented, the most refined woman he'd ever met. And she'd played the piano with flair, indicating a passionate, enthusiastic nature.

The attraction had not been one-sided, no matter what Fanny had later claimed. She'd been equally enthralled with Will, and had gone out of her way to win him.

Their courtship had been a blur. They'd attended the

opera, the theater and countless parties. Will had found the social whirlwind amusing, primarily because he'd known he was too dedicated to his business and his employees to have continued the extravagant lifestyle beyond that initial burst.

Just like the partygoing, happiness hadn't lasted long in his marriage either, less than a year. Pain and anger had replaced what Will had thought was love. Shouting had replaced the music in his home. Joy had all but disappeared.

Now, standing on the front stoop, listening to the sound of his children singing and laughing, Will realized how much he'd missed the music.

He wanted to be a part of it now. He prayed the memories, or at least the worst of them, stayed away so he could simply enjoy the moment with his children. And his mother. And, of course, Bridget.

Bracing himself, he twisted the doorknob and shoved inside the house. The music was louder in the entryway, jollier, his children's laughter happier.

Will swallowed past a lump in his throat.

Not wanting to interrupt just yet, he held perfectly still, listening. He recognized Bridget's soft, lyrical tone as she led the song. Her voice has been just as sweet in church yesterday. And now his children, with Bridget's urging, were attempting one of his favorite nursery songs from childhood.

He mouthed the words along with them. *How does my Lady's garden grow? In silver bells, and cockle shells and pretty maids all in a row.*

Caleb was pretty shaky of the first part of the song, but he had the last line down. His voice rose to a near shout as he sang, "All in a *row!*"

The music stopped, only to be replaced by clapping. "Oh, well done," his mother said with unmistakable glee.

The children giggled in response. "Again," Caleb demanded. "Let's sing it again."

Heart suddenly lighter than he could ever remember, Will wanted to be a part of the fun. He entered the room.

His gaze landed on his mother first. She was sitting in a chair facing the piano, still clapping her hands in enthusiastic approval. She looked remarkably refreshed.

He felt his eyes burn with relief, then quickly looked away.

Thankfully Bridget hadn't seen him yet, nor had his children. Sitting on either side of her on the piano bench, the twins were hugging her fiercely. Both of their spindly arms wrapped tightly around her waist.

For her part Bridget alternated between kissing their heads and praising their singing. A portion of a long-forgotten verse from Isaiah came to mind. *They shall obtain gladness and joy; and sorrow and mourning shall flee away.*

Will cleared his throat.

Bridget snapped her head up. Their gazes met and held. Her eyes shone with emotion, and then…

She smiled. Directly at him.

Will felt himself suffocating until he managed to drag in a gasping tug of air.

He'd once thought a woman could only be considered beautiful if her hair was perfectly coiffed and she was clothed in fashionable attire.

But now, *now,* Will realized he'd been woefully incorrect in that assumption. There was nothing more appealing than the sight of wild, untamed hair escaping from a long, thick braid, and nothing more striking than his children's arms wrapped around the waist of Bridget Murphy.

The scene was enough to give any man pause, especially a man with Will's disastrous marital history and determination to avoid a second mistake for his children's sake. Yet as he continued to stare into Bridget's pretty eyes he felt a sudden release. For that single, solitary moment in time he was free. Free from the anger and guilt of the past. Free to start over.

Free.

Chapter Eleven

With Will's intense gaze locked with hers, something very strange and unfamiliar began to swell in Bridget's stomach. Her lips parted in surprise.

The way Will was looking at her. It—it was so—enthralling.

Her arms automatically tightened around the children. Both squirmed in response, Caleb more than Olivia, but neither let go of her waist. They clung to her, their little cheeks pressed to her ribs.

Bridget dipped her head and whispered, "Your da is home."

Squealing with pleasure, they simultaneously jumped off the bench and rushed for their father. They shoved one another, jockeying to be the first one to cross the short distance.

Caleb, the stronger of the two, won the harmless competition.

"Papa." He vaulted himself against his father's leg. "You're home early."

"Papa, Papa." Olivia hopped from one foot to the other, raising her voice to be heard over her brother. "Miss Bridget taught us a song."

With excruciating tenderness in his eyes, Will

touched his daughter's cheek. "I heard." He lowered
to his haunches so his gaze was level with hers. "You
sounded wonderful."

"Miss Bridget said we get to learn another song tomorrow," Caleb declared. "After we play some games
outside."

"Splendid." Will's face broke into a wide grin. The
gesture took ten years off his face and made him appear far more relaxed than Bridget had ever seen him.

The man was dangerously handsome, especially
when he smiled so tenderly. Captivated, she filled her
gaze with his face, his shoulders, his hair. She couldn't
stop staring at him.

Talking over one another, the children told their father about the various adventures of their day.

Reminding them to take turns, Will sat on the ground
and allowed them to crawl into his lap.

The children chattered on.

"And then she made us take a nap," Caleb said, wrin-
kling his nose in disgust.

Will laughed deep in his throat. "I never liked naps,
either."

Olivia tugged frantically on his sleeve. "Papa, Papa.
I learned how to braid my dolly's hair."

Will nodded solemnly. "A most important skill for
a young lady."

"That's what Miss Bridget said."

The three of them looked so happy, and so very different from the sad little family she'd met in the general
store two days ago. Was this change due to her influence? Had the Lord brought her to this home, at this
precise moment in time, to make a difference for this
family, to help them overcome their grief and sorrow?

If that was true, why did Bridget feel as though she
was the one receiving the blessing? The smiles, the gig-

gles, the relaxed shoulders on the far-too-serious man, *these* were her rewards. Her eyes stung with gratitude.

Thank You, Lord. Thank You for bringing me to this home and to this family.

Looking away before a tear escaped, Bridget caught Esther's eye. The older woman smiled brilliantly at her, her own eyes shining.

Several moments passed before the children finally wound down. Will untangled himself and rose to his feet. Olivia skipped back to Bridget and plopped onto the bench next to her. The little girl leaned against her and released a dramatic sigh of pleasure. Bridget wrapped her arm around the child's tiny shoulders. It felt natural to have Olivia with her, while Caleb stayed close to his father's side.

Bridget felt a pang at the sight the two made. Man and boy, father and son, the perfect statement of family.

She felt a tug on her heart, a painful yearning that dug all the way to her soul. *If only they were mine.*

Her breath hitched as the thought whispered through her. She swallowed, knowing her wish could never come true. Will didn't want a real family, he wanted a wife in name only.

Bridget wanted so much more. She wanted it all. Love, family, *forever*—someday. When her heart had healed from all the damage Daniel had done.

"Papa?" Caleb tugged on his father's hand. "Can we keep her?"

Will looked down at his son. "Keep who?"

"Miss Bridget." Caleb pointed in her direction. "Can we keep her for forever and ever?"

A pause.

"Oh, can we, Papa?" Olivia hopped off the stool and ran back to her father. *"Can we?"*

Will whipped his gaze to Bridget's, his eyes perfectly unreadable. For a long, tense moment they simply stared at one another. It was a question neither was prepared to answer.

Will cleared his throat. "It's only been a day, Cal. We don't..." he swallowed "...need to..."

"Decide anything just yet," Esther finished for him.

Asserting herself, the older woman stood and then crossed the room with surprising agility. *"Now."* She put a hand on each child's shoulder. "Let's get you two washed up for supper while your father and Miss Bridget have a quiet moment to talk about the day."

The childish arguments began at once, proving just how far the children had come in one day. When Bridget had met the twins in the general store, neither would have raised their voices, much less protested a direct command. She wondered if their father realized the magnitude of the change in them.

One day. Nothing more than a handful of hours in Bridget Murphy's care and his children were already acting like...children. Will was so pleased he didn't have the heart to reprimand them for their whining.

His mother had no such qualms. "That's enough, both of you." Her voice had taken on the stern yet loving tone he remembered from his own childhood. "Upstairs, now."

Will recovered quickly from his stupor. "Do as your grandmother tells you."

Both children grumbled then trooped out of the room with slumped shoulders. He resisted the urge to call them back and hug them until those forlorn looks disappeared. No matter how pleased he was to see their very normal behavior, he couldn't reward disobedience.

Once they were out of earshot, he turned back to face Bridget. "You have won over my children completely."

She smiled at the empty doorway, a look of gratification lighting her eyes. "I'm afraid it's the other way around. They are very charming."

As are you.

He refrained from saying the words aloud. Barely. She was amazingly beautiful even with her disheveled appearance, and it was very distracting.

As though reading his mind, she smoothed an unsteady hand down her hair. The gesture drew his attention to her glorious face. The dark, loose waves were a perfect contrast to the flawless alabaster skin. A woman shouldn't be that stunning after wrangling two three-year-olds all day.

Will shook his head, only just realizing the heavy silence that had fallen between them.

This awkwardness would not do. Perhaps a change of scenery would help matters. "I would like to hear how the day went from your perspective," he began, pleased his tone was easy and businesslike. "Would you do me the honor of a short walk along the lane?"

"That would be lovely, Will."

The way she said his name in that soft Irish lilt made his steps falter. Recovering quickly, he strode to the entryway, waited for her to join him and then opened the door so she could lead the way onto the front steps.

As she passed by him, Will breathed in her scent, a blend of lavender and fresh air. She carried herself with poise and dignity, and not for the first time, he wondered about her background. Where she came from. Why she'd left her home. What her plans were now that she was in Faith Glen.

Determining how best to start the conversation, he directed her down the lane toward the town square. The afternoon heat hadn't yet dissipated, but there was a pleasant breeze kicking up.

"Tell me about your life back in Ireland."

She didn't answer him right away. And as he stared at her he realized her expression wasn't merely sad. It was grief stricken, as though she was working to hold back painful memories.

"You've lost someone recently," he said softly, wishing he could wipe away her sorrow but understanding there wasn't much he could do. Death was final.

"My da."

"And your mother? What about her?"

"She died ten years prior, during a terrible influenza epidemic."

"I'm sorry." He knew his words were woefully inadequate, but she graciously accepted his condolences with a nod.

"At Da's funeral Reverend Larkin promised we would see him again someday in a heavenly place, a place where there will be no more hunger or sickness."

The preacher at his father's funeral had said something similar. "That must have been a comfort."

"Not at the time." She pressed a fisted hand to her midriff and sniffed back what sounded like the beginnings of a sob. "Especially since we'd been turned out of the only house we'd ever known that very same day."

"How…" He wanted to say criminal, but he didn't know the particulars so he swallowed back the word and said, "That must have been terrifying."

"Terrifying? Yes, I suppose it was, but it was also grossly unfair. We'd worked the land alongside Da for years. It wasn't right, what Mr. Bantry did, kicking us off the land without warning. Maeve, my youngest sister, was the most upset."

"The one married to Flynn Gallagher, the doctor on the *Annie McGee?*"

"That's the one." A distant smile spread across her

lips. "Maeve said 'May God turn Bantry's heart, and if He doesn't turn his heart, may He turn Bantry's ankle, so we'll know him by his limping.'"

Will let out a short bark of laughter. "Can't say I blame her, under the circumstances."

Bridget bit her bottom lip as though trying to keep from smiling, or perhaps frowning. "She wasn't feeling very charitable at the time. None of us were."

If Will ever traveled to Ireland he would find Mr. Bantry and tell him exactly what he thought of the man's treatment of the Murphy sisters. Not usually prone to violence, Will felt a strong urge to punch the other man in the face. And then he would...

Best not to continue the rest of his thought.

"So you were tossed out of the only home you ever knew." Anger made his voice come out harder than he intended. He drew a breath. "And then the three of you decided to come to America."

The courage and faith required to make such a journey had Will admiring Bridget Murphy and her sisters all the more.

"Not at first." The distant expression filled her gaze once again and Will sensed she was no longer with him but back in Ireland. "When we started to pack our belongings Nora found a faded daguerreotype of our dear mother in an old worn frame. Behind the likeness we found a letter from a man named Laird O'Malley and a drawing of a home with a beautiful garden beside it."

Recognizing the name, Will stopped walking. "A Laird O'Malley settled here in Faith Glen a few years after I was born."

"That would be the same man." She looked up at him with shining eyes. "He told our ma that he would always love her, that he'd built a house that he would keep waiting for her. He put the deed to his home in our mother's name."

Will nodding in understanding, then resumed walking, matching his stride to her slower pace. "So you decided to come to America for the home awaiting you here."

The move only made sense, yet he still admired the courage it took the sisters to leave everything they knew behind and set off for a foreign land.

"We had enough money to live on for a month or buy three tickets to America." She smiled at him. "As I'm sure you have already guessed, we bought the tickets and placed ourselves in the Lord's care."

Her smile was enough to make his steps falter.

"Unfortunately when we arrived three days ago Sheriff Long said the house wasn't legally ours until we verified our deed against the one filed in the County Clerk's Office. He promised it was just a formality and agreed to travel to the county seat with us himself."

"Sounds like Cam."

"He and Nora left this morning, after dropping me off at your house. They took baby Grace with them."

Will silently wondered how Cam was coping with a woman and an infant in tow. It was a well-known fact that the big bad sheriff of Faith Glen was uncomfortable around children, especially babies. Will could see Cam squirming now, tugging on his collar and doing his best to pretend Grace didn't exist.

Will's smile faded as an image of Laird's house flashed in his mind. James Coulter had hurt his hip a few years back. The old man hadn't been the same since, but refused to admit he couldn't take care of his own home. As a result the house had fallen into a state of disrepair. Will had never liked the idea of the elderly couple residing in the house in its current condition. He liked the idea of Bridget joining them even less.

"Have you seen the house yet?"

"I'm afraid so." She stumbled over a small branch. He reached out, holding her steady until she caught her balance. Once she was walking once more, he let her go then offered his arm.

She accepted his assistance without question, as if they'd made this walk countless times before. The easiness he felt with her should have left him unsettled. Instead the rightness of the moment made speech impossible for several seconds.

Will forced himself to concentrate on the conversation once more. "So if I understand you correctly, you will know sometime later today if the deed you possess to Laird's house is legal?"

Her fingers flexed on his arm. "Aye, that's the way of it."

Although she'd been very forthright in all her answers, Will sensed Bridget was holding something back, a personal piece of her story she didn't feel comfortable sharing with him. "Any regrets leaving Ireland?"

"Not many." Her response came quickly, perhaps a bit too quickly. "I miss some of the people."

Some of the people, or one in particular? A man, perhaps? Just as he opened his mouth to ask, a mangy dog came into view. The hound stood several yards ahead of them on the path, his shoulders hunched in a slightly aggressive stance. Burrs and twigs were caught in his coat.

Will shifted in front of Bridget and put himself in the direct path of the animal. He rose to his full height and stared hard at the dog. Bridget's safety was in his hands, now.

The dog hunched lower and added an insistent bark, bark, bark in the process.

Will balanced his weight evenly on both feet, holding steady, ready for a sudden attack, prepared to strike if necessary.

He had the situation under control, or so he thought, until Bridget got it in her mind to join the scuffle. Speaking in a soft, sweet tone, she moved out from behind Will and told the mutt he was a "pretty boy."

"Stay back," he warned her, punctuating his command with an outstretched arm that barred her way.

She stepped around him, just as the dog flattened his ears against his head and increased the volume of his barks.

"Aren't you a sweet boy?" she cooed as though she were talking to an infant. "We aren't here to hurt you, you know."

Will knew better than to make any sudden move, but he couldn't stand by and watch Bridget step straight into danger. Filing through several possible scenarios, he eased toward Bridget. "You need to get behind me again so I can—"

"He's afraid of you," she whispered, her eyes still on the agitated animal. "Isn't that right, little doggy? The big bad man is scaring you."

"Little doggy," Will muttered under his breath. "He's at least seventy pounds." And was some sort of mixed breed with black, brown and possibly white fur. It was hard to tell under all the dirt.

Bridget took a tentative step forward.

The dog's ears lifted, just a bit, enough to tell Will that Bridget's tactic was working.

"That's right, boyo." She took another step. "I'm not going to hurt you."

The ears relaxed some more and then *boyo* belly-crawled toward her.

She stuck out her hand, slowly. "That's it."

The dog inched forward again.

This painful process of belly-crawl and soft encouragement went on for several minutes. At last, the animal raised himself to all fours then sniffed Bridget's hand tentatively.

Another moment passed and the mangy tail started wagging.

If Will hadn't been there to witness the full exchange, he would have never believed it possible. Bridget Murphy had won over a skittish dog in a matter of minutes. And she didn't look a bit concerned the outcome could have been less pleasant.

"You've done this before," he said, aware his voice was full of awe.

"Maybe a time or two." She smiled at the dog. "Put your hand out, slowly," she told Will, "so he can get a hold of your scent and know you aren't a threat."

"Who says I'm not a threat?"

"I do." She gave him a look that grabbed at his heart and tugged. In that moment Will would have done anything she asked of him. He'd never really understood Delilah's hold over Samson. Until now. A woman's smile was her most powerful weapon, and a man's ultimate doom.

"Go on," Bridget urged. "Make friends. Or we won't be able to continue our walk."

Knowing she was right, Will did as she suggested. One inch at a time, he stuck out his hand.

The dog dutifully sniffed and then licked his knuckles. Boyo was friendly enough, if a bit jumpy. Who could blame him? It was obvious the creature had been neglected and, Will narrowed his eyes, starved. A burst of indignation filled his heart. No creature should suffer ill-treatment like that.

"He needs food," Will said, eyeing the emaciated

frame, and the matted fur. "And a bath." He contemplated a way to accomplish both tasks without putting his children in danger when the sound of a wagon wheel crunching over gravel sounded in the distance.

The dog flattened his ears against his head, looked over his shoulder and then shot off like a bullet toward the forest.

"He's gone," Bridget said with a sigh. "What a shame."

Will wasn't so sure.

As much as it pained him to admit it, even in the privacy of his own mind, he didn't much like sharing Bridget's affections with a dog. He knew he had no claim on her. She was merely company. He liked her. Perhaps too much.

She's your children's nanny, he reminded himself. Why couldn't he keep that straight in his head?

Chapter Twelve

Soon after the dog disappeared into the woods, leaving a row of trampled wildflowers in his wake, Bridget heard the grind of wagon wheels approaching from the distance. Had the skittish animal heard the sound as well and sensed a threat? Had that been the cause for his hasty departure?

Whatever the reason, Bridget was sad to see him run off. Like Will said, he needed food and a bath, in that order.

Perhaps the animal would return. If he did, she would work to keep him close, then she would go about getting the poor dear some food.

Pleased by the thought, she felt a smile spread across her lips. But in the next moment her mind faltered and she paused to absorb what had just happened. Sensing danger, Will had put himself between Bridget and the dog. He'd been willing to sacrifice his safety for hers.

She wasn't used to that sort of care and protection from anyone other than her family and didn't know how she felt about it. Pleased, to be sure, but also uncomfortable and confused. Bridget took care of others. They did not take care of her.

The polite thing to do would be to acknowledge

Will's gallant behavior. She studied his profile. The sudden despair of knowing he would never be hers, not truly, lent urgency to her words. "Thank you, Will."

He turned to face her. "Pardon me?"

His strong jaw was shaded with dark stubble. She wanted to reach up and touch, to feel the rough prickles on her fingertips. She clenched her hand into a fist. "I… Thank you for trying to protect me from the dog."

He continued to stare at her.

"He could have been feral," she added.

Will blinked very slowly, his silvery-pale eyes filled with strangled emotion as he took her hand in his. "Praise God he wasn't."

"Yes, praise God." Instead of pulling her hand free she braided her fingers through his.

Something quite lovely passed between them, a moment of complete contentment that went beyond words. But instead of feeling delighted by the sensation, a wistful sadness crept through her. Will wanted the kind of wife she could never be for him, or for any man.

She dropped her gaze and sighed. She would not— *would not, would not, would not*—allow herself to want what she could never have.

Another moment passed and then someone shouted her name. "Bridget. Oh, Bridget, we have news. Good news."

Reluctantly pulling her hand free from Will's comforting grip, Bridget turned toward an approaching wagon. Cameron Long and Nora and baby Grace had returned.

Bridget had no doubt what that news was.

She should be beside herself with joy. Yet the sight of her sister with that wide smile spread across her face roused the most curious reaction. Annoyance. She was actually annoyed Nora had returned at this very moment. The strange, unexpected reaction constricted her lungs and she thought impatiently, *Why am I not more pleased?*

"Stop fretting, Bridget. Everything will work out fine." Will punctuated his statement by reaching out and giving her hand a gentle squeeze. An immediate sense of relief spread through her entire body.

She swallowed back her misgivings and looked up again, calling upon the faith that had brought her to this crucial moment in time. Bridget had been the most hopeful of all her sisters about this venture to America. She'd certainly felt the most confident when Nora and Maeve had wavered. Why was she not happier now?

What was causing her reservation?

Cameron pulled the wagon to a stop, nodded a silent greeting to Will, then smiled down at Bridget. "You will be pleased to know that all went according to plan."

She turned her gaze to Nora and lifted a questioning eyebrow.

"It's true," Nora said, her smile as radiant as Bridget had ever seen. "We own Laird O'Malley's house, free and clear."

Feeling oddly placid by the news, Bridget nodded. "So the deed is legal."

"That's what I just said."

At last—*at last*—Bridget's stomach gave a delighted leap. "Oh, Nora, this is wonderful news."

"I was wondering when you'd say that."

Hopes and dreams tangled together in her mind, weaving into a beautiful tapestry of possibilities. Bridget paused to sort through one wonderful reality after another. For the first time in her life her future was secure.

There was much work ahead, but she and Nora

would be repairing their own home and toiling on their own land.

It was all quite exciting.

She was suddenly aware of the man standing beside her, his silent presence far more comforting than she would have thought possible from a man she'd only met three days ago. She turned to face him again.

He smiled.

"You will want to go with your sister and discuss your next step." Although the words were uttered in a light vein, Will's eyes were alert, questioning.

"Not yet. The children will be expecting me." More than that, she wanted to see them through their suppertime and then read to them before they went to bed. Somewhere during the day the twins had stopped being a duty and had become her joy.

"Stay with your sister, Bridget. You have much to plan. I'll tell the children where you've gone. They'll understand."

Bridget wasn't nearly as confident. But what bothered her most wasn't what Will had just said but rather that he'd spoken in such a stunningly offhanded manner, as if he was used to making up other people's minds for them.

"No, Will. I appreciate the offer but I will return home with you." She took a deep breath and held her ground. "And only leave once the children are in bed."

He opened to his mouth to argue.

She cut him off with a raised hand. "And that's the end of the matter."

There was a flash of something in his eyes, something akin to amusement, as though he'd just come to a sudden realization that was a welcome discovery. "If that's what you want."

"It is."

"Then I'll make sure you are safely returned to the boardinghouse after the children are settled for the night."

Now that they had come to an understanding, Bridget wanted to make sure Nora was comfortable with her decision. Not that it would matter, but she didn't want her sister to feel abandoned. "You will be all right without me for a little while longer, yes?"

"Go on, Bridget, and take care of your charges." There was an odd note in her voice, an indulgent consideration that wasn't typical for Nora. There were also questions in her eyes, none of which Bridget knew how to answer just yet. Suddenly, a few more hours with the Black family seemed very attractive.

"We'll talk later tonight," she said in an even voice, hoping to send Nora on her way.

"Yes, Bridget," Nora replied, rearranging the baby in her arms. "We will talk later." Now *that* was the tone Bridget expected from her older sister, the quiet warning that promised much would be discussed once the two of them were finally alone.

When a heavy silence descended over their tiny group, Cameron took charge. He bid a friendly farewell to both Bridget and Will, and then asked if Nora was ready. She nodded.

The wagon rolled away with Nora gazing back over her shoulder. The insistent look in her eyes was enough to give Bridget pause. But not enough to make her think she'd made a mistake by staying with Will. Putting him and the children ahead of her desire to make plans for her own future seemed the right thing to do.

In that moment, she realized the Black family had already become a part of her heart. She prayed they didn't break it.

* * *

Several hours later Will sat in a chair beside Caleb's bed while Bridget's lilting voice filled the room. She read from the twin's favorite book, *Mother Goose's Melody*.

Will closed his eyes and listened. Her inflection was different than his mother's had been when she'd read to him as a child, yet just as soothing. Transfixing, even.

He opened his eyes and found himself watching Bridget's lips move as she spoke. She was achingly beautiful and something tugged at his heart. A breeze fluttered the curtains, creating a soft, pleasant feel to an already tender moment. Will tried not to read too much into the situation. Bridget was reciting nursery rhymes to his children as part of her job, nothing more.

Perched on the edge of Olivia's bed, near the foot, book spread across her lap, Bridget paused, looked up and caught him watching her. Holding his gaze, she continued narrating the story of Mary and her little lamb. All the while her beautiful eyes searched his, her gaze full of profound gentleness. No woman had ever looked at him that way before, certainly not Fanny. He swallowed a wave of unease.

She mercifully looked back to her book.

On surprisingly unsteady legs Will quietly left the room. Two steps into the hallway his mother grabbed his arm. He started to speak but she shook her head and pulled him away from the children's bedroom.

There was no sound in the house except the distant melody of Bridget's voice.

"I don't know where you found her, son, but that Bridget Murphy is a treasure."

He shot a look over his shoulder, a rueful affection filling him. "Yes, she is."

"She told me a little about how she ended up in Faith Glen. If you ask me—"

"Which I didn't."

"If you ask me," she repeated with deliberate slowness, "I'd say Bridget's appearance at such a time as this is a sure sign the Lord has smiled on our family at last."

Will didn't argue the point. Why would he? Hadn't he already decided that Bridget was indeed a gift from God?

Yet even as he silently admitted that he liked her, maybe even trusted her, discomfort spread through him.

Bridget was not a permanent fixture in his home, nor would she ever be. Her position was only temporary and still on a trial basis. She could still change her mind at the end of the week, and there was nothing Will could do about it.

Or was there?

What if he gave her no reason to leave? What if he gave her every reason to stay?

"...then she managed to coax Caleb into taking a nap, after she'd astonishingly convinced Olivia to hand over her unwanted crackers when Caleb had run out of his."

Will shook his head, only just realizing his mother had been speaking the entire time he'd been thinking about Bridget.

"What did you just say?" He thought he heard something about a nap and crackers? Did Bridget let the twins eat crackers in their beds?

"It was nothing important, just a little something about the children." A knowing smile hovered on his mother's lips, then spread into a grin as she looked over his shoulder. "Bridget, dear, are you finished reading already?"

"I am. The children are sound asleep."

Hearing the satisfaction in her voice, Will turned

around, hoping to get a glimpse of her smile. What he saw were drooping eyelids. "You're tired."

"Only a little." She released a soft laugh. What a wonderful sound, he thought, light and throaty. "I've had an amazing day."

Will liked knowing she'd found pleasure in her position with his family. "Let's get you to the boardinghouse at once, or you'll be too exhausted to return in the morning."

He lifted up a silent prayer that this woman would continue as his children's nanny. And then another that she was as trustworthy as she seemed.

After she said good-night to his mother, Will escorted Bridget outside then drew to a stop at the end of the walkway. "Wait here while I bring the carriage around."

She placed a hand to his arm. "It's such a lovely evening, Will, and the boardinghouse is so close. Let's walk."

"You aren't too tired?"

"Not at all. The fresh air has quite restored me."

"Well, then, Bridget, allow me to walk you home."

Bridget and Will made their way down the lane in companionable silence, turning together at the bend. Enjoying the sounds of the night and the unique smells that were familiar yet also foreign, she took a deep breath. The same sweet scent she'd smelled that first carriage ride into town filled her nose. "That aroma, is it from your mill?"

"It's the chocolate syrup, the byproduct of the melted cocoa powder." A smile tugged at his lips. "I'm so used to the smell I forget it's there."

She suddenly wanted to know more about his work,

about how he spent his days. "Tell me how you make chocolate."

As he described the process, she could picture him in his mill, his shirtsleeves rolled up, his powerful arms pouring cocoa beans between the millstones. She suspected he was a fair employer, one who expected the best out of his workers without demanding the impossible. When he explained the grueling process of heating the powder into syrup, she stopped him. "So you closed the mill early today because of the unbearable heat?"

"Partly, yes." He shrugged, looking a bit sheepish. "But I also wanted to see how you and the children were making out."

"You mean you wanted to check on me."

"I did." He paused a beat. "As well as the children and my mother."

Bridget wasn't offended by his admission—well, only a little. A man like William Black would want to ensure his loved ones were in good hands. How could she find fault in that? "You care very much for your family."

"I do." His tone was light but his eyes had taken on a very serious gleam. This was a man who would sacrifice everything for his family, even his life. Once again she experienced a strong desire to be cherished so completely, to enjoy the same care and concern that Will bestowed upon his kin. Earlier, he'd stepped up to protect her, but that had likely just been chivalry. What would it be like to have his devotion, his love?

Did she want those things from him, in particular, or would any man do?

It was a question she shouldn't ask herself, not now. Perhaps not ever. Will had made his intentions clear. Perhaps the death of his wife had left no more room in his heart for romantic love again.

Bridget looked down at her feet, swallowed three times, each time the beating of her heart grew louder in her head.

"We're here."

She looked up, having lost track of their route. "So we are."

Will set a hand on her shoulder and turned her to face him. "Thank you, Bridget." He reached up and touched her cheek. "Thank you for giving my children a lovely day and my mother a much-needed break."

Compelled, she leaned into his hand, trying not to sigh. It was all quite disturbing, this pull she felt for a man she hardly knew.

"It was a joy working in your home today," she said, desperately needing to remind herself she was this man's employee.

He dropped his hand to his side. "Would you like me to fetch you in the morning?"

What a lovely offer and completely unnecessary. "No. I can walk the two-and-a-half blocks on my own."

He took a step away from her. The added distance between them felt like a chasm. "Then I will see you in the morning."

"Good night, Will."

"Good night."

As she watched him turn and leave, Bridget remembered she was working for him only on a trial basis.

Why had she made such a condition? She didn't want to leave his employ. She adored the twins, and Esther, too. The thought of walking away from any of them—or from Will—brought physical pain.

There was a simple solution to the problem. She would give Will no reason to ask her to leave. She would make herself so indispensable he wouldn't be able to live without her.

Smiling at the thought, she turned and walked up the boardinghouse steps. She froze midway. Nora was waiting for her. "You just missed Flynn and Maeve."

"I'm sorry for that. How are they faring?"

"As well as two blissfully in love people can manage."

Bridget smiled. "The poor dears."

Nora laughed. "Flynn is considering the idea of opening a medical practice in Faith Glen and maybe even building a house so he and Maeve can be closer to us."

"Oh, Nora." Bridget clasped her hands together in excitement. They'd talked of this before, of Flynn and Maeve eventually making Faith Glen their home. But to hear it confirmed made Bridget's heart fill with joy. "That's wonderful news."

No longer smiling, Nora acknowledged her words with a distracted nod. "They plan to return for another visit Sunday afternoon. Flynn wants to check out Laird O'Malley's house before we move in."

"You mean *our* house."

"Yes." Nora nodded in satisfaction. "*Our* house."

"That's very kind of him." Bridget relaxed, but just as she commandeered the last step uneasiness stirred within her. Nora was alone.

"Where's Grace?" She caught her breath inside a gasp. "Did Maeve take her? Has someone come forward to claim her?"

"No, no." Nora waved off her concern with a flick of her wrist. "Rose is watching the baby."

Confused, Bridget continued forward, walking through the shadows that were dark pools of gray at her feet. "Why is Rose watching Grace at this late hour?"

"I wanted to talk to you, Bridget, without any chance of distractions cutting off our conversation."

That didn't sound good.

"Has something happened since we last saw one another?" Her mind went immediately to the deed, then shot to the house, rounded back toward the elderly caretakers. "Is it the house? The Coulters? The deed itself?"

"Come, Bridget." Nora took her arm and directed her to one of the rocking chairs. "Sit."

She did as requested, primarily because she had no other choice. Nora was pressing down on her shoulders.

She landed on the seat with a plop.

Towering over her, Nora planted her fists on her hips and scowled.

Bridget shuddered at the look in her sister's eyes. A lecture was in the making and, quite frankly, she wasn't in the mood. She'd had a long day, a happy one but long nonetheless. All she wanted to do was go to bed and relive the precious moments in her mind.

Bridget leveled a challenging gaze on her sister. "Out with it, Nora."

"I want to talk to you about William Black."

Bridget pretended surprise, then adopted an innocent expression. "Why do you want to talk about my employer?"

"Don't pretend you don't know what I mean. You've been uncommonly concerned with his situation, and that worries me."

Bristling, Bridget jerked her chin. "He's had a rough go of it lately."

"I realize that." Nora lowered in front of her and placed her hands on Bridget's knees. "You like him, don't you?"

"He's a good man," she allowed, refusing to give her sister any more ammunition than necessary. "*And* a fair boss."

"That's right. You're his children's nanny, Bridget. You need to remember that very important point."

"What are you implying?" It was a rhetorical question. They both knew what Nora meant.

Sighing, Nora settled in the chair next to her and began rocking. They were both quiet a moment, each lost in their own thoughts.

"Bridget." Nora took her hand and squeezed. "You give your heart so freely. *Too* freely, I fear. After what Daniel did to you, I couldn't bear watching you go through that pain again."

The mention of her former fiancé took her by surprise and she flinched. "What does Daniel have to do with Will?"

"Everything." Nora released her hand. "You were devastated for months after he left you at the altar."

Of course she'd been devastated. She'd planned to make a life with Daniel McGrath. She'd thought he'd shared her same hopes and dreams, as well as her desire to serve the Lord. She'd been wrong, so terribly wrong. Daniel hadn't wanted Bridget to serve the Lord; he'd wanted her to serve him.

She still wasn't sure what hurt more. His rejection or the way he'd broken things off, minutes before the ceremony.

"That was a year ago, Nora. I'm fine, now." As soon as the words left her mouth Bridget realized they were true. She wasn't devastated by Daniel's change of heart, not anymore. In fact, had she married him she wouldn't have left Ireland. She wouldn't have met Will and his family. She wouldn't—

"I don't want to see you hurt again," Nora reiterated, shoving her hair off her face. "Daniel was a selfish man, only concerned with his own interests. I fear your new employer is no different."

"Will is *nothing* like Daniel."

"Isn't he?"

"No." She shook her head vehemently. "You have no right making assumptions like that. Will cares for his family and puts their needs above his own." That alone made him different from Daniel.

"What about your needs, Bridget? Does he put your needs first?"

It was an unfair question. "I'm his children's nanny, my needs aren't important."

"Oh, but they are. Bridget, listen to me." Nora's mouth tightened. "You've always put others first, yourself last."

"What's wrong with that? Aren't we supposed to be humble and consider others better than ourselves? Isn't that the message in your favorite Bible verse, Philippians 2:3?"

By Nora's scowl, Bridget knew she'd hit her mark. "I won't deny that your tender, giving spirit is your greatest gift. But I see the way you are with William Black, the way you look at him. Bridget, you're headed for another heartache."

Now Bridget was angry. Nora had no right to lecture her on this matter. She didn't know all the facts. "I'll not quit my job because of something that may or may not happen in the future. No—" she held up her hand to keep her sister from interrupting "—let me finish."

Nora clamped her lips tightly shut.

"I've made a promise to William Black to care for his motherless children until he can find another woman to marry. I will follow through with my promise." And if she harbored a secret hope, deep in a hidden place in her heart, that things might work out differently, well that was none of her sister's concern.

Feeling the tiniest bit guilty for holding back a portion of the truth, Bridget rose from the chair and lifted her nose in the air. "And that's the end of it. I'll not discuss this again with you, Nora."

Finished having her say, she marched toward the boardinghouse, head still high. No one told Bridget Murphy she was wrong to serve a family in need. Not even her older sister.

"Bridget, wait."

She stopped with her hand on the doorknob.

"Don't you want to talk about our new house and all we have ahead of us? We need to plan our next step and we need to do so together."

Nora wasn't exactly apologizing for her meddling, but Bridget knew the change of subject was an olive branch nonetheless.

It was also the perfect topic to erase Bridget's annoyance. Excited about the possibilities that lay ahead of them, she returned to her abandoned rocking chair. "I have some initial thoughts."

Nora smiled. "I'd love to hear them."

Chapter Thirteen

Hoping to catch Will before he left for the day, Bridget arrived at his house early the next morning. She caught him on the front stoop, just as he pulled two sleepy-eyed children into his arms. Laughing at something Caleb mumbled in his ear, he kissed them both on their tiny heads.

Caught up in the moment, Bridget's throat clogged with emotion. The unmistakable love and affection in Will's voice as he told his children to mind their new nanny made the backs of her eyes sting. She placed her fingertips to her eyelids and swallowed hard, praying the moment would pass before any of them noticed her watching them.

Too late. Olivia shrieked her name. "Miss Bridget, you're here!"

Straightening, Will pivoted around to face her. His lips spread into a welcoming smile.

Her reaction was immediate. Everything ground to a halt inside her, her breath, her heartbeat, her ability to think. And then an ache of longing tore through her, one that nearly brought her to her knees.

Bridget was a talker by nature, or, at least, she'd always thought that to be true about herself. But around this man, with his marvelous eyes and intense love for his children, she found herself speechless all too often. Today was no exception.

Caleb rescued her as he sped around his father and catapulted himself into her arms. She had to move quickly to keep from dropping him. Bobbling under his additional weight, she laughed. "Hello, Caleb."

The little boy rubbed his cheek against her shoulder. "Good morning, Miss Bridget." So heartfelt, so sweet.

"I think he likes you," Will said over her head.

"It's a mutual affection."

He chuckled. "I see that."

Setting the child on the ground, she smiled up at her new boss. She felt an actual impact when their gazes met. "I'm glad I caught you."

"You are?" His voice sounded pleased.

"My sister and I have decided to move into Laird O'Malley's house, I mean *our* house, Sunday afternoon." She wasn't sure why she felt the need to inform him of her plans. He was only her employer. His confused expression indicated he was wondering the same thing. She paused, collecting her thoughts. "I just wanted you to know I don't plan to ask for a day off."

"I would have given it to you if you'd asked."

Of course he would have. "Nevertheless." She smiled despite her nerves. "I thought you should know."

"Thank you." He reached down and picked up a large leather case that she guessed was designed to house important papers. "I'll be home early again tonight."

And with that he was striding away from them, tossing one last goodbye over his shoulder.

Staring after him, her throat thick with emotion, Bridget smoothed a hand down her hair and breathed in deeply.

Caleb yanked on her skirt, practically vibrating with

little-boy eagerness. "What are we going to do today? Can we play tag?"

Not to be left out of the planning, Olivia pulled on Bridget's skirt from the other side. "I want to see the baby again, the one you had with you at church."

After much discussion and a bit of arguing between the twins it was decided they would do both, a rousing game of tag followed by a short visit to the Sheriff's Office to see how Nora and baby Grace were coping. "But before we start the fun and games we're going to march back inside, eat our breakfast and then practice our letters."

A chorus of mild-mannered grumbles followed her statement, but they obeyed.

By the time they were on the road to Nora's place of employment, Bridget had learned several interesting things about her new charges. They had exceptional patience for three-year-olds, never once fidgeting during their lesson, and their minds were like sponges. They remembered whatever she taught them after the first telling. The Black children were a pleasure to teach.

Holding their hands, Bridget drew up short at the sight that filled her gaze. A familiar young man was talking to Sheriff Long on the walkway outside the jail.

What was Gavin McCorkle doing in Faith Glen? He was supposed to be in Boston with his brothers and Mrs. Fitzwilliam. Had something happened? No, he didn't appear upset. He was quite animated, gesturing wildly with his hands as he spoke.

"Gavin? Gavin McCorkle?" She closed the distance between them. "Is that really you?"

"Miss Bridget." His face split into a grin, his blue eyes enormous in his freckled face. "I was just telling the sheriff about our journey across the ocean with you and your sisters. And he was telling me about your new jobs."

He paused, looked down. His grin widened. "This must be Caleb and Olivia Black."

"You know our names?" Caleb asked, his round little face full of wonder.

"I sure do."

"You talk like Miss Bridget. Did you come over on a ship, too? Like this one?" Caleb lifted the boat in his hand.

"Would you look at that?" Gavin gave a low, appreciative whistle. "It's the *Annie McGee* herself."

Caleb giggled, clearly delighted by the attention from the older boy. While he rattled off the various points of interest on the model boat he now knew by heart, Bridget looked over at Cameron Long.

The sheriff was leaning against a post in a leisurely manner, seemingly relieved Gavin was otherwise occupied. She hid a smile. From what she remembered of the oldest McCorkle brother, Gavin could be very enthusiastic when telling a story.

"Hello, Cameron," she said, giving him a sympathetic smile.

He tipped his hat. "Bridget, always a pleasure."

"Is my sister inside?"

"Yep." He pushed away from the post and gave Olivia an awkward pat on the head. "Nora's tidying the jail."

"Oh." Bridget hadn't fully thought through this impromptu visit and now she wasn't sure she should expose the children to an actual jailhouse.

"The jail cells are empty." He lowered his voice for her ears only. "Olivia and Caleb have been inside before."

"Well, then," she breathed in an audible sigh of relief, "very good."

Deciding she'd been ignored long enough, Olivia scooted in between Bridget and the sheriff. "Is baby Grace inside, too?"

"She sure is," he confirmed with a slightly caged look. The man really was uncomfortable around children.

"Can we go see the baby now?" Olivia pleaded. "Please? Oh, please?"

"In a moment." Bridget placed her hand on the girl's shoulder. "You'll have to be patient a little while longer."

Lower lip jutting out, Olivia gave a long-suffering sigh then plopped onto the bench outside the jailhouse, her doll cradled in her arms.

"As nice as it is to see you, I have to run out to the Phelps's place before lunch." Cameron looked down at Olivia then lowered his voice even further. "Mrs. Phelps claims someone tried to break into her barn last night."

Bridget swallowed back a gasp. "I thought you said this was a peaceful community."

"It is." He gave her an assuring smile. "She probably heard a raccoon rustling around, or maybe a stray dog."

Remembering the skittish animal she and Will had come across last evening, Bridget relaxed. "That makes sense."

He tipped his hat again, said goodbye to Gavin and the children, then was gone.

Once he turned the corner, Bridget returned her attention to the oldest McCorkle brother. "Gavin," she said softly. "I still don't know what you're doing in Faith Glen."

Smiling at Caleb, he handed the toy back to the boy then stood to address Bridget's question. "Mrs. Fitzwilliam sent me to find out how you and Miss Nora are settling into your new home."

Although the widow's interest in them was heart-warming, it made little sense. Yes, they'd created a bond aboard ship, but the older woman was far above the Murphy sisters' station. "I half expected her to forget us by now."

"No, don't say that, Miss Bridget. Don't even think it." Gavin shook his head vehemently. "Mrs. Fitzwil-liam has been very worried about all of you, even baby Grace. I'm not to return home without a full report."

Home. Bridget couldn't help but smile. The way Gavin said the word alleviated any remaining doubts she might have had about the boy's future.

"I'm also to let you know," he continued, "that she's successfully hired a private detective to search for Mary."

"Oh. Yes, of course." Bridget's cheeks grew warm. She'd been so caught up in her own life she'd nearly for-gotten about Mrs. Fitzwilliam's worry over her missing stepgranddaughter. "Has she had news, then?"

"None, so far." Gavin broke eye contact a moment. "It seems the girl has vanished into thin air."

"How disappointing."

"Yes, very."

Out of the corner of her eye Bridget watched Caleb set his boat beside his sister then jump from one plank to the next, reciting the alphabet as he went.

"But Mrs. Fitzwilliam has hired the best detective in Boston. We're very hopeful she'll find Mary soon."

Gavin sounded as concerned as his benefactor. Mrs. Fitzwilliam had obviously taken the McCorkle broth-ers into her heart, but so had they taken her into theirs. It was a lovely ending to a rocky beginning for all four of them.

"You are looking very well, Gavin." She paused to eye his clothing. The trousers and shirt were a far better quality than the ones he and his brothers had worn aboard the *Annie McGee*.

Blushing under the inspection, Gavin scuffed the toe of his boot on the sidewalk. "Mrs. Fitzwilliam has been very good to me and my brothers."

"I'm glad to hear it."

"She's even gone so far as to enroll me in school," he said, sighing heavily, his tone falling short of pleased. "She says it's important I better myself with an education."

"That seems like wise advice," Bridget said carefully, not sure what she heard in his voice. "Gavin, do you not wish to attend school?"

He shrugged. "I was never good with books. I'd rather be a lawman—" he looked over his shoulder in the direction Cameron had taken out of town "—maybe even a sheriff one day."

It took little imagination for Bridget to picture Gavin in the role. The boy had a very strong sense of right and wrong and knew how to protect others, as evidenced by the care he'd given his younger brothers. Yes, she could see him one day becoming a deputy. "Have you told Mrs. Fitzwilliam any of this?"

"A hundred times." He shrugged again. "She won't listen, says I'm far too smart to waste time on such a lowly endeavor."

Now *that* sounded like the high-handed widow Bridget remembered. Before she could comment any further Caleb hopped onto the plank next to Gavin, stopping mere inches from slamming into him. "I know how to say the entire alphabet," he declared, his little chest puffed out with pride. "Want to hear?"

Gavin ruffled his hair, seemingly fine with the change of topic. "Sure do."

Three verses later, minus a few letters in the middle, Bridget decided it was time to move along. "Come, children. You, too, Gavin. Let's find out how my sister and baby Grace are making out."

"At last." Olivia hopped to her feet, her eyes thrilled. The little girl was the first to enter the building, the rest of their tiny group following closely behind.

Since the first day Bridget had begun working in his home, Will had found a multitude of reasons to alter his daily routine. He'd closed the mill hours ahead of schedule—and only partially because of the stifling heat. He'd returned twice under the guise of having left important papers behind. He'd eventually quit making excuses and journeyed home to eat lunch with Bridget and the rest of his family.

And thus, as the noon hour approached on the fifth day of Bridget's employment, Will walked home with a smile on his face. Today was the end of her one-week trial. He would definitely be asking her to stay on.

Whistling the song she'd taught the children last night, he headed for the front door. Childish giggles dancing on the wind had him redirecting his steps toward the backyard. A familiar bark had him increasing his pace to a dead run.

When Will rounded the side of the house he froze.

Happy chaos reigned in the backyard of the Black home. It wasn't long before a laugh bubbled in his throat, begging for release. He let it come, let it flow out of him with welcome force.

Bridget had somehow managed to entice the mangy mutt they'd encountered earlier in the week into a tub of soapy water. The dog splashed around, tossing his head in the air, sending suds flying.

In their attempt to help, the children were as wet as the animal. Even Bridget hadn't escaped the madness. Her dress was half-soaked while her hair clung in wet tendrils around her face. She'd never looked more beautiful.

He watched her try to form some semblance of order amidst the bedlam. Or rather she tried and failed. Somehow, he didn't think she meant to succeed.

Will wanted to join the fun, but he wasn't sure adding another person to the fray was wise.

The dog settled the matter by jumping out of the tub and barreling straight for him. There was only time for impressions before his arms were filled with wet, wiggling fur. If an animal could smile, Will was certain this one was doing so, a big, loopy grin that included a hanging tongue. The same tongue that swiped across his face.

He laughed again. His suit was probably ruined, but all he could think was: *She's done it again. Bridget has charmed yet another unsuspecting creature.* At this rate the whole town would be under her influence in a month.

Looking over the dog's head, he caught her eye.

Her returning smile was enough to stop his breath.

"All right, boyo," he said, desperate to regain control over his emotions. "Let's get you back in the tub."

Will set the animal on the ground, clapped his hands and set out. The dog obediently followed.

"Papa," Caleb shouted. "We found a dog." He pointed unnecessarily to the wet animal practically dancing beside him.

Bridget gave Will immediate assurance that his children hadn't been in harm's way. Of that he had no doubt.

Not when he remembered the night they'd first encountered the dog and how quickly she'd soothed the nervous animal's fears.

Bending over, Will lifted the dog in his arms and set him in the tub once more. "Where did you find him?"

"Actually..." Bridget poured a bucket of water over the animal's soapy fur "...he found us."

A wide spray of water and suds shot through the air as the dog shook, and then shook again. Giggling, Olivia opened her arms and twirled under the impromptu waterfall. Caleb jumped up and down in his own version of the same dance.

Feeling unusually lighthearted himself, Will swiped water droplets off his face. "I'm sure there's a story behind this."

"Oh, there is," Bridget agreed, repeating the rinsing process.

Better prepared this time, Will took a step back before the animal shook himself free of the excess water.

By the third dousing every family member was as wet as the dog. No one seemed to mind, not even Bridget. She seemed entirely oblivious to her disheveled state. And that made her all the more stunning in Will's mind. Her face was bright and happy and incredibly beautiful.

He took another step back and nearly trampled over his tiny daughter. He caught her before she fell to the ground. Then, on a sudden whim, lifted her high in the air and spun her in circles. Around and around and around. She squealed in delight, kicking her legs wildly.

"Again," she demanded. "Do it again."

Will spun her around in the opposite direction.

The moment he set Olivia on the ground, Caleb lifted his arms. "My turn."

Laughing, Will obliged his son, tossing the little boy

over his shoulder after the third spin. He hopped around a bit then lowered him to the ground.

Once his feet were steady Caleb rushed back to the dog, now a very calm animal who was stoically enduring a vigorous toweling off from Bridget.

"Can we keep him, Papa?"

"Please, can we?" Olivia echoed.

"I have a feeling the matter is already settled." When both children simply stared at him, he clarified. "Yes, you may keep him, as long as he stays outside."

A chorus of cheers rose in the air. Sensing something significant had just occurred, the dog joined in the fun with a blissful *bark, bark, bark*. An impromptu celebration ensued.

Two children, one dog, lots of happiness.

Unable to remember a time he'd seen either of his children this uninhibited and natural, or when he'd felt this full of joy, Will glanced over at Bridget. Gratitude filled him. She had her head down, her hands busy pouring out the tub water onto the lawn.

Needing to thank her, he walked over to her, took her hand in his and laced their fingers together. Her soft intake of air was the only sign of her reaction to his bold move. He tightened his hold.

"You've done it again," he whispered.

She swung a startled glance up to his and then carefully drew her hand free. "I… I didn't mean to force the issue. The dog isn't a danger. He's—"

Will stopped the rest of her words with a finger to her lips. "I'm not angry."

Her mouth parted in surprise.

She looked so sweet, so innocent. So—kissable. He breathed in a sliver of hot summer air and nearly gave in to the urge to press his lips to her very attractive mouth.

She's your children's nanny, Will. Their. Nanny.

His instincts warned him to keep his distance, to remember why Bridget was in his home and that she'd refused to be his bride. She would not welcome his kiss—that had been made quite clear. "I better go change my clothes."

She said nothing, simply stared at him. Her hair hung loose around her face, the brown locks shot with red fire from the sun. The warm July air wafted between them and, still, she remained silent, blinking up at him as though deciphering a puzzle.

His arms itched to gather her close. He stepped back instead, and did so again for good measure. Each inch pulled him away from her, away from the temptation of doing something both of them might regret. Because no matter how many times he told himself this woman wasn't his, a rebellious part of him refused to accept that fact.

He turned on his heel and strode quickly to the house. His mother met him at the door. "My goodness, son, you're soaked through."

"Mother," he said in way of greeting, then rested his gaze upon her face. The purple shadows beneath her eyes were all but gone, the tight lines around her mouth smoothed away. "You look..." he searched for the proper word "...refreshed."

"Oh, I am." She ran a hand over her hair. "The daily naps Bridget insists I take have restored my tired old bones beyond my wildest hopes."

Once again Will found himself in Bridget Murphy's debt. Five days in his home and she'd worked wonders. His children were happy. His mother was no longer exhausted and he, well, *he* needed to change out of his wet clothes. He started off.

"Will, before you go."

He turned back around. "Yes?"

"Did you know Bridget and her sister are planning to move into Laird O'Malley's house Sunday afternoon?"

"She told me about the plans several days ago." And since that time he'd spent countless quantities of wasted breath trying to dissuade her from moving in so soon. But her excitement had been too great and she'd refused to listen to his arguments.

Although he'd eventually given up the fight, he still wasn't pleased with the idea of her living in that ramshackle house without a proper inspection first.

"I think you should assist the Murphy sisters with their move."

He'd like nothing better. It would give him a chance to check out the structure, assess any damage. But there was a problem, two of them to be exact. "The children—"

"Should stay home with me."

"Are you sure you're up to it?"

It was the precise wrong thing to say. "William Nathanial Black. I am not dead yet." Tiny as she was, his mother looked rather fierce. "I am quite capable of watching my grandchildren for a few hours."

He'd insulted her. That hadn't been his plan. "Of course you're capable."

"Then it's settled." Her tone brooked no argument.

"Yes." Will gave her one solemn nod of his head. "If Bridget wants my help moving into her new home, then I will be at her disposal the entire afternoon."

"Wonderful. Now go." She gave him a mock scowl, followed by a little shove. "You're dripping all over my clean floor and adding extra work for the housekeeper."

"So sorry." He strode swiftly down the hallway, thinking his day couldn't get much better.

Chapter Fourteen

Bridget was still disheveled, but thankfully composed by the time Will returned in a fresh set of clean, dry clothes. He looked handsome as ever, even with damp hair. She had to fight to regain her equilibrium all over again. There'd been a moment earlier, right before he'd gone inside, when she'd thought he might kiss her. He hadn't, of course. But now her insides were all quivering and she was struggling with an array of complicated, baffling emotions.

Her eyes met his from across the lawn and her stomach performed a slow, unexpected roll. Will was looking at her in that special way of his, as if he truly saw her, and she *truly* mattered to him.

Her cheeks grew warm and her hand lifted to her face. She brushed back a tangle of wet curls flopping across her eyes.

The dog caught sight of Will, did a few hops of joy and then raced straight for him.

"No," Bridget yelled after the animal. "No jumping."

Undeterred, the dog continued toward his target, but then he skidded to a stop, dropped to the ground at Will's feet and executed a quick flip, stopping once his feet were in the air and his belly was exposed.

Will gave the white fur a brisk rub. "You miserable mutt, spoiled already." He looked up, glanced around him, focused on Bridget. "Where are the children?"

"Upstairs with your mother." She angled her head toward the house. "Esther offered to bathe them while I clean up out here. He likes you," she said, indicating the happy dog at his feet.

"Have you named him yet?"

"I was thinking we could call him Winston, or maybe Gus, or, perhaps—" she narrowed her eyes and thought about the animal's propensity for uprooting bushes "—Digger."

"Digger, huh?" Will laughed, the sound a rich, hearty baritone. "I'm afraid to ask."

"Best that you don't."

They shared a smile.

Will straightened, the dog all but forgotten. "Bridget, about our agreement..." His words trailed off.

She tried not to stiffen at the sound of his serious tone. Needing something to do with her hands, she called the dog over and rested her fingertips on his head. "Our...agreement?"

Eyes dark and somber, Will stepped closer. "I'd like you to stay on as the children's nanny. For however long we can have you."

"Oh." That ridiculous stipulation of hers. How could she have forgotten? Perhaps because she felt so much a part of this family already, as if the matter had been settled long ago.

"I'd like to stay on." She stroked first one then the other of Digger's silky ears. "I'd like that very much."

"Then we're in agreement."

"We are."

His gaze dropped to her mouth.

Her lips trembled in response.

He drew in a long, hard pull of air. "There is one other matter I wish to discuss with you."

Her hand stilled on the dog. She swallowed and then ran her fingernails down his back.

Will's gaze followed the gesture. "I'd like to offer my assistance to you and your sister Sunday afternoon."

"You want to help us move?"

He must have sensed her surprise because his lips twisted in a grimace. "Is that so hard to believe?"

"No, but—" she pulled her hand back to her side "—what about the children? I don't think it would be wise to bring them out just yet."

She didn't add that she feared for their safety. That would only open up yet another conversation about her decision to live in a house that wasn't quite sound.

"My mother will watch them for us."

For us. Bridget's heart danced a happy jig against her ribs. Did he realize how that sounded?

She had to turn away so he wouldn't see the joy that surely must be in her eyes. They had more than enough hands already committed to the move. Nora, herself, Maeve, Flynn, even Cameron Long had agreed to be available for most of the afternoon.

Nevertheless Bridget found herself saying, "I would love for you to assist us on Sunday. Thank you for offering."

"No, Bridget, thank you." He reached out and placed a finger under her chin, adding pressure until she looked in his direction. "Thank you for bringing happiness back into this home."

"You're welcome, Will." She tried to keep her voice easy and bright, but the tension building inside her was like nothing she'd ever experienced. She was both hot and cold at the same time, all shivery inside and out.

Oh, Lord, what's happening to me? What is this strange, new feeling?

Will dropped his hand and shifted slightly away. "I better return to work."

"As should I."

"I'll be home at the usual time tonight." He reached down, acknowledged the dog with a quick pat then was gone.

Trying not to sigh, Bridget watched his retreating back until he disappeared around the house.

You like him, Nora had accused. "Oh, Nora," Bridget whispered to the spot Will had just vacated. "You have no idea how much."

Sunday afternoon brought rain, the kind of hard, pile-driving sheets of water that created mud puddles and bad tempers. And to think, the morning had started off so well. The sun had shone brightly in the sky. The church service had been both inspiring and moving, with another fitting sermon on faith and trusting the Lord.

God was trying to tell her something and Bridget was listening. Her future was in the Lord's hands. She simply had to have faith that all would turn out for the best, no matter what obstacles came her way.

Just like the week before, Bridget and Nora had sat with Will and the children in their pew. Esther had joined them, as had Cameron Long and—this one shocked them all—Deputy MacDuff.

More stunning still, Ben had spent most of the service whispering softly with Will's mother. Evidently the two were friends, *good* friends. It had been nice to see Esther smiling so liberally. When she'd giggled at something Ben had said to her, Will had caught Bridget's eye and grinned. He was clearly enjoying his mother's transformation.

With such a stellar beginning to the day, Bridget refused to be put off by the ill weather now. They were moving into their new house this afternoon and nothing, not even a little rain—all right, a large downpour—was going to stop them.

"It's just water, Nora," Bridget insisted when her sister grumbled a third time in less than a minute. "So we get a bit wet. We've been through worse."

"That's certainly true." Nora snapped open her umbrella and stepped out into the rain. Rolling thunder marked her progress to Flynn's carriage, where Maeve was already waiting with baby Grace in her arms.

Bridget followed her sister a moment later, picking her way carefully down the walk as she avoided first one puddle and then another. Raindrops fell in tidy rivulets from the points of her umbrella. Instead of feeling annoyed, she experienced a surge of excitement. Will had arranged to meet them out at the house. She was happy he would share this new beginning with her.

Flynn met Nora at the end of the walkway. Seemingly unaware of the rain falling down on his head, he took her arm.

"Is this all of your belongings?" He hitched his chin toward the top of the carriage where he'd finished tying off the second of their two trunks.

"That's it," Nora said.

"Then we should head out to the house without further delay." Although Flynn appeared somewhat impatient to be off, he helped Nora into the carriage then turned and took Bridget's arm.

Instead of allowing him to hand her into the carriage behind Nora she pulled out of his reach. "Flynn, wait."

Water dripping down his face, he gave her a questioning look.

"I have something I wish to ask of you, a favor, of sorts." When he didn't respond, she continued, "It's about my employer's mother."

"Your…employer." Flynn frowned, his expression no longer patient but somewhat stern. "You are speaking of William Black, the man from the docks, the one looking for his *bride*."

Her brother-in-law's face took on a troubled expression, and Bridget doubted it was because of the rain pounding down on his head. What exactly had Nora told him about Will?

She wasn't sure she wanted to know. "Would you mind examining Will's mother before you and Maeve leave for Boston later today?"

The doctor slid firmly into place. "Is she ill?"

"No. At least she seems well enough." In fact, now that Bridget thought about it, Esther had glowed with good health this morning in church. "However, she recently suffered what I believe was a bad case of exhaustion. It wouldn't hurt to make sure she's as well as she seems."

"If it's important to you then—"

"Oh, it is. Very important."

"Then how can I refuse? Now if that's all, let's get you out of the rain." He took her arm and steered her toward the carriage. This time, Bridget went willingly.

Once the women were settled inside, Flynn shut the door behind her with a firm snap. A moment later the carriage gave a hard jolt then rolled smoothly forward.

Nora chattered happily with Maeve, sharing details about their stay in the boardinghouse and the lovely people they'd met. "Oh," she said, cutting herself off in midsentence. "I haven't told you yet. Gavin McCorkle came to visit us this week."

"Gavin was in Faith Glen?" Maeve's surprise sounded in her voice. "Were his brothers and Mrs. Fitzwilliam with him?"

"No, he came alone."

"He came all the way to Faith Glen, by himself?" Maeve asked, wiping a droplet of water off the baby's blanket.

Bridget joined the conversation, explaining how the boy had stopped by the jailhouse. "According to Gavin," she added, "Mrs. Fitzwilliam has hired a private detective to locate her missing stepgranddaughter."

Maeve digested this information, her expression thoughtful. "The widow is certainly a woman of her word."

"And very determined, too. I predict she'll locate Mary within the month."

All three sisters nodded in agreement.

"What I don't understand—" Maeve sat up straighter "—is how did Gavin end up at the jailhouse? Why didn't he try the boardinghouse first?"

"As it turns out," Bridget said and let out a little laugh, "Gavin is interested in becoming a lawman one day."

"Oh. Yes." Maeve nodded. "I can see that."

"Bridget said the same thing," Nora confirmed in her big-sister voice. "And we all know she's very insightful about these sorts of things."

"That she is." Maeve pressed her toe to Bridget's and gave her an unreadable smile. "So tell me about your new job. Are the Black children better behaved than the Atwater girls?"

Something in Maeve's voice made Bridget bristle. "Why don't you ask Nora about her job?"

"I did earlier, when you were speaking with Flynn in the rain." Maeve rolled her eyes. "She said it was fine."

If Nora hadn't felt the need to expand, then neither would Bridget. "My job is fine, too."

Maeve sighed dramatically. "If you won't talk about your job, then tell me about William Black." Her voice held mild curiosity, an obvious ruse to cover the fact that she was mining for information. "From what I remember of the man, he seemed a bit severe."

That was the same word Nora had used when she'd described Will. He was many things, but severe he was not. He was kind, generous, loyal and honorable to the bone. Plus, there was no doubt he loved his children dearly and shared in all their joys and excitement.

Closing her eyes, Bridget called to mind an image of him rolling on the floor with the twins, and another of him tossing a stick for Digger to chase after, and one more of him sitting in a chair far too small for his frame while he listened to Bridget read to the children.

Severe? No, her sisters were wrong. Will was…he was…remarkable.

"When you first met him—" she began, feeling the need to defend him "—of course he seemed intense. He was concerned about his intended."

"That must have been it." Looking unconvinced, Maeve smoothed her fingertip across one of Grace's eyebrows. "What about his mother? How are you getting on with her?"

"Actually rather well." Before her sister could continue with her questions, Bridget added, "And I adore the children most of all. Stop worrying, Maeve, I'm quite happy with my position in Will's home."

Maeve's expression sharpened. "If you say so."

"I say so."

Grace chose that moment to let out an earsplitting wail.

Now that, Bridget thought with a large sense of relief, was the perfect ending to Maeve's not-too-subtle inquisition. They spent the rest of the ride discussing Grace's care and what was being done to find her parents.

By the time Flynn directed the carriage onto the road leading to Laird's house, the rain had stopped and sunbeams cut bold lines through several seams in the clouds.

Bridget looked out the window, bracing herself with a hand on the seat as they bumped and splashed along the unkempt path. Mosquitoes buzzed in her ears and she noticed gnats swarming in clumps around the puddles.

"You might want to cover Grace," Bridget warned, turning back to glance at her sisters. "The rain has brought out the insects." She swatted at a fly hovering close to her nose.

"I'll take care of it." Nora reached out her arms and took the baby from Maeve before settling a swaddling cloth around her tiny body.

Once the carriage came to a halt Bridget jumped to the ground ahead of everyone else. Steam rose off a nearby puddle and snaked around her feet.

Shrugging off the heat, she looked around her. Will's carriage sat off to her left, looking quite empty. Wondering where he could be, she turned to face the house. He was standing on the stoop, his arms hanging loosely by his sides.

The moment their eyes met something flared to life in his face, a look that Bridget knew was reserved solely for her.

She experienced a ridiculous urge to run to him.

He was so different from any man she'd ever known, strong, principled and very, very masculine.

A ray of sunlight caught on his hair, streaking a hint of gold through the black. He seemed to be silently calling her to him.

She started forward, slowly, inch by methodical inch.

"Well, I say." Maeve tugged her to a halt. "I'm a bit scandalized."

"What?" Bridget yanked her gaze away from Will. "Why?"

"That man on the stoop is looking at you rather—" she lowered her voice to a whisper "—*warmly* for an employer looking at his nanny."

"Maeve."

"Now don't go acting all outraged on me, Bridget Murphy. You're looking at him in the very same manner."

"I… I…" she sputtered and gasped and sputtered some more. "You can't possibly know… That is, I'm not…"

"Oh, stop it." Maeve slapped her arm affectionately. "You know exactly what I mean."

Unfortunately Bridget did know. She'd been staring at Will like a lovesick cow. "Please tell me I wasn't batting my eyelashes."

"Not quite, but close."

Bridget gasped.

"I'm only teasing you." Maeve patted her hand in a show of sisterly solidarity. "Now, come along, Bridget. I believe proper introductions are in order."

"You've already met Will, back in Boston. Remember?"

"Ah, yes, but I'm afraid we must begin anew. In fact, after what I just saw pass between you two…" Maeve gave her a haughty stare that rivaled any Mrs. Fitzwilliam had bestowed on them "…it's imperative I become better acquainted with your…employer."

Chapter Fifteen

Will had no idea what her sister said to Bridget, but he sensed it had something to do with him. Watching the two with their heads bent so closely together he saw the family resemblance at once.

Although Bridget's hair was darker and she was taller by a few inches, both women shared delicate bone structure and the same remarkable shape to their eyes. Their creamy, alabaster skin and symmetrical features reminded Will of Olivia's porcelain dolls.

They were both stunning women, but Bridget's beauty was softer, giving her a more approachable air.

The oldest sister joined them and the three locked arms. There was no mistaking the bold picture they made. Sisters, kith and kin, *family*. Remarkable women who had endured hardships together, and had not only survived their trials but had flourished. Their unity reminded Will of the Scripture from Ecclesiastes, *a three-fold cord is not quickly broken*.

Bridget stood between the other two, arms linked with her sisters, her eyes seeking his a second time.

When their gazes met again, he smiled.

She lowered her head and sighed. He liked her reaction. It made him feel very masculine and more than a little possessive. She was becoming a part of his life in ways he'd never imagined. He thought of her when he first woke in the morning and right before he drifted off to sleep at night.

He knew something important was happening between them, something he didn't want to analyze too closely just yet. She hadn't committed to him, had refused his proposal. She could leave him at any time. He had to remember that.

Enough stalling. Will started down the steps, just as Bridget broke away from her sisters. She met him halfway across the lawn.

"Thank you for coming today." Her hands twisted in the fabric of her skirt.

Was she nervous? Around him?

A prickly feeling tingled in his fingertips. They itched to touch her, to soothe away her anxiousness. He placed his hand on her arm. "I'm happy to help."

A movement behind her caught his attention and he looked over Bridget's shoulder. Her sisters were watching them intently, with what looked like suspicion in their eyes. He arched a brow, both annoyed and pleased by their loyalty. These women understood family, better than most.

Not wishing to upset anyone, he dropped his hand and took a step back. "The Coulters are inside, waiting for you to tell them if they should move out of their room to another smaller one upstairs."

Bridget's gaze snapped to his. "No. Oh, no. We don't expect them to move. I must speak with them at once." She hurried into the house, leaving him to stare after her.

Nora started forward as well, the baby tucked securely in her arms. She stopped next to Will and glowered at him. "What did you say to upset my sister?"

Her obvious concern for Bridget took away any annoyance on his part. It was good to know her family valued her as much as she deserved. "James and Agnes are waiting to be told where to move. I think they may have misunderstood your intentions."

"Oh, no." She hurried toward the house behind Bridget. Watching her rush off, he realized he hadn't told her about the cakes of chocolate he'd brought for her to use in her baking.

"Well." The third sister joined him at the bottom of the stairs and gave him a rueful smile. "You certainly have a way with women, Mr. Black."

He glanced over his shoulder, trying not to flinch when the door slammed behind Nora. "One would think I'd insulted them."

"One would think." Although her words came out flat and unemotional, this youngest Murphy sister regarded him with an amused twinkle in her eye. She seemed to understand his confusion. "What, precisely, did you say to them?"

"I merely told them that the Coulters are awaiting their instructions as to where to move their belongings." He lifted a helpless shoulder.

"Ah." Her eyes filled with wisdom far beyond her years. "That would do it."

He lifted an eyebrow, still confused.

The woman patted his arm in a gesture that fell just short of patronizing. "After what we went through those last few days in Ireland neither of my sisters would subject the Coulters to a similar misfortune."

At last Will understood. Bridget had told him about their Irish landlord's actions. Considering what they'd suffered, they would never expect the Coulters to relocate, not even to a different room in the house.

Maeve patted his arm again, this time with more

affection. "I had better go check on my sisters and the worried caretakers."

"That might be wise."

She walked past him, eyes fixed on the house. She climbed the steps a bit slower than her sisters had, but Will caught the urgency in her gaze. If he'd suspected otherwise, he now knew the truth. All three Murphy sisters were godly, kindhearted women who put the needs of others ahead of their own.

Evaluating the collection of emotions churning in his gut, Will decided one very important fact. He'd been blessed to have met Bridget Murphy. She was a special woman, born in a special family. He wasn't sure he'd ever be the same for knowing her, and was glad for the opportunity. What he would do next to make the most of that opportunity required some considerable thought.

For now, he set out toward the black, well-made carriage sitting a hundred feet away from his own. He eyed the man standing beside it, the one he'd met in Boston, the one who had declared his intended bride officially dead.

Flynn Gallagher watched his approach with an unreadable expression.

At the moment Will wasn't in the mood for a lengthy conversation with the other man. He'd just as soon forget about their last meeting, at least for today. "Put me to work."

Flynn met his gaze, smiled at last and then clasped him on the back in the universal male gesture of welcome. "Gladly, my good man."

While they were still unraveling the ropes, Cameron Long rode up on his horse. "Want another pair of hands?" he called out.

"Absolutely," they said as one.

Cam jumped down and then looped his horse's reins

over a tree branch near a patch of wet grass. The steed lowered his head and happily munched away. Introductions were made and the men took on the task of unloading the Murphy sisters' belongings.

Discussing the wonders of female packing habits—all the while marveling at how even women of modest means could collect a multitude of unnecessary items—the three men proceeded to unload bags, trunks and carrying cases.

They worked as a well-oiled team, as though they'd been toiling together for a lifetime. Will had a strange sense of homecoming, as though he'd finally found his place in the world.

That didn't make sense. He'd worked in his family's mill since he was a boy, had always known his future was there, making chocolate, providing jobs for others. Today, however, he'd been given a glimpse of something else, something equally permanent yet altogether different. Bridget Murphy was at the center, drawing him close, calling to a part of him long dormant that yearned for a richer sense of family in his life.

Uncomfortable with the sensation, he picked up a large trunk and made his way to the house without stopping.

Once inside he shifted his load and waited for instructions. Bridget pointed him in the direction of the staircase. "That goes in the first room on the right."

After a short nod he headed up the stairs, keeping his eyes cast down as he went. The house was clean, but the structure needed considerable repair. He avoided the third, fifth and seventh step. All three were warped and might not hold his weight. He wasn't sure about the rest. He would have to take a closer look. Before he left today, Will promised himself he would fix them and any other hazards that might appear.

With that in mind, he placed the trunk in the appointed room and then went in search of the other two men. He found them at the carriage, unloading the last of the bags.

"We have a problem," he said without preamble.

They both lifted their heads, but Flynn spoke up first. "What sort of problem?"

Will opened his mouth to explain then stopped himself. "Not here, where we might be overheard by the women. Over there."

He directed them toward a large shade tree where a neglected bench sat under a sign that read Colleen's Garden. He started to prop his foot on the bench then stopped himself. Like many of the stairs, the crumbling wood probably wouldn't hold his weight. "The house needs some immediate repairs."

Cam's eyebrows slammed together. The gesture gave him a ruthless look. "What kind of *immediate* repairs are we talking about?"

"You were in the house for all of five minutes," Flynn pointed out before Will could answer Cam's question. "How could you possibly know that?"

"Five minutes was long enough to discover that three of the stairs leading to the second floor are ready to collapse." Will shuddered at the thought of Bridget navigating them at night, without the benefit of decent lighting.

"I don't like the sound of that." Flynn looked up at the house, his eyes filled with concern.

Good, the man should be worried. He was Bridget's brother-in-law, her family. That made her safety his concern, too. But no matter how Flynn handled the situation, Will wasn't going to allow Bridget to live in a house where she could get hurt merely making her way up the stairs to her bedroom.

"What else?" This question came from Cam. He looked as worried as Flynn. "Is the kitchen safe?"

"I'm sure there are other points of concern, but as Flynn pointed out I was only inside a few minutes."

"Then our first step is to decide what's what." By the look on his face it was obvious Cam's mind was already working on a plan of action. "Once we decide which of the repairs need immediate attention we'll have a better idea where to start."

It was a solid suggestion, smart and logical. "And if we discover anything life threatening," Will added, "the women won't be staying here tonight."

Cam flattened his lips into a grim line. "Agreed."

Walking shoulder to shoulder, they took off toward the house. Two steps out Flynn moved into their direct path.

"Whoa, gentlemen, now wait just a moment." Feet splayed, he crossed his arms over his chest and held steady. "Not that I don't agree with you, in principle, but you boys are forgetting one very important point."

"What's that?" they asked in tandem.

"Other than my wife, Bridget and Nora Murphy are two of the most intractable women I know."

"What do you mean by intractable?" Cam asked in his most inflexible lawman voice. The unspoken message was that he could hold his own against a stubborn woman.

Flynn widened his stance. "You have to understand. The Murphy sisters have been single-minded about this house from the day they left Ireland. Now that it's theirs, you won't be able to convince them to leave tonight, maybe not ever."

Although deep in his gut Will feared Flynn was right, he also knew he had his own stubborn streak, especially when it came to protecting what was his.

And like it or not, Bridget worked in his home now. That made her one of his.

"Intractable?" Will repeated the descriptor the other man had used to define Bridget and her sister. "We'll just see about that."

"No." Bridget planted her fists on her hips and frowned at Will. How could he ask such a thing? When he knew how important this house was to her? "I am not leaving my own home. Don't ask me again."

"I'm not asking you." He towered over her, his face an immovable slab of hard angles and firm lines. "I'm telling you."

"Is that right?" She resisted the urge to stomp her foot. "Well, then, don't *tell* me again."

He softened his gaze and reached to her.

She took a step back. His hand fell away.

"Why are you being so stubborn?" He seemed genuinely confused by her resistance.

That hurt more than his words. "You know how important this house is to me."

"Bridget, listen to me. It's not safe." He spoke slowly, all impatient energy and suppressed power flickering across his face and tightening his lips.

She didn't want to be angry at him, and yet she was, very much so. "It's safe enough for the Coulters." She looked over her shoulder, as though searching out the elderly couple to prove her point. "If you're so concerned, why not insist they leave, as well?"

"They live in the bedroom off the kitchen." He moved closer toward her, his entire bearing begging her to give in.

Despite her annoyance at him, Bridget was captured by the fluid way he moved, the masculine vitality that encircled him. "What does the location of their room have to do with anything?"

"The first floor is sound enough." He spoke through a tight jaw. "It's the second floor that needs considerable repairs, especially the steps. I won't have you risking your neck every time you climb up to your room."

His explanation was not given smoothly, but with a rough sincerity that told her he wasn't trying to order her about as she'd first suspected. He was genuinely worried about her.

"You're concerned for my safety," she said, unable to hide the awe in her voice. No man other than her da had ever put her safety first, not like this, not to the point of arguing with her.

"Of course I'm concerned." He blew out a frustrated hiss, the sound reminding her he was a man used to taking charge. "I'll fix the stairs before I leave and Cam is already up on the roof mending the largest hole and—"

"Flynn is repairing the back stoop," she finished for him. "If you three complete those tasks today then I don't see what the problem is with Nora and me staying the night."

He frowned. "The *problem* is that there could be other hazards we've missed."

"There aren't any missed hazards." She raised her hand to stop him from interrupting. "I know this because you three men have been in and out of this house at least fifty times, up and down the stairs, scrambling on and off the roof, mumbling every step of the way."

"I can't let you stay in this house until I know it is completely safe."

She relished his fierce protectiveness for a brief moment. Will was so handsome, staring down at her with that stubborn, worried look in his eyes. Bridget felt a pleasant little ache in her stomach, a bone-deep yearn-

ing that she stifled. "You know the house is safe, or at least safe enough for Nora and me to live here with the Coulters."

He was shaking his head before she finished speaking. "I'm still not satisfied."

Now he was just being difficult. If she wasn't so flattered she might be frustrated with this stubborn streak of his. "*Like I said,* you, Flynn and Cam have investigated every square inch of this place, ten times over."

"Nevertheless…"

"Would it make you feel any better if I agreed to sleep down here on the first floor tonight?"

"No."

No? *No?* "If you don't want me living here, then what do you suggest?"

"I suggest—" he flashed her one of his bone-melting smiles that made her knees go weak "—you move into my house."

Chapter Sixteen

Bridget felt something akin to pins and needles running down her spine. Will wanted her to move into his home, as though she were a part of his family. A flush of warmth rose inside her, the sensation strengthening and thickening until she couldn't take a decent breath.

She tamped down her reaction and spoke with great calm. "I simply don't know what to say to such an offer."

"Say yes."

A sigh worked its way up her throat. "Absolutely not." But what a lovely, impossible request, one she had to squash at once, before she gave in. "My moving into your home, no matter the reason, would only confuse the twins."

He fell silent. His thoughtful scowl made her wonder if he even realized what he'd just asked of her. No, the request wasn't scandalous. Not when she considered the fact that his mother and children lived under the same roof as him. Bridget would simply be a live-in nanny, an employee and nothing more.

Except...

It would be much more for her. Somewhere in the past week she'd grown to care for this man, as much as she cared for his children and his mother. William

Black mattered to her, in a way she didn't want to analyze too closely, not until she was alone. One thing she knew for certain, to capitulate to his request now, no matter how sound his reasoning might be, would be far too dangerous for her heart.

"You're right," he said at last, speaking over her heartbeat drumming in her ears. "I can't risk the children's welfare like that. I will take you back to the boardinghouse."

Oh, no. No, no, no. "You most certainly will not."

"Bridget—"

"Rose rented out our room already. Nora and I must stay here tonight." She softened her voice. "There is no other answer."

His hand slipped up her arm, past her shoulder, stilled just shy of touching the back of her neck. "I don't want you in danger, not for a moment."

He dropped his hand.

Even without his touch, Bridget felt enveloped by warmth and noted with some surprise that she was finding it hard to form words in her mind. She brushed shaky hands down her skirt. Why had the Lord brought this man into her life, when there seemed to be so many obstacles standing between them? "I appreciate that you are worried, Will, I do. But I will be quite fine here with Nora and the Coulters."

"I cannot persuade you otherwise?"

"No."

His lips flattened. "You are a stubborn woman, Bridget Murphy."

She felt a twinge of tenderness for him. "So I've been told."

"You realize—" he took her hand and then braided their fingers loosely together "—that you have already turned down three of my requests in our short acquaintance."

"Yes, I have." She fought desperately to keep from touching him in return, from reaching up with her free hand and smoothing away his frown. "But never for a frivolous reason."

That earned her a smile. "No, never for a frivolous reason." His gaze turned serious, alarmingly so. "One day, Bridget Murphy, you will say yes to me."

She had no doubt of that. She only prayed that when she did it was to the right question.

"If you are determined to stay in this house tonight I had better continue working on the stairs." He ran his thumb over her knuckles before releasing her hand. "Twilight is fast approaching."

Without another word he strode around the corner and mounted the steps.

Bridget blinked after him, wondering what had just happened. There had been hidden meaning in their words, a promise to one another that had been silently understood, on a soul-deep level. She was still staring after him when she heard someone approach from behind. The light, airy footsteps warned her that the newcomer was her younger sister Maeve.

"He likes you," she said, her voice full of satisfaction and perhaps a small amount of amusement.

Bridget swung around to glare at her sister. Maeve was never one to judge, but still, to know that her sister had been eavesdropping on her and Will unsettled Bridget. "You were spying on us?"

"I couldn't hear anything, not with all that hammering coming from the roof." Maeve looked at the ceiling as if to make her point more succinctly. "And I averted my eyes once I realized you were having…a moment."

"Is that so?"

"I am a model of discretion." She waved her hand in a graceful arc. "I saw nothing out of the ordinary here."

There was an unfamiliar ball of something in Bridget's stomach, something that felt similar to panic. What if her sisters didn't like Will? Nora seemed to disapprove of him—did Maeve agree? And what if *he* didn't like *them*?

"Maeve," she began, considering her words carefully. She didn't want to alarm her sister, but she needed to know. "What do you think of Will?"

"What I think, is that we should have this conversation somewhere private." Maeve hooked her arm through Bridget's and steered her outside toward the overgrown garden. Bridget felt herself relax.

They made their way toward the tree indicating the entrance to Colleen's garden. The path was overrun with weeds, but it was clear this had once been a lovely spot.

There was a rickety old bench in the middle of the garden. Weeds were growing up its legs, tangling into a knot of twisted branches. The wood looked full of splinters and far too wobbly to support either of them.

Apparently Maeve agreed because she paced to the large oak tree and leaned against its massive trunk. "Now where were we?"

"You were about to tell me what you think of Will."

"Ah, yes." She tapped a finger to her chin. "But you must realize, my opinion isn't the one that matters. What do *you* think of the man?"

Bridget swallowed back her first response. She'd been about to give Maeve a superficial answer, something trite. But playing coy was an exercise in futility. Maeve knew her too well and would see through any attempt on Bridget's part to evade the truth.

"I think," she said, firming her shoulders and lifting

her chin a fraction higher, "that William Black is the best man I have ever met."

"You are in love with him."

Was she? Was it too soon to tell? Or entirely too late? "I... No... Maybe." *Probably*.

"But, Bridget, from what I understand he is only looking for a woman to be the mother of his children, nothing more."

Maeve was certainly well-informed. Nora must have filled her in during her first visit to Faith Glen, when Bridget had stayed late at Will's to read bedtime stories to the children. When she'd put his family and their needs above her own.

In a matter of days the Black family had become a part of her heart. The children. Esther. Even Will. *Especially* Will.

She might very well be in love with him.

"Oh, Maeve." She tried to smile, but emotion drenched her throat. "What does it matter whether I'm in love with the man or not? He's made it clear he only wants a marriage of convenience, one in name only, and I will settle for nothing less than an earth-shattering love."

"Oh, dear."

Indeed.

The sun had dipped dangerously low toward the horizon before Will felt comfortable enough to deem the house fit for Bridget, her sister and baby Grace to stay the night. Surveying his handiwork, he set down the hammer, rose and proceeded to test each stair one at a time.

Once he was satisfied, he went in search of Bridget. He heard the Coulters speaking with someone in the kitchen, but couldn't make out their words. The cooing noises indicated the baby was back there, as well. Will looked in and saw the older couple smiling over the child, playing with her tiny feet and hands.

Bridget was not with them.

Before either of the Coulters noticed him, he moved back into the hallway, ran his hand along the paint-chipped wall. They would have to address the decor eventually, but for now they had to focus on the basic structure before winter set in.

Will hadn't wanted to let Bridget win their argument this afternoon, hadn't wanted her to stay here until the house was completely put to rights. But she'd convinced him with the one point he'd been unable to deny. He couldn't move her into his home and risk confusing his children.

His entire family adored her. She had charmed him as well, somehow slipping below his defenses against his best efforts to remain guarded. She was fast sliding her way into his heart.

A hot ball of unease spun in his gut. Will didn't want to lose Bridget. And not just for his children's sake, but for his own, as well.

He longed for her, actually yearned to—

A twinge of unease had him slowing his steps. He'd made a promise to Bridget Collins months ago, and had planned to marry her without the benefit of meeting her. He'd nearly forgotten all about her. Shouldn't he be mourning the woman, at least a while longer? Yet a little over a week after discovering the terrible details of her death Will was falling for Bridget Murphy.

Lord, what does that say about me?

"Will?"

He reared back, his heart slamming in his chest. "Bridget," he said on a spurt of air, bracing his stance so he didn't run into her. "I didn't see you standing there."

"I only just arrived." She hovered in the doorway, her hazel eyes a vivid green mixed with golden brown. Her lips curved into a smile. "You were deep in thought."

"Got a lot on my mind." He spread his hands in a helpless gesture. "I was thinking about…the mill."

She gave him a dubious look but didn't question him. "The others are ready to leave. I've arranged to have Flynn stop at your house to check on your mother before he and Maeve return to Boston." She moved closer. "But only if that's agreeable to you."

Will gazed at her a moment, mesmerized. He suddenly understood why men wrote poetry. "You asked your brother-in-law to examine my mother?"

"He is a very good doctor, I assure you." She lowered her chin, breaking eye contact. "Although I believe Esther is feeling much better I thought it couldn't hurt to collect an expert opinion on the matter."

Staring at her bent head, Will experienced a sudden wave of tenderness followed by a strong desire to pull her into his arms and hold her close. In the next breath he gave in to the temptation and drew her against him, resting his cheek against her soft hair.

She relaxed in his embrace and all he could think was how good she felt, soft yet solid, yielding yet strong.

"Thank you, Bridget." His throat grew tighter, clogging with some unnamed emotion until he had to force the rest of the words past his stiff lips. "Thank you for caring about my mother."

"I care about all of you." She splayed her fingers against his chest and rested her cheek on his shoulder. "So very much."

There was a wistful note in her voice and his arms tightened around her. "I know."

Of its own accord, one of his fingers twined in her hair, the silky locks smooth against his skin. He went motionless, all but his hand. His heart pounded in his chest.

"Bridget?" A deep, masculine voice called from the back of the house. "Are you in here?"

Reluctantly, slowly, Will disentangled his hand from her hair and set her away from him. He took a second step to provide a safe enough distance to keep from pulling her back to him again.

Bridget blinked up at him, her eyes slightly glazed. Then she sighed deep in her throat. Will liked that rich, throaty sound. He liked it a lot.

"Bridget?"

Still looking somewhat bemused, she glanced over her shoulder and called out, "I'm in the hallway with Will." She sounded short of breath.

Will suffered a similar affliction.

Several loud, purposeful footsteps later and Flynn Gallagher entered the tiny space. Eyes narrowed, he looked from Will to Bridget then back again.

"Maeve and I are ready to depart." He spoke in a tone full of silent warning Will had no problem interpreting. "I'll need you to lead the way to your house."

"Certainly." He held the other man's stare without flinching. "I'll meet you outside in a moment."

Flynn looked ready to argue, but then shook his head and left without another word.

"Well," Bridget said, "that was a bit awkward."

Will felt a smile tug at his lips and almost fell in love with her right then. Leave it to Bridget to state the obvious in such a matter-of-fact manner, as though she was speaking about nothing more important than the weather.

Despite reminding himself to keep up his guard, he felt something deep in his soul shift, a softening. "Your brother-in-law is rightfully protective of you."

She laughed. "So it would seem."

"Come." He took her hand without thinking, the gesture as natural as breathing. "We should join the others outside, before we give Dr. Gallagher cause to come searching for you again."

"Heaven forbid."

They walked hand-in-hand down the corridor, as easy with one another as though they'd been together for years. Like a couple. It was a stunning realization that had Will pulling his grip free of hers before they stepped outside.

Cheeks turning a becoming pink, Bridget rushed ahead of him and took the baby from her younger sister. She positioned the bundle in her arms and turned to face him. "I'll see you first thing in the morning."

Glad for the squirming shield between them, he nodded. "Tomorrow."

He gave Flynn a brief nod, tossed out a few general directions to his home and then headed for his own carriage.

After climbing aboard, he lifted the horse's reins in his hands and patiently waited for Flynn to do the same. He let go of the reins after several moments passed, realizing he wasn't going anywhere just yet. Bridget and her younger sister were in the midst of a lengthy goodbye.

Her older sister was off to his right, under a large shade tree, poking her finger into Cam's chest. The woman did not look happy. In fact, as Will leaned forward for a better look, he realized her face was scrunched into a frown.

Cam, seemingly unaffected by the woman's obvious frustration, suddenly threw his head back and let out a belly laugh. Whereby Nora swung around and stomped off, her hands balled into two tight fists. Cam immediately stopped laughing and gaped after her retreating back in utter astonishment.

Good old Cam, Will thought with a shake of his head, *charming the ladies like always.* Clearly, the sheriff of Faith Glen needed a few lessons on how to talk to women. Not that Will was the one to school him on the subject. He wasn't much better, as evidenced by his inability to talk Bridget into leaving this ramshackle house tonight.

As he caught Will's eyes on him, a dark scowl spread across Cam's face. He pushed away from the tree and headed in his direction. "You got something to say to me?"

"Just watching the show." Will grinned. "What was that about, anyway?"

"It was the strangest thing." Cam shrugged. "Nora suggested I hire some eighteen-year-old kid I met last week, one of the passengers she knew aboard ship."

"And you laughed at her." Will shook his head. "Badly done, my friend."

"I thought she was fooling with me." Cam slapped his hat against his thigh. "But she really wants me to hire the boy on as my deputy."

"You already have a deputy."

"Yeah, that's what I told her." He ran a hand through his hair. "That's when the finger poking began."

Will tried not to smile at his friend. Focusing on the practical points of the discussion helped. "Can Faith Glen afford another deputy?"

"The city can barely afford Ben."

Cam looked about as miserable as Will had ever seen him. Despite his gruff exterior the man hated letting people down. Will gave it one week, maybe two before Cam was in possession of a new deputy sheriff. And if the city couldn't pay, Cam would do so out of his own pocket. "I'm confident you'll work it out."

"Yeah, I will. *Right now.*" He strode purposely toward the house.

Watching him go, Will almost pitied Nora Murphy. She was about to discover the consequences of walking away from Cameron Long when he wasn't finished having his say. But after watching their previous interaction Will figured she could hold her own.

He turned back to check on the others.

Bridget pulled out of her sister's embrace. The fading sun caught her hair just right, hugging her in a ray of soft, golden light. The effect was so stunning Will had to swallow back the sudden lump clogging in his throat. She looked beautiful with the overgrown garden as a backdrop, approachable as always, yet warmer and more inviting than before they'd met in the hallway.

They'd crossed a line in their relationship and Will wasn't altogether sorry for it.

But if he allowed the pretty Irish lass to squirm her way deeper into his life there would be unforeseen repercussions. He had his children to think of, as well as his mother and a load of dark memories that made it necessary to guard his heart more carefully than other men.

Yet for one brief moment when she turned her head and smiled over at him, all Will could think was: *Yes.*

Flynn Gallagher sauntered into Will's study an hour later. Will wasn't surprised the doctor was alone. The man's pretty wife had lured the twins into a game of marbles as soon as they'd arrived.

After being shooed out of his mother's room while Flynn conducted his examination, Will had taken the opportunity to review a stack of invoices. Now, as Flynn shut the door behind him, Will shoved the pile aside and looked up expectantly.

"Your mother is extremely healthy for a woman her age." He flashed a broad smile. "Correction, she's extremely healthy for a woman of any age."

Will's heart contracted in relief. "So she is out of the woods at last."

Flynn moved deeper into the room, his gaze lingering a moment on the dog sleeping contentedly on a makeshift bed of worn blankets. Will glanced ruefully at the snoring animal. So much for his stipulation that Digger remain out of doors.

"I didn't say your mother was out of the woods," Flynn corrected. "I said she was healthy."

Will rose, came around the desk, every movement precise and controlled. "What, exactly, does that mean?"

"It means that you must ensure she continues eating regular meals and resting whenever she's tired. Under no circumstances should she overtax herself."

Good advice, in theory. But Esther Black was a stubborn woman. "How will I know if she's overdone it?"

"I'll leave a list of the signs to look for."

"Good. Anything else I should know?"

"No. However—" the doctor stuffed his hands in his pockets and leaned back on his heels "—I can't stress enough the importance of rest."

Mulling this over, Will nodded. "So I need to bully her."

Flynn chuckled. "If that's what it takes, yes."

"Fair enough." Rubbing a hand down his face, Will wondered why he wasn't more relieved by this report. His mother had been suffering from a simple case of exhaustion. This was good news, yet something in him couldn't let go and rejoice.

Flynn reached down and ruffled Digger's fur. "Your

mother claims she's been feeling better ever since Bridget became the children's nanny."

"Your sister-in-law's influence on my family has been nothing short of remarkable."

And that, Will realized, was the problem. His mother's recovery was directly due to Bridget's appearance on the scene. If they lost her, or if Will ran her off, the Black household would fall apart again.

His family had become completely dependent on Bridget Murphy. His children adored her. His mother was growing stronger by the day. Even the stray dog owed his position in the household to her.

As if to punctuate this last point, Digger kicked out in his sleep and gurgled a sort of happy dog laugh.

"What about you?" Flynn asked, his voice no longer sounding like a doctor but a protective older brother. "Has Bridget made an impact on you, as well?"

Will had no idea what to say. Not because he was hedging, or stalling, but because he simply had *no idea what to say.* "There are many ways to answer that question."

"How about going with the truth."

The truth. Bridget deserved nothing less. "Yes, she's impacted me, as well. More than I thought possible."

Flynn's piercing stare seemed to probe all the way down to his soul. "I have one final question for you."

Bracing himself, Will nodded.

"What are your intentions toward my sister?"

Astonished at his reaction to the question, Will had to fight back a rush of tangled emotions twisting through him—anger, guilt, hope, despair. His roving gaze landed on Bridget Collins' baggage.

Flynn's gaze followed his, and then narrowed in recognition. No wonder, the doctor had been the one to sign Miss Collins's luggage over to Will.

"Just one week ago you were set to marry another woman, a woman you'd sent all the way to Ireland for." The man's face was full of hard, intense lines. "You cannot be thinking of replacing her with my sister-in-law."

When spoken that plainly, in that flat tone, Will realized the terrible repercussion of his attempt to "hire" a bride. He should have never sent for Bridget Collins, no matter how desperate he'd been. He should have had more faith and allowed the Lord to reveal his next step. Instead, Will had taken matters into his own hands.

"No," he said at last. "It is not my intention to replace my intended bride with your sister-in-law."

"Then what is your plan?"

A valid question, one he could have answered a week ago but not today. "I...don't know."

Flynn moved closer, continuing forward until he was standing toe to toe with Will, his arms crossed over his chest in angry deviance. "You better decide soon."

An unspoken warning hung in the air between them.

Although Will knew Flynn was right—he did need to decide what he was going to do about Bridget—he bristled at the man's aggressive stance. "And if I don't make up my mind?"

"I'll take her away from you, and Faith Glen, if need be. I'll move her to Boston, anything to prevent her from being hurt again."

"Again?" Will picked up on the word like a dog on point. "Who hurt Bridget?" He nearly grabbed the man by his lapels. "Tell me."

As though realizing he'd said too much, Flynn stepped back, hands spread in a show of capitulation. "I can say no more. It's not my story to share."

"Tell me."

"It happened a year ago, back in Ireland, before I

knew her." Flynn took another step back. "I don't know all the details, only the main points. What I do know is that it was quite a scandal, and…she was devastated."

Dread chased across his spine. Will knew all about scandal, the pain, the whispers and, yes, even the devastation. What had Bridget endured? "Tell me what happened."

No longer on the offense, Flynn gave him a sympathetic grimace, as though he knew the information he was about to share would change everything.

"Bridget was left at the altar."

Chapter Seventeen

When Cameron Long dropped Bridget at Will's house
the next morning before proceeding to the jail house
with Nora, Bridget discovered Will had already left for
the day. Disappointment spread through her and all she
could do was stare at Esther in silent regret. She'd arrived early for the sole purpose of seeing Will again.

"Bridget, dear." Esther crossed to her and set a hand
on her arm. "Are you ill? You look pale."

She forced a smile onto her lips. "I'm perfectly well."

She lied, of course. She wasn't well. She was full
of frustration and sadness and a strange sense of loss.
She'd wanted to see Will this morning, needed to assure
herself they were still on the same easy terms as yesterday. When he'd pulled her into his arms, and buried
his face in her hair, and then whispered his gratitude
in that sweet, gruff, serious tone of his.

"Bridget?"

"I… There is nothing wrong… I just…"

Thankfully the sound of doggy toenails clicking
on the floor spared her from responding further. She
dropped to her knees and flung her arms around the
animal. "Digger, my big furry friend," she said a tad
too brightly. "Good morning."

Caleb and Olivia rounded the corner next. Bridget opened her arms wider to include the two sleepy-eyed, rumple-haired children. Next thing she knew the four of them were rolling on the floor. It was a very inelegant, undignified moment, but when she swept a glance in Esther's direction the older woman was smiling at the four of them.

After another moment of play, Bridget scrambled to her feet, leaving the children and the dog to finish the game without her. Afraid to assess the damage, she ran a hand down her hair. Most of her curls had fallen free of her bun. Sighing in resignation, she pulled out the rest of her pins and let her hair tumble past her shoulders.

"We're going to do something different today," she declared, clapping her hands a few times to gain the children's attention.

They looked up at her, their little faces expectant. Caleb spoke for them both. "We are? What?"

"A picnic."

Heads tilted at a confused angle, they simply stared at her. Had they never been on a picnic? How sad. "We're going to eat our lunch outside, on a blanket under a tree, *and*—" she had a stroke of genius "—we're going to steal your father away from the mill so he can join us."

"What a lovely idea," Esther said, pressing a corner of her apron to her eyes. "He'll like that."

Caleb jumped to his feet. "Can we eat by the river?"

Pleased by his excitement, Bridget nodded enthusiastically. "I think that can be arranged, unless your father has another suggestion."

"I'll bring my boat, just in case."

"Splendid idea."

"Can Digger come, too?" Olivia was still on the floor with the dog, her arm looped across his shoulders.

Bridget smiled softly at the child. "It wouldn't be a family picnic without him." She turned her smile onto Esther. "Will you join us, as well?"

"I think I'll stay home and rest."

At the strange note in Esther's voice, a terrible thought came to Bridget's mind. Flynn had been here last night. Had he found something wrong, something concerning Esther's health? She was desperate to ask, but not in front of the twins.

"Children, I need you to go back to your rooms and wait for me." She used her firm, no-nonsense voice. "I'll be there in a moment to help you pick out your clothes for the day."

They opened their mouths to grumble.

Bridget spoke over them. "It's important you wear the right clothing for our adventure."

Showing his displeasure at being sent away, Caleb scuffed the floor with his foot. Olivia sighed heavily. But they soon turned on their little feet and shuffled toward their room. Digger followed in their wake.

Once she was certain the children were out of earshot, Bridget got straight to the point. "Esther, when Dr. Gallagher came by last night, did he find—" she stopped herself, not quite sure how to phrase the question "—something wrong?"

"Oh, no, dear. I am quite well." Esther waved a dismissive hand. "I'm healthy as a horse, according to the doctor."

That didn't sound like something Flynn would say. "If that's true then why won't you come on the picnic with us?"

"Because…" Esther fiddled with her apron, not quite meeting her gaze. "I have other plans."

Other plans? In all the time Bridget had worked in

this home, Esther had never had *other plans*. "You do? With whom?"

"A friend." When she continued avoiding direct eye contact, Bridget couldn't help but wonder about the identity of Esther's friend.

It wasn't any of her business, of course. Yet she liked Will's mother and worried about her. The older woman seemed to be hiding something, something secret.

It is none of your business, Bridget reminded herself. "If you are certain—"

"I am."

"Then I won't press any further."

A loud bang came from the other side of the house and was followed by an equally loud bark.

Esther looked positively relieved by the interruption. "That doesn't sound good."

Bridget sighed. "I had better go see what's happened."

"Very wise, my dear." Esther practically shoved her out of the room.

Bridget shifted out from under her hands and touched the older woman's arm. "You are truly feeling well?"

"Yes, Bridget." She patted the hand on her arm. "I am well, but I thank you for worrying. It's very kind of you."

"I care about you, Esther." It was the simple truth.

"I know, dear. You are a sweet girl and I—"

Another louder bang rang out, practically rattling the windows. And then came a very loud, very heavy thud.

"Miss Bridgeeet," Caleb shouted at the top of his lungs. "Come quick. Digger broke Olivia's chair."

"Oh, my." She released Esther's arm and hurried off.

The moment Will spied Bridget and the twins standing in the doorway of his office his heart tumbled in his chest. The picture they made personified family, a very happy, normal one.

The mangy dog leaning against Bridget's leg added the final touch to an already perfect scene. In fact, the mutt looked healthier than ever, and he appeared to be grinning at Will as if to say: *Look what we have, old boy, a real, genuine family of our own, isn't it grand?*

Yes, it was grand. And Will felt something move through him he hadn't experienced in years. Happiness. The kind he wasn't sure he deserved.

"What's all this?" he asked in a hoarse voice.

"We've come to take you on a picnic," Bridget declared, her eyes shining bright.

Staring into that beautiful, mesmerizing gaze, Will was tempted to pull her into his arms and bury his face in her hair as he had yesterday afternoon. How could any man leave such a kindhearted, lovely woman at the altar?

For the third time in his life, Will felt the urge to punch another man. The first had been Harcourt Smythe, Fanny's lover, the man she'd abandoned her family for. The second, Bridget's Irish landlord. Now when he thought about the pain and humiliation Bridget must have suffered from her fiancé's callousness, he wanted to inflict permanent damage to the rogue's face. Will wasn't normally prone to violence. Or so he'd always thought.

Swallowing back his rising fury, he lowered his gaze, locking it on the basket hanging from her arm. She carried a blanket tucked up under the other.

A picnic. Bridget wanted him to join them on a picnic.

He ran a hand down his face, drew in a hard breath. He thought briefly of praying, but he wasn't sure what he should lift up to the Lord. A prayer of thanksgiving for bringing this woman into his life? A prayer for strength so he could remember his goal wasn't to find a woman for himself, but to provide stability for his children?

Or perhaps he should just let down his guard for a few precious hours and enjoy time with his family.

"You haven't eaten already, have you?" Bridget's question brought him back to the matter at hand.

"No, I haven't." Even if he had, he wouldn't admit it now, not with his children's eager faces staring up at him and Bridget's encouraging smile warming his heart. "Let me put away these ledgers and we'll go."

"Lovely."

"I know the perfect place for our picnic," he said as soon as they were heading down the hallway toward the back door.

"Then we'll let you lead the way."

Once outside, Will directed their small party toward a shade tree near the riverbank. Olivia skipped alongside him, her dolly clutched tightly against her. She chattered away, her words tumbling over one another so quickly she wasn't making much sense. Will wasn't sure it mattered.

Caleb carried his boat in one hand while he threw a stick for Digger to chase after with the other. A languid breeze rustled through the trees. Birds chirped, frogs croaked, the mill's wheel churned in the water. It was a beautiful, mild summer day. Perfect for a family picnic.

At their destination, Will retrieved the blanket from under Bridget's arm and laid it carefully on the ground. As soon as he'd smoothed away the wrinkles, Olivia plopped down and proceeded to recite a nursery rhyme to her doll.

"No, Caleb," Bridget called out. "Don't go down by the water on your own."

The little boy threw her a scowl. "But how am I to sail my boat?"

"Your da will help you after we eat." She turned to Will. "Isn't that right?"

"Absolutely. I can't think of a better way to spend the afternoon." His words were directed at Caleb, but they carried far more meaning than he'd intended.

Still scowling, the little boy muttered something under his breath but obediently trudged over to the blanket and set down his boat near Olivia. She shoved it aside with a careless flick of her wrist.

"Don't hurt it!" he yelled in outrage.

She lifted her tiny shoulders. "Don't put it in my way."

"*You're* in the way." He puffed out his chest in angry, childish frustration.

"No, you are."

"You are."

Just as Will stepped forward to intervene, Bridget moved in between the twins and picked up the boat herself. "Why don't I just put this over here, next to the picnic basket where it'll be safe?"

"Excellent idea," Will said, aligning himself next to her, shoulder to shoulder.

Looking from one to the other, Caleb opened his mouth to argue, thought better of it, shook his head roughly, then sighed in defeat. "I guess that'll be all right."

Nodding in satisfaction, Bridget set the boat where she'd indicated. She wiped her palms together in a gesture that said the matter was settled. "Now, Caleb. Please chase down that naughty dog and bring him back over here."

"Digger." Caleb ran toward the animal. "*Digger,* no. Naughty boy. Naughty. You stop that right now."

The dog, Will noted with a suppressed grin, was proving true to his name. He was digging frantically in a bed of wildflowers on the other side of the tree. Tiny stars of color flew in every direction. Caleb continued to scold the animal.

In that instant, if anyone had asked him, Will would have said there was nowhere else he would rather be than right here, with his children and Bridget and that crazy hound. The thought brought a moment of peace, followed by a sudden wave of regret.

For his entire life he'd been a man of action, committed to seeing matters through to the end. When he'd needed someone to care for his children he'd done the logical thing. He'd drawn up a list of specific criteria and then designed a plan to find a woman who would meet his requirements.

A little more than a week ago he'd been willing to marry a stranger and have her care for the twins. At the time his reasoning had made sense. With her erratic behavior Fanny had put them through years of instability. Her inconsistent schedule and ultimate abandonment had left Olivia and Caleb unnaturally reserved. They'd wound up trapped in abnormally good behavior.

Considering all that had transpired, Will had believed his children needed permanency above all else. Now he knew better. They didn't need consistency as much as they needed unconditional love, the kind that Bridget had shown them.

Today, as he sat on the blanket and watched Bridget unpack the picnic basket, he realized his lack of foresight. And, of course, faith.

Bridget Murphy was an extraordinary woman. Her heart was so pure, her compassion so strong, she gave all of herself. She deserved a man who could give her the same level of devotion she would provide him in return. She deserved a man who would give her his entire heart, and hold nothing back.

Will was not that man.

If he made an offer of marriage to her again, and she accepted, he feared he would let her down eventually. As he had Fanny, and Bridget Collins.

No. He couldn't risk hurting her.

But how could he allow any other man to have her?

His heart lodged in his throat, and a portion of his previous joy left him.

Then Olivia crawled into his lap and rested her tiny head against his chest. Overwhelmed with love, he pulled his daughter close and dropped a kiss on the top of her head. He was thinking too hard. This was supposed to be an easy, carefree day. "Having fun, darling?"

"Oh, yes." She let out a happy sigh. "Quite a lot, actually."

Will's stomach twisted. His daughter had sounded just like Bridget, all the way down to the sweet Irish accent.

Olivia turned her face to his. "Are you having fun, too?"

He caught Bridget's eye before answering. She gave him a quick, almost imperceptible wink. The intimate gesture sent his pulse beating in a fury.

Bewildered at his reaction, he shifted his gaze to a spot just over Bridget's shoulder. "Yes, my darling." He kissed Olivia's head again. "I'm having a lot of fun."

"Oh, good," she said, then jumped up as Caleb and the dog returned.

Will endured the rest of their picnic with a smile on his face and a stoic resolve in his heart. No matter how hard he tried to enjoy the afternoon, his mind kept rounding back to one very important question, the one Flynn had posed last night.

What were Will's intentions toward Bridget Murphy?

As Bridget helped prepare the children for bed later that evening, she was acutely aware of the man working silently beside her. Something had altered in their relationship this afternoon, but she wasn't precisely sure she knew what. Will seemed especially careful with her tonight, and overly cautious, as if he didn't want to do or say the wrong thing.

But that made no sense. Will was not a man to tiptoe around a difficult situation. What had changed? Had she said something this afternoon? Had she crossed some sort of invisible line?

The wink. It must have been the wink. He probably thought the gesture had been too bold for a woman in his employ.

Swallowing in dismay, she focused on pulling Olivia's arms gently through the sleeves of her nightgown. The child smiled up at her and Bridget responded in kind, her heart wrenching at the sight of all that innocence staring back at her.

This nightly custom was always the best and worst part of her job, a bittersweet time when she felt the closest to all four of the Blacks yet not quite a part of their family. Sadly the sensation was magnified tonight.

Will hadn't looked at her once. Come to think of it, he hadn't looked at her since arriving home tonight, not even during the evening meal.

With this strange new tension between them, she was grateful it was Will's turn to read tonight. Bridget wasn't sure she could speak without her voice cracking.

She only hoped she gathered her emotions into some

semblance of control before it was time to kneel beside the twins for their bedtime prayers.

Will's soothing baritone eventually filled the room and Bridget found herself relaxing, despite her nerves. The man had a lovely voice. She could listen to him read for hours. But all too quickly the story came to an end and he set the book down on the floor at his feet.

Without having to be told Olivia and Caleb knelt beside their individual beds, folded their hands together then rested their elbows on the mattresses in front of them.

Bridget joined them. Will came to her side, brushed his fingers across her sleeve before lowering to his knees, as well.

Heart pounding, afraid to see what was in his gaze, she squeezed her eyes tightly shut.

"Dear God," Caleb began. "Please feed the hungry, clothe the poor and—" he paused "—and, oh, yes. Please, if You have time, can You make Digger come when I call him?"

As if hearing his name, the dog raced down the hallway, his toenails striking the floor with a *click, click, click*.

Thankful for the interruption, Bridget quickly rose and caught the bundle of fur before he charged into the room. She held him in place while the children continued praying.

"My turn now," Olivia said without looking up, her forehead resting heavily on her clasped hands. "Dear God, please give us rain for the garden and sunshine for the plants. Please bless Nene and Papa and Caleb."

"And Miss Bridget, too," Caleb reminded her.

Olivia opened her eyes and shot him a scowl. "And of course Miss Bridget, too. And, God, please, oh, please—" she lifted her face to the heavens "—*please* make Miss Bridget our new mommy."

Bridget's hand flew to her throat. Her heart pounded hard against her ribs, so hard she was sure everyone could hear the rapid staccato. She couldn't breathe, couldn't think.

Her gaze shot to Will. He rose and joined her in the doorway, his eyes dark and full of emotion. It wasn't shock she saw looking back at her, but an apology. Did he think he had to apologize for Olivia's prayer?

Bridget wanted to assure him that she understood how children thought. If not with words, with a touch or a look, but she couldn't force herself to move. God save her, she wanted the same thing Olivia did. She wanted to be the children's mother. She wanted to be Will's wife.

Holding back a sob, her lips moved in a soundless whisper.

Gaze softening, Will touched her arm. Overwhelmed with emotion, she quickly looked away and caught Caleb and Olivia staring at them.

"Those were lovely prayers," she said, hoping her voice didn't register her nervousness.

"Yes, they were," Will agreed, dropping his hand. "Now hop in bed, both of you."

"Can Digger sleep with us tonight?" Caleb asked.

"Yes." Will nodded. "That'll be fine."

What? Bridget blinked at him in surprise. He must have been taken off guard by Olivia's prayer, more than he was letting on. Yes, he'd given in and allowed the dog inside the house, but he'd never allowed the animal to sleep in the children's room before.

Throat tight, Bridget watched Digger crawl atop Caleb's bed, circle three times, then settle in. She took great care settling the covers around Olivia's shoulders.

When she leaned down to kiss the child's cheek, Olivia whispered in her ear, "I meant what I said. I want you to be my mommy."

Bridget shut her eyes and squeezed back the tears. "Me, too," she whispered back, knowing how inappropriate it was to promise such a thing, yet unable to censure herself.

She shouldn't get this child's hopes up, or her own. But maybe, *maybe* there was a way to make Olivia's prayer come true.

Bridget couldn't marry Will, not given his current restrictions. But she could stay on in the role of the children's nanny for as long as possible, indefinitely if necessary.

What if Will asks you to leave? What if he finds another woman to marry, one who meets his stringent requirements?

Well, if that travesty occurred…

No, it simply would not happen. Bridget wouldn't let it.

Chapter Eighteen

Bridget didn't remember walking out of the children's room. Nor did she recall saying good-night to Caleb, although she was confident that she had. She probably even gave him a bedtime kiss on the forehead as always.

Yet, now, only moments after entering the kitchen behind Will all her mind could focus on was him and the fact that his deep blue eyes were full of piercing intensity.

Bridget pressed her lips together, determined not to break the silence between them this time.

Olivia might have prayed for her to become her mommy, and Will might have failed to tell the little girl that her request was impossible, but he hadn't encouraged her, either. In truth, as Bridget reviewed the past few minutes in the children's room, she realized Will had ignored the situation entirely.

Would he continue to do so now that they were alone?

She had her answer the moment he opened his mouth. "I brought home some special chocolate I want you to try."

Turning his back on her, he moved toward the counter directly behind him. "My chocolatiers are working on a new recipe." He picked up a package wrapped in plain white paper and then pivoted back around. "I want you to tell me what you think."

"It's...grayish-brown."

He laughed, them pinched off a bite-size piece and handed it to her. "Taste it."

She stared at his hand. "You want me to eat that? By itself? Won't it be bitter?"

"Not if we got the formula correct."

"Oh." She gave him an exaggerated smile as she took the piece of chocolate. Rolling it around in her fingers, she realized the texture was much softer than the large cakes he'd left at the house yesterday. The color was lighter, too.

Prepared to hate the taste, she closed her eyes and popped the confection in her mouth. The chocolate melted on her tongue, the sweet flavor both a shock and a pleasant delight. "It's...quite good."

Her answer didn't appear to satisfy him. "But not great."

Bridget thought for a moment, remembered the full, rich flavor of Nora's famous chocolate cake. "No," she admitted honestly. "Not great. Not as good as some of the sweets Nora makes. Although the piece you gave me was far better than I expected, something is—"

"Missing?" he finished for her.

"Yes," she agreed, surprised he could read her mind so well. "Something is missing."

"Can you think what?" He seemed genuinely interested in her opinion.

Honored, and touched by his trust in her, Bridget closed her eyes and thought for a moment. She could think of nothing. Not one thing. Of course she was a bit out of her depth here. "Unfortunately, no, but my sister could. Nora's a baking genius."

"Why, yes she is." A booming voice sounded from behind them. "I can vouch for that myself."

Surprised to hear the familiar gravelly voice in Will's home, Bridget turned quickly. Her gaze landed on Deputy MacDuff standing in the doorway grinning at her.

"Your sister is a cooking marvel," he said, winking at her with his wide grin still firmly planted on his face. "Hiring Nora was the best decision that boy Cameron has made in years." He patted his belly with satisfaction. "Maybe ever."

Confused, Bridget blinked at the older man. What was Ben doing here at this hour?

As though he were equally confused, Will's eyebrows pulled together. "What are you doing here, Ben? Is there a problem I don't know about?"

Perhaps Ben was here because of Bridget. Had something happened to Nora? Or baby Grace?

"Now don't you two start worrying, there's no problem." Esther maneuvered past the deputy and entered the kitchen with a smile. "Ben is here visiting me."

"You," Bridget and Will said simultaneously.

"We're having coffee and scones."

Will stared at his mother, blinked down at Bridget, then turned back to stare at Esther again. "You're having scones and coffee, at night?"

"Oh, honestly, Will. Don't look at me like that." Esther made a frustrated sound in her throat. "Ben is an old friend of your father's, and mine. We haven't talked in a good long while. It's time we did some catching up."

Will continued blinking at her, as did Bridget, their mutual silence an indication of their common surprise. An image from the day before filled Bridget's mind. She remembered Ben and Esther at church, heads bent together, whispering softly to one another. Was there something more happening between the two, something sweet and possibly—romantic?

Lips pursed, Esther took Will's shoulder in a firm grip. The bold gesture spoke of her continued healing.

"William, *son,* I think it's long past time you escorted Bridget home for the night." With a flick of her wrist she turned him around to face the back door, then motioned to Bridget. "Now run along, both of you."

Before either could utter a word they were unceremoniously shoved onto the back stoop and enveloped in twilight. The door shut behind them with a firm bang.

A moment of shocked silence fell over them.

Then to her horror, a laugh bubbled out of Bridget's mouth. Esther had certainly made her intentions clear, quite boldly in fact. She slid a covert glance in Will's direction. Was he pleased by this unexpected turn of events?

"Think my mother wanted to be alone with Ben?" he asked, amusement in his voice.

Another giggle slipped out. "That would be my guess."

Joining in the laughter, he took her arm and steered her toward his carriage. "I'm glad. She deserves some masculine attention after all her years of loneliness."

"Your mother was positively glowing."

"That she was." There was genuine pleasure in his tone.

They walked side by side, smiling at one another, the tension gone between them. The moment was light and happy and yet surprisingly intimate.

Bridget glanced to the sky, a ribbon of pink mixed with orange rode along the horizon. The moon had begun its initial ascent in the sky, a fat, glowing crescent that hadn't fully taken shape. Croaking frogs sounded their nocturnal presence. A soft breeze swept over them.

Several feet away from the carriage Will abruptly stopped walking. Nearly losing her balance, Bridget was forced to do so, as well. When he pulled slightly away from her, she looked up at him and waited for—well, she didn't know what she was waiting for him to do.

As he turned to face her, his strong warm fingers took hold of her hand. There was no more amusement in his eyes, only serious attentiveness. He was staring at her with such purpose her blood ran molten in her veins. Yet she shivered.

"Will?"

He continued staring down at her, saying nothing, his gaze filled with gleaming, silvery-eyed intent.

That look. It made her knees go weak. She should pull away, move apart from him, but she took a step forward instead, closing the distance between them to mere inches.

The wind kicked her hair around her face, obscuring her view for a moment.

Hand reaching out, he pushed the tangles away from her forehead. "Bridget, my beautiful, beautiful girl."

The words sent another shiver whipping down her spine. Beautiful? He thought she was beautiful?

He raised her hand tenderly to his lips, pressing a soft kiss to her knuckles before cradling it against his chest. His heat seemed to echo through her, to the very core of her heart.

She closed her eyes and simply breathed in the moment.

"Bridget," he whispered her name again, this time in a low, rough voice that was no longer steady. "What am I going to do about you?"

She shivered a third time, looking down as she flushed.

"Oh, Will."

A second passed, and then another. He placed his fingertip under her chin and then lifted her head with gentle pressure.

The kiss shouldn't have surprised her. She saw it coming, saw the intent in Will's eyes before he lowered his head to meet hers. Yet it still made her heart pound and her head swim. She sighed into the kiss, marveling at the rightness of the moment, and the contentment flowing through her.

This was where she belonged. With this man.

All too quickly he pulled his head away.

Her hand reached to her mouth of its own accord. *"Oh, my."*

"My thoughts precisely." He brushed a fingertip down her arm, the gesture both casual and intimate. His smile was so tender she nearly lost her footing again. Surely, with that look in his gaze, he was about to say something important to her, something that would change her life forever. Indeed, the yearning look on his face seemed to confirm it. But his expression was so uncertain. Surely he didn't doubt her feelings for him.

He touched her cheek. "Let's get you home."

What? That was it? The man had just kissed her oh-so-tenderly, had looked at her as though she was the most important thing in his life, and all he could say was *let's get you home?*

Wasn't this the moment when he was supposed to make a declaration or a promise or—something?

Eyes blinking rapidly, Bridget waited for him to begin again and make the moment special. Instead he said nothing. He took her arm with solicitous care—she'd give him credit for his impeccable manners—and then helped her into the carriage.

And *still* he said nothing.

When Daniel had kissed her he'd given her flowery words and endless promises. He'd meant none of them.

What was worse? she wondered. Words that had no meaning? Or no words at all?

Fighting back an onslaught of tears, Bridget waited in stunned silence as Will walked around to his side of the carriage. Had she done something wrong?

She desperately wanted to ask. But she couldn't find it in her to look at him just yet, not directly. Staring straight ahead, feeling hollow and bleak, her vision blurred as the truth hit her at last.

Even without the words, even without the promises, Bridget realized she was in love William Black, desperately, unequivocally in love with the man. If his current dreadful silence was any indication, he didn't feel the same way about her.

Lord, what have I gotten myself into?

Will gripped the horse's reins tightly in his hands, his knuckles turning white from the effort. He knew he was handling the situation badly, knew he needed to tell Bridget he loved her, wanted to make her his wife. In short, he needed to tell her the truth.

Yet the words wouldn't come. Not even when she looked at him with that lost, confused expression.

Lord, what have I done?

Without thinking about the consequences, without caring about the possible repercussions, he'd given in to temptation and had kissed Bridget soundly on the mouth.

One moment he was thinking happily about his mother huddled over coffee with Ben, the next Will was letting his emotions take over without any of the logic or careful consideration that usually guarded his decisions.

He should have left her alone, should have stepped back before he'd given in and kissed her. Hadn't he decided she deserved better than him?

He'd been incapable of resisting. Because right or wrong, good or bad, he'd wanted to show Bridget how he felt. The kiss had seemed the most natural step.

Now he needed to explain himself.

He wasn't sure where to start.

Hoping for an idea—any would do—he cast a glance in her direction. She looked sad and confused and so completely adorable he wanted to grab her and never let her go. He refrained. Her brother-in-law had made a valid point last night, one that had haunted Will all day, even during their picnic.

He had been committed to marrying another woman for very specific reasons, reasons that were still important to him. How could he know for sure he wasn't replacing Bridget Collins with the first suitable prospect that came along?

The thought made his stomach roil. The woman sitting by his side was so much more to him than a substitute for a bride he'd never met. Bridget, this Bridget, *his* Bridget had brought music and laughter back into his home. She'd brought joy back into his heart and had won over the children within moments of meeting them.

How could he not want her for his bride? How could any man not want her?

A disturbing memory came to mind, one that had him reaching out and closing his hand over hers. "Tell me about your fiancé and the day of your wedding," he said. "Tell me what happened."

Her shocked gasp and swift yank on her hand out from under his warned Will he'd hit on a highly sensitive subject. Flynn had told him only the basics.

She was devastated.

Right, *now* he remembered that very important part of the story. A minute too late. He shouldn't have blurted out the question.

"You…you know about Daniel? You…" Her voice hitched on a sob. "How?"

"Your brother-in-law told me last night."

A lone tear escaped from her eye and trailed down her cheek. "He shouldn't have said anything. It wasn't his place."

"Probably not." Will reached up and caught the next rogue tear with his thumb. "If it makes you feel any better I forced the issue. And he didn't give any details."

She looked away, put a trembling hand to her mouth and sighed. "Well, I suppose that's something."

"If you tell me where the man lives I'll hunt him down and beat him to a pulp."

Instead of making her smile, the statement unleashed an onslaught of sobs. Tears rolled unchecked down her cheeks.

Excellent, Will, now you've made her really cry.

Hurting for her, he pulled the carriage to a halt.

"Bridget." He spoke her name on a whisper. "I didn't mean to upset you."

"I know." She looked to the heavens, waved her hand in a fanning motion by her face to no avail. The tears kept coming.

Will couldn't stand it. He simply couldn't stand seeing her in such misery. He tugged her into his arms and held her close. "I'm sorry he hurt you."

"He said he loved me. But he didn't, not really. Not enough to follow through with his promise to marry me." The words tumbled out of her mouth in a choked, hiccupping rush of air. "He claimed he loved me…" She let out another sob. "But he didn't…even…understand me."

Unsure what to say, or how to say it, Will stroked his hand along her spine in a soothing up-and-down motion.

Slowly, stroke by stroke, she relaxed into his arms. "We'd known each other all our lives. He'd seen how I was with our neighbors, helping whenever I could, doing whatever was needed. Yet, in the end, he said I gave too much of myself to everyone else. He feared I wouldn't have anything left for him, so he decided to marry Amy Doyle, a woman he claimed would put him first."

Will's hand stilled. What a selfish clod.

"How could Daniel think I didn't love him enough?" she said into his shirt. "The capacity to love isn't finite. It's a growing, expanding gift from God that only grows larger and fuller with use."

Not always. But in Bridget's case, that was true.

There was a certain fierceness to her capacity to love that went beyond what others had within them. She would never withhold an ounce of her devotion, not from her husband or from any living creature on this earth. Will had a mangy, very spoiled dog sleeping in his children's room to prove that particular point.

The man Bridget eventually vowed to love till death do them part wouldn't get a portion of her, he'd get the very best of her.

"The scoundrel didn't deserve you," he said through a tight jaw.

She held silent a moment, then turned her face up to his. "You really believe that?"

Lost in her watery gaze, he nodded slowly. "I do."

"Do you know what hurt the most?"

He shook his head.

"My life with Daniel had been nothing but a lie. He'd allowed me to believe he loved me and that my future was with him. Then he broke his word at the very last moment."

She clutched at Will's arms, as though hanging on for dear life. But then her eyes took on a distant gleam. "How could he have done that? How could he have lied so completely? To me, a woman he'd known all his life?"

"I don't know," Will said, his gut churning with rage. How could her fiancé have done something so heinous? A man was nothing without his word. *Let your yes be yes and your no be no,* that had been the Biblical principle Will had lived by all his life.

"Will?" Bridget said his name very softly. "Do you think I give too much of myself?"

"No, I don't."

Her fingers dug into his sleeves. "Truly?"

"Bridget, my darling." He drew in a breath. "The Bible teaches us everything we need to know about love. Above all, it's supposed to be selfless. When we truly love someone we should want to serve that other person. It's not about what we get from them in return. It's about what we give."

"Is that how you love?" She reached up and cupped his cheek, her eyes full of tenderness. "Are you a man who gives rather than receives?"

Wanting to answer her truthfully, he closed his eyes and concentrated on her question. As a parent his answer was an unequivocal yes. He would give anything for his children, even his life. But as a man, one who'd been served the ultimate betrayal by a woman he'd vowed to spend the rest of life with, he wasn't sure anymore.

And until he knew the answer he couldn't make any promises to Bridget. She'd been lied to before. The result had broken her heart. Will would not subject her to that pain again.

He opened his eyes and stared into her beautiful, trusting face. Even after what her fiancé had done to her she was still willing to give of herself. She was the most incredible woman he'd ever met.

Afraid he might lean down and kiss her again, he pulled slightly back. "I'm a man who wants the very best for you." He set her out of reach and took hold of the reins. "At the moment that means getting you home before the sky turns completely dark."

Chapter Nineteen

An eerie stillness hung over the road as Will steered his carriage down the lane leading to Bridget's house. They hadn't spoken since he'd set the carriage in motion. Bridget couldn't help but think the silence between them was excruciating, painful even.

No one would ever know they'd recently shared a sweet, tender kiss that had changed her life forever. Or that Bridget had revealed her darkest secret only moments before and Will had responded by saying just the right words to help her release the shame from her heart at last.

Sighing, she dropped her gaze to his hands holding the reins. He had strong, sure hands, capable of such tenderness, the kind that made a woman feel protected and adored at the same time.

Head still down, Bridget cast a covert glance back to his face. Will kept his gaze fixed straight ahead but she could see that his eyes bore signs of quiet distress.

There would be no declarations from him tonight, no renewal of his marriage proposal. After what she'd revealed about her past, she should be thankful he didn't attempt to give her empty words or false promises. After all, he knew exactly how much Daniel's rejection had hurt her.

Will's steadiness of character ought to be awe-inspiring. By not saying anything, he was showing her the greatest sign of respect.

But right now, at this very moment, Bridget wanted to hear Will say he cared. For her, only her. He didn't have to say he loved her, nothing so earth-shattering, just that he cared what happened to her, that their kiss had meant something to him.

She'd thought the Lord had brought her to this man and his family for a purpose. Had she been wrong? Was more grief in her future?

Before that terrible thought could creep into her heart and settle, her new home came into view. Although the repairs the men had begun yesterday weren't nearly enough to make the structure attractive, the soft glow of twilight cast the building in a more flattering manner than ever before. Bridget felt the weight of her troubles lift ever-so-slightly.

Nora met them on the stoop. She was alone and smiling, a clear indication she'd had a good day. *At least someone had,* Bridget thought.

"Hello, Bridget." Without waiting for a reply she directed her gaze to Will. "Mr. Black, won't you come inside a moment? I have something I'd like to show you." Her voice was filled with satisfaction.

Seconds ticked by before he responded. For a shocking moment Bridget thought he would refuse Nora's request and thus leave her to explain his rude behavior. Instead he allowed a small smile to spread across his lips and let out a dry chuckle. "That sounds ominous."

"Not at all." Nora took his arm and led him into the house ahead of Bridget. "I've been working on a cake recipe with the chocolate you left yesterday. Since you're the expert I want to get your opinion on the mix of flavors."

Following behind at a slower pace Bridget didn't catch all of his reply, but she was pretty sure she heard him mention his chocolatiers attempt to formulate a soft candy and ask if Nora would be interested in helping them.

Despite knowing Will was simply being a smart businessman, Bridget felt her chin tremble. Why was he so easy with Nora, so comfortable, when only moments before he'd been distant and silent with her?

She wasn't jealous of her sister, not precisely—well, maybe, but that wasn't the point. *The point,* Bridget realized as she knuckled an errant curl out of her eyes, was that she loved Will—it scared her how much—and from all outward appearances he did not return her feelings, at least not on the same level.

She never expected falling in love would feel like a physical blow. She'd always prayed the Lord would gift her a capacity to love that would overflow abundantly and increase daily. To Bridget's way of thinking, a person could never love too much or too hard.

But this new type of love with its very real pain in the vicinity of her heart, was nearly too much to bear.

"Bridget," Nora called from the kitchen. "Get in here. Will and I want your opinion, too."

Guard your heart, Bridget.

The silent warning came entirely too late.

The following Saturday morning, Bridget woke with a dark sense of foreboding. Although she'd been feeling off-kilter ever since Will had kissed her, the sensation was stronger today. Perhaps avoiding him all week had been a mistake.

Or perhaps not.

Bridget had needed the time apart to understand this all-consuming love she felt for the man. The strong emotion was still so new, both frightening and thrilling at the same time, but mostly frightening. Mainly because she had no idea how he felt in return.

Her solution to the problem was to avoid thinking about Will altogether. And their kiss. And the way he'd held her tenderly in his arms and let her cry into his shirt over Daniel's betrayal. He'd helped her heal, when she hadn't known she still needed to do so.

Will is your employer, she reminded herself. *And you're his children's nanny.* That kiss had been…it had been…

Glorious.

No. No, no, no. She was not thinking about that particular event this morning. Today she and Nora were welcoming their first official guests to their new home. Mrs. Fitzwilliam and the McCorkle brothers were due to arrive sometime before noon.

Thankfully Gavin had ridden over to the jailhouse two days prior, and alerted Nora of the impending visit. Apparently he'd stayed much longer than necessary, plying Cameron with questions about possible job openings in the Sheriff's Office.

The young man clearly knew what he wanted.

Bridget did, too. She wanted a family of her own, with Will as her husband and the twins as the first of their many children. Surely he wanted the same things. She'd caught him watching her with considerable longing in his eyes.

So what was stopping him from declaring himself?

She knew he cared for her. After all, he'd been very gracious when she'd asked for the morning off to prepare for Mrs. Fitzwilliam's visit. When Bridget had impulsively asked him to come, too, and meet her friends, he'd readily agreed, smiling into her gaze in the way she treasured. He'd promised to bring Olivia and Caleb along, as well. Perhaps even Esther.

The sound of a hammer banging on the roof interrupted her musings. Bridget lifted her head toward the sound and smiled. Cameron must have decided to work on the house today.

Despite the sense of unease she felt, Bridget wanted today to be a happy one full of blessings. With that in mind, she finished tying the laces on her boots and lifted up a prayer. *Oh, Lord, may today bring only joy.*

Shrugging off the last of her somber mood, she hurried down to the kitchen. Nora was already busy rolling dough.

"I'm here to help," Bridget said, spreading her arms wide. "What do you want me to do first?"

"The pies." Nora handed over the rolling pin.

Bridget got straight to work.

Several hours later with most of the preparations complete and the pies baking, she took Grace outside so Nora could have a break. Setting the baby on a blanket under a large shade tree, Bridget knelt down beside her.

She positioned herself so she had an unobstructed view of the lane. It wasn't long before she was rewarded with the sight of Will's open-top carriage coming around the bend. He looked as relaxed as she'd ever seen him, holding the reins in a loose-fingered grip. Two giggling children and one large dog rode alongside him.

Her family. And yet, not.

Swallowing back a pang of yearning, Bridget lifted her hand and waved. Will returned the gesture, a smile sliding into place. Her heart gave a little skip and she quickly broke eye contact. Would she ever get tired of looking into that handsome face?

Would she ever stop hoping the man was hers?

Sighing, she tickled the baby's belly. Grace responded with a merry kick of her legs. Laughing, Bridget bent at the waist and kissed the flawless cheek. "You're a good girl, aren't you?"

One day, she silently prayed. *Oh, Lord, one day may You bless me with a child of my own.*

As Will watched Bridget leaning over the baby something in him released, unwound. For weeks he'd been fighting the inevitable. Now he accepted the truth. He loved Bridget Murphy. He didn't know when she'd taken up residence in his heart. Long before he'd kissed her, that much he knew for certain.

The beautiful Irish lass with the sweet smile and unruly hair was everything he wanted in a wife. Ever since Fanny's tragic death he'd been afraid to love again.

But then Bridget had shown up and changed everything. Will had to tell her how he felt about her. How she'd changed him, and taught him to open his heart. He had to tell her today. But not now. When they were alone. When there wouldn't be anything to distract either of them.

As if to solidify his point, Digger leaped out of the carriage before Will pulled the horse to a complete stop.

"Digger, no." Caleb attempted to follow the animal, leap and all, but Will grabbed the boy by his shirt.

"Wait until we've stopped."

Practically bouncing in place, Caleb obeyed. The second Will swung open the door the boy jumped to the ground and ran after the dog. The ridiculous animal had stopped midstride and was now chasing his tail, literally. Caleb joined in the game.

Olivia departed the carriage in a more regal manner. But just like her brother, the moment her feet hit the ground she launched herself forward, this time in

Bridget's direction. Sinking to her knees near the baby, she began an onslaught of questions. Bridget responded with her characteristic patience.

"Hey, Will," Cam called down from the rooftop and then rubbed the sweat out of his eyes with his sleeve. "You gonna cool your heels all day or get up here and help with the man work?"

Will turned to Bridget and lifted an eyebrow.

Reading his silent query correctly, she laughed and waved him off. "Go on. I have things under control here."

"Be right there," he shouted up to Cam.

Three steps later a stately carriage pulled by two perfectly matched white horses rolled to a smooth stop. Digger and Caleb froze in the midst of their game. The dog moved in front of the boy as if to shield him from an unknown threat. The animal didn't growl, but he dropped to his haunches, appearing ready for a sudden attack.

In that moment Digger became Digger Black in Will's mind, a permanent member of their family. Just in case the animal decided to pounce on Bridget's friends, he crossed over to stand next to dog and boy.

A tall, imperious-looking woman exited the carriage first. Dressed in a fashionable emerald silk dress, with a perfectly coordinated hat on her auburn head, she looked completely out of place in the country. Nose in the air, seemingly oblivious to the heat, she took a slow, methodical turn, surveying the area with what Will thought was a highly critical eye.

"Needs considerable work," she declared.

"Mrs. Fitzwilliam." Bridget rose to her feet in a quick, fluid movement. "I'm so pleased you could make it."

The older woman hesitated then smiled. The gesture

softened her otherwise hard features. "Well, Bridget Murphy, you are looking very well. Very well, indeed. But this house…" She waved her hand in the general direction of the front stoop. "It's ghastly."

"It's coming along," Bridget said defensively, her shoulders flinching. "We'll have it in shape before winter."

The older woman sniffed indelicately. "I should hope so." Nose back in the air, she shuffled over to the blanket, caught sight of the baby and smiled broader than before. "My, my. That child has grown."

"Several pounds, at least." Bridget picked up Grace, introduced Olivia, and then the three proceeded to fuss over the baby.

Will started over, more intent on protecting Bridget from further censure than meeting the widow, when a movement from the carriage caught his eye.

He turned and watched as three boys jumped to the ground in rapid succession and headed toward Bridget. The first two were considerably smaller than the third, but they all had the same eager smiles, red hair and pleasant, honest faces. These had to be the McCorkle brothers Bridget had told him about.

Deciding he liked the look of the boys, Digger rose to his feet and barked a happy greeting. The younger two immediately changed directions.

"A dog," one of them declared, nearly tripping over his own feet in his haste to greet the animal.

"A *big* dog," the other one announced, moving at a more lumbering pace.

Chest out, chin high, Caleb beamed at the approaching boys. "His name is Digger. And I'm Caleb. Want to play with us?"

That was all the encouragement the McCorkle brothers needed. They introduced themselves as Sean and

Emmett. Will wasn't sure which was which. Before he could sort it out the three boys were wrestling on the ground with the dog.

Laughing at their antics the older brother crossed to Will. "I'm Gavin. Gavin McCorkle."

Will shook the outstretched hand. "William Black."

Recognition lit in Gavin's eyes. "You're Miss Bridget's employer."

"That would be me."

"Pleased to meet you, sir." He started to say more but then his gaze landed on Cam's horse. "Sheriff Long is here?"

"Up there, working on the roof." Will angled his head to where Cam was engrossed in fixing shingles. "I was just headed up there myself."

"I'll come along."

"Suit yourself."

Before heading out, Will approached Bridget and introduced himself to Mrs. Fitzwilliam.

Eyes narrowed, the widow looked him up and down and back again. Knowing this woman meant a lot to Bridget, Will remained unmoving under the rude appraisal.

She continued to take his measure, as if she were determined to find him wanting. Holding steady, he shot a quick glance at Bridget. A wordless message passed between them, one that was filled with apology on her side and amusement on his. His mouth curved into a slow, easy smile and Bridget blushed.

Catching their silent interaction, Mrs. Fitzwilliam's gaze widened. She looked from Will to Bridget and back again. After a tense moment she gave one firm nod. "You'll do, Mr. Black. Yes, you'll do quite well." With a toss of her head she dismissed him. "You may go now."

His amusement increased. Apparently he'd passed the test. He gave the widow a slight bow, touched his daughter's head with the tips of his fingers and then strode off.

With a stab of surprise Will realized he was whistling. Prior to Bridget's arrival in his home, he'd never whistled before in his life.

With so many people in attendance, and the day milder than usual, Nora made the decision to serve lunch outside on the lawn. The men had quickly set up a table to accommodate the adults, while the children sat happily on the ground.

Bridget found herself seated directly next to Will. Instead of feeling scandalized she experienced a warm, happy glow of contentment.

Something had changed this morning. Or rather something in Will had changed. He'd been overly attentive since arriving, whenever they were in the same room, at times visibly affectionate. A slide of his fingers over hers, a hand on her back, a secretive smile just for her, he was making his intentions clear. In front of her family and friends. Despite Nora's occasional scowls, and Flynn's silent warnings, Bridget couldn't have been happier.

The two youngest McCorkles and Caleb finished eating first. After seeking permission, the three boys set off toward the front of the house for a game of hide and seek. Olivia squirmed onto Bridget's lap and promptly fell asleep in her arms.

Bridget smiled at Will over the child's head. With everyone else involved in their own conversations, she decided to ask him a question that had been weighing on her mind since his arrival. "Esther didn't want to come with you today? She was more than welcome."

"She sent her regrets." He leaned in closer. "When the children and I left she was preparing a special lunch for Ben. The deputy had been left all alone to fend for himself at the jailhouse."

Bridget shook her head in mock chagrin. "That poor man."

They shared a laugh.

Will started to say more, but Mrs. Fitzwilliam's booming voice cut him off. "Although this house isn't up to my usual standards and the grounds need considerable work, that pretty, wild sort of garden around the side of the house caught my eye."

"That's Colleen's Garden," James Coulter said, setting his fork down with deliberate slowness. "Laird planted it for the girls' mother. Agnes and I plan to restore it to its original grandeur once my hip is better and she's feeling stronger."

"A fine idea," Mrs. Fitzwilliam said in an approving voice, then swung her gaze around the table as if looking for her next victim or rather the next person to engage in conversation. Her eyes narrowed on Will.

Before the widow could open her mouth—no telling what she would say—Bridget spoke first. "Mrs. Fitzwilliam, how is the search for your stepgranddaughter progressing?"

The older woman blinked, drew in a single, catchy breath then sighed heavily. "Not well, not well at all. Although there is evidence Mary set off for America with that no-good boyfriend of hers, the detective has been unable to determine precisely where the two settled."

"So she is not in the Boston slums as you feared?"

"Apparently not."

Was that good news or bad? Bridget wondered. "Perhaps the girl is in a much better situation than you feared." And wouldn't that be a blessing?

"Perhaps." Mrs. Fitzwilliam took a slow sip of her tea, her gaze growing distant. "Or perhaps my step-granddaughter is in a far worse predicament."

Nora touched the widow's arm. "We're keeping her in our prayers."

The older woman set her cup on the table, shook her head, then pinned Cameron with a glare. "You." She jabbed her finger in his direction. "Am I to understand you are the sheriff of this town?"

Cam leaned his forearms on the table. "That's me."

"So you're the one putting ideas into my boy's head." She indicated Gavin with a hitch of her chin. "Offering him a chance to be your apprentice when he's already enrolled in school."

Nora gasped in surprise, effectively pulling his attention to her. "You actually did it? You offered Gavin a job?"

He lifted a shoulder. "Yeah, well, he wore me down."

Bridget sensed there was more to the story. Cameron Long was not the type to be worn down by anyone, especially not an eighteen-year-old boy. By the way the man smiled at Nora, with that lopsided grin of his, Bridget suspected pleasing her sister had been the real motivation behind the unusual hire.

When Cam continued smiling at Nora, all but ignoring Mrs. Fitzwilliam's loud huff, the widow swung her angry gaze in the other direction. "Explain yourself, young man."

Gavin cleared his throat. "I've told you, Mrs. F. I don't want to go to school." He threw his shoulders back. "I want to be a lawman."

"Well, I like that." She sounded outraged, but Bridget saw the hurt in her eyes. "After all I've done for you and your brothers."

"You've been very generous." Sincerity filled

Gavin's gaze. "But Emmett and Sean need the schooling, not me. Like I said, I'd rather—"

A commotion on the other side of the house silenced him.

"Papa, Papa," Caleb shouted, running straight for the table of adults, Digger and the McCorkle brothers hard on his heels.

The dog barked frantically, spinning in circles. Caleb was breathing hard. The other boys were babbling, something about a horse.

Will jumped up and rushed to Caleb. "Calm down, son." He took the boy's shoulders and then turned his gaze to the older boys. "Tell me what's happened."

The taller of the two gulped in several hard breaths. "We tried, Mr. Black. We really did. But we couldn't stop him."

"Stop who?"

"The boy. The one stealing the sheriff's horse."

Chapter Twenty

To everyone's surprise Gavin McCorkle was the first
to run down the horse and rider. He'd raced ahead of
Will without breaking stride, passed Cam without much
more effort, covering ground in a fleet-footed flash of
speed. Will had never seen anyone move that fast.

With shockingly quick reflexes, Gavin reached out
and grabbed the horse's reins. It was a gutsy move. No
fear. No hesitation. He was going to make a good lawman one day.

Taking charge of the situation, he ordered the thief
off the horse.

The boy refused to relinquish the reins. Will couldn't
see the kid's face due to the shadows cast by his hat.
From the look of his small stature and painfully thin
shoulders he was probably fourteen, maybe fifteen, full
of youthful defiance and bad attitude.

Will squinted into the glaring sun. There was something odd about the way the kid fought to maintain his
seat, hunched over and wobbling, his grip on the reins
almost delicate.

"Get down. Now," Gavin ordered.

"No."

An ill-thought-out tug of war ensued, where Gavin

proved as stubborn as the boy. "Get off that horse. He's not yours."

A string of high-pitched oaths followed, and Will found himself reassessing the thief's age. Clearly, he was younger than fourteen. His voice hadn't changed yet.

Cam, knowing better than to get too close, watched the fray next to Will with tight-lipped intensity.

Will knew that look. His friend was barely holding on to his anger.

"How long you gonna let this go on?" he asked.

"Not a second more." Cam stepped forward. "Gavin." He lifted his voice above the fray. "Pull back, now, you're spooking Fletch."

The warning came a second too late. The horse snorted, tossed his head back in panic, then reared, his front hooves punching the air with vicious intent.

Screeching in fear, the thief flung himself forward and hung on to the horse's neck for dear life. The sudden motion sent his hat to the ground.

Long, curly hair cascaded down his—*her*—back.

Gasping in shock, Gavin's hand slipped from the reins and he lost his footing. He went down hard.

As one, Cam and Will rushed forward and grabbed him. They tugged him away from the horse, moving as quickly as possible. There was a moment when time stood still. And then...

The horse's hooves slammed to the ground, landing inches from Gavin's face.

In a whirlwind of angry snorts, female screams and flying dust, horse and rider galloped away.

Cam took off after them, yelling something over his shoulder about needing to borrow one of Will's horses to pursue the girl.

Will paid more attention to Gavin, who was still

sprawled on the ground. He was checking for injury when Bridget and Mrs. Fitzwilliam careened around the house. The children and the Coulters tried to follow, but Nora held them all back. "Give them room," she ordered, barring their way with an outstretched hand.

"Gavin." Bridget dropped to her knees. "Talk to me. Are you hurt?"

Will helped the boy to a sitting position. He wobbled a few seconds then collapsed back to the ground, groaning.

Bridget turned her concerned gaze onto Will. "What happened?"

"Gavin took a tumble," he said, but didn't expand. Bridget was already shaking with concern. He would not add to her anxiety.

Besides, the boy was fine. Or he would be, once he gained his bearings. Best not to tell her how close he'd come to disaster. Had Will and Cam been a shade too slow, had the horse swiveled a few inches to his left, Gavin would be dead.

"Praise God you're all right," she said to the boy.

Mrs. Fitzwilliam echoed the sentiment. She'd been studying Gavin with equal parts fear and frustration. "This just makes my point. School is where you belong."

Moaning, Gavin lifted to his elbows, swallowed hard, then collapsed back to the ground a second time. "I'm not talking about that now."

"Fine." The widow relented, for now, but her tense shoulders and pursed lips said the conversation was long from over.

Will predicted Gavin was in for an earful on the ride back to Boston.

Seemingly unconcerned with his fate, Gavin sighed. "Did you see her?" He blinked up to the sky. "That marvelous face, all that gorgeous long curly hair, I've never seen anything, or anyone, so beautiful."

"Long curly hair?" Bridget glanced at Will in confusion.

"The horse thief was a girl," he said.

"A *beautiful* girl," Gavin corrected, wiping the back of his hand across his mouth but making no attempt to sit up a third time.

Moving to her left, Mrs. Fitzwilliam stared off into the distance, as if she could see horse and rider through the dense forest. "My stepgranddaughter had long curly hair." She shook her head almost wistfully. "All that beauty wasted on a ruffian."

Will wasn't sure what the woman's stepgranddaughter had to do with the situation. He dismissed the thought, deciding she was still thinking about the girl because of the earlier discussion at the table. He turned back to Gavin, who was still mooning over the female horse thief. He'd gone into a litany of her fine attributes.

Maybe the boy wouldn't be a good lawman, after all. He seemed entirely too distracted by a pretty face.

"Right." Will shared a look with Bridget. "Let's see if we can get him to stand."

With Bridget's help they had Gavin on his feet a few moments later. He took four full steps before his knees buckled. Will ducked under his right arm. Bridget did the same under his left.

Leaning heavily on them both, Gavin half stumbled, half dragged himself back to the house. Whereby he was surrounded by fussing women and a myriad of questions from the children.

The boy took the whole incident in stride. Now that he'd had a taste of adventure he seemed more committed than ever to begin work as Cam's apprentice.

Less than fifteen minutes later Cam returned with both horses in tow and no thief.

"I found Fletch, unharmed, grazing in a patch of grass halfway down the lane." His lips tightened along the edges, the only outward sign of his true reaction to the incident. "I wanted to return your horse before I continued searching for the girl."

"I'm coming with you." Gavin rose to his feet, winced, but then righted himself.

Cam eyed him a moment, then nodded. "Not a bad idea. Might as well get you started as my apprentice."

"You're still going to hire me, even after I let the girl get away?"

"We all lose a few." Cam clapped him on the back. "From what I saw you have the instincts and speed necessary for the job, but we're going to have to work on your discipline. You're far too impulsive for your own good."

Gavin let out a whoop. "I'm going to be a sheriff one day."

Mrs. Fitzwilliam had a few things to say about that. "Not so fast, young man. I haven't given my approval."

A litany of reasons for the job—these from Gavin—and just as many against the job—these from the widow—ensued.

Moments into the argument Will had no doubt Gavin would win, eventually.

Wanting to focus on his own unfinished business, he went in search of Bridget. He found her with the twins, sitting on the ground in the backyard. Digger was spread out beside her, his head lulling in her lap. As Will drew closer he had to set his jaw against a quiver of emotion.

The children were listening intently to whatever tale she was spinning for them.

Will was enthralled himself by the tranquil picture his family made. By the way the sunlight spread fingers of burnished fire through Bridget's hair. By the gut-wrenching desire to join them on that blanket and get lost in the moment.

He felt a lot of other things, as well—hope, longing and a fierce need to ask Bridget to become a permanent part of his life.

Bridget's mouth went dry. Will was approaching her and the children with his gaze full of intense emotion. He was a sight to behold. She felt time slow to a crawl, and then certainty took hold. This was the man for her, the one the Lord had brought into her life at this perfect time.

"Hello," she said, proud of the fact that she kept her voice even. Somehow, she managed a smile.

He did not smile back. In fact, his eyes were very serious. Was he about to say the words she'd been waiting to hear? Was he going to declare his feelings for her now? In front of the children?

"Bridget," he said, his voice giving nothing away. "Would you come home with me?" He looked down at the children, "I mean, us. Would you come home with *us* today?"

That wasn't what she'd expected him to say. "But the day is already half over."

"The children are tired, they need their naps and I'd like you to come with us." He crouched in front of her, took her hand and kissed her knuckles. Right there in front of his children.

"I have something I want to say to you," he continued, "and I'd like us to be alone when I do. I'll get you home before dark, if that's what concerns you."

Oh. Oh, my. He was going to propose again, and

this time for all the right reasons, she saw the truth in his eyes.

How could she possibly say no, when she loved him so much and wanted nothing more than to be his wife? "Yes, of course I'll come home with you. I just need to let Nora know where I'm going and when I'll be back. I—"

"But, Papa." Caleb jutted out his bottom lip. "Do we have to go now?"

Will's eyes never left hers as he rose and stretched out his hand. "Yes, son, we have to go home now. It's time."

Why did she sense his words had a double meaning?

"But I want to play with Emmett and Sean some more."

"They'll be leaving soon, too." He helped Bridget stand, and didn't let go of her hand once she was firmly on her feet.

Mesmerized by what she saw in Will's eyes, she couldn't look away. "Don't worry, Caleb," she said without looking at him. "You'll see the boys again."

"Promise?"

She smiled. "Promise."

"Papa?" Olivia pulled on his pant leg. "How come you're holding Miss Bridget's hand?"

"Because I like her."

"I like her, too."

He chuckled. "Then take her other hand."

Olivia did as her father suggested. Hand in hand in hand, they walked back toward the house. Caleb and Digger meandered behind them in a crisscross pattern.

The next half hour passed in a blur. Bridget barely remembered saying goodbye to Mrs. Fitzwilliam and the two youngest McCorkle brothers, or the many promises she'd uttered to see them all again before too long.

The parting was very anticlimactic after the dramatic events of the previous hour.

A moment before Will helped her into his carriage Bridget flatly denied Nora's request to speak with her a moment, *alone*. She refused to allow anything to dampen the rest of her afternoon, especially not a well-meaning lecture from her overprotective big sister.

The ride back to town was filled with effortless camaraderie. It was as if the children sensed something exciting was about to happen. Will seemed remarkably relaxed.

How could anyone think him severe? He was one of the most calm, tender, compassionate men she knew. It would be a joy to spend the rest of her life by his side.

A thread of doubt tried to braid through her excitement and a renewed sense of foreboding took hold of her heart.

Where was this reservation coming from? Will cared about her, Bridget saw it in his eyes and in the way he reached out to touch her hand.

When they turned onto the road leading to his house, Will's hand closed over hers again. His thumb moved in a gentle sweep across her knuckles. The touch caused her to take in a quick, disjointed breath.

"We're nearly home," he said.

Home. With Will and the twins. Her pulse went wild, thrumming hard against her ribs. Bridget lowered her head and clutched Will's hand tighter. She'd journeyed to America with hope bursting in her heart. At every turn she'd clung to the Lord, knowing He was leading her to a new life and a new home. She never dreamed her destiny would include this incredible man and his adorable children.

God's plan for her life had been larger, grander and

far richer than anything Bridget could have imagined for herself.

She sighed. They were a few hundred yards away from Will's home when she noticed Ben coming toward them on his horse. His face was scrunched in a grave expression, his eyes filled with urgency.

Bridget had never seen Ben look so grim. He must have heard about the horse thief and was on his way to meet the sheriff. But then he came to a stop alongside their carriage.

Will let go of Bridget's hand and pulled his horse to a halt, as well. Apparently recognizing the older man's unusual shift in mood, he leaned forward, his gaze sharp. "Ben? Has something happened?"

The deputy whipped off his hat and wasted no time with pleasantries. "Your mother sent me to find you."

Motionless, Will glanced briefly at Bridget. She saw the barely concealed panic in his eyes. Hoping to calm his worries, she closed her hand over his arm and asked the question they both feared most. "Is Esther unwell?"

"No, nothing like that, it's…" He shot Bridget an apologetic grimace then made a specific point of speaking directly to Will. "You have a visitor."

"A visitor?" Will echoed, sounding as confused as Bridget felt.

"That's right. It's a—" Ben glanced at Bridget again "—a woman."

Why was the man looking at her like that, as though he pitied her? Apprehension dug deep, all the way to the depths of her soul.

Ben placed his hat back on his head and heaved a sigh. "You'll understand once you get to the house."

He rode off toward the center of town without another word.

Esther met them at the door, her hands wringing

over one another, her gaze darting over her shoulder every few seconds.

Digger raced for the kitchen, probably in search of his water bowl. In their attempt to tell their grandmother about their day, the twins started talking over one another.

"...and then Papa talked Miss Bridget into coming home with us today. They've been holding hands the *whole way,*" Caleb announced, proving nothing got past his little-boy eyes.

"Oh, Bridget, my dear girl." Unease rang in Esther's voice while her hand wringing increased. "I didn't realize you were coming home with Will and the children this afternoon. This makes everything all the more awkward."

It wasn't the actual words the older woman spoke but the quiver in her voice that sent panic shuffling through Bridget. Her hands coiled and flexed.

"Mother, what's going on? Ben mentioned something about a visitor." Will lifted a dark eyebrow. "Perhaps you would care to explain."

Esther looked pointedly at the children, who were staring up at her, mouths gaping open. She cleared her expression and smiled down at them. "Olivia, Caleb, I made you a very special treat while you were gone. Run along into the kitchen and wait for me there. I'll be right behind you."

Her voice was low and strained but the children didn't seem to notice. They rushed to the kitchen as quickly as Digger had, loudly speculating over what their treat might be.

"William, son, I..." She drew in a tight breath. "I put your visitor in your study."

Will straightened his waistcoat with a hard snap, a

sure sign of his agitation. "Who is this visitor? Why the secrecy?"

"Her name is Bridget." Esther glanced at him with chagrin. "Bridget Collins."

"Collins?" He sputtered out the name. "No. Impossible."

"It can't be true," Bridget whispered, her mouth dry with the tinny taste of fear. "It just can't be."

Yet deep down in the part of her filling with despair, she knew Esther spoke the truth. Bridget Collins was alive.

And she was here, in Will's home.

Bridget glanced at him, her heart beating as though it would leap out of her chest. But he wasn't looking at her. He was staring at his mother in stunned silence.

"I'm sorry, son." Esther touched his arm, then turned to Bridget. "I'm sorry for you both."

"No, Mother." Will wrenched his arm free of her grip. "Bridget Collins is dead. Flynn Gallagher verified it himself."

"I'm afraid the doctor was mistaken." A thin, dark-haired girl wearing a shabby dress and a tortured expression ambled down the hallway. She kept her hand flat against the wall, looking as though she would fall without the added support. "I am very much alive."

Will swung around to face the newcomer. *"Who* are you?"

The girl stumbled under his angry glare. Cloaked in shadow, she looked frail, defeated even, and Bridget's heart went out to her. Clearly something horrible had happened to her in recent days.

"I asked you a question."

A shudder was her only response.

Couldn't Will see he was scaring the poor girl?

Bridget touched his arm, hoping to calm his anger. After a few tight breaths, he visibly relaxed.

"Who are you?" he asked again, this time in a softer tone.

"My—my friends call me Birdie. But my real name is Bridget." She lifted a shaky hand to her forehead, brushed the hair away to reveal a stricken expression. "Bridget Collins."

"You cannot be her." Will's voice was full of shocked grief, the same emotion Bridget felt herself.

"Oh, but...but I am Bridget Collins. And I—" she raised her trembling chin a fraction higher "—I can prove it."

Chapter Twenty-One

Will escorted Bridget Collins—Birdie—into his study and shut the door behind them. Closing his eyes, he rested his forehead against the warm wood and desperately tried to gather his thoughts. The last image of Bridget, *his* Bridget, played in his mind. Her eyes had been filled with grief, mortification and sheer unhappiness. The same painful mix of emotions he struggled with now.

He'd planned to tell her he loved her this afternoon.

How could he declare himself now—when he was, apparently, still engaged to be married to another woman?

Perhaps there was still a way to fix this debacle. He and Bridget were meant to be together. With love and the Lord on their side no problem would be too big for them to conquer.

But if this young woman was truly Bridget Collins, they weren't facing a problem. They were facing a quandary. There were no solutions to quandaries, only strategies to manage the worst of the consequences. Until he knew what he was dealing with, there was no reason to despair.

Determined to uncover the truth, Will shoved away

from the door and turned to face Bridget, *Birdie.* She would never be Bridget to him. "Show me your proof."

His words came out hard and unforgiving. Without the calming influence of the woman he loved by his side, without her comforting touch, he was unable to temper his emotions. He regretted that, regretted that he couldn't try harder to listen without judgment. This girl was both ragged and miserable, that much was clear. Wherever she'd been in the weeks since departing the *Annie McGee,* she'd not had an easy time of it.

He tried to remember that as he spoke again. "Birdie." He kept his voice soft. "You said you have proof of your identity."

Dropping her gaze, the young woman nodded. "I—I have all the letters you sent me."

"Show me."

She reached into a tattered reticule, pulled out a handful of papers and set them on his desk.

He recognized his own handwriting, but didn't reach for the letters. "You could have stolen those."

"I may have done terrible things of late, unforgivable things—" her lips quivered "—but I am *not* a thief."

Will said nothing. He'd sent her considerable funds to make the journey to America, yet she hadn't fulfilled her end of the bargain. What was that sort of behavior, if not stealing?

As though reading his mind, Birdie looked away. Bottom lip stuck between her teeth, her gaze darted around the room, then locked onto the battered suitcase the ship's authorities had given him, proof of the dead girl's identity. Or so they'd all thought.

"That's my luggage." She turned to face him. "I can describe its contents."

"Perhaps you better." He retrieved the case, set it

on his desk and then opened the lid, making sure she couldn't see inside. "Proceed."

In a halting voice she gave an accurate accounting of every item, all the way down to a pair of scuffed slippers.

Will lowered the lid and secured the latch, closing off his emotions as firmly as he shut the case. She might look remorseful, but looks could be deceiving.

"All right, Miss Collins. You have convinced me. But the question still remains. Where have you been these past two weeks?"

"I...met a man aboard the *Annie McGee.*" A tiny, almost imperceptible shudder revealed far more than her words had.

Just like Fanny, this girl had turned to another man instead of trusting Will to understand her plight.

Pride warred with a growing sense of pity. This woman, the one he'd mourned with equal parts guilt and sadness, had *met a man.* By the looks of her now Will already knew how the story ended. Nevertheless, he said, "Go on."

As though the floodgates had been opened Birdie's story tumbled out of her mouth. "Cyrus was so handsome. He said he loved me. He made promises." She wiped her eyes with a quick swipe of her wrist. "I believed him."

No matter what lies the man had told her, Will had a hard time feeling sorry for Birdie. She'd made her choice, before ever having met him. "So you ran off with Cyrus once the ship docked."

"He said he would marry me." Will saw the humiliation in her gaze, and the pain. The same look Fanny had in her eyes the day her lover had sent her packing.

"I'd planned to tell you once we docked," she claimed. "I figured you'd understand."

Thinking about the man he'd been back then, just over three weeks ago, before Bridget had come into his life, Will wasn't sure he would have understood. But he wouldn't have tried to change Birdie's mind either, not after Fanny.

"I had it all figured out. I knew exactly what I would say. But then that girl fell from the forecastle and..." She sighed. "I knew her, you know."

How would he know that?

"She had the bed next to mine," she explained. "She was a timid girl named Bethany, or Brittany or something like that. I'm ashamed to say I never learned her name. I was too caught up with... Cyrus."

Was Birdie as contrite as she sounded? With so much at stake, Will reserved judgment. "I'm still unclear how you managed to switch identities with the girl."

She clasped her hands together. "When the authorities came asking if anyone knew her, I told them she was Bridget Collins. I gave them my luggage and said it was hers. They didn't question me any further. So with that simple exchange, the girl became me. And I became her."

Will shoved a hand through his hair. Her story made a sad sort of sense, except for one very important detail. Why had Birdie been in a bunk in the first place?

"Miss Collins, I sent you enough money to purchase a stateroom."

"Yes, well, I..." She broke eye contact and brushed her palms down her skirt. "That is, my family needed the money more than I needed a stateroom."

Frustration filled him. Will would have sent her more money had she asked. But that wasn't the important point here. "What happened with... Cyrus?"

Her face went dead-white. "He found a better prospect."

Of course he had. His kind always did.

"All those promises meant nothing to him." She wiped her nose on her sleeve and sniffed. "*I* meant nothing to him."

"And so you came back to me."

"I have nowhere else to go." She ran to him and clutched his sleeve, her hands curling into fists. "I have no money, no job. If...if you don't take me back... I... I don't know what I'll do." She gulped in huge gasps of air and tears welled in her eyes. "I... Please, Mr. Black. Have mercy. Don't turn me away."

Will had seen that same desperate look in another woman's gaze. Fanny had been similarly distraught, her threat almost identical in nature, uttered mere hours before she'd thrown herself off a cliff.

His gut wrenched as memories came flooding back. The agony on Fanny's face. Him reaching her moments too late.

How could he toss Birdie out of his home, knowing the possible consequences of doing so? He'd made a promise to her. And as hard as it was to think about what he would lose if he followed through, he was responsible for this woman. He was the reason she was in this country. He couldn't turn his back on her.

But what she'd done, switching identities with a stranger and then running off with another man when she'd promised to marry Will, those were grievous acts. Had Birdie's actions been driven by a temporary error in judgment, a youthful indiscretion? Or were they signs of her true character?

Only time would tell.

Fingers still clutching his sleeve, Birdie choked out a strangled sob. "I made a mistake. Please, Mr. Black, give me a chance to fix this terrible wrong."

How could he refuse her request when he'd made his

share of mistakes? As the Bible said, *for all have sinned and fall short of the glory of God.* No matter what she'd done, or why, he would not send her away and risk another tragic ending.

"All right, Birdie." He spoke without inflection. "You may have a second chance."

Even as he said the words he wondered how he could ever marry Birdie, especially with her character still in question. She could just as easily run off again. How could Will put his children through that pain a second time, the pain of wondering where their mother was, wondering if they were loved as completely as they deserved?

And more important, what sort of lessons would a woman like Birdie teach them? Nothing but sadness. His children deserved to know happiness and joy. Olivia and Caleb—and maybe even Will, himself—deserved a woman like Bridget in their lives.

Wincing at the repercussions of his actions, Will shoved a hand through his hair. This current disaster was of his making. Out of desperation he'd trusted in his own power to solve his problems instead of waiting on the Lord.

Now he had a woman in his home he didn't completely trust.

Unaware of his internal battle, Birdie let go of his sleeve. "So I am to stay here, in this home, with you and your family?"

"Yes." *For now.*

"Thank you." She collapsed to the ground with a sob, as if all the fight had left her. Sitting there, staring up at him with those large round eyes she looked very, very young. And extremely pitiful.

Sighing, Will lifted her in his arms and set her in one of the leather, wing-backed chairs.

Her stomach growled.

"When was the last time you ate?"

She brought a shaky hand to her throat. "I don't remember."

"Right." He found a blanket folded neatly on the settee and wrapped it around her shoulders. "I'll have my mother bring in some food."

He headed for the door.

"Will...will you be coming back?" she asked in a panicked voice.

"Eventually. I have something I must do first." He didn't expand. The fact that he was about to break the heart of the woman he loved wasn't any of this girl's concern, no matter what role she eventually played in his life. Or in this home.

As if understanding finally dawned, Birdie's eyes widened. "That woman in the hallway with you earlier, who is she?"

"My children's nanny." Again, he didn't expand.

"You won't need her anymore, now that I'm here."

Sorrow slammed in his chest. "I know."

He left the room without uttering another word.

Bridget heard Will's approach before she actually saw him enter the kitchen. His dark hair stood in disarray around his handsome face, as if he'd been running his fingers through it over and over again.

His gaze found hers. Oh, the grief she saw in those clear blue eyes. Her heart lurched with unspeakable pain for him. She wanted to run to him, to throw her arms around him and tell him everything would work out. That God was in control.

She didn't have that right. He wasn't hers anymore. He'd never been hers. And that was the saddest part of all.

He reached out to her, casually, as if it was the most natural thing to do. Her heart took an extra hard thump but she didn't go to him.

Lowering his hand, he looked around the room. "Where's my mother?"

"She took the children and the dog for a walk."

Bridget moved closer to him, unable to help herself, and touched her fingertips to his face. She would never forget this man. "Is that girl in your study, is she…your intended?"

He leaned into her open palm. "She is, indeed, Bridget Collins."

"And you're going to honor your promise to her."

Sorrow drained out of him and slammed into her. "I can't send her away."

Of course he couldn't, Bridget thought. Nevertheless, her insides turned cold and she dropped her hand to her side.

"I'm sorry," he said.

She wanted to tell him he had nothing to apologize for. After all, he wouldn't be the man she loved if he sent Birdie away. But she couldn't make the words come.

"I'll take you home now."

Even through the thick haze of her regret she couldn't let him do that. "I think it will be best if I have Ben escort me."

"Please, I have things I need to say to you."

Her common sense fought a hard battle with her desire to spend a few more moments in his company. "No, Will, it wouldn't be wise."

The haunted way he looked at her reminded her of the man she'd first met on the docks in Boston. He'd come so far, her handsome, serious-minded Will had learned to laugh. And even whistle for no good reason.

She wanted to weep in frustration at all they'd lost

in a single afternoon. "We both know how the conversation will go. You'll tell me you care about me but—"

"I can't walk away from Birdie right now." His mouth became a grim slash.

Hearing him speak the words aloud was like a solid punch to her heart. "I know that," she said very softly. "You would never break your word."

And she loved him all the more for it.

Will rubbed the bridge of his nose between his thumb and forefinger. "What you don't know is *why* I can't walk away."

"But I do." She pulled his hand away from his face. "It's because you are a man of integrity."

"There's more to it than that, another reason why I can't throw her out of my home. My wife, Fanny, she hated life in Faith Glen, hated being married to me and despised being a mother." He swallowed. "After the twins were weaned, she found solace in another man's arms."

Bridget could see how hard this was for him. She laid a hand on his shoulder in a show of comfort. "You don't have to tell me this."

"Yes, Bridget, I do." He covered her hand with his, squeezed, then moved away to lean against the doorjamb. "The short version is that when the man decided he'd had enough and tossed her aside, something in Fanny snapped. She ended her misery by jumping off a cliff. I was there, but I'd arrived too late to save her."

"Oh, Will." The horror he must have felt, the helplessness, the guilt.

"Now do you understand? Fanny chose death over life. She didn't want me or the children." His eyes went dark and turbulent. "Maybe if I'd tried harder to make her happy, she would still be alive."

"You can't know that."

"I let her down in the worst possible way. She's dead because of me."

"No, Will, your wife made her own choices. She could have turned to the Lord for comfort, or she could have sought godly counsel. She could have done any number of things. Instead she turned to another man who was not her husband to ease her unhappiness. And when that didn't work she chose to jump off that cliff."

"If I had only been there sooner..."

"Your presence might have made a difference, or it might not. Listen to me, Will, you have to forgive yourself."

Head down, he didn't answer her for a very long time. Then he looked up and glanced directly into her eyes. What she saw in his gaze made her heart twist. "Thank you, Bridget."

Although he didn't say the words, she knew, in that moment, she *knew* he was on the road toward forgiveness, for Fanny, and maybe even for himself.

"I won't make the same mistakes with Birdie." The weary resignation in his voice told its own story. "She's suffered a similar rejection as Fanny."

How...horrible for them all.

Bridget took one long breath and accepted the truth at last. The man she loved was promised to another woman. "I need to say goodbye to the children."

Nodding, he reached inside his coat and pulled out a leather wallet with a grim twist of his lips. When he tried to hand her a wad of bills, she simply stared at him, appalled.

He might as well have slapped her. "I don't want your money."

"These are the wages I owe you, for services rendered as the children's nanny." His voice was so businesslike, so distant.

Humiliation sliced through the fabric of her control. For one black moment Bridget was tempted to tell him what he could do with his *wages* in a very unladylike manner. "It's too much."

"Consider it my thank-you, for...everything."

"Your words are enough."

His jaw clenched so tightly a muscle jumped in his neck. "Bridget, you and your sister need the money for repairs to your house."

"We'll make do."

He tried to stuff the money into her hand. She reared back, hands splayed in the air. "Stop it, Will."

He cast her a quick, pained look. "Then let me offer you a job at the mill. I'm still responsible for you."

Therein lay the problem. She didn't want him to feel responsible for her. She wanted him to love her. "Will, I am not alone in this world, nor am I destitute. I have a home now, and a garden that will supply food, eventually. I also have family." *Just not your family.*

"Bridget, please, allow me this honor. Let me help you."

"I won't take money from you." She threw her shoulders back. "I won't."

A thousand unspoken words passed between them. Then he shook his head sadly. "You might understand how to give of yourself, but you have no idea how to receive."

"It's better to give than receive," she shot back, hurt by the censure she heard in his voice. "You said so yourself."

"Yes. But how can you truly understand God's grace if you can't accept earthly help from someone who cares about you, someone who has no ulterior motive?" He crumpled the money in his hand. "How can you understand the depth of the Lord's sacrifice if you never admit to your own need for help?"

He had a point. A valid one, but she couldn't accept his charity, no matter what argument he used. "Good-bye, Will."

Eyes fixed on the doorway, Bridget walked past him. At the last possible moment she reached out and touched his arm gently with her fingertips.

Surprisingly she managed to hold her emotions in check when she found the children playing in the front yard. She stayed in control as she told them goodbye and promised to see them at church the next morning. For fear of breaking, she avoided Esther's gaze altogether.

The older woman didn't press the issue.

With Ben filling her in on the missing portions of Birdie's story, Bridget remained stoic and brave throughout the ride back to her home. She even managed to hold it together during Nora's rapid-fire questioning over why she'd left with Will earlier in the day, putting off her sister by saying that she was tired, but would tell her everything after resting.

It wasn't until she was in her room, with the door firmly shut behind her that she finally gave in to her grief. Alone at last, Bridget folded her arms around her middle and wept. She wept for all that could never be, for the family that had almost been hers but now belonged to Bridget Collins.

Oh, Lord, she whispered into the darkened room, *how will I ever survive without Will and the children in my life?*

Bridget woke to find Nora sitting on her bed, her warm gaze staring down at her with unveiled concern.

"Nora?" She rubbed her eyes, then noticed the sky was still a cold, gloomy gray. "What time is it?"

"Early," she said. "Not yet six in the morning."

"Oh." She rolled onto her side and cradled her head with her hands. "Why are you here?"

"I heard you crying."

Those four simple words brought back all the misery of the day before. Breathing in slowly, carefully, she squeezed her eyes shut and told Nora the worst of it. "Bridget Collins is alive."

"What?"

Bridget struggled to sit up, but the effort was too great and she collapsed back on her pillow.

"I don't know all the particulars, but she apparently switched identities with that dead girl we thought was her."

"Why would she do something like that?"

"So she could run off with another man." Bridget spoke each word with deliberate slowness so as not to start crying again. "Now the other man doesn't want her and she's back to claim her position as Will's bride."

Nora processed the tale in silence. Then her face scrunched into a frown. "What an awful, selfish girl."

Bridget wasn't so sure. "Oh, Nora, I wish I could dislike her, too. But the girl I met yesterday was so utterly defeated. I just can't find it in me to hate her. And besides, it's her right to claim what was promised to her."

At that, Nora had a few choice things to say, but Bridget couldn't make out the words through the blood rushing in her ears. Her throat closed on a miserable sob.

Muddled thoughts coursed through her mind. She couldn't face Will and the children at church today, not if Birdie was sitting between them. She'd never experienced jealousy before. Now it ate at her.

She wanted to cry out in agony but then she heard

Nora turn her anger onto Will. "How dare he hurt you like this?"

"No, Nora, you don't understand. Will made a promise to the girl long before he met me. He has to follow through. He's a man of his word. That's one of the things I love about him. And yet…"

She promptly burst into tears.

"Oh, Bridget." Nora smoothed her hair off her face. "No matter what you say to defend the man, he carries some of the blame."

Bridget's entire body stiffened. "He has reasons for honoring his promise, reasons that go beyond his inherent integrity, reasons I can't tell you."

Nora remained unmoved. "Is that so?"

"He's trying to make things right, for Bridget Collins and for me, in the only way he knows how." Why hadn't she seen that sooner, why had she been so insulted by his kind gesture? "He offered me money and then a job at the mill."

"And you refused both."

Something in Nora's voice, something that sounded far too much like censure, had Bridget gaping at her. "Why are you so sure I refused Will's assistance?"

"You never accept help, not even from family."

"I…" She frowned. "Never? Surely that can't be right."

"Sadly, it is." Nora slid down on the bed next to Bridget and stared up at the ceiling. "Your refusal to lean on your loved ones in times of crisis is your most frustrating quality, dear sister."

Bridget twisted the edge of the blanket between her fingers and stared up at the ceiling. "Will said something similar. He said that I knew how to give but not how to receive."

Nora snorted in agreement. "He knows you very well."

The echo of a smile trembled on her lips. "Yes, he does."

After a moment Nora rose and helped Bridget up, as well. "What are you going to do now that Will is determined to honor his promise to that awful, awful girl?"

Bridget cringed at Nora's hard tone. "Don't, Nora. Don't judge her so harshly. She's had a hard go of it."

"So have we all. But sometimes we don't always get what we want."

"I know. Oh, Nora, I know."

Nora pulled her into her arms and gave her a tight, sisterly hug. "You deserve happiness, Bridget. And so does Will."

"I thought you didn't like him."

"I thought so, too." She stepped back and shook her head. "But he has goodness in him. I was so busy looking for flaws I missed that at first. It wasn't until I saw the way he was with you and the children yesterday that I changed my mind. He adores you, Bridget. He would have made you happy."

Futile disappointment tinged her vision. "It doesn't matter anymore. All I can do is step aside and try to build my life without him and the children."

"The twins. Oh, Bridget." Nora's hand flew to her mouth. "What are you going to do about Olivia and Caleb? You can't walk away from them, not after all they've been through."

A cold, thin pain slid through her heart. "No, I can't."

Bridget would not abandon the twins like their mother had. She had to stay in their lives and, if necessary, when the time came, she would slowly ease away. But *only* if necessary.

Surely Will would understand her need to stay in the children's lives.

For their sake, he had to.

Chapter Twenty-Two

Less than a week with Birdie in residence and Will's home had lost much of the joy Bridget had so effortlessly restored. It wasn't that Birdie was a terrible person. She was simply miserable. And no matter how hard she tried she couldn't seem to snap out of her melancholy.

At least she put on a brave face around the children. The three of them got along well enough, but there was no real connection. Impromptu picnics were a thing of the past. There was no more spontaneous laughter at meals, no more musical performances or rousing games of tag. In four short days, Olivia and Caleb had reverted back to the overly polite, well-behaved children they'd been before Bridget had come into their lives.

The only time the twins showed any signs of enthusiasm was when Ben came by and took them on a ride in Cam's rickety wagon. Because they were usually gone all afternoon Will suspected Ben took them to see Bridget.

He would have to thank that old coot one day.

And Bridget, as well. Even when he'd pushed her out of all their lives, she hadn't abandoned the children. Sitting behind his desk in his study at home, Will leaned back in his chair. The sun was finally setting, marking the end of another disastrous day. A kaleidoscope of moving shadows flickered across the floor, creating an eerie picture—a perfect accompaniment to his grave mood.

He couldn't marry Birdie. That much he was ready to admit to himself. He could never subject his children to a lifetime with a woman even more unhappy than their mother had been.

Nevertheless she was his responsibility.

Lord, what am I to do?

The obvious answer was to set her up in her own home and provide her a job, either at the mill or somewhere else. There were other options as well, including sending her back to Ireland. The problem he faced was that he had no idea what Birdie wanted. All he knew was that she was wretchedly unhappy in his home.

A tentative knock jolted him out of his reverie. Will called out, "Come in."

The door creaked open and his mother's head of silver-white hair poked through the opening. He motioned her forward.

As she stepped deeper into the room a burning throb knotted in his throat. The purple smudges were back under her eyes. A clear indication Will had made a mess of all their lives.

His future bride was supposed to have taken the burden off his mother, but Birdie was too caught up in her own pain to provide much help. Bottom line, she was no Bridget.

Bridget. His beautiful, wild-haired, Irish lass with the tender heart and…

No, Will. Bridget Murphy is not yours, not anymore.

He closed his eyes and offered up a silent prayer

for discernment. Hope for the future drifted just out of reach.

"We need to talk," his mother said in a firm voice that belied the look of exhaustion in her eyes. "About Birdie."

He nodded, reconciled with the inevitability of the impending conversation.

"I understand why you brought the girl into this house, but you must realize how unhappy she is. She doesn't want to be here."

No, she didn't.

He forced himself to rise from his chair and make his way around the desk. "As much as I value your opinion, this is my misstep to unravel."

"But you *will* unravel it, son. Promise me."

"Yes, mother." He took her by the shoulders and pulled her into a gentle hug. "I promise."

She slumped against him in relief. "You'll do so soon?"

"No, not soon." He flattened his lips into a determined line. "Now. This very minute."

He released her and started for the door.

His mother stopped him with a hand on his arm. "I know that look in your eyes. You've come to a decision, haven't you?"

"I have." Or at least he was close to doing so. There were a few points he needed clarified first.

"What are you planning to do?"

Several options came to mind, long-term solutions. But before he made any move he had to discover where Birdie stood on several matters, including their supposed marriage. "I'll know more once I speak with the girl."

"No need to seek me out, Mr. Black." The door

creaked on its hinges and Birdie pushed into the room. "I'm right here."

Not taking his eyes off the girl, he said, "Mother, will you please excuse us."

Esther gave a heavy sigh but made her way out of the room without argument.

Will held his tongue until he was certain he and Birdie were completely alone. "I think you will agree that our current arrangement is not working out."

"No." Her lower lip trembled. "It is not."

"I have several possible solutions. But first I want to ask you a question." He took her hand and guided her to a nearby chair. "Do you wish to marry me?"

Her gaze widened at his blunt question, making her look very young, more child than woman. "No, Mr. Black. I do not."

He forced himself to speak calmly. "You are sure?"

"Yes. I *never* wanted to marry you." She clasped her hand over her mouth as though shocked the truth had slipped out.

"It's all right, Birdie. You may speak plainly with me. There will be no penalty for speaking your mind."

She lowered her hand, swallowed hard. "Our marriage was a way to make money for my family. They didn't want me to do it—" a sob wrenched past her lips "—but I told them I wanted to help. Money was so scarce…"

What a terrible situation for them all. And Will had played his part. He'd made the offer, had sent the money. He winced at his own shortsightedness.

Forgive me, Lord.

Now that he knew the truth, Will would do his part to rectify the situation. He would give Birdie the second chance she needed. And he would do so generously.

"You are sure, Birdie?" He asked the question very

slowly, very carefully, giving her one last chance to state her wishes as truthfully as possible. "You are absolutely sure you do not want to marry me?"

"I—I want to go home." Two fat tears fell from her eyes. "Please, Mr. Black, send me back to Ireland."

Bridget tried to move on with her life as best she could, but the brave face she presented to the world was a lie. Every day without Will became harder to bear than the one before, and with each new dawn came a renewed internal struggle. Should she yank the blanket back over her head and remain there all day? Or should she buck up and pull herself together?

As Nora liked to remind her, Murphy women never gave in to defeat.

And so, like all five mornings prior to this one, Bridget forced herself to climb out of bed and dress for the day.

Her fingers were clumsy, her eyes gritty from lack of sleep. There was no denying she missed Will desperately. She actually longed for him as though a part of her very soul had been ripped out. Even her afternoons with the children were bittersweet because he wasn't there to share them.

It had been Esther's idea to send Olivia and Caleb to Bridget for a few hours every afternoon, a way to help ease the transition for them all. Ben had been kind enough to offer to transport them out to the house every day.

Bridget wondered what Will thought of the arrangement. Surely he knew. Ben and Esther would never go behind his back. Would they?

Mind working through the question, wondering why she sensed he'd been kept in the dark, she stepped into the kitchen and poured herself a cup of tea. Perhaps she should seek him out this next week and tell him. It would give her a chance to see him, to—

No. That would only make matters worse.

Sighing, she looked up. The incessant banging indicated Cameron was already hard at work on the roof. He seemed determined to spend every free moment he had helping them prepare the house for the coming winter. Was he acting out of simple kindness, or something more? Something to do with Nora?

Smiling for the first time in days, Bridget glanced out the window to where Nora and Agnes were weeding together in the garden. Well, Nora was weeding. Agnes was perched on a bench, chattering away, baby Grace in her arms. The older woman looked happy, so did Nora, except when she glanced toward the roof. Then she looked uncertain, nervous even, uncharacteristically so.

Bridget's smile widened, just as a movement off to the left captured her attention.

Doing his part, James shuffled back and forth between the house and garden, clearing away the piles of weeds when Nora's stack grew too large.

Watching the Coulters and Nora get along so well, Bridget thought about how far she and her sisters had come in less than two months. The journey across the ocean had started out with little hope and a lot of prayer. All the fear and uncertainty had been worth it in the end. They'd found a home and life in a new country.

Meeting Will and his beautiful children, getting to know and love them, had been an added blessing. The Lord's plan for her life wasn't entirely clear in her mind anymore, but Bridget had no regrets.

Not...one...single...regret.

Then why the wrenching gasps of agony? Why the

burning throb in her throat? Giving in to her misery, she buried her face in her hands and let the sobs come.

And then she heard someone say her name.

Will. Will was here. "Please, go away. I can't speak with you right now. I—"

Strong arms gathered her close.

"Bridget, my love, don't cry." His deep voice washed over her, soothing her.

The simple pleasure of being wrapped in his arms made her feel so much worse. The sobs came harder, faster, louder. She tried to push him away, humiliated, but his hold tightened and he began murmuring words of comfort, the meaning of which she couldn't seem to make out.

For several seconds he stroked his hand down her hair, then brushed his lips against her forehead. "There's no need to cry."

She quivered, caught between yearning and lost hope.

Will's hand worked small circles along her back, up and down, round and round. All the tension drained out of her and she relaxed into him. She just wanted a moment with the man she loved, just one, but then sanity returned and she pushed him away with a hard shove.

The air between them pulsed with tension.

Bridget studied his face, surprised to see the stubble shading his strong jaw and the tangled hair on his head. Will never left the house disheveled. What had happened?

What did it matter?

She wiped the tears off her cheek and closed off her heart. "You can't hold me like that ever again. You're to marry another woman. Being here, with me, like this." She waved her hand between them. "It's wrong."

"Felt right to me." The flare of love that flashed in his eyes sent her pulse rioting out of control.

I love you, too, her heart whispered. Longing filled with hope reared, lingered, but she fought the painful emotion back. A torrent of words came rushing forward, none of which made it past her lips.

Eyes softening, Will wordlessly reached for her again. She leaned forward a little then caught herself and took a pointed step back.

A deep frown etched his forehead. "You're making it hard to tell you how I feel."

"I don't have the right to hear it." It would hurt too much. "And you don't have the right to tell me."

"I'm botching this." He rubbed his face with both hands. And for the first time since he'd arrived Bridget realized he wasn't simply disheveled but fatigued, as well.

"Will?"

"I put Bridget Collins on a ship back to Ireland early this morning, before dawn."

Bridget's heart stumbled. "You—you what? Why?"

"She wanted to go home."

"She—she didn't want to marry you?"

He gave her a wry smile. "Not in the least. Praise the Lord, she'd never wanted to marry me. The arrangement had been a way for her to make money for her family."

Bridget nodded in comprehension. After the potato famine many families had resorted to all sorts of creative means to survive. But for Will to have to hear from his bride's own mouth that she didn't want to marry him, that must have been painful. Bridget had lived that humiliation herself.

Except Will didn't look sad or embarrassed or hurt. In fact, he was grinning at her.

"You're not upset Birdie didn't want to marry you?"

He roped her body against his and bent his head so that his mouth landed just shy of hers. "Not in the least."

He pressed his lips to her forehead, then her cheek, then her mouth, where he stayed put for a while.

"You've ruined me for other women, Bridget Murphy."

She liked the sound of that, very much.

He kissed her nose. "You brought music and joy into my home again. You are a mixture of grace and strength, a woman who gives all of herself and holds nothing back. You taught me to enjoy life again and to love with all that I am."

Her heart stopped altogether and then started beating faster, harder, leaving her happily dizzy. "Oh, Will, the capacity to love has always been in you. You've never held back with Olivia and Caleb."

"But I did with everyone else. I shut off any desire to love again. You broke down my defenses, with your sweetness and giving nature." He nipped tenderly at her ear. "I love you, Bridget Murphy. I think I have from the moment I first saw you on the docks."

"I love you, too," she whispered in return. "And I *know* it was from the very moment I first saw you on the docks."

He chuckled. "Marry me. Be my wife and the mother of my children. We'll let God direct our path. And I promise, I'll no longer try to control every outcome on my own."

This wonderful man declaring his love for her was full of surprises. Her hand stole up the side of his face. "And I'll no longer refuse your gifts, tangible or otherwise. I want you to take care of me, Will, in the same way I'll take care of you. I want to receive all that you have to give to me, as well as give all that I am to you."

"Is that a yes?"

"Yes." She kissed him on the mouth. "Yes, yes, yes. I'll marry you."

"As soon as possible?" he asked.

"As soon as possible."

Setting her out of his arms, his manner seemed easy and relaxed but his eyes were full of emotion. "Come, Bridget." He reached out his hand to her. "Come greet the rest of our family."

He guided her outside. Waiting in his carriage were two very excited children and one rambunctious dog.

Her sorrow instantly vanished. Yes, Bridget thought with happy tears welling in her eyes, this was her family now.

Epilogue

Years after the blessed event, Bridget knew she would remember her wedding as a happy affair shared with family, friends and many of Will's employees. The event had come together seamlessly, thanks to the welcome assistance of her sisters and future mother-in-law.

Now she was standing in front of the preacher, with Will by her side reciting his vows as she'd done herself moments before.

Smiling into his eyes, Bridget fingered the light blue silk of her dress. Maeve had supplied the lovely hand-made creation as a wedding gift, with the help of Ardeen Nolan and her aunt Mrs. Kennedy's skillful assistance. Not to be outdone, Nora had created a special cake—a chocolate one, of course—for the celebration after the ceremony.

Will squeezed her hand as he finished his vows. "…until death do us part."

The preacher nodded, then took a moment to impart a bit of sage advice. "Wise couples recognize that they're going to see things differently, and this will cause them conflict. The solution will be loving compromise."

Bridget shared a meaningful look with Will. The day after asking her to marry him he'd hired a work crew to rebuild the stairwell in her house. She'd not only accepted his gift, but had sent him a thank-you note that was so full of gratitude he deemed it the sweetest love letter he'd ever received.

Oh, how she adored this man. He looked especially handsome in his black frock coat, matching trousers and crisp white shirt. A shiver of anticipation traveled up her spine. The ceremony was almost complete. She was moments away from becoming Will's wife.

As her groom slid a beautiful diamond ring onto her finger, Bridget cast a glance at the children standing at the front of the church with them. Olivia and Caleb were behaving beautifully.

Of course the very moment she had the thought, Caleb began fidgeting.

Bridget couldn't really blame the little boy. The ceremony must seem impossibly long to a child his age. Despite several whispered orders from his grandmother to stand still, it was clear Caleb had had enough of minding his manners.

Eyes dancing with mischief, he reached out and pinched his twin sister. Olivia pinched him back.

Instead of stopping the misconduct, Bridget shared a secretive smile with Will. Their children were back to normal, at last.

As soon as Bridget slid the gold band onto Will's finger, Caleb swiveled his head toward the back of the church and let out a war whoop. Before either parent could grab him, he tore down the aisle. Olivia was one step behind.

Neither had been given their cue.

Squealing in delight, the twins dodged outstretched hands and all other attempts to slow them down. They were met at the end of the aisle by a very handsome, well-groomed dog that had somehow broken free of his restraint.

The preacher's eyes widened at the mayhem erupting right in front of him. "I—I now pronounce you husband and wife."

Seemingly undaunted by the uproar brewing at the opposite end of the church, Will pulled Bridget into his arms and kissed her soundly on the mouth. "I love you."

She smiled into his blue, blue eyes, lifted on her toes and kissed him right back. "I love you more."

"Not possible." His arms slid around her and he went for another kiss.

The preacher cleared his throat and they laughingly broke apart. Arm in arm, they began their walk back down the aisle, heading straight for their children.

Bridget's gaze landed on so many dear faces. Mrs. Fitzwilliam and the McCorkle brothers. Ardeen Nolan and her aunt. Ben MacDuff. Esther. Standing in the front row, Maeve winked at Bridget. She returned the gesture then smiled at her sister's handsome husband. Flynn smiled back. Although the Gallaghers had been married less than a month, they were no longer the reigning newlyweds in the family. As of today, that honor belonged to Bridget and Will.

Three sisters, but only two happy endings.

A burst of unease shot through Bridget and her steps faltered. Nora was alone now, left to build her life in America without her sisters. She had Grace, but for how long? The baby's family could claim her at any moment. Surely Nora deserved her share of happiness, too. She'd guided their family through lean years after their mother's death, and had held them together when all seemed lost.

What would become of Nora now that Bridget and Maeve were married?

As if to drive home the point, Bridget caught Nora's eye at the very moment a tear slid down her older sister's cheek.

Bridget's steps faltered. But then Cameron Long moved into view and whispered something into Nora's ear.

Nora laughed in response, the gesture transforming her face.

Bridget sighed. This time the sound was full of hope. Perhaps her sister would be all right after all.

Will continued guiding Bridget down the aisle. Each step pulled her away from her past and closer toward her future, the one she would share with her husband. *Her husband.*

She turned her face to his.

He planted a tender kiss on her nose.

At the end of the aisle he turned and looked out over the crowd. "Please, everyone, follow us back to our home and celebrate our new family with us."

Smiling at Bridget in a way that nearly made her swoon, he escorted their entire family into the carriage waiting for them outside the church.

Once everyone was settled, Will kissed Bridget again, on her lips, longer and with more enthusiasm than he had in the church.

When he finally pulled away, his eyes were full of promises. Promises she knew he would fulfill down to the letter.

"Ready to go home, Mrs. Black?"

"Oh, yes, Mr. Black." She reached out and pulled both children close. "Oh, my, *yes.*"

To Bridget's way of thinking, the journey across town was more than an exciting adventure. It was the perfect beginning to her new life as Mrs. William Black.

* * * * *

WE HOPE YOU ENJOYED THIS BOOK!

Love Inspired® SUSPENSE

Uncover the truth in these thrilling stories of faith in the face of crime from Love Inspired Suspense. Discover six new books available every month, wherever books are sold!

LoveInspired.com

SPECIAL EXCERPT FROM

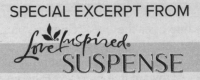

*When a rookie K-9 cop becomes the target of a
dangerous stalker, can she stay one step ahead of this
killer with the help of her boss and his K-9 partner?*

Read on for a sneak preview of
Courage Under Fire *by Sharon Dunn,*
the next exciting installment to the
True Blue K-9 Unit miniseries, available in
October 2019 from Love Inspired Suspense.

Rookie K-9 officer Lani Branson took in a deep breath as
she pedaled her bike along the trail in the Jamaica Bay
Wildlife Refuge. Water rushed and receded from the shore
just over the dunes. The high-rises of New York City,
made hazy from the dusky twilight, were visible across
the expanse of water.

She sped up even more.

Tonight was important. This training exercise was an
opportunity to prove herself to the other K-9 officers who
waited back at the visitors' center with the tracking dogs
for her to give the go-ahead. Playing the part of a child lost
in the refuge so the dogs could practice tracking her was
probably a less-than-desirable duty for the senior officers.

Reaching up to her shoulder, Lani got off her bike and
pressed the button on the radio. "I'm in place."

The smooth tenor voice of her supervisor, Chief Noah Jameson, came over the line. "Good—you made it out there in record time."

Up ahead she spotted an object shining in the setting sun. She jogged toward it. A bicycle, not hers, was propped against a tree.

A knot of tension formed at the back of her neck as she turned in a half circle, taking in the area around her. It was possible someone had left the bike behind. Vagrants could have wandered into the area.

She studied the bike a little closer. State-of-the-art and in good condition. Not the kind of bike someone just dumped.

A branch cracked. Her breath caught in her throat. Fear caused her heartbeat to drum in her ears.

"NYPD." She hadn't worn her gun for this exercise. Her eyes scanned all around her, searching for movement and color. "You need to show yourself."

Seconds ticked by. Her heart pounded.

Someone else was out here.

Don't miss
Courage Under Fire *by Sharon Dunn,*
available October 2019 wherever
Love Inspired® Suspense *books and ebooks are sold.*

www.LoveInspired.com

LISEXP0919

Looking for inspiration in tales
of hope, faith and heartfelt romance?

Check out **Love Inspired®** and
Love Inspired® Suspense books!

New books available every month!

CONNECT WITH US AT:

Facebook.com/groups/HarlequinConnection

 Facebook.com/HarlequinBooks

 Twitter.com/HarlequinBooks

 Instagram.com/HarlequinBooks

 Pinterest.com/HarlequinBooks

ReaderService.com

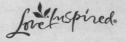

LIGENRE2018R2

SPECIAL EXCERPT FROM

Love Inspired

*Could a pretend Christmastime courtship
lead to a forever match?*

Read on for a sneak preview of
Her Amish Holiday Suitor, *part of Carrie Lighte's
Amish Country Courtships miniseries.*

Nick took his seat next to her and picked up the reins, but before moving onward, he said, "I don't understand it, Lucy. Why is my caring about you such an awful thing?" His voice was quivering and Lucy felt a pang of guilt. She knew she was overreacting. Rather, she was reacting to a heartache that had plagued her for years, not one Nick had caused that evening.

"I don't expect you to understand," she said, wiping her rough woolen mitten across her cheeks.

"But I want to. Can't you explain it to me?"

Nick's voice was so forlorn Lucy let her defenses drop. "I've always been treated like this, my entire life. *Lucy's too weak, too fragile, too small, she can't go outside or run around or have any fun because she'll get sick. She'll stop breathing. She'll wind up in the hospital.* My whole life, Nick. And then the one little taste of utter abandon I ever experienced—charging through the dark with a frosty wind whisking against my face, feeling totally invigorated and alive... You want to take that away from me, too."

She was crying so hard her words were barely intelligible, but Nick didn't interrupt or attempt to quiet her. When she finally settled down and could speak normally again, she sniffed and asked, "May I use your handkerchief, please?"

"Sorry, I don't have one," Nick said. "But here, you can use my scarf. I don't mind."

The offer to use Nick's scarf to dry her eyes and blow her nose was so ridiculous and sweet all at once it caused Lucy to chuckle. "*Neh*, that's okay," she said, removing her mittens to dab her eyes with her bare fingers.

"I really am sorry," he repeated.

Lucy was embarrassed. "That's all right. I've stopped blubbering. I don't need a handkerchief after all."

"*Neh*, I mean I'm sorry I treated you in a way that made you feel…the way you feel. I didn't mean to. I was concerned. I care about you and I wouldn't want anything to happen to you. I especially wouldn't want to play a role in hurting you."

Lucy was overwhelmed by his words. No man had ever said anything like that to her before, even in friendship. "It's not your fault," she said. "And I do appreciate that you care. But I'm not as fragile as you think I am."

"Fragile? You? I don't think you're fragile at all, even if you are prone to pneumonia." Nick scoffed. "I think you're one of the most resilient women I've ever known."

Lucy was overwhelmed again. If this kept up, she was going to fall hard for Nick Burkholder. Maybe she already had.

Don't miss
Her Amish Holiday Suitor *by Carrie Lighte,*
available October 2019 wherever
Love Inspired books and ebooks are sold.

www.LoveInspired.com